Patricia Reynolds

Keeper
of the
Souls
SERIES

A SCATTERING OF CLOUDS
BOOK THREE

KEEPER OF THE SOULS SERIES - A SCATTERING OF CLOUDS
BOOK THREE

Published by Old Crow Publishing WASHINGTON
Copyright © by Patricia Reynolds 2022
ISBN: 978-0-9998348-4-8
LCCN:

Cover design by Damonza.com
Edited by: Roberta Edgar

Praise For The Previous Works Of Patricia Reynolds

Reading Keeper of the Souls series, Book One. I experienced a plethora of emotions. I was excited to meet the characters, however, went from being happy to sad and then mourning. I flew from smiling to crying out loud and back to exhilaration. Patricia Reynolds has done an extraordinary job bringing a voice to the plight of the Lakota Sioux children.

Cheryl Acosta –
Owner of Gathered: A Native Made Marketplace

This book (Book One) was way by far one of the most impactful books I have come across. I couldn't put it down. Myself being an Apache, have related to this book in many spiritual ways. Although this book is historically fiction, it touched on a lot of different detailed perspectives and actual historical events that took place. Native Americans, my ancestors, were taken away from each other and it has been ignored for many years, so on a personal level, I am very grateful to the author for bringing this book to us. I look forward to seeing what else Patricia Reynolds brings to us.

Donna Johnson-Hucke

CHAPTER ONE

SOUTH DAKOTA

OLIVER WHITE CLOUD headed northwest on Highway 44 in a red and white '61 Pontiac Firebird, en route to the Badlands on his way to the Black Hills, and then on to Los Angeles. His Auntie Bell warned him to be careful driving such a long distance in the old heap – that at nineteen years old it might break down.

Oliver floored the old Pontiac as he barreled down the two-lane road, dodging potholes and rocks, caught up in his misery and guilt. He paid no mind as the engine whined… pushing the odometer past seventy as the scenery flashed by in a blur of rolling hills and plains. He rolled down the window and took a deep breath.

He felt his life begin to unravel as emotional scenes flashed through his mind of his sixteen-year-old brother, Swift Bear, who had been killed by a hit-and-run driver as he walked home from school after a basketball game. The boy's body was discovered lying in a ditch. Anger and despair overwhelmed Oliver as he beat his fist on the steering wheel in frustration. Riddled with guilt, he thought, *I should never have left home to live in New York after our father disappeared. If I hadn't, maybe Swift Bear would still be alive.*

Oliver's father, Looking Spirit, disappeared a few years ago, on his way to Wyoming to buy a Kiger Mustang, known for its compact, muscular body and classic Barb head. It was supposed to be a short trip, only about fifty miles from the South Dakota reservation, but the days turned into weeks, then months, and now years. He never returned.

Stomping on the accelerator, Oliver tried to outrun his demons, and roared even faster down the deserted highway, his mind in a blur as he headed northwest. He felt compelled to go to the Badlands where he used to go with his father when he was younger.

Oliver cracked the window open and listened to the winds whistle across the plains. The buffalo grass swayed to and fro – as if caught up in a seductive dance. In the distance, the prairie drifted off into rolling hills. Today was a scorcher – over 100 degrees, and it wasn't yet noon. So, Oliver rolled the window down even further, slung his arm over the door, and let his long black hair buffet against the wind, which, ironically, soothed his tormented thoughts. Spotting Route 24 up ahead, he turned down the deserted road heading toward the badlands – a thick layer of dust billowing up behind.

Startled by the shadowy figure he saw in the rearview mirror, he pushed even harder on the accelerator. The whirling dust grew thicker and wider, keeping pace. Oliver thought he saw a shimmering silhouette of his brother's face smiling widely in the thick cloud of dust and gasped in astonishment. But before he could look closer the image disappeared. Sensing it was his imagination that had conjured up his brother's face, he choked back his sorrow.

He was unprepared when the road suddenly took a sharp curve. The old Pontiac rounded the corner, fishtailed, and skidded over a rough patch of gravel before sliding with a loud crunch into a gaping pothole. A rusty wheel cover went flying off into the brush and the car fizzled to a stop. He cranked the engine over and over, but the old Pontiac wouldn't start. Cursing his luck and stupidity, he slammed down the hood and leaned against it. "Damn!" "I should've paid more attention to where I was going." *At least I'm not far from the Badlands,* he thought. So, Oliver grabbed his brother's backpack and a canteen, and headed toward his father's favorite spot high up in the hills.

Oliver climbed the large boulders and rocks and scrambled along through the maze of twisting trails and buttes, then winded his way alongside a steep canyon. He was surprised that he could remember the way, deep into the backcountry… it was a strenuous trek, but Oliver didn't care. He couldn't wait to find his father's special place once again, that overlooked the valleys and mesas. His father called it "Mako Sica," the name the Lakota gave to the Badlands, meaning 'land bad.'

The two would sit for hours, sometimes not saying a word, letting the land speak to them as they watched bald eagles soar gracefully overhead, bighorn sheep climb the treacherous hillsides, and prairie dogs stand on guard. They would build a fire and cook fresh trout his father had caught along the way. Oliver's favorite time was when they would camp overnight in the summer and sleep out in the open using the stars for a blanket. He would listen eagerly to his father talk late into the night. Oliver used to imagine that he could reach out and touch the stars they were so close – especially Venus, the brightest of them all. By early morning a spectacular display of reds, pinks and golden hues would emerge over the horizon and shimmer on top of the vista.

One night as they sat stargazing, admiring the Milky Way and other planets that circled overhead, his father had asked Oliver, "Can you feel your ancestors out in the ethers, my son? They are near."

Oliver shook his head no, as he looked around, wide-eyed and intrigued.

"You must first listen with your heart, my son, then you will hear the voices of our ancestors out among the valleys. They will tell you many things if you ask and then quiet your mind. Your Grandfathers are heroes of our people. Hold the courage in your heart and see their strength in your mind. They will guide you on your journey in this life."

Oliver smiled as he remembered those times with his father. Then his thoughts turned somber, as he walked on, remembering his brother's funeral, and brushed away a tear. He had buried him on their property, near a stand of cottonwood trees where Hidden Spirit and Morning Star were lain to rest long ago. It was a peaceful place filled with June grass and yellow primroses.

Holding hands with his mother and Auntie Belle, he lit a bundle of white sage and let the smoke curl over them and onto Swift Bear's grave. Auntie Belle said a prayer in Lakota and the three sat there in silence until the wee hours of the morning – remembering the boy and honoring his young life.

His mother had told Oliver that while he was living in New York, Swift Bear spent most of his time in the old cave near the house, writing stories about our ancestors. He loved the tales about Hidden Spirit and his mystical horse, Ghost Dancer and their daring escapades. Lily told him that he should go to the cave and look at his work… so he did. Oliver had no idea his brother could write like this. He wished he could have told him how proud he was of him – and how much he loved and missed him. Right now, the pages of his book were all he had left of his brother. He had to find a way to share his story with the world. To tell the people about the horrific abuses at the boarding school where the children were forced from their homes, and the harsh treatment they endured… especially he wanted them to know about the tyrannical Preacher Jim, who ran the school.

Oliver was struck by the warmth of the cave when he stepped inside. A flood of emotions filled him as he looked around the peaceful space. He inhaled the lingering aromas of pine and sage and sat down on his grandfather's old buffalo robe. His mind was still reeling from his brother's death. He built a fire and stayed in the cave for three days, not eating or drinking, searching for answers in his troubled mind. Then he felt himself slip into a dream-like state… awake and asleep at the time. He jumped when he heard a haunting cry, and felt a shadowy form wrap around him like a velvet blanket, soothing him. A sweet smell of tobacco wafted by, and he heard a faint whisper. "Mi-thakoza," floated past on a breath of air. Next, he heard, "Go to the City of Angels."

His eyes flew open. Jolted out of his stupor, he stood up and filled his brother's backpack with his writings, then left the cave. He told his mother, Lily, and his Auntie Belle he was leaving for a while… he had some things to take care of. His old '61 Pontiac still ran pretty well, and he grabbed his keys hanging by the door, then kissed his auntie and mother goodbye. They both gave their blessings along with their tearful farewell.

*

Oliver reflected on his life growing up on the reservation. It was hard, but wonderful at the same time. The family lived in a cozy old wooden house, far enough away from town – surrounded by the serenity of nature and land. This was the same house where his famous grandparents, Hidden Spirit and Morning Star had lived. His father still had Broken Feather's teepee set up down by the stream, which Oliver and his brother loved to sit inside for hours. Their house was filled with wonderful memories from their famous ancestors and elders.

Oliver's mother, Lily Rosebush, was from the Lakota tribe. A slight woman, barely five feet tall, Lily always smelled of fresh picked lilies and sweet roses, no matter the time of year. Lily loved to garden and was adept at coaxing her squash, potatoes, beans, and sweet peas to flourish like magic in the hard soil. She would talk to each seedling as she carefully put them into the ground… ecstatic when the shoots would appear. Not a day went by that she didn't say a prayer and bless the food. Their home always smelled of wild herbs, onions, mint and other freshly picked herbs. Oliver's favorite smell was from her homemade bread, that was filled with berries and nuts and shoots. He could almost taste the warm bread coming out of the oven, smothered with butter and fresh honey from their hives.

His father, Looking Spirit, had made an outdoor oven for his beloved Lily, who enjoyed being out in nature in every season, spring, summer and fall… even in the freezing winters. She loved to dance and sing as she cooked all her specialties for her family and anyone else who might drop by. They all used to sit outside waiting until the moon rose high in the sky and listen to the chorus of crickets, frogs, and katydids explode into the night while fireflies twinkled past – appearing as glowing lanterns flittering into the air. They had little in the way of money but were rewarded by an abundance from Mother Earth.

Looking Spirit was Hidden Spirit's grandson. He was adept with a bow and arrow and had a knack for finding enough food for his family and others… as his elders had done before him. Behind their home, Looking Spirit had built a sweat lodge, used to cleanse his body, and say his prayers. He smoked his grandfather's old peace pipe, knowing his prayers would be sent to the Great Spirit on the trail of smoke.

*

Oliver walked deeper into the valley and wound his way up a steep ravine, balancing between huge boulders as he traversed the steep hills and crevasses. After walking for what seemed like hours, he noticed a glint of sunlight reflect off a trickle of water coming from a crevasse tucked inside the rocky hillside. The water was cool and soothed his parched throat. A group of cottonwood trees stood a few yards away and the thought of resting under the welcoming branches, was just what he needed. He felt the sturdy bark, and smiled, recalling the story of the cottonwood tree.

"Black Elk called it, 'the talking tree,' his father had told him. "The rustling leaves are like a prayer sent to the Great Spirit, even in the slightest of breeze. That is why we use the sacred tree for our Sun Dance ceremonies."

Oliver leaned against the tree and was soon lulled to sleep by the rustling leaves. He dreamed he was surrounded by a cloud of smoldering mist. But as he tried to brush away the haze to see, it became thicker and dark –mysterious and otherworldly. The cry of, "Hoka Hey," melted out of the mist.

Oliver bolted up gasping for air covered in sweat. The dream unnerved him. He rubbed his eyes and ran over to the water splashed it over his face to revive him, and then continued on his trek, hoping he was near. He finally made it to the highest peak and gave a sigh of relief. He couldn't believe he found the same spot where he used to sit with his father on this plateau. The scenery was staggering, and the view was endless. He was again struck by the beauty of the badlands as his gaze wandered slowly across the spires and peaks of the valley. Standing motionless and without thinking, he held his hands out to the sky and closed his eyes. He felt compelled to ask the Great Spirit for answers that had plagued him for so long. He cried out, "Why did you take my father? He prayed to you every day and night. He was all that was good in this world. And now you take my brother, as well?" Swept away by his emotions, he squeezed his fists into a tight ball. His eyes welled with tears as memories came flooding back in tremendous waves. He had put thoughts of his father out of his mind for so long, because all the years he was missing, it was too painful to think about. He wanted to forget the past and the pain and go somewhere where he didn't see signs of his father everywhere he looked. That's why he had left the reservation for New York. While living there, he never forgot the words of his father that stuck in his mind… *"Alcohol is a poison the white man brought to our people. It destroys our souls and makes us weak — makes us forget who we are. Do not fall victim to the poison or you let the white man succeed. Always remember, we are still warriors of the plains, even if we live on reservations. I see many of our brothers not wanting to be of this life. We are people of the earth, connected to our Mother in ways that is a mystery to the white man."*

Wistful, Oliver sat down on a ledge that jutted far out over the valley and looked across the horizon. He leaned out over the side in awe of the spectacular sight and clung to the edge and then listened. Through the stillness, he thought he heard a faint cry in the distance. He was curious and leaned out even further. It looked like the outline of a gathering of his people wearing flowing head-dresses, carrying long pipes… calling to him. A chill surrounded him. He could feel their presence whoosh along on the currents of the breeze, fluttering deep into the valley. His ears pricked when he heard, "Oliver," whoosh across the vista.

Am I going crazy? he wondered, as he looked around in apprehension. Then he heard his name being called again. "Oliver!" Suddenly, feeling himself being elevated he screamed out. His screams turned to wonder as he found himself floating over the steep canyons and ravines, and into the horizon — then effortlessly drifting off into the currents. Floating high enough to touch the clouds, he started to shiver uncontrollably. Then, suddenly he was calm. He was now one with the air, and the wind, and the sky, and the earth. His eyes widened when he saw a luminous face emerge from the scattering clouds — that of a man with a long ponytail and three eagle feathers loping down the side, fluttering in the breeze.

Oliver gasped and called out. "Father! Is that you?" Tears threatened. He felt lost in a dream, lost in a veil of smoke. "I have been in turmoil for so long… I don't know who I am anymore." He paused. "What happened to you, father? Where are you?" He reached out to touch the image and felt the whisper of a kiss.

A faraway voice sang out. *You are brave, my son, like your grandfather, Hidden Spirit.* A faint reddish glow crackled against Oliver's skin. *You make me proud.*

Oliver sucked in a breath of air, to make sure he was really alive and held out his hands, hoping to capture his father's essence. He wanted to wrap his arms around the velvety cloud and tell him to please come back. But before he could call out, he felt himself floating back to the ledge of the canyon. He lay on the ground, heart hammering in fear and awe. *Did I really see my father?* Oliver wondered. He had a thousand questions he wished he could've asked, but the form vanished before he could get the words out.

Oliver remained on the plateau the rest of the night, pondering the vision. He sat staring at the sky until the morning star disappeared into the pink horizon. He was stiff and thirsty, but oddly, he felt at peace. He took one last look across the valleys, hoping for another glimpse of his father.

Moments later, he was setting off down the steep canyons on his way to the Black Hills. He perused the landscape. *Got about a hundred miles or more to go. Maybe I could hitch a ride part of the way. Gonna be a really long walk if I don't.*

At the bottom of the ravine, he found a tiny creek with just enough water to fill his pouch and quench his thirst – and to douse his long black hair. He pulled his red T-shirt over his 6'3" frame, revealing ripples of muscle, scars and lean hips. His sculptured face and square jaw was set off by high cheekbones and silky eyebrows that looked like painted feathers forming gracefully above his startling blue eyes. He rinsed his T-shirt in the trickle of water, wrung it out and put it back on. A few hours later, with his water in hand and his backpack, he made it to the main road.

Past noon now, the sun was blistering hot, scorching the soles of his worn boots. It was like walking on burning embers. The temperature had soared well past 100 and showed no signs of letting up. It was hard to breathe in the stifling air and he soon lost track of time. Nothing but miles and miles of empty road lay ahead.

To keep his mind off his burning feet, he let his thoughts drift off to when he was sixteen and he started paying more attention to girls, who reciprocated but chided him when he spoke his language, especially when he talked about the Great Spirit. The one girl he fancied, Shayna Long Deer, teased him. "Why do you still believe in the old ways, Oliver? Don't you know times have changed? I think you're pretty hot, you know, but you lose me when you talk like some old medicine man. I'm too hip for that crap anymore."

That's when Oliver started to dismiss his father's teachings and traditions. He stopped going into the Badlands with him and going into the sweat lodge, praying to the Great Spirit. He even gave up hunting with his father. He thought at the time that his father was just an old Indian, nostalgic for the past. He remembered thinking, *That's not for me, I'm not like my grandfathers – dancing around the sick, chanting prayers, beating drums, watching feathers fly. I'm cool now. Girls like me. I'm gonna leave the res and set out on my own. Maybe cut my hair and forget who I am… forget my famous ancestors. After all, this is the '80's. Then my father disappeared a couple years later. I forgot about being cool. I forgot everything and sunk into despair. That's when I left the reservation and headed to New York to stay with a cousin.*

Oliver's boots stuck to the pavement – jarring him out of his thoughts. He looked at the surrounding landscape and breathed in a hint of cool air. The sun was starting to set in the west over the distant hill. There were a few more trees along the way now as he wound his way off the main road and found a secluded spot to rest for the night. His feet burned, his head pounded, and his breath was ragged. He took a drink of water, chewed on a piece of jerky, lay down near a clump of bushes, and fell asleep, still chewing.

The next morning was crisp and cool. Oliver wanted to get an early start, before the heat set in. He was hoping to hitch a ride. It didn't take long for the sweltering heat to arrive —even fiercer than yesterday – he wiped his forehead with his kerchief and slung it around his neck. He stared at the waves of burning rays on the pavement imitating a sultry, undulating dance, and stared at the hypnotic rhythm for hours until he fell into a trance-like state in which he imagined a pool of water waiting for him to dive into. The sun was climbing even higher now. Sweat poured off him like a spigot… he felt like he was walking on molten lava.

Then off in the distance Oliver heard a truck come rumbling down the deserted road. He stopped and stuck out his thumb. The old beat-up pickup truck pulled up alongside him with an old man and dog in the front seat. The old man said, "Can I give you a lift son? Hotter'n a pistol, I'd say. Where ya headed?"

"Anywhere near the Black Hills would be fine." Oliver said, wiping the sweat from his brow.

The old man shook his head and motioned for him to get in the back.

Oliver hopped in the back and said, "I appreciate the ride." He sighed, leaned back, and let the wind whip across his face and body. It felt so good as he pulled off his boots and shook loose a couple stones that had lodged inside. A big blister formed on his ankle, so he pressed his kerchief against it. Exhausted, he lay back against the bed of the truck and closed his eyes, wishing he hadn't been so reckless with his car. *I've got a helluva ways to go,* he thought, *till I get to Los Angeles. Gotta be more than a thousand miles yet.* He had never been there before, but wasn't sure about the name, "City of Angels." He heard the air was dirty and the pace was fast… one could get lost in a city of dreams… even swept away in them, Oliver surmised, but that's where he had to go.

After a few hours the truck came to a stop. "I 'spect you're not too far from the hills over yonder. Here ya go." The old man looked at him in concern. "An' watch yer back, young man."

"Thanks," Oliver replied with a wave, and hopped out of the truck. It was mid-afternoon now, and he felt rested as he headed toward the Black Hills.

When Oliver was young, his father told him the story about Mt. Rushmore, a time before the president's heads were carved into the granite hills. "We used to call the mountain, 'The Six Grandfathers.' There were six sacred directions: west, east, north, south, above, and below. It was said, the directions represent kindness and love, full of years and wisdom…like our grandfathers before us," he told him sadly. Then they desecrated our hills with four presidents.

George Washington became the first president of the United States of America, but here in the Black Hills he was known as the "Town Destroyer," who decreed an extermination of the Iroquois people in 1779 and called for the destruction of their lands.

Our third president, Thomas Jefferson, declared that all Indians should be driven beyond the Mississippi, and he worked aggressively to acquire the Indian land.

President Abraham Lincoln ordered the largest mass hanging in U.S. history of thirty-eight Dakota Indians.

Theodore Roosevelt famously said, "I don't believe that the only good Indians are the dead Indians, but I believe nine out of ten are."

Oliver remembered climbing Mt. Rushmore when he was eleven years old, and the story of the Six Grandfathers was fresh in his mind. He shouted at the white faces that were carved in the sacred hills at the top of his lungs, "You don't belong here, wachicus. This is our land… our sacred hills. The granite hills belong to our people, not where your ugly heads are stuck." Then he let a steady stream of urine rain down on their heads. Oliver smiled at his rebellious nature and thought, *it was quite a climb to get there, but well worth it.*

Oliver walked on. He was hoping to make it to the Crazy Horse monument before dark. The monument wasn't completed yet, but he didn't care. He wanted to be near his idol… the fierce warrior that defied death at the battle of Little Bighorn. He felt a need to be there, to feel the energy of his people. He walked into the trees and breathed in the cool air. There was a stream up ahead, where he took a long drink of the cool crystalline water and lay down in it for a few minutes, enjoying the rush of water across his body. He felt energized by the mountains that were home to his ancestors and took in a deep breath of the sweet air. He got to his feet and walked on. His long strides took him up the hills where wild bergamot bloomed, and Sunflowers dotted the landscape. Struck by its beauty, he bent down, plucked a Sunflower – and ate the seeds.

After walking nearly four hours, he finally made it to the Crazy Horse monument. Exhausted and elated, he walked over and touched the enormous head and thanked the great warrior for his courage and his willingness to defend his people and their lands. Falling to his knees, he grabbed a handful of red clay, and put it to his lips. He could taste the gritty feel of the earth as he stared in awe at the mammoth statue – and swore he could hear the war cries of his people. For a long while, he sat there in silence and stared out at the vast expanse of wilderness, full of trees, rivers, and wildlife.

It was nearing dusk now, so he made a small fire and lay down. Looking up at the sky, he noticed a flicker of Venus, big, bright, and sparkly, rising in the east. He leaned back and stared at it for a very long time. A sense of calm filled him for the first time in years. Being back in his homeland, in the Black Hills, he felt at peace. The feeling surprised him. He had thought he never wanted to return to the reservation. But now – he was wavering.

In the morning, he awoke feeling invigorated. He took a handful of earth, stuck it in his pocket, said goodbye to Crazy Horse and walked slowly down the hills, enjoying the tranquility of the hills and the scent of the spruce trees and quaking aspens.

On the main road, Oliver looked across the stretch of plains where the buffalo grass swayed gently with the wind. The sun was low now, setting off a splash of red and purple hues, that bathed the twilight sky with its glorious colors – dazzling the senses with its brilliance – creating a feast for the eyes. Glad for a reprieve from the heat of the day as evening time approached, he shifted his backpack, ready for the long walk. A lone crow was circling overhead and, without thinking, he waved at the bird. Soon more crows appeared overhead.

As he walked along, he saw the glimmer of the first star appear in the deep blue twilight. Soon, it was joined by thousands of stars – flickering and dancing and blanketing the ever-deepening night sky.

Up ahead, Oliver saw a speck of light that morphed into a fast-approaching truck – its headlights shining intensely and blinded him momentarily. Quickly he moved over to the shoulder of the road, as the truck zoomed by. He was sure he heard the words, "Careful, Oliver…"

The truck screeched to a halt and then grinded into reverse, as the tires skidded on the hot pavement, and idled by Oliver's right side. The smell of burning rubber lingered in the air.

Oliver squelched his apprehension and did his best to ignore the guys in the truck.

The driver rolled down his window and hollered out, "Howdy there. Lookin' for a ride?" He squinted at Oliver to get a better look and yelled out at him. "Hey, you a redskin?"

Oliver didn't respond. He kept his head down and walked a little quicker, his unease growing with each step.

Keeping pace with Oliver, the driver revved the engine, sending thick fumes wafting in the air.

Oliver heard the two guys laugh, as the truck moved slowly alongside him, but he continued to ignore them.

The driver appeared to be in his early twenties, with long blond hair hanging out of a black Stetson, cowboy hat. Introducing himself, he stuck his hand out the open window. "I'm Hank," he said. "How about a slug of firewater to quench your thirst? Get ya itchin' an a twitchin'. Know what I mean?"

Oliver ignored his offer and kept walking – focused on the road ahead.

"You some sort of stuck-up Injun or somethin'?" Hank scowled, not liking being ignored. "You're not being too friendly, you know, and it hurts my feelings." He swerved the truck in front of Oliver, almost knocking him over.

Oliver heard country music blaring over the truck's radio, as the old Ford spit and sputtered – fumes drifting from the tailpipe.

"So, tell me – what are you doing out here in the middle of nowhere? You lost? I think you wandered too far from your rez," the young cowboy said with a chuckle. "I'm gonna give you a friendly word of advice. Miners Gulch is a ways up ahead. If I was you, I'd stay away from there. Dangerous place for an Injun to wander into. We got us a God-fearing sheriff in town, and he keeps law and order by keepin' the lowlifes outa there. Ain't that right, Jimmy Dean?"

Oliver could smell whiskey on the cowboy's breath, from where he was standing.

"Oh, and in case you hadn't noticed, you're out here in cowboy country. That's God's country. There's a lot of folks here that wouldn't take too kindly to seeing an Indian on the loose." Hank took a gulp from his bottle, and grinned. "This here is my sidekick, Jimmy Dean. We don't mind Injuns much, Jimmy Dean and I, and we hate to see you out walking in the dark. "Tell you what. Since we're neighborly fellas, and I'm a neighborly kinda guy, I'll give you a ride. Where'd you say you were headed?"

"Los Angeles," Oliver said, feeling his gut tighten and his fists clench. He wasn't sure why he told them.

"Los Angeles!" Hank hooted. "Wait till they get a load of you. You should fit right in with those beatniks and hippies out there. Hear they got a real loose-running crowd." Hank took another long, slow drink of whiskey and wiped the dribble from his chin. "Sure about the ride? Like I said, ain't gonna bite you."

"Thanks for the offer, but no thanks."

"Suit yourself. Just make sure the boogey man ain't the one keeping you company at night. Never know what he might do when he's riled up. "Ole boogey-woogey might just slide up and slit your Injun throat." he snorted. "Maybe even scalp ya. And that'd be a real shame. Hey, Jimmy Dean. This here redskin don't want to ride with us."

Jimmy craned his neck to look at Oliver. "I guess he must be one of the stupid ones… turning down a free ride and all. To Hell with him, Hank! Let's get going!"

"Well, last chance, partner. Give you a ride for about forty miles, so hop on in before I change my mind."

Oliver eyed the red pickup truck. It looked familiar. He rubbed his hands along the side of its bed, then walked around the back and looked at the bumper where he saw an old sticker that was partially worn off, visible from the taillight. He rubbed the dirt off and squinted at a faded war bonnet on it with the partial word: "…wow!" inscribed. The first part of the sticker was gone. Feeling the dent in the fender brought back a memory. *I did that when I was eleven years old… when I backed into a big tree.* The revelation jolted him. *This must be my father's truck.* He was curious why this cowboy had it and he had to find out why.

Hank came up from behind and gave him a smack on his

back. "Whatcha waiting for? Either get in or get lost! Ain't waiting no longer. I'm out of liquor and I'm bone dry."

Oliver's gut told him not to go with these guys, but he didn't have a choice. He was on a mission.

"Hang on," Hank hollered, as he started the engine. "I'm a wild guy and like to drive fast, so get ready for a wild ride." Oliver couldn't believe he was in the back of his father's truck – yet there he was – flying across the bed as it sped off down the road. He heard howls of laughter up front as the truck swerved sharply to the right, onto a gravel road – almost turning over as it skidded precariously on two wheels and started to spin in circles. "Yee-haw," Hank shouted crazily, "Hold on to your britches, Red." Watching Oliver in his rearview mirror being hurtled back and forth spurred Hank to drive even faster.

As the pickup came to a sliding halt, Oliver thought he'd better jump out. He heard Hank holler. "Hey, pow-wow. How'd you like your ride so far? I was just having a little fun, is all. I'll take it a little easier on ya…" Then he stomped on the accelerator and sped off with a loud snort.

Just then a ribbon of lightning circled the truck. Hank slammed on the brakes, the glare blinding him. "Hot damn! That was so close I could feel it in my boots all the way to my fingers." Hank wanted to get out of there, but barely a second later another burst of lightning struck the ground, sizzling hot and lighting up the night sky.

"Get your arm inside," Jimmy Dean whimpered in fright, "before we're cooked to a crisp inside this chunk of scrap metal." He wiped the smoke from the window. "That was the weirdest thing I've ever seen," he said. Checking the rearview mirror, he shouted to Oliver in back. "Get your ass fried, back there?" He grinned nervously, showing a row of perfect white teeth.

"Say, Hank," Jimmy Dean said, scooting around to look at him. "I don't see him back there. I think he's gone."

The ground still smoldering bright red, Hank jumped out of the truck, cursing, and raced around back to find Oliver missing. He swatted the air in frustration.

"Well, I'll be a ding-a-ling. Where do you suppose he went, Hank?" Jimmy Dean said.

Hank smiled as he spotted Oliver running into the scrubs. "Let's get that bastard, Jimmy Dean." He hopped inside the truck, gunned the engine, and took off after Oliver.

As the truck headed toward him, Oliver took off in a sprint, pleading to the Great Spirit for help.

Out of the smoky dust a group of crows in flight began to nosedive in his direction and surrounded him protectively. Adrenaline kicked in and with a sudden burst of energy, Oliver was running on the wind – zipping along the road.

The pickup truck was on Oliver's tail. He felt the bumper knock against his legs, shoving him forward into a stumble.

Hank slowed slightly, put the gear in neutral and revved the truck for show. "Ain't gonna finish the Indian off just yet, Jimmy Dean. Wanna have some fun… make him squirm a bit before I do."

Oliver's legs wobbled from the pace, as Hank hollered after him. "Look who's trying to get away from me, Jimmy Dean! Better hurry, Red, before I run your ass over."

Hank revved the engine, and ran a little harder into Oliver, making him lurch forward. "Look at his legs go, will ya? Got him running now, huh?" Ready to step on the gas, he gasped at the sight of a big fat crow with enormous yellow eyes as it landed on the hood of the truck with a "ker-plunk." Its long sharp beak snapped a warning.

Hank and Jimmy Dean looked in disbelief at the unnerving sight.

"Say, partner," Hank whispered, almost afraid to speak. "You see what I do?"

As beads of perspiration formed on his forehead, Jimmy Dean choked out his answer. "Looks pretty dangerous, Hank. Get your gun and blast the nasty thing."

Before Hank could get his gun or close the window, the crow flew inside the truck. As feathers and wings were flapping wildly, Hank yelped in alarm and Jimmy Dean dove to the floorboard, covered his head, and screamed. "Get away!"

Hank swatted at the big crow and missed. Cawing loudly, the crow skittered on the dash, flashed its enormous yellow eyes, gouged Hank's arm, and flew out into the night.

As Hank peered out the window a thick plume of dust came out of nowhere – swirling like a cyclone.

Scratching his chin, Hank sat in wonderment. "There wasn't even a cloud in the sky a while back. That sonofabitch blew in from out of nowhere and brought in a storm. Pa said we weren't due one for a week or more."

Hundreds of birds were flocking out of the dust – beaks pecking, wings thrashing, feathers flying. Hank pulled out his gun and aimed to fire when he heard a sudden pop. A huge crack formed down the middle of the window as claws, and wings, and beaks swarmed around the pickup truck, whirling and spinning. The speed of their movements made Hank dizzy. *Is it the booze or am I going crazy?* His shaking hands tightened on the steering wheel, and he started to drive – blindly swerving the truck back and forth, trying to ditch the crows.

"Where the Hell are all these birds coming from?" he screamed. "I can't see a blasted thing in front of me!"

The crows landed on the hood of the truck and on the roof – their jittery talons tapping like a rainstorm.

A terrified Jimmy Dean grabbed Hank's leg and squeezed. "Hurry, Hank. We gotta get outa here. Remember the movie, *The Birds*? Everyone in it got killed. We're gonna die, just like those movie stars did."

"Shut up about dying and some stupid movie, Jimmy Dean." Hank gripped the steering wheel harder, thinking he might faint or get pecked to death. Maybe, both.

Hank was sick of these damn birds, so he yanked his shotgun from the back window, and jumped out of the truck – firing off several rounds of shots before the chamber was empty. By now, the crows had disappeared.

Still pointing the empty gun, Hank looked around cautiously. "I think the coast is clear," he said in a hushed voice, looking over his shoulder, as if the crows might hear him and return. The dust and wind seemed to have settled down by now and all was silent, except for Hank's ragged breath. Satisfied they were alone Hank shook his head and shoved his gun back into the truck. "We're getting the hell out of here before more weird shit happens," he said nervously. "And I'm gonna find that Indian and finish what I started." He hurriedly cranked the ignition, shoved it into gear, slammed his foot on the accelerator, and squealed off. "He's not getting away from me." But as soon as he saw in the distance the swarm of crows circling above, he changed course and headed back to town.

"I sure as hell don't know what happened back there, but I do know I shouldn't have stopped to give that damn Indian a ride. Just wanted to have some fun. You know what I think?" he said with bravado. "I think those Injuns are a whacked-out bunch of goons. No wonder people call them crazy, doing all kinds of supernatural stuff..." He looked over at Jimmy Dean, who was too shocked to speak, and poked him in the chest. "What you think it was, Jimmy Dean? And... you best not mention this... this... crazy shit that just happened... not to anyone! I'll knock your noggin right off your scrawny shoulders if I catch wind of it. You hear?"

Jimmy Dean shook his head emphatically. "I ain't mentioning a word of this, Hank. Don't you worry none about that. I don't know what it was back there, neither. I told you about that movie… they did the same thing to all those nice people. And… and… nobody ever knew why, neither."

"Shut up about that damn movie, will you?" He turned up the radio and stomped the pedal to the floor – anxious to get back to Miners Gulch, more than ready for a serious drink. He'd never felt this nervous before.

CHAPTER TWO

MINERS GULCH

OLIVER STOOD MOTIONLESS on the side of the ditch as he watched the truck drive past and barrel into the distance. He heard a bottle crash on the road, as a Willie Nelson tune blasted on the radio.

Oliver sank into the ground as the pounding in his ears eased up. He had a lot to absorb tonight after seeing his father's '54 Ford pickup truck – and then the crows and the wild sandstorm. For a moment, he held his head in his hands, then slowly stood and brushed off his jeans. He noticed his T-shirt was ripped and he felt the sting of a cut on his arm. He was stiff and sore and started to walk gingerly down the dirt road – thinking. *I know that was my father's Ford. He loved that truck and took very good care of it. I remember him putting on that powwow bumper sticker. Then, when I backed the truck into a tree, all he said was, "It just adds a little character, son."*

Oliver was exhausted and lay back, as he stared at the dazzling sky. A moment later, a scattering of clouds drifted overhead, heading to the west. Then thousands of stars shone and glimmered in the dark night. He smiled at the thought of those crows heeding his cry for help. He remembered his father once saying, "We have mystical abilities in our blood, son. More than once, the crows helped Hidden Spirit – and saved his life." Those were Oliver's last thoughts as he drifted into a deep sleep and dreamed his father warned him to be wary of "cowboys and a hanging rope."

Oliver woke at dawn, covered in a thick coat of dust and surrounded by mounds of tumbleweed. He sat up slowly, brushed the dust from his clothes, wiped the crust of dust from the corners of his eyes and took notice of a red glow in the east, promising a beautiful sunrise. Without thinking, he closed his eyes. As he sat in silence, he had a feeling someone was watching him, so he cracked open his lids and saw, off in the distance, a lone crow with a bright silver wing watching him intently. The crow opened its beak and tilted his head back, twisting it around in circular motions. Oliver wondered what it was doing and started to walk toward it, but the bird flew onto a nearby branch and made a short series of clacks with its beak. Thinking he heard the word, "Miner," his ears perked up. Was the bird telling him to go there? Oliver did believe in signs from the spirits. His father taught him that. Those guys last night in his father's truck talked about Miners Gulch and he had already heard stories about the town and knew it was a dangerous place to wander into, especially if you were an Indian. But dangerous or not, he had to do some digging around in that town or he might never learn what happened to his father.

Sheriff Joe's reputation was widely known, and most Indians kept their distance. It was rumored he had a "hanging judge" at his beck and ready.

Oliver was angry seeing Hank and Jimmy Dean in his father's truck. Did they steal it from his father – did they kill him? The truck wasn't worth much, and he had nothing on him of any value. Nonetheless, the questions haunted him.

Looking up to the sky, he called out to his hero. "I ask to be as brave as you in battle, Crazy Horse. I ask the Great Spirit for strength and wisdom to face the enemy – to guide me on my journey. Wopila tanka!"

Oliver stood solemnly looking at the sky. He closed his eyes and felt his courage swell. Breathing out, he straightened his shoulders. "I will find the answers," he said. "I will do it for our people."

He looked around to get his bearings and headed toward the main road. *It shouldn't take long to get to Miners Gulch*, he thought. *Maybe a couple days.* As he walked, the crow flew overheard. He smiled.

"If you were sent to help me, and I believe you were," he said, "I thank you." The crow flew down a little closer and perched on a willow branch. "I'm going to Miners Gulch," he called out, "and I have a feeling your help could come in handy." He felt kind of silly, talking to the crow, asking for help. He couldn't help but smile, amazed by the fantastical occurrence of the crows scaring away Hank and his friend. He had heard stories about the crows helping his grandfather… I guess stranger things have happened.

The crow flapped its wings, flew overhead in circles, and dropped something shiny at Oliver's feet. He bent down to pick up the object – an unusual stone in the same brilliant shade of blue as Oliver's eyes. The stone seemed to exude power and to hold a secret. He had never seen anything like it before, and he turned it over in his hand – wondering why the crow had given it to him. He looked up to thank the bird, but it was gone.

Once he arrived at the main road, Oliver looked at the empty stretch of highway and headed southwest. Not many cars were out, so he could see one coming from a long way off. But he was in Wyoming, and off the reservation. He needed to be vigilant. So, he decided to stay away from the main road for a while. If a cowboy or rancher had the inclination, they could shoot him for target practice – just for being an Indian.

He was also concerned those two guys from last night might come back looking for him. Gazing into the distance, looking for any signs of the crows. For some odd reason, he felt the crow with the silver wing was going to be crucial on his journey. *I wish he hadn't flown away.*

Oliver rummaged through his backpack and found a couple pieces of jerky. But his water pouch was empty, so he walked toward a small creek flowing to the west. He filled his pouch, sat under a tree, and ate a few bites of jerky. The coolness and gurgle of the stream had a calming effect on him, and he stayed for half an hour. While enjoying the tranquility, he couldn't help but think about last night – it seemed surreal. *I guess I better be prepared for what lay ahead. I hope the crows come back.* He stood and stretched, feeling refreshed.

Oliver shifted his backpack to the other shoulder and started walking. A few miles down the road, he saw a worn sign: Miners Gulch. 40 miles. Turn left on Route 44.

For the next couple of hours, Oliver walked without seeing a car or truck on the road. It was getting past noon when he thought he heard the rumble of a truck with a noisy muffler come roaring down the road. His hair rose at the back of his neck. Recognizing the sound, he quickly slid into a nearby ditch and lay down. The truck was moving slowly as it rolled to a stop a few yards from where Oliver was crouched behind a large tumbleweed. He wondered if the two men spotted him. He dared not breathe.

"Gotta take a whizz – like a racehorse," said Hank. "Had too many Buds, I guess. Hold tight. I'll just be a minute. Then we'll go back to where we were last night and look for signs of that Injun. Any damn crows flying around, and I'll shoot 'em dead."

Oliver heard Hank get out of the truck, undo his zipper, and urinate on the road while Jimmy Dean cranked up a Willie Nelson tune on the tape-deck. Totally off-key, Hank yodeled out, "Yer a good hearted…" and continued to hum as he zipped up his fly, then bent down to inspect the tires – making sure to kick the left rear for emphasis. "Looks like this baby's getting pretty worn," he said, as he walked around the truck, fanning himself with his black Stetson hat. "Say, Jimmy Dean. You wanna get laid tonight? I ain't hardly ever seen you with a girl. And I got my hands so full of them I gotta swat them away – like pesky flies. Guess that old football trophy is still working its magic."

"Have a bit of a time getting a girl to go out with me," Jimmy Dean said, unenthusiastically. "I prefer my friends, anyhow," he said, as Hank climbed back inside and cranked up the engine. "Less trouble."

"Well, wouldn't mind sharing Sally with you, if you want. She'd do anything I say," he said wickedly.

Jimmy Dean sat there with a glum look and no answer.

"Always thinking of my friends," Hank grinned, as he slapped Jimmy Dean on the shoulder. "Okay, then. Let's go hunting some wild Injuns. Got my shotgun loaded and ready for action."

The red pickup truck grinded into first, then rumbled down the road, with music blaring and Hank singing, "…must beee love…"

Oliver heard the crash of a beer bottle and Hank say, "We should've picked up more long necks. Might run out… at the rate we're going."

From behind the tumbleweed, Oliver stood and watched the truck disappear into the horizon. *Miners Gulch,* he thought apprehensively, as he felt his insides burning - but continued on.

Two days later he was on the outskirts of Miners Gulch, where he waited until dusk before making his way through the town. His heart pounded wildly as he summoned his courage.

A few minutes later he was in the center of town, easing his way along the sidewalk. Creaky boards groaned under his step as he walked gingerly past the storefronts, trying to keep to the shadows. He thought about his great-grandfather, Hidden Spirit, and how he could make himself invisible. Feeling a sudden shiver, he wished he could disappear right now.

When he was a teenager, Oliver's father had told him, "The powers to become invisible are already in us, my son. First, you must still your mind, and tap into your ancestors' wisdom. Then focus with all your strength. We are all descended from the Great Mystery, but along the way, we have forgotten our path. We tried to be more like the white man – fat and lazy and let our minds dull – but it destroyed our soul."

Oliver recalled Looking Spirit's words. "We must remain true to who we are and where we come from – the earth and the sky. Once you believe that, your gifts will start to appear. Remember our prayers, our dances, our songs – they keep our spirit alive. As we go into new times, living amongst the whites, we must get along – but not lose ourselves.

Further into town, Oliver continued down the main street, which was deserted. *There must be at least thirty cars and trucks here,* he thought, but one stood out amongst the battered pickup trucks and rusted cars. A bright red Chevy Camaro with fancy wheels. He wondered who owned it and where all the people were. A block down on the left side was a gas station with a garage. A half dozen trucks sat parked out front, with hoods raised.

Next to the garage was a brick building, Bank & Trust, with a tattered nondescript flag flying in front. The empty lot next to the bank was filled with broken beer bottles and cigarette butts. Further down the street a used car lot's huge flashing yellow sign said: HANSON'S CARS – COME ON IN. An old barbershop next door had about three chairs inside and a diner. Oliver looked across the street, where most of the trucks and cars were parked in front of the Blue Sky Saloon, according to the big sign painted on the side of the building. A faded blue sign hung above the door that read: Cowboy Heaven. Something illegible was carved below the sign with splotches of red.

As a couple of guys came outside the bar cracking jokes, Oliver ducked into an alleyway. The jukebox was cranked up high, and the sound of country music floated out from the open door. The two guys staggered down the street until one stopped and leaned against a post. "Woo-wee. Think I'm a little drunk, and I gotta piss so bad it hurts. You don't see no one coming do ya, Wilbur?"

Not waiting for an answer, the drunk unzipped his jeans and peed on the post.

"Damn, Sonny, you coulda done that inside. You know how Sheriff Joe hates it when folks piss like that on the street."

"It was either piss on the post or piss my pants. And it ain't sanitary to piss my pants."

After Sonny finished, the two guys continued down the street, telling jokes and tall tales. Holding onto each other for balance, they flicked their cigarette butts across the road seeing who could flick the furthest.

They were just a few feet away from Oliver when they heard a whistling wind buzz past. They jumped in unison, swatting at their heads.

"What the hell was that?" Sonny staggered, falling backwards.

"Sounded like a hive full o' bees got loose. You see any flyin' 'round, shoot 'em dead," Wilbur said, snickering, as Sonny yanked out his gun, taking aim at the darkness. "Well, let's get on outa here. There's a groovy party going on at the trailer park. Some hot broads over there want us to come an' *par*-tee." He shook his torso for show. "Don't give a shit 'bout a bunch o' bees. I'm getting me some honey tonight."

Oliver waited in the alley until the two guys left.

At the end of Main Street, he saw a large store that had to be over a block long with an equally large sign:

HERSHEL'S GROCERIES - SUNDRIES-HARDWARE-FEED STORE.

A dim light burned from within, and Oliver peered inside, where he saw a teenage girl sitting at the counter, counting money from the cash register. She had short black hair with bangs and dark glasses and looked to be serious. As he scanned the ample space, he saw neatly lined rows of canned goods in shiny glass jars. Laid out in long rows beside the counter were freshly baked breads of several varieties, and to the side, ripe apples, pears, bananas, and loads of fruits and vegetables. Deeper into the store, in an aisle leading to the back, were piled bags of flour, rice, coffee, and beans up to the ceiling. Another aisle was too far over for him to see. At the sight of the sheriff's office across the street, his heart skipped a beat. He had seen enough of Main Street for now and was relieved to find it so quiet as he turned down a side street and passed a church on the corner with a sign on the grass announcing services. The church was large for the size of the town and had a house connected in the back. He walked softly through the back part of town where a streetlamp at the end of each block barely illuminated the sidewalks but helped to block him from view. A few people were sitting on their front porch talking as he passed them by, unnoticed.

At the end of the street, he found an alley riddled with potholes and garbage cans. It had a strange feel, he noticed, as he walked on – and he had an inkling something was off. He poked around and wound up in the back of the Blue Sky Saloon. It had a dim lamp in back and a large sycamore tree with sturdy long branches. Beside the tree was a fire pit with chairs lined around it. Music was coming from the bar. On closer inspection, he saw several notches carved out of the tree with unreadable drawings. He ran his fingers over the notches and felt a jolt. His hand involuntarily went to his neck. He heard a moan. He wondered who was there. As he slid around the tree, he heard a whisper through the branches. "Oliver." He felt himself go rigid, as the branches started to sway. In his bones, he knew something bad had happened here. A lump caught in his throat. As he ran his hands over the rough bark, he could barely breathe. *It could be that one of these notches was my father's fate,* he thought. *I wish it could tell me what happened.* He leaned in close to the tree, feeling the energy pulse against his hands and his body. The large sycamore seemed to sway with his sadness. As he leaned into it, he felt droplets of water that rained down from the branches. He hugged the tree for comfort as his face leaned against the bark and his own tears mixed with the droplets. He stayed like that for a few minutes, then whispered, "I miss you, Father."

Looking Spirit was kind and wise. He loved his people, and he loved all life – especially the animal world and the buffalo he called his "brothers." He walked the earth a proud man – proud of who he was. No man could make him ashamed to be called an Indian. He thought there was power in that name. He was Lakota, and no matter how many times he was spit upon or mocked, he still held his head high and walked with pride.

Oliver's emotions swirled crazily. He had so many questions. He whispered, "Is this why I keep seeing a rope in my vision? Did they hang you, Father?" He felt the branch lurch against his back – as if in response. He wanted to scream until he was hoarse. His despair was so great.

The familiar rumblings of a pickup truck drew closer and stopped in front of the Blue Sky Saloon – the muffler letting off its characteristic pop. He eased his way around the side of the building. "There it is – my father's truck." He watched the men get out and walk into the saloon and he waited a moment before rushing over to the truck and peering inside the open windows. The smell of beer and stale cigarettes assaulted his senses. He stared at the garbage and beer bottles on the floor. His face burned with rage. Without thinking, he slid into the driver's seat, shut the door quietly, and lay his head against the steering wheel for a moment.

The rearview mirror looked empty without Looking Spirit's dream catcher of three silver feathers and red beads wrapped around it. He told the young Oliver, "The Great Spirit infused each feather with his love. When the wind blows it sends prayers across the land. So, whenever you look at it, know it's filled with love and prayers for you. And then thank Him for the blessings."

Seated next to his father, Oliver used to love to watch the feathers fly in the wind when they would go for a ride in the truck with windows down. He wondered if he would find the dream catcher in this mess he was rummaging through. Then his fingers touched something silky, and he knew his wish had come true. Here, still intact, was his father's dream catcher. "I can't believe it!" he whispered to himself, carefully wiping the crud from the beads and delighted to see the feathers were still smooth and silky. He ran the feathers across his face and felt a tingle of warmth and smiled. For a moment he had lost himself in better times.

Just then, the car door yanked open, and there stood Hank, scowling, with Jimmy Dean behind him. Hank reeled backwards and whipped out his pistol. He hollered in disbelief.

"Well, I'll be damned if this ain't the same Injun we been looking for, Jimmy Dean. He didn't even thank us for the ride. He's not just uppity – he's a damn thief, besides." Hank snorted loudly. "Fix that soon enough," he said, looking into Oliver's startling blue eyes that stared coolly back at him and made him squirm. He cocked his pistol and said, "Run and get Randy – and tell him to bring some rope. Gonna tie up this thief and charge him for trying to steal my truck. Don't like Injuns and especially don't like Injun thieves. To prove his point, Hank shoved his pistol into Oliver's chest.

Hank's family owned a large cattle ranch that spanned a hundred square miles throughout the Wyoming territory. Hank Jr. had always heard growing up that the Indians were a nuisance and a bunch of drunks. His father was a powerful man and wielded a lot of influence. "Injuns are just in our way, son," he would tell Hank. "They got all this land they don't do squat with… they're hogging all the water we need for our cattle… and you can't trust them as far as you can shoot them."

Hank Jr. was his father's favorite – and only – son. He was great at sports and a football star in high school for which he won a scholarship to a college back east. Ranching was not in his blood like it was in his father's and his grandfather's. Football was his life. So, in '76, he packed his bags and headed east. After he left home, the proud, but sad, Mrs. Williams cried for a month. All the girls adored Hank Jr., so, in his absence, they sent him love letters to his address. To their minds, he was everything a girl could want – tall and muscular with blond wavy hair and eyes the color of sweet amber beer. In his sophomore year as a star quarterback, he fractured and dislocated his shoulder in a game against Penn State. It was a crucial game, but he was injured in the third quarter. His dream of an NFL career died right there on the field, and that was the last time he played. After that, he lost interest in school, his grades plummeted, and he fell into a depression. He stored his anger deep inside, where it waited to erupt – and he drank and partied until all hours of the night. At the end of the semester in Boston, he came back home, and continued drinking and partying. He couldn't get over the fact that his lifelong dream was gone. Not long before, he had been a beloved football hero, and now he was just another guy who didn't make the grade. Increasingly bitter, he unleashed his anger in different ways. Sometimes he would target girls; namely, Sally Bennett, who made a habit of excusing his forceful and aggressive behavior. Other times, it was a local who inadvertently said something he didn't like or, in his mind, looked at him the wrong way. But it could have been anyone at random he felt deserved the back of his fist. The one thing that numbed his feelings in a hurry was alcohol. So, naturally, he indulged accordingly.

Hank, Jr. had already drunk his fair share for the night when he found Oliver inside his truck. *He stares at me like he's not one bit afraid. I'll remedy that soon enough.*

Jimmy Dean came hustling out of the saloon with Randy, carrying a coil of rope – his Wesson Colt with the pearl handle strapped to his waist. His hands generally shook when he held the gun, which scared him to death. He only carried it because Hank had given it to him. One time he tried shooting it and blew a window out of his house.

Jimmy Dean was barely 5' 7" – with his boots on. He had a hawkish face with a pointy, boyish nose and was so devoted to Hank, he would do his bidding without question, and was always by his side.

"Hey, Hank," Randy hollered. "I hear you caught yourself a redskin. What you gonna do – shoot him or tie him up? We could bring him on in the saloon and have us a little fun. Maybe raffle him off or use him as a dartboard." Grinning, he uncoiled the rope.

Oliver snapped. He envisioned all the legendary warriors he admired, and quick as lightening he whirled around, fist like iron, and punched Randy solidly in the jaw. Randy's head swiveled sharply to the right, knocking him backwards into Hank with such force, they both slammed into a post. Hank's gun went flying.

Hank was stunned by the strength of the slender Indian, who punched him in the gut, knocking the wind out of him. He rolled over backwards, moaning, "Jimmy Dean! Don't just stand there! Shoot! Do *something*!"

Scared and confused, Jimmy Dean shouted, "You savage beast!" He raised his fist, ready to land a punch, but swung wildly, whirled around, stumbled over his feet, and landed on his backside. He pushed himself back up ready to try again, but before he could ball his fist, Oliver shoved him back with his boot – slamming him into a truck.

Curses and shouts erupted. Hank was furious. He didn't like being made a fool of by anyone, especially an Indian. He was the guy to never mess with, and here he was, knocked to the ground by a savage.

Randy staggered tentatively toward Oliver – his head still reeling from the previous blow. *This Indian is half-wild*, he thought breathlessly, as he went at Oliver, who was a vastly more skilled fighter. But Randy didn't care – he had to help his friend and he loved a good fight.

Oliver was bursting with adrenaline and fought like a grizzly – hammering Randy repeatedly in the head.

In the meantime, Jimmy Dean was frozen in place. He didn't want to get hit again but he had to impress the guys, mainly Hank. Taking a blind swing, he hit Randy on the head.

Randy whirled around, furious. "What the hell you doing?"

Embarrassed, Jimmy Dean caught Hank giving him an exasperated look. Without thinking he pulled his Wesson from his belt but tripped over his feet and then his gun fired and hit a tire on a nearby Chevy truck. Jimmy Dean squealed in alarm and dropped the firearm. The thing made him nervous.

Randy snatched Jimmy Dean's smoldering pistol and threatened. "Make another twitch, and I'll end you right here.

Hank shoved his cowboy boot into Oliver's back, and knocked him hard to the ground, and kept him pinned down. "You're a wild sonofabitch, but gotcha now, redskin! You ain't goin' nowhere." The guys stood for a moment to catch their breath. Hank wiped his face with the back of his hand. He hadn't been prepared for this.

"Holy shit," Randy said, in admiration. "That Injun fights like a bear. Took two and a half of us," he winked at Hank, "to wrestle that skin to the ground. Good thing I came out to help." He held his jaw that was already starting to turn a deep purple. "Let's get him tied up before he gets loose. Not ready to take him on again right now."

Jimmy Dean found the rope that got tossed into the street during the melee, unwound it, and handed it to Hank. "Here ya go," he said meekly. "I could use a drink."

"A stiff one sounds pretty good right about now, cause that's how I feel." Hank groaned, holding his ribs. "Hope you didn't get hurt too bad."

"Naw," Jimmy Dean said, sheepishly.

"Let's drag his ass into the saloon," Randy said. "Got a whoppin' headache. "Give me a hand." He motioned to Hank and pulled Oliver off the ground.

Randy's hair was matted, and his face was bruised with blood oozing down his cheek. Hank sported a black eye already swollen shut.

Jimmy Dean followed behind. His throat was red from Oliver's fierce grasp and his rib cage was sore to the touch.

Oliver was left with blood oozing from his swollen lip and a slight gash above his eye.

CHAPTER THREE

BLUE SKY SALOON

RANDY RANG THE bell as they entered the smoke-filled barroom. "Caught us a wild Injun," he hollered, strutting like a peacock – pulling Oliver behind him.

No one really noticed at first, as the jukebox was blaring out a sultry tune. The dance floor was packed as couples shuffled around, bumping into each other on the small dance floor. But no one minded as they swayed back and forth enjoying the moment.

The bar was filled with locals and ranchers, and tired cowboys still wearing spurs on their boots, while cozying up to boozy women sipping drinks and smoking. They sat at wooden tables, telling the ladies wild stories of their week, exaggerating tales of corralling wild buffalo and other wild critters out on the range, as they happily doled out their wages for a good time. It was Friday night, and people had driven in from miles around to meet up with old friends, gossip a bit, and talk ranching, horse trading, and this year's harvest. Some hoped to dance a little with a fair-haired maiden, treat her to a drink or two, and get a kiss or more in return.

The one person no one paid attention to was the good-looking, well-dressed young guy sitting alone at the far end of the bar, wearing a bright red Dodgers baseball cap pulled down low over his forehead. Fully engaged with a tall gin and tonic, he observed the crowd with curiosity.

The long bar stretched almost the entire length of the saloon – smooth as a baby's belly and oiled to a sheen so bright you could even see your reflection. If you happened to drop a cigarette on the polished wood, the meticulous Randy would threaten to shoot you, then escort you out the door.

The long wooden bar had an unscrupulous past with a few names scratched into it. It was told that Buffalo Bill sat at this very bar and shot a couple holes through the wall. The bar had been around for almost as long as Miners Gulch, which was founded in the 1870's as a mining town. It was a lawless place, with slews of brothels and gunslingers and riffraff drifting in from all parts of the country as word spread of wild shootouts that became so common on the streets, no one blinked when someone was shot and killed right in front of them. "God and Guns," the sign boasted. Another weather-beaten sign, sitting at an odd angle with wooden slabs and painted bright red clarified the townsfolk's sentiments about Indians: "Shoot 'em on sight! $10.00 for scalps or the full head – as long as they aren't breathing."

Miners Gulch had once been touted as the best place to live in the west – assuming you liked guns and bars. The folks didn't like outsiders then, and they didn't now, either. They frowned on them snooping around town and judging their way of life. The laws here reflected their belief system, and you did not want to violate them.

Sheriff Joe Jenner was about six-foot-two and had been the sheriff of Miners Gulch for a long spell. He looked like a bulldog with his thick neck and big jowls, and with a rowdy laugh that sparked uneasiness and lacked sincerity. Sporting a wide girth, the sheriff had a penchant for rich food and hefty women. "Like my women with some meat on their bones," he used to say. "Not those scrawny broads that poke you with their skinny-ass bones." When evening time rolled around, Sheriff Joe liked to frequent the Blue Sky Saloon. And when the tunes started to roll there, he'd click his fingers and wiggle his wide girth to the music. Then he would grab a gal to dance with if a Waylon tune or Don Williams song played. "Loved to get the women all worked up and hot to trot," he would laugh wickedly.

Sheriff Joe loved women, but thought, "Marriage is a load of crap, set out to hook a poor sucker. Some crazy female scheme." He said some broad back in the '60s claimed he knocked her up and tried to get him to marry her. He was having no part of that – that's for damn sure. "When the marriage part didn't work, the bitch tried to weasel my hard-earned money outa me." He told her to get her ass back to Montana and to find a doctor and deal with it. She ignored his advice and had a daughter she named Mary. He had not heard from her in a spell, and thought, *good riddance.* But, instead, he discovered the broad died – and then their sixteen-year-old daughter showed up at his door. What could he do? As an upstanding sheriff, he had obligations, he said. "It's my duty as a Christian to take in the girl. So being "a God-fearing man in a God-fearing town, gonna do what's right, you see."

Now, his daughter Mary… she was another story. "Despite her good Christian name," she did exactly as she liked – "stubborn as hell and opinionated," according to Sheriff Joe. "She even had the unholy gall to start calling herself some weird-sounding hippie name – Indigo. *That* apple didn't fall far from its tree – a clone of her hippie-dippie ma."

Sheriff Joe liked to collect favors, and he wrote copious notes on everything. He could pry information from someone with ease and beguile you with a wicked grin. Most people never noticed. He was giddy with power, with his disarming charm and swagger.

Having been sheriff of Miners Gulch for over thirty years, he knew the most meticulous details of every secret, grudge, or feud in town. The place was jam-packed with scandal, and none of it eluded Joe. He was an observer of people, always listening in on conversations, overhearing bits of gossip. He discovered people liked to talk, especially about each other – and the more defamatory the better. Joe had judges and lawyers in his pocket, so when the ranchers needed more land, he was the one to go to for favors. He knew the ropes and even used them on occasion – like the time some Indian with a broken-down truck came to town. "Put an end to that in quick order."

The town was rugged, surrounded by lots of open land with large cattle ranches, wild mustang horses, hunters, and a couple of open mines. Lots of good folks lived here. Sheriff Joe liked a peaceable town, and he kept it humming. Any stranger that made their way here was suspect.

One time some "slant eyes" came to town. "Had to run those 'chinks' right back on outa here." They were sniffing around some nice river property. There was no way in hell he was going to let that happen. "Showed them the end of my gun, and that put a quick end to that notion." Besides, Hank Jr.'s father wanted that land, *real* bad. Right now, Indians had rights to the land. It was on their reservation, and he was figuring a way to get it away from them. It was just a matter of time – like always.

Sheriff Joe was particular about who he allowed in his town. "No hippies, Jews, or coons in my neck of the woods," he would say. "With one exception – that money-grubbing Jew family running the mercantile store. They charge a high price for their goods, so I charge them a little commission on the side. Makes for a nice healthy profit to my pension plan and keeps their store open for business." But the one race of people he would not abide – above all the rest – was "those devil-trompin' redskins… free-loadin' sonsabitches…" Sheriff Joe tried to barter with them about some grazing land of theirs, but they were a stubborn lot and refused to budge. Wouldn't give him an inch or an acre. When he pressed the issue, the tribe gave him trouble. So, three Cheyenne Indians came to town to negotiate. He didn't like their demands or their "high and mighty" attitude. They were in his territory now, and he would teach them a thing or two. So, he arrested them, had the judge come to town for a quick trial, then took the bunch out back behind the saloon and hung them on the old sycamore – for "due cause" – whatever *that* was.

Sheriff Joe called it "the hanging tree," and he nailed a cross on the side as a constant reminder to the people of Miners Gulch as well as to outsiders how the sheriff of this town dealt with undesirables and lawbreakers.

But on this night, with Sheriff Joe out of town, Hank, Randy, and Jimmy Dean had dragged Oliver into the bar and joked about taking the law into their own hands. "Just doing the sheriff a favor," Hank said, bragging. They shoved Oliver into a seat at the bar, wound the rope around him tight, and tied him to the bar stool. No one paid much attention at first. It was noisy and the dance floor was crowded.

When the song came to an end, people clamored back to their seats, lit cigarettes and sipped their drinks. Mike Stull, the banker, blinked his bleary eyes a couple times to make sure he was seeing straight. "What the devil…? Serving up some 'firewater,' for the Injun?" he asked with a laugh.

The patrons joined in, slapping their knees at the sight of an Indian in their bar. Some wondered why he would even dare come to their town. It set off a buzz of speculation.

Someone piped up, "I could bring my dog if you're lookin' for more customers. Wouldn't stink as bad, neither." The bar erupted into laughter. More drinks were ordered and soon the jukebox cranked out a Merle Haggard song, sending the locals scurrying back to the dance floor.

Hank, Jimmy Dean, and Randy went to the kitchen out back

where Randy's mom, Gladys, was tossing some cheeseburgers onto the grill. She slapped mayonnaise on the buns and pulled some French fries from the deep fryer. As she turned around, she was so startled, she almost dropped the fry basket. "Good Lord! What happened?" She hurried over to her son to inspect his face, turned it to the side and gasped.

"Had a tussle with some redskin, Ma. Fought like crazy, but we got him in his place now. He's tied up at the bar. Got some peroxide and bandages handy?"

Gladys ran for some towels and a frozen burger. She soaked the towel in cool water and handed the frozen patty to Hank. "Looks bad. Don't count on seein' outa that eye by tomorrow." She wrung out the towel and started to wipe the caked blood from Randy's face.

"I can do this, Ma. Tend to your burgers. Gotta full house tonight, so I need to get back out there and relieve Ollie. He's good in a pinch, but only for so long. Plus, got that Injun out there, too, and… who knows…? Could get a little rowdy." Randy went back out front toward the bar and grabbed a double-barrel shotgun on his way.

The bar was starting to hop. It was only nine o'clock and had a long way to go before closing time. Randy thanked Ollie for looking out for the bar. "I think I can handle it from here. Give you a holler if I need more help. And, hey, pop a long neck… it's on me."

Randy looked over at Oliver, who seemed oddly at ease. It flustered him to see the Indian sitting there unrattled. So, he strutted over, pointed his shotgun, and shoved it up against Oliver's face. "Listen up! You try anything smart or look at me crooked, and I'll blow a hole clean through you. And I won't lose a wink o' sleep over it, neither." He lowered the shotgun and put in under the bar, giving the unruffled Indian a warning glare and watching him out of the corner of his eye.

Randy had to admit to himself that he grudgingly respected

that Indian for his stoical demeanor, although he was puzzled by his aloofness. He snuck another peak out of the corner of his eye, envying Oliver's sinewy muscles, and broad shoulders. Every ounce of him oozed strength and stamina. Randy eyed his long hair, pulled into a ponytail tied with red leather strips. He thought it suited the Indian. When he caught himself envying the guy, he quickly dismissed the thought. *Good God! What's wrong with me? If anyone found out how I feel, they'd laugh me outa town. No, worse.* Randy poured a shot of whiskey and downed it in one swig.

The lone stranger sitting at the far end of the bar called to Randy, pointing to his empty glass. "Tall gin and tonic with a slice of lime."

Randy swiveled his neck around to get a look at this guy. High and mighty with fancy duds – not from these parts, Randy surmised, as he walked the drink over to the customer, banged it down on the bar, spilling some of its contents and throwing the slice of lime on the counter for emphasis. "That'll be three bucks, Slick."

"Name's Sam." Catching Randy's glare, he put down a five. "Keep the change."

Randy eyed the money, then scowled at Sam. He didn't trust this one.

"Get into a fight with that fellow over there?" Sam asked, pointing to Oliver. "You got a mass of blood on your face. I bet it hurts like hell."

"You just mind your own beeswax, partner. Don't like strangers sticking their nose where it don't belong. And no, it don't hurt. Takes more than a fist to make me holler." Randy snatched the five, walked back to the cash register, put it in the drawer, and slammed it shut – giving the stranger another dirty look.

Sam sipped his drink slowly, wondering about the intriguing young Indian tied up at the bar. *He seems almost indifferent to his situation – which looks dire.*

Oliver turned his startling blue eyes to Sam.

Sam nodded in acknowledgement and tipped his glass to the Indian. He was thinking about going over to talk with him, find out what happened, when a shaggy blond-haired guy came out from the back holding a burger to his eye – a slight guy following behind looked pretty banged up. Sam grinned. *That Indian must have beaten the crap out of those guys.* He pulled his hat down lower to cover his eyes and watched. This was getting interesting.

Hank sat down near Oliver and smacked him hard on the back. "Your sorry Injun ass is gonna be in for a treat tonight," he laughed. "Ain't that right, Jimmy Dean?"

Jimmy Dean smirked. "You got *that* right, Hank. His sorry ass is in big trouble."

"And look at this… ponytails, with ribbons… like a girl." Hank leaned in close. "You're gonna be a sorry sonofabitch, coming to this town, Red. Not many Injuns make it out of here, especially ones looking to steal my truck." He lowered his voice to an ominous snarl. "That's about as bad as stealing a man's horse… we hang folks for that one. Gonna put another notch on that great big tree out back, and when your legs finally stop twitchin', gonna throw your worthless carcass out to the wolves. So, enjoy yourself, Injun, while you're still breathing." He shoved Oliver's head onto the bar with a loud thud.

"Say, Randy. Grab a Hamm's brew for me, would you? And one for Jimmy Dean, too." Hank looked over at Jimmy Dean. "You thirsty?"

Jimmy Dean nodded enthusiastically. "Parched to my toes," he said with a wide smile.

Hank slapped him on the shoulder. "How're you holding up, pal? See you got punched pretty good."

"A little sore, for sure, but had to help my friend." Jimmy Dean clinked bottles with Hank, giving him a pat on the back.

Randy came over and set a big bottle of Old Crow on the bar

and poured a shot for Hank, Jimmy Dean, and himself. "Here's to snagging a loose Injun off the ole rez." The three raised their glasses, and Randy and Hank emptied their own.

Jimmy Dean took a small sip, trying to act cool. But, as the drink went down his throat, he felt it burn. He coughed hard, his face turning a bright pink. "Whew! Pretty potent stuff."

Hank slapped him on the back and laughed. "That's what real men and cowboys drink, Jimmy Dean."

Jimmy Dean's face turned scarlet, and he forced another sip of the wicked-tasting whiskey. "Well, *I'm* a real man… so, here goes." He held his breath and drank, hoping the burning liquid would stay down.

Randy smirked watching Jimmy Dean struggle to get the whisky down. "Whaddaya think the sheriff's gonna do to that Indian, Hank?" he said, "when he gets back to town."

"Think I'll save him the trouble of going to court," he said. "But, for now I'm gonna let loose and have a little fun. Been a helluva week. My dad's been working me real hard on the ranch, and my butt is dang sore. Been sitting in the saddle from morning till night, out driving the cattle."

"Well then, how about another beer, Hank?" Jimmy Dean asked.

"Take you up on that one," Hank said. "Hey, if you want to earn a little extra cash, I could take you along next week. One of our ranch hands got injured, so he's off for a spell. It's tiring work, but if you can sit in the saddle all day and keep an eye on the strays, might be a good gig. Plus, Jake's getting on in years and he's not much company."

Jimmy Dean tried to hide his excitement, being out on the range with his – his hero. All he could do was nod. He looked at the remaining whiskey in his glass, thinking, *I best get used to this stuff.* Holding his breath, he swallowed the remaining whiskey and let out a "Whoo-whee! Sounds great! I'm not too steady on a horse, as you know, but I'll get the hang of it… with your help." His face flushed as he considered the possibilities.

"There's an old cowboy saying," Hank said with a grin. 'If you climb in the saddle, be ready for the ride. I'll tell my dad we've got another hand."

Randy overheard the conversation and chuckled at the prospect of Jimmy Dean out there in the range, roping cattle and such. He always thought the guy was a little off, but what the heck? He was Hank's friend and that was good enough for him. He poured himself another Old Crow, and said, "Salute! to the boys. Hank clinked bottles with Jimmy Dean and they both hollered, "Salute!" back to Randy.

Just then, two girls walked into the bar. One wore a short skirt and a tight top and the other a plain dark dress that fell below her knees. Jimmy Dean's smile faded as he saw Hank's neck do a fast swivel and his eyes pop out at the sight of the sheriff's scantily clad daughter. She called herself, Indigo. Hank couldn't get used to the name, but he thought, *what the hell… who cares about a name with a body like that… makes a man melt.* He whispered to Jimmy Dean, "I've gotta get close to her, cause she's the sweetest thing I've ever laid my eyeballs on. Check out that body – like one of those cheerleaders back at college… but even better."

Indigo stood five-feet-nine with auburn hair that fell in luscious waves past her shoulders. Her emerald-green eyes slanted at the corners and could make most men fall to their knees.

Hank was smitten. Jimmy Dean was perturbed.

Indigo breezed on past Hank and Jimmy Dean without a glance. Her long auburn hair looked ablaze as it swayed seductively while she strolled lightheartedly through the bar.

Hank thought he must have died and gone to heaven as she whooshed past him, leaving behind her lingering fragrance. He could only imagine the delights hidden beneath that brief skirt. Oh, sweet Lordy, he wanted her so bad he could taste her.

Boozy eyes followed her through the smoky haze. She sparkled and was full of sass. No one paid any attention to her friend, Janet Hershel, with her large-frame glasses and plain looks. Plus, she was a Jew. Most folks would have told her to leave, but the sheriff gave his 'okay' because Mary would put up a fierce fight for her. He didn't want to deal with her crap, so Sheriff Joe backed down. He had never run into anyone as stubborn or as fearless as her. Secretly he was proud of that trait… figured those genes came from him.

The girls were close enough to nineteen, which was the legal age for drinking, and nothing was said, anyway, if they fell a bit short of that figure. Besides, considering who her father was, no one would dare question Mary or her friends.

Sheriff Joe thought "broads," were good for business, and *nothing's better for business than a pretty gal sitting at a bar.*

Indigo and Janet found a small table set back in the corner by a slightly worn pool table. A few locals were placing bets on the table, ready for a game of nine-ball. Indigo's eyes scanned the room, then wandered toward the bar. She stiffened when she saw someone tied up in a chair. Noticing the guy's long hair and bronzed face, she gasped, poking Janet. "Oh my God, Janet. They've got some Indian guy tied up. What do you suppose he's doing here? I hope they don't hurt him."

Janet arched her neck to look at Oliver. "That's awful. Who knows what these guys will do – especially when they get drunk and rowdy?"

"It doesn't look good," Indigo said, scrunching her eyes to see what he looked like, and taken aback when he turned his head and looked directly at her. She couldn't believe how handsome he was, nor how calm he appeared. *He can't be much older than me,* she thought. A lump started to form in her throat, and she felt tears prickling in her eyes. She sensed something unusual about him, as he sat staring back at her, looking as cool as a cucumber. *What on earth is he doing in this town? Doesn't he know it's a dangerous place for him?*

"I'm going to see what's going on, Janet. Hank is at the bar with Jimmy Dean. I bet they had something to do with this." She pushed her chair back, walked up to the bar, and stood next to the Indian, where she boldly stared into his gorgeous face and his unusual deep blue eyes stared back at her. She felt a prickling of apprehension as she stood there. In a low tone, she asked him, "What happened to bring you to Miners Gulch? This is a dangerous place to be, I hate to say – if you're an Indian. I'm sorry."

Oliver's unsettling blue eyes stared with such intensity and distrust, that Indigo backed away from the fierce gaze.

No wonder they're called warriors, she thought in admiration.

Hank slid his chair back, fuming, and quickly shoved his way between Indigo and Oliver. He smacked him up the side of his head. "Best be staying away from our ladies, Red. Talking to white girls will get you in a whole bunch of trouble. Stick to your squaws…" Then he cocked a smile at Indigo and tipped his black Stetson hat. His eyes wandered over her body in admiration, and his white teeth lit up the smoke-filled room. "Well, hello there, Mary darlin'. I haven't seen you in a spell."

"My name is Indigo. Not "darlin'." And not Mary. Indigo."

"Well, excuse me, Mary… uh, Indigo. Be careful around this Indian," Hank said, cocking his thumb at Oliver. "I caught him snooping around my truck… trying to steal my ride. He may look innocent, but he's got a real mean streak in him. So don't get too friendly with him. You know how this town feels…" He let his words drift off with a wink.

"Don't tell me, what I can or cannot do," Indigo said angrily, and shoved him hard.

Hank stumbled backwards and Jimmy Dean caught him before he landed on the floor. "Whoa, big guy. Almost landed on your backside." His face flushed as he felt Hank's hard body.

Hank jerked himself upright and brushed off his shirt. "You don't need to be so uppity," he said to Indigo, holding back his anger. "Your pa's outa town, so we're gonna handle this matter ourselves."

Jimmy Dean poked his head around Hank and spoke up, "Sure the hell are, Mary."

"Shut up, Jimmy Dean," Indigo said. "My name is Indigo. You must be deaf as well as stupid."

Jimmy Dean's face burned with indignation. He swallowed hard, looking at Hank, and itching to smack her pretty face.

Hank said. "You're cute as hell when you're mad, Indie, but don't go steppin' in places that don't concern you."

"This guy was skulking around town, looking hard at Hank's '54, Mary," said Randy. "Most likely he's a drunk and a thief. Probably planning to rob the bar, too. I know the sheriff wouldn't tolerate this kind of goings on, especially while he's away."

"You guys can't take the law into your own hands," Indigo said.

Hank grinned at the feisty girl. She just made him want her even more than he already did. "Your pa may be the law in these parts, but I know he'd thank us for saving him the trouble of dealing with this… petty annoyance here. So, I decided, we're gonna have us a little hanging tonight." He started to put his hand to her shoulder, but she shoved him away, eyes smoldering with disgust.

"You can't hang someone just because you *think* he might steal your old truck. That's why we have courts and judges. You need evidence!"

"Look Mary… uh, Indigo," Randy said, trying to placate the girl. "This is Wyoming. We have our own set of rules here. *You* know that. There's a big sign outside of town that warns: 'Indians are not welcome here. Enter at your own peril.' And, for Chrissakes, in case they miss that one coming in, there's an even bigger sign in front of the bar that says, plain as daylight: 'No Indians allowed.' How I like to think of it is, 'you come a walkin', you won't leave a talkin'. How much plainer can we be? It's like they're asking for trouble when they come around, so that's what they're gonna get."

"Oh, shut up. You guys are as ignorant as you are malicious…"

"Oh, come on, Indie," Hank said, with a big grin. "Let's forget about all this nasty stuff for a while. You just graduated. Let's celebrate on the dance floor. Show you some of my hip moves." Hank started to slide his hips back and forth and do a quick-two-step.

"I wouldn't dance with you for a hundred dollars," she said, fuming. She turned her back on him and placed an order with Randy. "Tequila sunrise and a cherry coke."

Drinks in hand, Indigo stomped off, back to the table, and placed the cherry coke in front of Janet.

"Thanks, Indigo," said Janet, taking a sip.

"This town makes me sick!" Indigo said. "These *men* make me sick. Hank and Randy and that idiot Jimmy Dean are talking about hanging the Indian guy tonight."

"Oh no," Janet said, paling at the news.

"Sheriff's out of town. Can't quite get the word, 'father' out, without feeling like gagging. Not even sure where he went… not that I care. But maybe if he was here, I could talk him out of letting this thing get out of control. If those guys are drunk, there'll be no stopping them. It's like part of their stupid culture."

Janet was stunned silent, shocked they might make good on their threat. After a moment she found her voice. "Oh, my God! We've got to stop this. This is crazy!"

"Look Janet, you know this town. You know how these people are. They don't like outsiders – especially those with a different skin color."

"I *do* know how these people are, and that's why I'm so scared."

Just then, Sally Bennett walked in, sporting a black eye. The girls waved her over and she signaled she was on her way. But first she stopped at the bar and ordered her favorite – a rum and coke. She looked over at Hank, who turned his head toward Jimmy Dean. They both started laughing.

Sally glumly picked up her drink, walked over to the girls, and sat down.

In unison, Indigo and Janet said, "What happened to you?"

Sally took a gulp before answering and made a face. "I'm guessing my makeup didn't cover it up.

"Oh, Sally," Indigo said, annoyed. "It had to have been Hank, again. Why do you still see him? He just uses you…"

"I know, I know. But he's just so damn cute… plus, he didn't mean to hurt me. It was my fault for getting so mad at him for seeing other girls. It drives him nuts when I get whiny."

"Oh my God, Sally. You deserve so much better than him."

"Well, then, who do you think I *should* date? That simpleton, Jimmy Dean Hinkle… or as your dad calls him, 'Sausage Link?'" To break the tension, she giggled.

"That's mean," said Janet, reprimanding her friend.

"Well, that's what he looks like."

"Look, Sally. You're a talented artist with a promising future. You don't need to belittle yourself with a creep like Hank. But now we have a big problem. Hank says he and Jimmy Dean found this Indian in his truck nosing around, accusing him of trying to steal it. So, he and Randy and Jimmy Dean have a plan hatched up and they're talking about a hanging. We just can't sit by and do nothing."

"Wow!" Sally said, straightening up, taking a better look. "Shame to let a handsome hunk like that get his neck snapped at the end of a rope. Do you see his rockin' bod and that head of hair? Holy shit! I could go for that!"

Janet rolled her eyes and gave Sally an exasperated look. "Is that all you can think about at a time like this?"

Indigo's eyes wandered to the far end of the bar and the good-looking stranger seated there. "Okay. I'm not sure what's going on here tonight, but… see that guy, that hunk sitting at the end of the bar with a baseball hat?"

"I see him," Janet said, curiously. "That makes two strangers in town, *and*, on the same night."

All three girls turned their attention to the gorgeous creature sitting alone, seeming to observe everything.

"Who is he?" Sally said, gushing.

"Yeah, I wonder where he's from," Janet said, "and what's he doing here."

"Well, we're going to find out. I can't stand not knowing." Indigo said.

"Ooooohh! Two gorgeous dudes in one night," Sally said.

"Let's wait a minute and watch him… see what he's up to," said Janet.

"We can't appear too anxious, can we?" Indigo said, as the girls sat huddled together, sipping their drinks, watching and waiting.

Hank was standing at the bar, stewing and observing Indigo. "Wouldn't you know it… the one night that Mary's here that damn Sally's here, too. My luck. Better be careful calling her Mary, huh, Jimmy Dean? Might get in trouble. But it bugs the shit outa me… she's always acting like she's better than me. That just gets my goat," Hank said with a grumble, taking a big swing of his beer. "She knows I would've been a famous NFL star if I hadn't gotten injured and messed up my chances. Sure, my shoulder's always acting up… but I'm still tall in the saddle, if you get my drift." Hank snorted, elbowing Jimmy Dean. "It stinks what happened to me," he said, looking toward the floor. "All I've got going for me now is working on my Pa's ranch…"

"Which will be yours someday," Jimmy Dean said, reminding him.

"Yeah… Guess it's not all that bad, huh, partner?" Hank smirked, downing the rest of his Hamm's.

"Well, I'm glad you're back, and I'm sorry for what happened to you, but it just wasn't the same around here… uh… *you* know… without you." Jimmy Dean reached around and rubbed

Hank's back. "I'd say you're one lucky dude. All the guys like you… and all the girls want you… Well, maybe, except for that Mary-Indigo-Whatever she calls herself. She doesn't deserve you and she certainly doesn't appreciate your good qualities. You're… handsomer than most, you're rich, you're popular, you can still pack a pretty good punch – even with that busted shoulder, and, most important, Sheriff Joe likes you. So, I don't know… your life seems pretty darn sweet to me. A lot sweeter than mine… that's for dang sure. Plus, today, you caught a wild Indian. Besides, unlike me, you don't have to live with your Granny. I don't mean to complain, because I love my grandma. She needs my help, and I'm happy to lend a hand. And I sure don't mind cooking and cleaning up a bit around the house… Long as I can get out with you and have some fun, I'm good."

"That's what I like about you Jimmy Dean… always got my back. Now let's get stinkin' drunk. Randy pours that cheap shit, Old Crow. I'm gonna get us some of that fine-tasting Gentlemen Jack whiskey. Feeling kinda frisky tonight so, what the hell… let's celebrate while the night is young."

"Yeah, love that Gentlemen Jack. Bet he's a real upstanding guy."

Hank looked over at Oliver, who was quietly watching him. "Say, what are you staring at, Red?"

Oliver didn't answer.

Hank grabbed hold of his hair, gave it a yank, and twisted it tight. As he looked him square in his eyes, he was instantly taken aback by his fierce gaze. Hank fumbled before finding his voice. "Gonna take care of you later. Teach you for coming around here, messing where you don't belong!" And he yanked harder. "Hey, Randy. We gotta keep an eye on this skin. He's a sneaky one. I can see it in his thieving eyes."

Randy nodded. "Sure thing." He was busy making drinks

for customers and for Leah, who worked on Friday and Saturday nights.

"Let's see what's going on at the pool table. I'm feeling lucky tonight, with ole Gentlemen Jack by my side, and, of course, my partner in crime." He punched Jimmy Dean good-naturedly in the arm. "Let's go relieve those cowboys of their wages."

Oliver remained still, warily watching the crowd of people. His eyes fell on the lone guy at the end of the bar – wondering what he was up to and why the guy had been staring at him. It wasn't a menacing or angry stare. More like a look of "how can I help?" The guy looked sophisticated… probably from a big city. Oliver watched him as he stood up and headed toward the restroom and then looked back and gave the peace symbol.

There was more to Sam Colton than his Dodgers cap. He was dressed in a navy blue fitted blazer with a light blue T-shirt underneath and pressed Levi blue jeans and tasseled loafers. With short dark brown hair, he was slim, well-built, and stood close to six feet tall.

En route to the restroom, Sam passed near the table where Indigo, Sally, and Janet were seated. "Hello, ladies," he said with a slight bow, tipped his baseball cap, and continued on.

Indigo smiled brightly. "That guy is definitely not from these parts, and I want to get to know him. Had enough of these stupid cowboys to last a lifetime."

"Did you see his smile?" Janet asked the girls. "He could certainly make a woman swoon, just by looking at her."

"Well, he's not quite as cute as Hank," Sally quipped. "He seems too proper to be a regular guy. I bet he's a real snob."

Indigo's heart was racing. "I don't know why I feel so strongly about him. I can't help it."

Hank pranced around the pool table, bragging about the redskin he had bagged who was sitting at the bar, and pointed to Oliver.

"Hell, you could skin him and use him for skunk bait," a local cowhand said, drunkenly.

"Gonna have some fun first," Hank said, "then… we'll see." He chalked the tip of his pool stick, eyes following the newcomer as he passed by the girls and paused. He saw Indigo smile at the stranger and felt his blood boil.

"We got us a pansy ass in town, Jimmy Dean," Hank said, jealously.

Jimmy Dean couldn't help looking at the stranger, admiring his physique.

Hank cursed and hit the two-ball with such force it flew off the table. "Bet he's a faggot, sashaying around with those swishy tassel shoes. If you're any kind of a man around here, you wear your cowboy boots and strap a big ole gun to your…" He stopped as Sam came up to him and stuck out his hand.

"Sam Colton is my name."

Hank just stared at him with a sneer and said, "So what? Why don't you take your tassel shoes and get lost?" And he turned away.

"Well, here's twenty bucks for the next game," Sam said, pulling a bill out of his pocket.

Hank turned around and said, "Well, now, I don't mind taking money from a sucker. They say there's one born every minute, and you, I can see, are a big one."

Sam just smiled. "Give a yell when you want to play."

The music stopped and it seemed like everyone hurried to their tables, sat down, and lit a cigarette – blowing thick plumes of smoke that filled the room.

Sam walked up to the bar and stood next to Oliver. "Looks like this is the wrong bar in the wrong town for outsiders," Sam said lightly. "My name's Sam, by the way."

Oliver's blue eyes flashed over at Sam, and he nodded. "I'm Oliver."

"Nice to meet you."

Indigo shoved her chair back, got her nerve up – determined to find out what was going on with the Indian who was tied up and also to introduce herself to the cute guy with the baseball cap, who made her heart skip a beat.

She walked boldly up to the bar and looked Oliver straight in the eye. "Looks like you've landed in a bit of trouble," she said with a slight nod, showing a bright smile. Not waiting for him to answer, she turned to the guy standing close, who made her nerves tingle. Her voice wavered slightly as she asked, "You two know each other?"

"We just met. His name's Oliver. I'm Sam… Sam Colton."

"My name used to be Mary, but it sounded like a nun's name, so I changed it to something – you might say – more colorful – Indigo. My *favorite* color actually," she grinned. "My dad's the town's sheriff. I hate to admit it, but I felt you should know. He's somewhere out of town right now, which is always a good thing. Not sure why I'm blurting all this out, but for some reason I just want to be straight. That wanna-be stud you met over there at the pool table is Hank. He and the other guys are planning to hang Oliver. I know this sounds crazy and I'm sorry about all this."

"Whew!" Sam said. "Quite the introduction. Nice to meet you, Indigo."

Oliver looked warily into Indigo's eyes, nodded his head, and said, "Hi."

"What made you come to this place…?" Her voice trailed off as a swaggering Hank sidled up next to her.

"Say, Indie. I don't think it's safe for you to be up here talking to this Injun. Besides, anything you want to know, you could just ask me," Hank said with a stupid grin. "You know I'd do anything for you…"

"Just shut it, Hank. You reek of whiskey and, you're unlawfully restraining this man. You can't hang someone without proof he committed a crime. The only thing you're proving is that you're a bona fide ass."

Hank's face turned livid. "Look, Indie. This wild Injun came at me with a tomahawk when I told him to get out of my truck. These people aren't normal, and they fight like savages on the warpath. He jumped Jimmy Dean when I turned my back and tried to kill Randy when he came out of the bar. Assault is cause enough to hang him."

"You're full of crap, Hank."

"Hey, Jimmy Dean," Hank hollered out. "Get over here!"

Jimmy Dean hustled over to the bar, face flushed.

"Tell Indie here that this redskin tried to kill us."

"Hank told it right," Jimmy Dean, said. "That Injun is a thief and tried to kill us."

Indigo had a strange feeling about Jimmy Dean. She never trusted him. "You'd say anything Hank asked you to." Turning to Hank, she said, "Let him go before you do something crazy."

Hank grinned. "I'm a crazy kinda guy, Indie." He winked flirtatiously, and said, "Let's go dance and forget about this nobody. I'm feeling all warm and fuzzy being next to you. Can't help myself. That's what you do to me, and I'm…" Before he could finish, he felt his hat knocked off and his face slapped.

Indigo stomped off to the pool table and slammed a quarter down. "I'm next."

A couple of ranch hands just finishing up their game looked at Indigo in surprise. But they didn't question her. They knew enough to stay away from her. It was well known in town that Indigo and the sheriff weren't close, but she was his daughter and anything that belonged to the sheriff was off limits. No one dared argue with that notion except Hank. His dad, Hank Sr., was a powerful man in these parts, and he and the sheriff were tight.

Hank scurried over to the pool table, and told the two ranch hands, "Move it," and racked the balls. "Okay, Indie. So, you won't dance with me, I'll play you a game of pool. Got 'em all set up."

Indigo shrugged her shoulders, as Hank slammed the cue ball hard, scattering the balls across the pool table, and knocking three into pockets.

"Solids," he called out. He meticulously eyed each ball, and with great concentration, he hit every solid into a pocket, intentionally missing the last one. "Didn't mean to hit them all in, so I'll give you a chance to catch up. Maybe you'll get lucky."

Indigo ignored him. A good pool player, she studied her remaining shots, then managed to sink four balls in a row, missing her next shot.

"Well, now, Indie. You did pretty good for a girl, but I can't let you whip me in front of all the guys, now. So, hang onto your panties and watch how it's done." He strutted around the table and called out, "eight ball in the corner pocket." With one swift motion, he shot the ball in the pocket. "Woo-hoo, Momma's stew! Give you another chance if you want."

Hank's eyes narrowed as Sam walked up to the pool table and challenged him. "Like I said earlier, I'll play you for twenty," and set it on the table. "We can double that, if you like."

"The table is taken, so go back and sit your ass back down," Hank said, grabbing the twenty. "For that matter, why don't you go back to wherever the hell you came from. We don't like nosey strangers coming to our town, snooping around."

Sam didn't back away or blink an eye as Hank glared ominously at him. He just smiled and said, "Just looking for a friendly game of pool is all."

Hank snorted, looking Sam up and down. "You hear that, Jimmy Dean? Well, we ain't looking for friendly around here." Hank poked Sam in the chest. "So, git your fancy ass an' tasseled shoes outa here."

Indigo saw trouble and quickly stepped in between them. She

looked at the handsome stranger, and said, "Well, I like tasseled shoes and I welcome newcomers that come to town. We don't have that many coming this way, so I'll play for your twenty that Hank's holding." She held out her hand. "Hand it over, Hank."

Hank's face burned purple as Indigo grabbed the pool cue from his grip along with the twenty. She stood her ground, daring him to make trouble.

Jimmy Dean hustled next to Hank. "Best not start any trouble with Mary." Hank grudgingly turned away.

Indigo turned to Sam and said sweetly, "Here you go," and she handed him the pool stick.

Hank stalked over to the bar and looked at Oliver, who was watching the scene at the pool table. He slapped him across the face. "Don't be looking at that white girl, Injun. Stick to your own kind… dirt-digger."

Jimmy Dean leaned in close to Oliver and slurred in his ear. "You heard right, Injun. Keep your eyeballs straight ahead." He watched Hank watching Indigo shoot pool with the handsome stranger, then grabbed a whiskey and gulped it down – choking from the power of the stinging brew.

Sally swayed up to Hank at the bar and looked at him with longing – hating herself at the same time. "Hi there, Hank. Wanna dance?" she asked sheepishly. "Merle is playing your favorite tune." To entice him, she started to dance.

Hank looked at her, and grimaced. "Well, why don't you get on out there and dance with Jake? Looks like he's lonely. Got other things on my mind right now."

Sally felt embarrassed and humiliated by the guy she adored. "Looks like someone gave you a real big shiner – just like the one you gave me."

"Why don't you shut your trap."

"You musta run into a fist that had had enough of your shit," she mocked – then, seeing the fury in his eyes, backed away to the other side of the bar and ordered a rum and coke. There she stood watching Hank, his eyes never leaving Indigo. She couldn't help feeling jealous of her friend, who attracted all the men in town. She knew Indigo didn't like Hank… quite the reverse. She just wished she didn't care about him. As it was, she felt lucky he noticed her at all. Resigned to disappointment, she set down her drink and, to the sound of Earl Thomas Conley's music she dragged that scrawny Jimmy Dean to the dance floor. Jimmy Dean looked awkward, as he gyrated around the floor, stomping his boots like he had a nervous condition.

Maybe this isn't worth it, she thought, as she danced seductively in her tight skirt, moving her hips real slow, hoping Hank would notice. But Hank paid no attention, so, when the song ended, she brought her drink back to the table and sat down next to Janet, who seemed amused by Indigo's pool game with the intriguing stranger.

"Well, isn't he a hunk?" Sally mused, and nudged Janet. "Wonder where he's from and why he wandered in this town of all places."

"He must have made a wrong turn on his way to somewhere else." Janet said, sipping on her drink, trying to listen to pieces of their conversation.

Indigo set the balls and did the first break – knocking one in the side pocket. She looked over at Sam curiously. "So, Sam Colton. Where are you heading to? I know you said you were just passing through, but I'll bet you'll regret stopping off here."

"Well, this town is something, that's for sure. So, your dad is the sheriff?"

"Yep. He's a real winner around her. His favorite slogan is: Remember, this is cowboy country," said Janet.

"Sounds like a real nice guy." Sam said under his breath as he missed an easy shot.

"Well, I hope you can dance better than you can play," said Indigo as she easily put a couple balls in the corner pocket.

"Probably not much better," Sam said slyly, as he aced the remaining balls.

"How about that?! You were holding out on me," Indigo said with a grin.

Hank was still watching Indigo and Sam shoot pool. "She's flirting with that bag of scum," he told Jimmy Dean, seething. Downing another shot of whiskey to soothe his misery, he almost choked at the sight of Indigo touching Sam's arm and cringing when she gave him a big smile. *That's the kind of smile that makes my knees go weak*, he thought bitterly. He rushed over and crossed his arms. "Hey, tassel toes! Why don't you play someone that can teach you a thing or two. I got twenty bucks that says I can whip your ass! How about it?" He racked them up quickly, hoping for a yes.

Sam looked evenly at Hank, ready to play, when Indigo slid up beside him. "Sorry, Hank, we're going out on the dance floor." She looked at Sam with pleading eyes.

"I'll take you up on your offer… after this dance," Sam said to Hank. "Here's my money." He put a twenty-dollar bill on the table. "Hold it till I get back."

Hank bristled at the thought of Indigo dancing with this guy. He seemed a little too at ease for his liking.

Merle Haggard was singing, "That's the way loves goes…" and Indigo was feeling intoxicated from her drink and from being so close to this charming stranger. "Must be a dream come true," she breathed out, and wrapped her arms around Sam's neck. "You're like a breath of fresh air in this stifling haven for cowboys and creeps. How long are you staying?"

Sam smiled as he looked into Indigo's emerald-green eyes and held her gaze for a moment. "Leaving tomorrow," he said softly, pulling Indigo close and breathing in her scent. "You feel nice. It's a shame I have to leave, but…" He let the sentence dangle.

"I don't blame you for wanting to leave. I would like to leave myself… This town has little tolerance for newcomers. We've got a sheriff who's a bully and a church to keep everyone in line. People are like sheep around here. Everyone follows the pack and does what they're told. Sorry, I don't mean to be a downer, but, as you've surmised by now, I hate this place with a passion. Like I said. You're a breath of fresh air…"

They were quiet the rest of the dance, enjoying the closeness of each other.

Indigo wasn't one to be swept off her feet by any man, but this guy was somehow special. She wanted to find out more about him so she could discover what that 'special' was. *Maybe it's his easy way, charming and sophisticated. Or maybe it's just that he's got a mind of his own. Probably, both.*

Just as the dance was ending, Sam asked, "Do you think these guys will carry out their threat against this Indian? I overheard the bartender say they were going to take the Indian out back after closing and watch him dance on a rope."

Indigo stiffened at the words. "Oh, my God! I hope not. Hank's a hero in this town. Everyone blindly looks up to him…"

"Well, maybe they're just trying to show off their manhood…"

"That could be. Hank's as cocky and arrogant as they come. Been spoiled all his life. His father is powerful and rich, and he thinks he can do whatever he wants around here. He likes to brag and strut about – especially if someone new is in town. Plus, it didn't help that you were dancing with me. He can't stand that… which is a big waste of his time," she giggled. Her smile faded as she considered the facts. "Still… have to keep my eyes on these guys. They're known to get real crazy when they're drunk."

"And they're *really* drunk." Sam held her close and whispered in her ear. "I'll watch my back – and yours." He squeezed her hands as they walked to the pool table where Hank was holding a shot glass full of whiskey. "Here's to losing your shirt, Slick." He tossed it down in one gulp.

Sam said, "I hate to see you drink alone. Be right back." He hustled up to the bar, next to Oliver, and spoke in a low tone. "How're you doing? I hope they're not serious about a hanging… but if they are, I'll be around to help however I can."

Oliver looked at Sam in amusement. "I guess you're not from these parts. These ranchers pay off local law enforcement and get away with anything they like. So, what do *you* think? They hate us Indians. Still think we stole their lands… if you can believe that."

Randy walked over and looked Sam in the eye. "I told ya to leave this Injun alone. You're not to be talking to him."

"Just wanted another drink is all. Tall gin and tonic with lime," Sam said, politely. When Randy was out of earshot, Sam hunkered close. "The sheriff's daughter said she and her friends will help, too."

Oliver shook his head. "Not sure what the girls can do, but if *you* try to help me, they'll string you up as well… or run you out of town. So, drink your gin and tonic with lime… and then, leave."

"I don't get it. Why did you come here, knowing this place was so dangerous?"

Randy stormed over, and slammed Sam's drink on the counter. "That'll be ten bucks, Slick."

Sam said, "The last one was three bucks."

"Price goes up after ten o'clock. So, pay up or leave!"

Sam put a ten on the bar and Randy snatched it up. "You best mind your own business, or you'll be a sorry one." He turned, walked to the cash register, and shoved the bill inside.

Sam took a sip and persisted. "So why *did* you come here?"

"That's my father's '54 Ford truck out there. He's been missing for a few years. My guess is, they got him *and* his truck. I saw it as I was walking down the road. Hank was driving. They stopped a couple nights ago and offered me a ride in the back. I hopped in, and they tried to get rid of me, but I managed to get away."

Hank slid up and gave Sam a rough slap on his back and

yanked him off his chair. "Say, whatcha doing messing in affairs that don't concern you. This one's a criminal, so leave him and everyone in here alone. And that goes for the fair maiden you were dancing with. I'll get the sheriff to lock your ass up in the jail if you don't watch your p's and q's around here. This is cowboy country. We don't take to slick city folk poking their noses into where they don't belong. Take that as a warning! Now if you want to play pool, get on over there."

Sam acquiesced without a word, picked up his drink, and went to the pool table.

"Got your twenty, tassel-toes?"

Sam pulled another twenty out of his pocket and set it on the pool table.

Hank cracked the balls, scattering them across the table. Nothing went in.

The girls were glued to the pool table. Indigo's eyes were peeled on Sam. Sally was watching Hank – her hands twitching nervously. Janet's eyes flew back and forth and watched both of them. Jimmy Dean stood by cheering Hank on, as Sam chalked up his pool stick, studied the position of the balls and went to work, methodically hitting every shot. The last was the eight ball. "In the corner, cowboy," said Sam, and slammed it into the pocket.

Hank didn't say a word. He reset the table and glared at Sam with a snarl. "You come sailing into our town, trying to be a big-shot. So put a fifty down if you think you're so damn good." He looked over at Jimmy Dean and slurred. "Get me 'nother of that Gentlemen Jack, Jimmy Dean. A double this time." He turned to Sam. "Why don't you have a real man's drink? Like a whiskey."

Sam said, "I'm good."

"You drink a sissy drink… an' you wear ribbons on your shoes. Ha! We got us a pansy fellow in our midst, boys." A blend of snorts and jeers came from the onlookers. A few more guys came over, curious, and stood near the table watching Hank play the newcomer. Someone yelled out, "Whatcha do, skin a croc for those shoes?" Howls of laughter erupted. Then a Johnny Cash song played on the jukebox. Soon, boots were stomping and things were starting to get rowdy in the Blue Sky Saloon, as some sang along drunkenly: "I fell on a…"

Hank cleared his eyes trying to focus on the game. He couldn't lose to this guy. So, he racked the balls, and didn't wait for Sam to start. He hit the center, and sent the balls flying across the table, knocking in two solids. Then he proceeded to hit four more in a row. Next one, he missed.

Sam stepped up to the table, and methodically hit each ball in. "Game," he called, winking at Indigo.

Hank was livid and his face burned bright red. He wasn't used to anyone beating him at anything. He was an athlete – strong and confident. He was also used to getting what he wanted, and by whatever means necessary. So, he balked in outrage. "I think we've got a stinkin' cheater amongst us." He glared at Sam. "I ought a shoot your sorry ass. First for cheating, and second for coming into our town. You're not welcome here, so get your sorry ass gone."

The bar went quiet. All eyes were on Hank, waiting to see what might happen next.

Indigo stood bravely and walked over to Hank. She said, "I, for one, didn't see him cheat. Did any of you?" She whirled around and confronted Jimmy Dean. "Did you see this guy cheat, Jimmy?"

Jimmy Dean's mouth was dried up. He took a quick drink, wiped his mouth, then said, "Well, uh, if Hank says he cheated, then he cheated."

Indigo walked up to Jake. "Did you see any cheating?"

"Well, looked to me like he was kinda cagey… the way he shot that pool stick… just didn't look right to me." A few others chimed in. "Yeah, looked like a cheater to me."

"Girls," Indigo said, "Did you see this guy cheat? Janet! Did you?"

Janet spoke evenly. "No. He didn't cheat."

"Sally, did you see Sam cheat?"

Sally said, "I couldn't see real good, so I'm not sure…"

Indigo hissed. "That's a load of crap, Sally."

Indigo turned to Hank and said, "Don't be such a sore loser. Besides, it's just a game. Why don't you play another round and see what happens? See if he cheated." She glanced at Sam, pleading with her eyes to lose.

Sam was defiant and walked up to the table. "I am not a cheater, and I didn't cheat you. So, if you're up for it, let's play again and see."

Hank took on the challenge. He told Jimmy Dean. "Get me another Jack."

Jimmy Dean looked at his friend and said, "Say, partner. Do you think you should cool it on the drinks for a spell?"

Hank gave Jimmy Dean a shove. "Don't tell me to cool it, you little dick. You ain't my ma, so don't act like one. Now get my drink."

Jimmy Dean meekly obliged and went to the bar.

Hank stumbled as he walked up to Sam's face. "You must be looking for trouble, tassel-toes. Put up a hundred for the next game."

Sam said, incensed. "That's fine by me, but you haven't paid up for the last two." He reached into his pocket, pulled out a roll of bills, and put a hundred on the table.

Hank sneered. "What ya do, rob a bank… or you just like flashin' cash around…?"

Sam ignored him, sipped his drink, and looked over toward Oliver.

Oliver's arms were starting to go numb, and he tried his best to stretch his fingers and wiggle them. He heard a buzzing sound. He looked carefully around the smoke-filled room, paying attention to every detail – trying to figure out where the sound was coming from. Instinctively he closed his eyes, and then gasped. He sees the image of his father's face as it floated past. He opened his eyes, but the vision faded, so he closed them again and was soon swept away into the vision of his beloved father. Words began to dance before his eyes. "I see you have found me. This is where my bones are scattered. Take me home, my son."

Oliver's eyes flew open as he felt a wet rag smack him across his face.

Randy said, "Wakey-wakey, Red. Ain't no sleeping at the bar. Gotta stay awake for your big shindig. You're guest of honor."

Gladys came from behind the bar, opened a bottle of beer, wiped her brow, and smiled at Randy. "Hot as Hades in that kitchen. Think I'm gonna close shop. Cooked enough burgers for the night. Feels like my arms are about to fall off." She took a long draw on her beer, sat it on the counter, looked over at Oliver, then back to Randy. "So, what are you gonna do with the big Indian boy? Give him to the sheriff to deal with?"

"Hanks got a plan for later when things settle down around here. Wants to have some fun first, then, *whack!*" Randy gestured by hanging his head to his chest. He picked up his guitar and started to sing, "Another One Bites the Dust."

Gladys took a big swig of her beer, lit a cigarette, and took a long, deep draw – blowing hazy plumes of smoke in the air. "The joint's really rocking. I'd say we're having a record-breaking night."

Randy nodded, put his guitar down, and started washing the stack of beer glasses. "We're busier than a whorehouse on nickel night."

Gladys chuckled. "Where'd you hear that kind of malarkey? Sheriff Joe, I'd wager." She lit another cigarette from the butt of her smoke and perused the bar.

Oliver watched Gladys's smoke curl up, drifting across the

bar toward him. The smoke expanded and encircled him as he sat. Oliver closed his eyes and prayed, calling on all the ancient powers. He felt comforted – as though someone was hovering nearby. It seemed as natural as breathing.

I will never let my prayers go again, he thought. Praying with such intensity and passion, he felt swept away with the power. He began to hear songs from long, long ago. Songs he had never heard before – songs that held power. He envisioned his grandfathers, Broken Feather and Hidden Spirit, form a protective circle around him. He could feel his body lift off the chair, then falter. Regaining his focus once again, he felt as light as the air as he hovered near the back door. A sudden whoosh and he slid out into the night – landing on the old sycamore's massive limb. A trail of feathers flittered from a nearby branch.

A striking face full of wisdom and warmth appeared before him – that of an old Indian wearing a full headdress and eyes of immense strength and courage. Then in a flash the image transformed into a young, powerful warrior speaking softly in his Lakota language. Oliver could not quite understand the words until he heard, "Concentrate my son. Concentrate on the figures in the shadows… feel your body sail in the wind, light and free…" Following the whispery voice, as the image faded in and out, he was now light as the wind, hovering, as he continued to pray and stare into the eyes of the ancient warrior.

Then he heard his name called out. "Oliver." His vision blurred. An Indian that looked as old as the hills held his arms out to him.

Oliver was so startled that he lost his concentration and faltered. His vision blurred and he heard…

"Hank! Where the hell's that redskin?"

Oliver wavered. He heard shouting. People were milling around the bar.

"Why're you asking me, Randy? *You're* supposed to keep an eye on him. *You* let

him escape. Get your ass out here and help me look for him."

Hank turned to Jimmy Dean and cursed. "That sonofabitch got loose."

Pandemonium broke out as Hank shouted for everyone to help find that Indian. Loud, drunken curses erupted, and half of the crowd staggered out the door.

Jake asked, "What the devil is going on?"

A slurred voice answered, "Don't know an' don't care. Came here to have some fun. Heard some Injun escaped… or some shit like that."

Jake tossed down the rest of his Bud and said, "Why didn't he just shoot the guy when he had him? Hell, I just want to get back to partying."

CHAPTER FOUR

TO THE RESCUE

S AM'S EYES WERE peeled on the bar. He couldn't believe that Oliver was gone. It was odd. He thought he could still see his shadow lingering, but just couldn't figure out what had happened. *How did he manage to get free? Those ropes were tied so tight his wrists were chaffed.* Sam wanted to shout, "Hats off to you, man," but, instead, he kept the words bottled inside. "Amazing!" was all he could say, watching in confusion and wonder. He brimmed with relief.

Sam wasn't at all sure how he could help Oliver without getting himself killed in the process. He could get Hank really drunk and lose a game of pool if he had to. *I'd rather bash his face in with a pool stick,* he thought, as he felt the sturdy pool cue that weighed heavily in his hand. *Knock that smug grin right off his drunken face.* He remembered that he could count on Indigo's help.

As he stood deep in thought, Sam felt a flutter around his head – and his hat lifted slightly. His hackles rose as he felt a buzzing sensation, which ended abruptly and left him confused and rubbing his chin. He heard himself say, "Stay hidden, my friend."

Indigo walked up to Sam at the pool table and put her

hand on his. "Are you okay? You look like you just saw a ghost or something."

Sam didn't reply for a moment, still taking all this in. "Oliver was sitting here a moment ago… and then he just disappeared. He couldn't have walked out without my seeing him…" Sam looked puzzled and said under his breath, "weird…"

"I guess everyone had their eyes focused on the pool table to pay any attention to Oliver." Indigo flirted, touching his arm. "I can't seem to take my eyes of *you*, either. But, I do wonder how he could have disappeared like that."

Then a shot went off in the bar. Randy shouted in bewilderment, "There he is. Hank! Get your ass back to the bar!"

With a loud *whoosh and a thump,* Oliver had slipped back into his body, still tied to the chair.

Hank came flying inside. His eyes did a doubletake when he saw Oliver sitting there at the bar in the exact same place and cool as a freaking cucumber – like nothing ever happened. His innards quaked. *First it was those damn crows. Then that lightning that almost fried my ass and now this. I've had enough of this… this witchcraft. What else could it be? I don't know… maybe it's that injury I got playing football… seeing all kinds of shit that isn't there, and all….*

Gladys choked. "I thought I was gonna faint. One minute I looked… and he wasn't there… and then the very next… there he is, big as life." Her hands shook. "Look at him, just sitting there with a smile. I either need my eyes checked or a stronger drink."

The bar was in a total uproar, as the crowd stumbled back inside the bar. Pairs of bloodshot eyes peered at Oliver. To make sure he was real, a couple of ranch hands went up and poked him in the back. But the Indian was the last thing on their minds. These guys had women to seduce and beers waiting to be drunk.

One of the drunks shouted. "Put on some damn music. I came here to drink, damnit, and have some fun."

"Yeah," Jake said, stumbling inside. "Let's get some Waylon goin'. Who gives a shit about a stinkin' Injun, messin' where he oughtn't."

Soon, everyone was back to drinking, dancing, and smoking – glad to forget all that nonsense.

Hank was fuming. He felt a bit foolish, and some were hinting how that Indian sure got the best of him. His face burned as he hightailed it over to Oliver and pulled out his six-shooter. "You try some of that weird shit again, and I'll blast your brains over the bar." He shoved the barrel of the gun hard against Oliver's temple. "You get the message, Tonto, or do you need a smoke signal?"

Oliver didn't flinch or move a muscle. He just stared straight ahead. A slight smile tugged at the corner of his mouth.

Hank was seething at Oliver's indifference. "You ain't gonna find anything funny later on."

Sam walked up to the bar beside Hank. "Say, are you gonna play pool, or did you change your mind and chicken out?"

Hank whirled around so fast, he had to grab the bar so he wouldn't topple over. Scowling, he said, "Who you calling chicken shit, pansy ass outsider? I had problems that needed tending to, is all. Like this Injun, trying some wild stunt in here. Just letting him know it ain't gonna end well for him, no matter what he tries. And he ain't gonna fool me again

"I think he's already fooled you." Sam grinned. He couldn't resist the jab.

Hank snarled, "If you know what's good for you, you should mind your own beeswax and get your ass on outa town by morning."

"Sam bristled. "Last I heard cowboy, this is a free country."

Hank rubbed his six-shooter across his chin, glaring at Sam. "Guess you've never been to this part of the country before, Slick. Free is a word used pretty loosely around here." Hank jabbed Sam in the ribs with his gun. "Not so sure *you're* so lilywhite, neither.

Hard to tell sometimes. Lotta half-breeds around these parts… best not be one of them." He pointed his gun to the table. "Meantime, get your hundred bucks where I can see it… right over there." He checked Oliver's rope and growled. "No more funny business. Try that again… whatever the hell you did before, and I'll plug you so full of holes they'll use you for a waterspout."

Hank pounded the bar to get Randy's attention. "Keep a close eye on this cagey bastard. If you think he's gonna do something, plug him good… and get me a drink while you're at it. Worked up a thirst.

Randy said, "No problem." He set the Gentlemen Jack on the bar and poured a hefty shot.

Hank drank it down and poured himself another. "This one's on Slick over there. See he pays up." He turned and walked toward the pool table, then stopped. "Hey Randy. Best make sure slick pays up before he slides on outa town."

Randy smirked as he looked nastily at Sam. "You got yourself quite a bill racked up. Best not leave before paying up… might land yourself in jail."

Sam swallowed his fury. "What do I owe?"

Randy puffed up his chest as he sauntered over to the adding machine, and plunked on the keys.

While Randy was busy on the adding machine, Sam leaned in close to Oliver. "That was really something you did earlier. It was crazy and amazing all at once."

Oliver's eyes smiled.

As Sam was studying the impressive Indian, he felt a strange power emanating from him. It was puzzling, and yet somehow familiar. *He seems more like a warrior to me.*

Randy walked over to Sam with a smug look on his face. "The tally's fifty-five buckaroos, pal."

Sam felt the urge to tell him to stick it, but instead took the bills from his pocket and slapped the money on the bar. "I'll take my change this time."

Randy picked up the money and held it to the light for inspection. "Looks about right," he said, and put it in the cash register, not bothering to bring back any change.

Sam shrugged and walked to the pool table, muttering under his breath, "asshole." Things had calmed down considerably, as everyone went back to partying, forgetting about the Indian. They had tall tales to tell – bragging about the cattle they had rustled earlier this week and a buffalo Jake lassoed.

Indigo smiled at Sam, as he picked up his pool stick. Her smile did not go unnoticed by Hank, who strutted up to Sam, and glowered. "You best stay away from our women, too. That's the sheriff's daughter you've got your eye on, and he wouldn't take kindly to your messing around with her. So, keep your eyes on the game, Slick… the one you're about to lose."

Indigo approached Sam. "This is for luck – from the sheriff's daughter." She planted a light kiss on his lips.

Sam was surprised at her willful nature and all he could think to say was, "Thanks." He knew it was for show, but *WOW!* His heart did a jump and tingled with pleasure.

Indigo rubbed his smooth cheek and said, "I'll be cheering you on."

Inspired by Indigo's boldness, Sally jumped up, sashayed over to Hank, and kissed him hard on the mouth.

Hank pushed her away angrily, wiping his mouth. "Don't want you to jinx my game. Go sit back down." Then he said as an afterthought. "You can cheer for me though."

Sally's face burned with humiliation as she sat back down at the table, sulking.

Janet looked at her, shaking her head. "Why do you keep doing this to yourself? He just uses you… and it makes me mad.

He may be cute but he's a player and he has no respect for you. So, pleeease stop."

Sally didn't answer. She kept her eyes peeled on the game, and mainly on Hank.

Hank was off to a roaring start. He had remarkable accuracy, considering the liquor he had consumed. On his last shot of the game now, he was feeling pretty cocky as he strutted around the table. Aware he had everyone's attention he took aim – and then missed the eight ball by a hair. A groan went up.

Sam had a lot of catching up to do. He skillfully measured each shot and, one by one, the ball fell into the designated pocket. Then on to the eight ball. He knew he should probably let Hank win the game, but he just couldn't do that. He loathed men like Hank, and he was determined to beat him… he had to. So, he carefully took aim, hand steady, and dropped the eight ball into the left rear pocket. For a moment, a stunned silence took hold. Then, Indigo ran up to Sam and gave him a big hug and another kiss – this one more lingering. Pulling away, she gushed breathlessly, "That was really impressive, Sam. I see you city boys know a thing or two about pool."

Jimmy Dean was floored by the outcome. Hank was an impressive pool player and he usually let the other player make a couple of wins before he went in for the kill. *I guess it didn't work this time. Well, he's still a winner in my book,* he thought with a tinge of longing. He worried about Hank's reaction losing to the good-looking stranger and hurried to his side, and said with conviction. "That was a great game, Hank. Now, how about you and I have a little fun? We'll shoot a couple games, then I'll put some Merle on the jukebox… maybe take some girls for a twirl on the dance floor."

Hank was sore as he glared at Jimmy Dean. "What the hell you talking about – a little dance, or a friendly game of pool? Can't you see I ain't in a friendly mood? Best get out of my way," he threatened and shoved Jimmy Dean out of his way. Hank stormed up to the bar, banged on the countertop, and shouted. "Anyone here ever see a redskin dance?"

The voices dimmed to a low buzz.

"Listen up. I'm gonna have this here Indian give us a little show… a pow-wow dance. And now we got us a cheatin' smart ass over there. Just wanted to warn ya in case he asks you to play pool with him. Don't. Seems kinda strange and a little fishy, they're both here on the same night. Must be in cahoots on something. But first, we're gonna see an Injun dance. Gonna have us a little entertainment to liven up the joint." Hank slurred as he pulled out his six-shooter.

A few whoops and shouts filled the air. "Here's to seein' a war dance, Hank," said Jake, as he raised his glass in the air and laughed, waiting to see what would happen next.

Hank cocked his gun and put it to Oliver's head. "You're gonna get your devil-makin' ass out there on the dance floor and give us a show. Hear me?" he hissed, yanking his hair back.

Oliver simply stared back at Hank. His deep blue eyes glimmered with fury.

Hank hollered to Jimmy Dean, "Untie the bastard, 'cept his hands. There's a slipknot around his waist. Just yank it on the end and it'll slip right off. Learned that from ranching. Gonna have to teach you a few tricks."

Jimmy Dean did as he was instructed.

Hank clicked his gun, ready.

Randy grabbed his shotgun from behind the bar and pointed it at Oliver.

Everyone was watching Hank, as the bar went quiet, jukebox silent. He yanked Oliver off his chair and shoved him toward the dance floor. Hank's hand swayed slightly as he held his gun. "Give us a good show out there or I'm gonna shoot your pigtails right off ya. Better shake it real good!"

The crowd formed a circle around the dance floor, anticipating the entertainment. "Leave it to Hank to do something like this," Jake whispered to his buddy. "This ought a be real good."

Everyone's eyes were glued to Oliver on the dance floor, standing tall and unafraid.

Someone in the crowd hollered, "Show us what you got, buckskin."

"Yeah," another snickered. "Do the pow-wow-woo-pah-woo-hah!"

Jake yelled out, "Sounds just like the real thing. Get out there and show him how it's done." Harold stepped onto the dance floor, and slurred drunkenly, "This is how ya do it… ain't it?" Putting his hand to his mouth, chanting, "Ompah-oompah…" he hopped around, from one foot to the other and stumbled over himself.

A chorus of laughter went up in the jeering crowd.

Hank gave Oliver another shove, prodding him with his gun to move. "Okay, boy. Getta shakin'!"

Oliver didn't budge.

Hank growled. "You best do as I say, or I'll drill some holes in you right here. Trust me, nobody's gonna give a shit if I shoot ya or hang ya… your choice. The rope 'll just give ya a little longer to hang out." He laughed out loud at his joke.

Oliver squared his shoulders back in defiance, eyes flashed fearlessly and said with an air of calm. "Shoot me then."

Hank, not to be outsmarted, took his six-shooter and let off a blast into the air, sending the crowd ducking for cover.

Something in Sam erupted as he watched this scene unfold. His eyes were on fire. He was not a fighter, but it triggered something deep inside him. He felt a wild new sensation rise up – almost like a warrior spirit full of courage. He had no idea where that came from, but he wasn't going to stand there and watch his new-found friend with the ice-blue eyes being ridiculed.

In Los Angeles, Sam had never mentioned to anyone about his native roots – that his mother was Arapaho. It sounded strange to think about it now, but he recalled always being embarrassed to mention that he was part-Indian. If anyone would ask, he would say, offhandedly, he wasn't sure what he was – that maybe he was Italian or French, or whatever – but he never uttered the word, Arapaho.

Now, for the first time, he felt strong and brave, and proud of his heritage. "Arapaho," he whispered, as the name rolled off his tongue like liquid. It must have had something to do with seeing Oliver sitting at the bar being heckled by Hank and those loud-mouthed cowboys. It didn't bother Sam that he might get killed in this place. Nothing mattered right now, except saving Oliver from these vile people. It struck a chord deep in his heart, and he could feel his own heart thunder in his chest. So, he shoved his way through the crowd, knocking over tables and chairs in his wake. Without thinking, his fist went flying at Hank's face, grazing his bruised and swollen eye.

Stunned by the sudden hit, Hank fell backwards toward Jake, who quickly righted him. "Whoa there, big fella," he cried out. "Gotcha."

Hank regained his balance and this time swung and hit Sam's shoulder. Sam managed to stay upright. His strong slender frame was quick and easily sidestepped another incoming blow from Hank. Then he lunged at the unsteady guy, letting loose of all those suppressed feelings he had held back since he was a boy. Sam was hopping around the floor like a dancer, dodging blows, while managing a few powerful jabs of his own.

He looked around at the crowd that circled the dance floor and shouted. "What's the matter with you people…?"

Before he could finish, Hank flew clumsily at Sam, throwing a furious punch, which Sam barely managed to duck.

Even drunk, Hank was a vastly more skilled fighter than Sam who had managed to keep him off balance for a while. Then Hank swung a fist into Sam's shoulder, sending him flying across a table, scattering beer bottles and cigarettes onto the floor.

Indigo was afraid for Sam and ran to the table where the girls were watching in alarm. She cried out, "This is crazy. Fighting Hank is just looking for trouble… serious trouble. We've got to stop this before it really gets out of control. Plus, who knows what the others will do. Maybe they'll hang him, along with Oliver."

Janet was equally alarmed. "You could be right. No one in this town would dare go against Hank. No matter what he does. Plus, they could care less about an Indian!"

Indigo wrinkled her brow, "You know the new young pastor that came to town last week? Percy Goodwin. He seems like a really nice guy and he's the only person I could think of to go to. Not sure if he can help, but maybe he could calm everyone down a bit.

"Yeah. A preacher coming into a bar trying to talk peace and love to this crowd, is about as crazy as Sam fighting Hank," Sally laughed. "Are you nuts, Indigo?"

"Maybe. But it's worth a try. Got any other suggestions? He may be our only hope to stop this craziness."

Janet said, "Do you want me to come along?"

"No. See if you can get one of the ranch hands to… I don't know… do something. I'll be back as soon as I can." Indigo took off in a sprint out the door.

Pastor Percy Goodwin's house was just a few blocks down the street, right behind the church. Indigo raced over there, but it seemed to take forever. Standing at the front door panting, she banged as hard as she could, yelling, "Pastor Percy! Please open up. Hurry! I need help!"

She tried to control her fear and hold back tears that threatened, as she continued to yell. "Please hurry!"

Then, a flash of light came on inside the house and the door flew open, with a startled Percy peering into the darkness. Before he could ask what was so urgent, Indigo grabbed his robe with her fist and talked as fast as she could. "Pastor Percy. Hank is going to shoo-shoot a... an Indian, and ki-kill Sam," she said, stumbling over her words. "I didn't know who else to turn to."

Percy had a hard time trying to make sense of what she was saying. "I'm not sure what you mean but give me a minute to get dressed."

"You're fine how you are. Please hurry, Pastor. There's an awful fight brewing at the saloon, and it's going to end in bloodshed."

Percy tightened his robe, grabbed his Bible and ran out the door, flannel pajamas flopping in the breeze as he followed the distraught girl as they scurried down the street.

Running at top speed, Indigo looked sideways at Percy holding his Bible and couldn't help but ask, "What do you plan to do with your Bible at the bar?"

"It helps me remain strong in the face of madness," he smiled.

"Well, that's a relief," Indigo said with a hint of sarcasm. "Madness is not the only problem in this town. But it's definitely up there..."

As they rushed inside the Blue Sky Saloon, Indigo wondered about her hasty decision to recruit the Pastor. *Not so sure Pastor Percy is the right man for the job. Too late now,* she moaned.

What they saw inside was all-out pandemonium. Fists were flying, bottles hurtled with abandon, then crashed across the room, and chairs were thrown haphazardly – smashing into Randy's liquor-stocked shelves and walls. Indigo was shocked to see Pastor Percy climb onto a tabletop, trying to get people's attention. No one paid any mind to the guy, so he threw off his robe, and, in a flash, ran right into the middle of the brawl, raising his Bible in the air and shouting. "God commands you to stop! This instant!"

No one paid attention to the harried pastor, so, fists raised, Percy dove into the melee. A dozen or so men were falling over each other to get at Oliver and Sam, but there were so many men in the mix, it was hard to tell who, was who, and who was getting punched and by whom. Sam managed to fight off blows as best he could while Oliver quietly squeezed free from his rope. He shook his hands to regain circulation and then swung at the nearest guy, who happened to be Jake. The blow sent Jake hurtling against a table and sliding across the top, knocking into overflowing ash-trays and glasses and slamming into Jimmy Dean knocking the wind out of him.

After letting loose a curse, Jimmy Dean picked himself up from the floor and stumbled away from the chaos – holding his arm and sore ribs.

Percy was still in the middle of the fight when he whacked Hank's jaw with his Bible, which didn't even faze him. Then Harold threw a wild punch at Percy, propelling him backwards with such force that he cartwheeled head over heels, landing in a heap in the corner, and leaving him panting and dazed.

A door slammed open, and three rounds of shots were fired. Eyes agog, with blood dripping and sweat streaming, the brawlers looked to see who had done the shooting. Someone shouted, "Who the hell fired those shots?"

Sheriff Joe yelled, "I did, you wild-ass sonsofbitches. I want order in this place or I'm locking up every one of you drunks for disorderly conduct. I can't even go out of town without worrying you'll start some kind of ruckus. Now, someone tell me what the hell's going on here."

Hank extricated himself from the center of the pile, cut and bruised. With blood spouting from his nose, he walked stiffly up to the sheriff.

"Well, sheriff. Here's the deal. Caught me an Injun around here earlier, rifling through my truck… no doubt, trying to steal it. Then another city dude, over there, just happened to be in town on the very same night. I would bet my Stetson that those two are in cahoots, maybe trying to rob the bar or even the bank. Either way, they're fishy, for sure. So, I thought to save you the trouble of hanging 'em."

"All right, Hank. That's enough. Got the picture. Now, all of you get your hats and asses and bags and whatever else you got and get on outa here – and I mean pronto. Party's over."

Wyoming was a rugged place with ranchers, miners, hunters, trappers, and real good folks living around here. The sheriff liked a peaceful town and needed to put an end to this malarkey in the Blue Sky Saloon. His eyes scanned the saloon and cursed. "And where the hell is my deputy?"

The young pastor came up to the sheriff in his torn pajamas and holding his ripped Bible close to his chest. *At least I still have my grandmother's Bible,* he thought gratefully, *even if it's a bit tattered.*

The sheriff scrutinized him with disdain and spoke irritably. "I'm not sure with you being a pastor and bar-fighting is setting a good example for our community, Percy. I brought you here because of that little issue we had with our other pastor," he said lowering his voice, "with him looking at naked women… doing… well, it didn't sit well with some of our townsfolk and most of the ladies. Had to let him go… and now this!" He threw his hands up in disgust.

Percy Goodwin was shaking from the pummeling he received and held his stomach gingerly. *And now he had to endure the sheriff's angry lecture.* He tried to still the trembling in his body, but the thought of a wild-west-style hanging had him frustrated. He couldn't believe that people would try to take the law into their own hands. Percy was from the east and abhorred this display of lawlessness. But he couldn't say anything or go against Sheriff Joe Jenner. He had already heard the rumors about him and didn't doubt a one.

Percy considered himself more of a free-thinker and he wondered if he had made a mistake in coming to this town. He liked rock and roll music, and when no one was around he played it on the church piano, with gusto. He knew most lyrics to the Elton John songs. He even has a taste for fine bourbon, which he found relaxing, *when indulged in moderation, of course.* Now, here he was, trying to save an Indian from a lynch mob. Percy's slight five-feet-seven frame was wobbling, as much from his injuries as from Sheriff Joe's glare. His head began to throb as Sheriff Joe continued to admonish him. "You best stick to praying and preaching and keeping the parishioners in line with a Hellfire-and-Damnation sermon. And make sure you pass out that collection plate twice at every service… once for sinning and the other for salvation. You got that, Pastor?"

Percy bobbed his aching head yes, but he was taken aback by the sheriff's fury, eyes blazing. Luckily for him, Sheriff Joe turned his attention to Jimmy Dean and Hank. Sheriff Joe cleared his throat and said, "Hank, bring over those two guys." He was in a fit of fury. Purple veins popped on his cheeks and red splotches appeared over his entire face. "Make sure you tie them up together and march their asses over to where I can see them."

The crowd was thinning out in the bar, as the patrons staggered toward the door, looking back curiously at the sheriff – wondering what was going to happen.

Outside, Jake grinned, limping from a kick to the knee. "Helluva fight in there! I don't even know who won or who got the shit whacked out of 'em. Gotta say, I'm pretty sore."

Amos slurred his response. "So many folks piled up, I don't even know if that Injun got whooped or not. He looked like a tough son-of-a-gun."

Jake said, "Well, I think that pastor got it good. Right in the ole snout." A chorus of laughter echoed along the sidewalk. "Imagine bringing a Bible to a fight! It's like trying to kiss a mule and expect him not to kick."

Harold snorted, "Well, I don't know what yer talking about,

but sure was fun. Didn't mind landin' a few punches on Hank. He's a real smart ass sometimes, thinking he's real cool cuz he's a football star."

Jake corrected him. "*Was* a football star. Cuz he sure as shit ain't one no more… just a royal pain in the ass now."

Snickers and grumbles died down as engines roared to life. The guys all sat in their pickups and rusted-out Chevys rehashing the night for the final time.

Inside the bar, Sheriff Joe hollered to Randy. "Bring me a Bud and a shot of rye. Double, with two cubes. The sheriff slicked back his hair and smoothed it into place. He loved to use loads of Brylcreem and sing the snappy slogan. Looking straight at Jimmy Dean Hinkle with cold eyes, he said, "Go find my deputy."

Not all that keen on the scrawny kid, he liked to call him, "Link-o-sausage," because he was pinkish in color with thin skin. He could tell Jimmy Dean didn't like being called a sausage. His face would burn and he would stiffen at the sound of it. *Like to rattle people*, the sheriff thought with a grin. *Keep them off guard and never let 'em know what comes next.* But still, for the life of him, he couldn't understand why Hank took such a liking to that scrawny kid. *Something's off with him and I'm going to find out what it is*," he thought as he watched him walk out the door and blinked hard. *Was that a sashay I just saw?* He shook his head and slugged down the rye. "Bet he's a faggot," he muttered. "Yeah, no doubt about it."

Randy sat down and poured himself a drink, and asked Sheriff Joe, "You want ma to cook you up a big juicy burger and fries?"

Sheriff Joe sipped on his icy cold Bud and wiggled his empty whiskey glass. "Give me another," he said, "and tell Gladys burger and fries sounds good. I'll thank her later."

Randy nodded and found Gladys in the kitchen cleaning up. "Sheriff 'll have a burger and fries, Ma."

Gladys just grimaced and set about getting everything ready.

Sheriff Joe eyeballed those two troublemakers sitting on the nearby barstools. He handed his handcuffs over to Hank, and said, "Cuff those two."

Glancing over at the stranger wearing the Dodgers baseball cap, he grimaced. *He must be from LA… Hell, I hate those Dodgers. They couldn't hit a ball if it stopped right in front of them and said hello. Bunch of liberal pussies out there, anyway…* He dearly wished a few more of those folks would pass this way. He'd kick their asses from here to China. *Then they could commiserate with those yellow-skinned commies they like so much. I'd show 'em how the cowboys tamed the west — with a fist, a gun, and a rope. We can ride a bull, throw 'em to the ground, and shovel enough shit to fill all of LA. Yep. I'd like to stick my boot right up their asses*, he thought, getting riled up and glaring at Sam.

Getting Randy's attention with a wave, he pointed to his empty glass. Then he sidled up to Oliver – his belly jiggling from the sudden movement. As he yanked his face around, he was staring directly into startling blue eyes. He thought, *this is damned peculiar – an Indian with blue eyes. His momma must've tangled with a white boy.* That thought infuriated him, so when he spoke with Oliver, he carefully chose his words.

"Heard you're in town looking to steal from our hard-working folks. I'd say you aren't too swift or smart to come here." He smacked his head hard with his beefy fist. "You got anything up there?" he asked sardonically. "Maybe you got shit for brains," he said with a laugh. "Ain't that right, Hank?"

Hank stood next to the sheriff with a shiner and blood still dripping from his nose. "I'd say, he's lucky to have that much, sheriff," he said, itching to slam Oliver's head against the wall.

"So, tell me Hank… what you saw and whatnot?"

Hank winced as he touched his eye, then growled. "Walked outside to have a smoke with Jimmy Dean when I heard something that sounded like a squeak of a truck door being opened.

My ears perked right up. So, I motioned to Jimmy Dean to be real quiet and I snuck around the side of the building where I saw someone rifling through my stuff. I got madder than a hornet when I figured he must be trying to steal my truck. So, I went up to him and asked him what the hell was he doing?' He never answered. Just stared at me with those wicked eyes. So, I yanked his butt on outa there, and we got into a bit of a tussle. He's mean as hell and fights like a savage. Said he was going to kill me. Jimmy Dean ran and got Randy, and the three of us wrangled him to the ground… like a wild bull. Then we tied him up and brought him into the bar. I thought a hanging would set things right… like we do with horse thieves. I thought since you were outa town, you wouldn't mind if I…" He let his voice trail off, as the sheriff glared at him. "Well, what I mean is… save you the trouble. I didn't see Ben around, so…"

"All right, Hank. I'll take it from here." Sheriff Joe scooted over to Sam, yanked off his hat, and looked at him close-up – their noses almost touching. "I see your fancy car out front… and your fancy clothes. Whatcha doing around here, boy? You're a long way from the city of lost angels."

Sam leveled his gaze and spoke as politely as he could muster. "Just passing through is all."

Sheriff Joe grunted. "You're a helluva long way from nothing. Out here are ranchers, cowboys, and miners. You don't look like none of those. And you tell me you just happened to be in town on the very same night as this Injun. Now, that don't add up, you see… unless you two were planning something sneaky-like. Matter of fact, the whole thing stinks to high heaven. And I got a real good sniffer." Pointing to his nose.

Sam kept his gaze directed on the sheriff.

Sheriff Joe pulled a toothpick out of his pocket and twirled it. "Now, what kind of blood you got in you, anyway? You don't look white. You got that black-as-spades hair, and eyes to match… evil eyes, far as I can tell. So, what are you? Wetback?" Not waiting for an answer, he continued. "Half-breed? Bad blood in the mix far as I can see… You mutts are just as bad as full-breeds."

Sheriff Joe looked up as Gladys sat a platter of fries on the bar and a huge cheeseburger piled high with the works.

Sheriff Joe nodded his thanks, and took a big bite of the burger, spilling some droplets of sauce on the counter. He grabbed a fistful of fries, and chewed hungrily, never taking his eyes off Sam. Another fistful of fries, dipped this time in ketchup, followed by another big bite of burger sent juice dribbling down his chin, onto his shirt. He meticulously wiped his mouth and chin with the paper napkin Gladys had provided. After a few more bites, the sheriff continued. "Made a big mistake ending up in this town, boy. Should've pointed your compass in a different direction. Out here, we're a God-fearing bunch and we obey His laws. Now, when we see a stranger come to town, sniffing where he shouldn't, could land you in a heap of trouble." The sheriff took another bite of his burger and chomped away. "Say, Gladys," he called out, "you outdid yourself tonight on the burger. Best one yet. I'll give you a proper 'thank you' later." The sheriff wiped his mouth, belched, and pushed away the empty plate, then turned his attention back to Sam who sat quietly. 'Well, you know what I think? I think you and your friend here just landed yourselves in some real hot water. *Real* hot." He drained the last of his Bud, then stared Sam down, intent on shaking him up. "I'll give you a little jolt that might wake you up a notch. How about we have us a little hanging party? You and Tonto will be the star attractions, and the whole town 'll be there. It'll be quite a shindig. Haven't done that in a spell… So, how does that tickle your fancy ass?"

Sam shoved his worries down. "Guess it wouldn't matter what I say, sheriff. You wouldn't believe me if I told you. But there are laws in this country, and I have rights…"

The sheriff cut him off. "Don't talk to me about laws and

rights, big shot. I'm the law here, and your rights are what I say they are. So, if I were you, I'd clamp it shut while you still can."

Indigo, Janet, and Sally were huddled together in the back, listening to this scenario in horror. Indigo said, "I can't believe what I'm hearing. I'm going to talk to my disgusting father. Can you both come with me?"

Sally squirmed and said, "I don't know, Indie. Your dad… uh, I mean, Sheriff Joe… can be pretty rough. Half the town's scared of him, and the other half admire him. But they all like a big ole tough guy running the town."

"I have to be careful, Indigo, around the sheriff," Janet said. "You know what he thinks of my family being Jewish and owning a business here. He hates us. If we did the slightest thing that he could blame us for, he would run us out of town." She lowered her voice and continued. "My parents are really strict about staying out of his way… they still have nightmares about those years they spent in the concentration camps. They feel very fortunate to have come here, thanks to my Uncle Horace. The store has been in the family for nearly a hundred years, and we must not lose it. I don't mean to be selfish… but on the other hand, I couldn't stand by and do nothing. And there is no one in this town that could or would stop the sheriff from hanging these guys… not that anyone would dare try.

Nervously, Indigo said, "I tell you what. Just come with me. You don't have to say anything. I just need your support. Truth is, he scares me, too, even though I try to hide it. Besides, Sam is… I know I just met him, but something about him feels right. I feel a connection, and I know he felt it, too. Honestly, Janet, I wish I could hug him… tell him I'm sorry he came to this town, and I'm sorry for the piece-of–shit that happens to be my sperm donor." She smiled over at Sam and whispered in Janet's ear. "On the other hand, I'm so glad he's here."

Indigo had big plans to leave Miners Gulch as soon as she

could. She felt it was no coincidence she met the gorgeous stranger – that it was meant to be. She had always dreamed of going to Los Angeles. *A place where dreams come true.* She had no money and no way to get there, but now… *My dream just might come true, after all,* she thought giddily.

The three girls quietly made their way to the bar, their eyes wide with fright. Indigo tried to steel her jitters as she tapped tepidly on her father's back. Sheriff Joe swung around, and his eyes popped when he saw her – and then the two others. "What in the blazes are you doing here?" he exploded. "I told everyone to leave and that included you and your friends here. Don't think, just because you're my daughter, you get any special pass."

Indigo fidgeted, took a deep breath, and then blurted out. "You can't hang these two guys… they have rights, even if their skin is not pearly white. And – they did nothing wrong!"

Sheriff Joe was stunned by her audacity, and another vein popped at his right temple.

Hank saw the look on the sheriff's face and chimed in before he could blow up. "Now I know you mean well, Indie, but this here Injun tried to steal my truck. I caught him red-handed. As for this LA dude," his eyes swiveled to Sam, "he's suspicious no doubt and I'm sure he had to be in on it, so…"

Indigo interrupted with an irritated "Shut-up, Hank."

Sheriff Joe stood fuming at his daughter, "I'll handle her. Now go find my deputy and get his britches over here. Where's Jimmy Dean? Must've gotten lost."

Reluctantly, Hank got up and headed toward the door.

The sheriff hollered after him. "Go to Tucker's place. Tell Deputy Willis we got prisoners to lock up. Tell him he's staying at the jail tonight, too!" He turned back to Indigo and looked at her. "Been meaning to ask. What the hell kinda name is Indigo anyways? The one decent thing your ma did was name you after my mother, and now you disrespect her and me, too?"

Indigo shoved her shoulders back, indignant. "I happen to like my name. I wouldn't expect *you* would, but I don't care!" She stood firm, staring back at him. "And what's my name got to do with these two guys you want to lynch? They are innocent," she shouted with unrestrained fury.

Sherriff Joe cut her off abruptly, "Kindly shut your mouth," and turned his attention to Sally and Janet. "And you two… I'd advise you not to get involved in this mess." He pointed his finger directly at Janet. "You know, I give your parents leeway around here, even though they're Jesus-haters. Lots of folks wouldn't mind if I was to run the bunch of you out of town. The only reason I don't is they're real regular with their payments and keep their big snouts to themselves. They do know how to order the goods, and I swear to God they can squeeze a nickel so tight it bleeds orange juice.

Janet was shaking. Her insides felt that they would erupt. It took every ounce of her willpower to stay quiet.

Sheriff Joe slugged down another shot of rye and spat out. "Now, you get involved in any of my business, I'll send you and your gold-digging family back to wherever you people came from."

Janet shook her head. She couldn't believe the venom that spewed from him about her family. It was like she was dreaming a nightmare. She wanted to run and hide from this monster, but instead, forced herself to remain calm – expressionless.

Then the sheriff turned to Sally. "Now Sally," he said, "be a good girl and go on home. It's getting late."

Sally breathed a sigh of relief. She had been shaking the whole time and felt lucky he didn't berate her or worse. Her father worked in a mine outside of town. Not much nickel was left in there, but enough to keep it open. Hank's dad owned a share of it as did the sheriff. Mining was hard, dirty work, but he managed to eke out a modest living much of which went to booze for him and Sally's mother. That's when the fights would start. On those drunk nights, Sally would usually stay with Indigo or Janet.

Maybe I'll stay with Janet tonight, she thought wryly.

Sheriff Joe said, "Get going, girls. As for you, Mary..." he smirked nastily, "and don't think I'm going to call you by that hippie name. And a little advice to you, Miss Smartie Pants. Keep your nose out of my official affairs... you hear?"

"Well, this may be 'your' town, but these two deserve a fair trial. If you deny them their rights, I'll call the newspaper over in Billings, and tell them what you're doing. That'll make front-page news. Maybe even get you fired... and then have charges filed against you."

Sheriff Joe was so furious he thought his insides might explode. At that moment, he literally hated his daughter. He struggled with thoughts of ringing her neck until she apologized. Hard as it was, the sheriff kept his temper in check. "You want a trial," he snarled, "I'll give those two a trial... a fair one, too. So, tell that to the newspaper in Billings. Judge Ellis will come on a moment's notice. I do abide by the law of the land. And consider yourselves lucky I let the three of you in here for a little underage drinking. You don't seem to mind *that* perk from me, do you? I let all that slide so you gals can have a good time and as a special favor for the boys. They like coming in here and finding something better to look at than a bunch of cowhands. Even a Jew, they told me, was better looking than a longhorn. I said I wasn't so sure I agreed, but... whatever keeps the boys happy around here, I like to oblige."

Tucking in his rumpled shirt and smoothing down his hair, Deputy Ben Willis, came bursting through the door. "I hear we got us a real problem here, sheriff."

"Well, if you'd been at your post, you might have caught this here Injun thief. Lucky for you, Hank caught the guy sniffing around his '54. We all know that truck's his pride and joy... being a gift from Hank Sr. and all. Would've been a real shame if it was stolen. Now, I want you to take these boys over to the jail and lock them up. Gonna have us a trial. Now, get your gun out, and don't take it off them. Got them cuffed together so they shouldn't be a problem. But if there is, shoot. And watch out for the tall quiet one. They're the most dangerous kind. Ole L.A. here's got some big fancy words to say about the law. We'll see about that at trial." He looked over at Indigo with a steely glare. "No one can claim I didn't give them a fair trial." He was still fuming about his daughter and her big mouth. *Well, I guess that little bitch is just like her mother.*

"Now get outa here, girls. Party's over and it's getting late. I still got some work to do… a lawman's work is never done – not easy."

Deputy Ben pulled out his pistol and cocked it. "Okay, Hollywood. You and Red, scoot your asses outa the chair real slow, an' head out the door. Going to the clinker to get some of our old west hospitality."

Indigo kept her eyes peeled on Sam, her insides quaking with emotion. *I'll find some way to help him… I have to… but right now the Sheriff doesn't trust me… me and my big mouth. I'd better lay low and stay out of his way. I can't let him find out my feelings for Sam. He'd never let me anywhere near the jail, not that he would anyway.* Her thoughts were chaotic.

*

The century-old jail was rock solid. Sheriff Joe and Deputy Willis each had a desk and occasionally they would have Mildred, a fifty-eight-year-old widow, come over and handle the phones. Not a lot went on in Miners Gulch. Sheriff Joe made sure of that. The jail had three cells – each with a cot, a piss pot, and a bucket for water. "No sense putting in a toilet," Sheriff Joe said. He had Deputy Willis empty it out back in a covered hole. Worked just fine.

So, when the cold steel bars slammed shut, a hollow boom echoed down the hallway. Sam looked over at Oliver in the next cell and said, "You don't really think they'll hang us… do you? I feel like I just stepped back in time…straight into a nightmare."

Oliver said bitterly, "I guess you don't know much about this part of the country. These folks around here despise us Indians, and the judge will likely do whatever the sheriff wants. No one really cares. So, sleep on that one." Oliver stretched out on the hard cot, his feet hanging over the edge.

Sam paced nervously back and forth in his cell, as a sinking feeling filled him. "Will they allow us a phone call? I could get some help to get us out of here."

"Good luck on that," Oliver said. "The sheriff's reputation for being a tough sonofabitch is not an exaggeration."

Sam asked curiously, "Was it worth it to come here to find your father's truck. What were you going to do when you found it? Steal it back?"

"My father disappeared a few years ago. He was headed north of here to look at a horse, a mustang. He knew about this town and its reputation and wouldn't have come anywhere close unless something happened. Then he vanished. That's not like him. We hadn't a clue… until now. When I found his truck, I had to look for anything I could find out about him… even if it meant risking my life. Not knowing is far worse."

Sam wanted to ask him more but thought he should wait until morning. Then the lights went out and darkness filled the room.

The half-moon shone through the small window. Oliver noticed the reflection on the wall. He saw the outline of a crow standing on the ledge of the window clacking its beak – its eyes bright as the moon. He smiled.

Suddenly, Sam called out, "Did you see that crow, Oliver?" He jumped up from his bed rubbing his eyes. "I swear it was right at the window, looking in… staring at me with its enormous eyes. I must be really tired, seeing things and all."

Oliver didn't reply at first. He wasn't sure how much he should tell Sam about what happened. He needed to let everything settle in for a bit. Then after pondering a few moments, he sat up and decided to tell Sam what happened to him. He recounted the story about the crows coming to help a couple nights ago, when Hank and Jimmy Dean offered him a ride. "That's when I discovered they were driving my father's truck., then they tried to run me over… that's when the flock of crows swooped down and saved me."

Sam was wide-eyed with interest and urged Oliver to tell him more.

Oliver recounted about the voices he heard in the bar talking to him, like they were right next to him and the next thing he knew, he was floating out of his body.

"I know it's a lot to take in let alone comprehend right now… and to be honest so much has happened my thoughts are jumbled. I remember when I used to go camping with my father in the hills. He told me stories about the crows and their many gifts they possessed. He said, "they're so smart they can read your thoughts, and help you in times of trouble." I didn't believe it at the time, but I liked listening to him. He was a good storyteller. But now… I know the stories were true and not just some made up magical tale." He could feel his heart racing in excitement. "I should've paid more attention."

Sam hopped up, as though a light bulb clicked on in his head. "I just thought about you sitting at the bar, and for a second or two, I swear, you weren't there… just the outline of you lingered. I was really blown away. I've read a lot of stories about the old medicine men and their powers. Every time I read some of that stuff, it rang true for me. I could feel goose bumps rise on my arms. My mother was Indian. Her name was Singing Dove," he said softly. "I'm not sure what tribe she was from, but I remember her singing to me all the time. I can still feel her hugs… so full of love." Tears filled his eyes. "I was four when my father dropped me off at my aunt and uncle's house. He was a white dude my mother met when she was fifteen. His name's Jesse. He liked to drink and gamble and spent most of his time in bars. I remember that he would hit my mother and call her a lazy squaw. Then I'd cry and run to her. He got real tired of that… thought she coddled me too much. He felt she should've been taking better care of him and his needs. So, one day in a drunken rage, he grabbed me from my mother's arms and threw me into his truck and sped off. I can still remember her calling and screaming for me to come back. Jesse told my Aunt Alice that my mother was crazy, and I'd be better off living with her and Uncle Fred. When I started crying for my mother, he smacked me upside the head so hard, I saw stars. My Uncle Fred hurried over and picked me up trying his best to console me. Then, a couple months went by, and Jesse sent a letter to their house. Aunt Alice told me that my mother had died. My father didn't say how. I cried myself to sleep for a long time. I always hoped she would come back to get me, but… he let his words trail off. "My father did come to see me a couple times. He didn't seem upset with her passing when he told me, 'Your ma was whining about seeing you all the time. Got sick of listening to that shit. Then she croaked. So now you got a real nice place here with your Aunt Alice and Uncle Fred. Lucky you!' I hated him and wished he had been the one to die."

Sam lay back on the cot and was quiet for some time before he spoke. "My Aunt Alice lives around sixty or seventy miles from here. That's where I was headed. I wanted to see if I could find out more about my mom – maybe where she was buried and, while I was here, learn something about my Indian culture, including what tribe I come from. I used to be embarrassed to say I was part Indian, so I'd make up stories and tell people I was part Italian or French… romanticize my background. Then I started reading stories about Chief Joseph and Sitting Bull and others. I was fascinated. They were brave men, and their hearts were good. They loved their lands and their people. I wanted to be more like them. I looked at my life and it felt useless. I wondered what I was doing and was sick of living in Los Angeles, so I came back to see Aunt Alice and Uncle Fred. They were good to me, and I never really thanked them. So that's my story. Not sure why I told you all this, but thanks for listening. It feels good to tell someone." Sam was quiet for a while and then said, "If we get out of here, I will help you… any way I can. Maybe the girl I met tonight might help us." He said her name softly. "Indigo." He liked the sound of it. "She's gorgeous plus she's really nice. There's something about her eyes that I like."

Oliver said, "That's nice. Better try and get some sleep. Need to be on our toes tomorrow."

Sam yawned. "I'll see if I can get ahold of my friend in Los Angeles. Maybe he could get us an attorney and we'll be out of here in no time." But a bad feeling crept inside him that he couldn't shake. It took a long time for him to fall asleep.

In the morning, Oliver and Sam awoke to a loud clanging on the bars. Deputy Ben, said, "Wakie, wakie, boys. Hope you had a pleasant night," and couldn't help but snicker at the irony of his comment. He rattled his keys and opened the cell door just a crack, then shoved a bucket of water inside – first in Oliver's cell, then Sam's.

"Thought you might be thirsty. Can't let our prisoners think they're not being taken care of." Slamming the door shut, he said, "When you're finished drinking, you can bathe in it if you want. Double duty, and all." He smirked. A glint of sunlight streamed in the small window, highlighting his pock-marked face.

Still groggy from the little sleep, Sam sat up, tousled hair falling across his forehead. He pushed it aside as he stood. "Hey, wait a minute. I'm entitled to a phone call – and I'd like to make it now. This is my right under the law."

Deputy Ben snickered and looked at Sam with contempt. "Look, Hollywood, here in Wyoming, we are the law, so if I were you, I wouldn't go threatening anything in this town. The sheriff says when he gets here this morning, you'll get your call. So, shut up about rights and stuff. We know what's what around here. Besides," he grinned, "we're not the ones sitting in jail." Deputy Ben turned and slammed out the door.

Oliver paused a moment before saying, "I wouldn't be so sure about that phone call – or about getting out of here. The sheriff isn't going to let that happen… but it's a nice thought."

Before Sam could respond, he jumped, hearing several shots fired behind the jail cell. Oliver and Sam quickly hopped up on their beds and looked out the small window. Deputy Ben was out back shooting a row of cans he had lined up on a fence for target practice. His aim was perfect and didn't miss a single one. Then he walked over and set the cans up again. This went on for over an hour.

At about ten o'clock, Sheriff Joe came banging through the door. "Howdy, boys. You sleep all right in here?" he grinned wickedly, turning to Sam. "Now, my deputy was telling me you know the law pretty good. Well, it's mighty fine you do. We like big shot out-of-towners coming here spouting what they think they know. Real impressive!" He threw a set of handcuffs inside Sam's cell and growled. "Put these on, and then you can come out and make your phone call."

Sam did as he was told. Sheriff Joe unlocked the cell door, checked the handcuffs, and then squeezed them a little tighter. "Come on in the office."

Sam followed the sheriff to the outer room, where the sheriff motioned for him to sit, and shoved the phone at him.

"Now, you go making any more threats around here about your rights and the law, and I'll shove this here receiver right down your big mouth. Understand, Slick?" The sheriff grabbed his chin and squeezed. "I don't mess around. So, make your call and be quick. You got five minutes."

Sam picked up the phone and dialed his friend in Los Angeles.

He'll surely help, he thought. When he finished dialing, he waited and waited, but there was no activity on the other end. He dialed again. This time, he heard nothing but static. Then he dialed the number again, this time slowly. Still nothing. Puzzled, Sam said, "Sheriff. I don't think your phone is working. Might need to get this fixed. Is there another phone I could use?"

Sheriff Joe looked at Sam with his steely gaze. "Working just fine a while ago. Maybe you dialed the wrong number."

Sam glared back at the sheriff and dialed once again. A buzzing sound pinged through the phone. Sam banged the receiver on the desk in frustration. "Look sheriff, I think you know that this phone isn't working," he fumed. "You did this so I can't make a call."

"Best be careful boy what you say. I don't take kindly to accusations, so watch your big mouth. Can't help it if the phone doesn't work. You can try a little later. Meantime, I have a little more news for you. I'm impounding your fancy Camaro out there. Saw some stuff in your car I didn't like. I found this Nazi magazine in the front seat," and slammed it on the desk. "You a commie, come here to incite trouble? That a crime itself, so I'm taking your car as collateral. Now it's time you get back to your cell." He gave Sam a shove down the hall. "You had your rights, so sit your ass back down and keep your trap shut. Gladys 'll bring some lunch over." He clanged the cell door shut and motioned for Sam to stick his hands through the opening to remove the cuffs.

Sheriff Joe looked at Oliver and said, "Looks like you won't be making your call right now… phone's outa order."

CHAPTER FIVE

SHERIFF JOE

SHERIFF JOE HIKED up his pants and walked into the Blue Sky Saloon, clicking his fingers and singing, "Brylcreem, a little dab 'll do ya…" He ran his fingers through his greasy hair as he eyed Gladys, who was sitting at the bar going over paperwork, and he sashayed over, humming his silly slogan. Gladys lit a Pall Mall cigarette, took a deep draw, and blew smoke circles in the air.

"Those things are gonna kill you if you're not careful, Gladys," the sheriff said jokingly, giving her a pinch on her cheek as he jerked his hips back and forth, still humming the Brylcreem tune.

Randy was sitting behind the bar, strumming his guitar, singing a Willie Nelson tune.

The sheriff listened a moment, then banged his fist on the bar, rattling Gladys's ashtray. "What the hell are you playing that law-breaking hippie's music for? That guys a no-good scoundrel, smoking that marijuana crap, and all. If he ever finds himself in my neck of the woods, I'll string him up faster than you can say, 'pothead.' Not that you can play a shit's worth of nickels, anyway."

Sheriff Joe rubbed Gladys' back, digging deep into her shoulders with his beefy palms, and bending down to nuzzle her neck and whisper in her ear. "Why don't you come over a little later, and I'll give you a bit more than a massage. Been known to perk you right up. It's been a while since you've been over, honey bun, and I missed you last night." For emphasis, he pinched her behind.

Randy was watching the sheriff as he plucked on his guitar and switched to a Jimmy Hendrix tune.

Sheriff Joe covered his ears and glared at Randy. "What the hell is wrong with you? You got shit for brains? Playing that pot smoking bandit was bad enough… now you're playing that black hippie jigaboo's music. So don't disrespect me while I'm in your bar. The only reason you got this place is because ole Sparky fell dead… for no apparent reason far as I could tell," he intimated. "Now, I let all that slide by as long as you and your ma, here," he said, giving Gladys a wink, "pay up my half of the earnings," rubbing his fingers together. "Nope. I've got no problem with that old codger being gone. Wasn't as beholden to me as he should've been. But if I was you, I wouldn't be getting all cocky like… playing that jigaboo crap in here. For chrissakes, play some music God would approve of… like George Strait or Hank Williams. Now those guys, really know how to sing the tunes." The sheriff started clacking his fingers together while humming "Doo-dah-diddle-dum…"

The sheriff cozied up to Gladys. "Come on, honey buns. Let's take a spin…" Not waiting for an answer, he pulled Gladys off the barstool and swung her around the dance floor. "I wish I could sing as good as Jonny Cash… get the ladies begging for a look. He hugged Gladys and asked, "Think you could rustle up some grub for those two felons sitting in the jail, honey buns? Give them any leftovers you've got. Can't let them starve, can I?" He looked at Gladys and let off a loud snort. "They might think I don't care about them." He continued to swing her around the dance floor.

Gladys eyed the sheriff, then pulled herself out of his beefy grip. "Sure, I don't mind for the boys. I'll have Randy take it over to the jail, if he isn't too busy."

"Busy?" the sheriff laughed. "You coddle him too much, for chrissakes. He's close to twenty-five, ain't he? And still living at home, with you still taking care of him. I say shove him off the roost, or you'll make a sissy out of him." Sheriff Joe looked up as the bar door swung open and in walked Hank Jr. and Jimmy Dean. "Speaking of sissies, that Jimmy Dean takes the prize. The way he follows Hank around, always looking at him with his big bulging eyes… something ain't right. I got a feeling 'bout that guy, so I keep my ears and eyes sharp." He winked at Gladys. "Good thing it's just his eyes bulging out, if you get my drift."

"That's not nice, Joe. Jimmy Dean's a real nice boy. Always polite and pays his tab without any trouble. I don't care if he's fond of Hank," Gladys said as she walked into the kitchen. "He's not hurting anyone."

Hank and Jimmy Dean sat down at the bar. Hank nodded to the sheriff and said, "Helluva night, huh, sheriff?"

Sheriff Joe looked at Hank's black-and-blue eyes that had swelled to the size of walnuts, with cuts and scrapes covering his face. Then he noticed Jimmy Dean fidgeting. "Say there, big fella. Did you get into the tussle, too, or did you hide behind Hank?"

Jimmy Dean's face burned scarlet, and he shifted in his seat. "No sir. I got right on into the thick of stuff. Fists were swinging every which way…"

Sheriff Joe rolled his eyes and turned his attention to Hank. "Mighty good work, catching that thief and his sidekick. I should have hired you for my deputy instead of Ben," he paused, then said, rubbing his chin, "but Ben's real faithful. He'll do anything I ask. A little on the lazy side, but still, he could shoot the front tooth off a jackrabbit, while its hopping away at full speed."

Hank nodded. "Yep, he's a real good shot, for sure. Need to

have someone like that working with you. A straight shooter that's got your back when you need it."

Gladys came out from the kitchen and threw a couple platters of burgers and fries on the bar. "Jail order to go."

Sheriff Joe smiled. "That was fast. Thanks honey buns."

Hank gave a big sniff, nose quivering over the plate. He picked up a burger, ready to take a bite, when the sheriff slapped it out of his hands.

"Take these over to the jail, would ya? When you get back, then we'll eat. Maybe Gladys 'll come up with something special for us. She knows what I like, ain't that right honey buns?"

Without a word, Gladys shot him a look, then walked back into the kitchen.

Hank handed the platters to Jimmy Dean. "Let's go. I'm starving and my head feels like a sledgehammer whacked at it." They headed toward the door, and Hank opened it for Jimmy Dean. "See you in a couple minutes, sheriff."

As soon as they stepped outside, they heard a rally of shots blasting near the jail, and Jimmy Dean slid to his knees, to keep the food from spilling, hands shaking, aghast.

Hank did a double take as the sheriff went tearing out of the saloon and hollered. "Good God. I bet those bastards might've escaped." Without another word, he scurried off toward the jail.

Hank jumped a couple feet in the air, ready to fight, pulling out his six-shooter, and ran after the sheriff, gun ready.

Everyone stopped in their tracks halfway down the street near the jail, jaws dropped in dismay. There was Deputy Ben Willis, with his guns drawn, blasting away at the air, cursing, "Damn birds!"

Sheriff Joe cried out in dismay. "What the hell are you shooting at? Did the prisoners escape?"

Deputy Ben was all excited and he hopped around like a swarm of hornets were after him. "There was a huge flock of crows swarming around the jailhouse. I went outside to see what the ruckus was, and the crows came swooping down at me, chasing me like they were going to attack me. One big bird got ahold of my shirt, ripped it, and took a bite out of my arm." Panting, he showed the sheriff his bloody wound. "I thought they might kill me or peck my eyes out. I must have fired a hundred shots and didn't hit a single lousy crow." He looked at the sky in disbelief. "And you know I can hit anything that moves. If those crafty buggers come back, I'm gonna have me some crow pie." *Strangest damn thing I've ever seen…* he thought warily, looking at the sky.

The sheriff about came unglued as he stared at his deputy. "Look Ben! All that uproar about a bunch of birds. You had me thinking those felons got loose or someone was robbing the bank. I don't give a rat's ass about a bunch of crows. You're wasting those bullets on the taxpayers' money. I should make you pay for those," he huffed, then stomped off down the street, heading back to the saloon – a sheepish Ben following behind.

Indigo and Janet came around the corner, and quickly ducked behind the barbershop to avoid the sheriff. They waited until he left and saw Jimmy Dean and Hank heading toward the jail. Indigo poked Janet and said, "Let's go." And they went running up to them. Out of breath, Indigo said, "Hi Hank. Where are you going with the food?"

Hank scowled, still sore at Indigo from the previous evening. "It's for the felons! The ones sitting in jail… you know, Mr. LA dude… the pansy you cozied up to last night. You wouldn't even give me a dance neither. Not so sure I'm happy about that."

Indigo said as sweetly as she could muster. "I've been meaning to ask… how is your eye? Looks pretty swollen and sore. Hope you can see okay. Did Sam do that?" She stifled a giggle and scooted even closer to Hank, pulling Janet beside her.

"Don't know which of them did it, but they're the sorry ones that landed in jail, not me."

Indigo bristled at Hank's remark. "I'll walk with you a bit, if you don't mind?"

"Suit yourself, Indie."

In just a few minutes they were at the jail. Hank eyed, Indigo suspiciously and said, "You best stay out here. Don't want those felons to bother you. I'll be but a second, and you can walk with me some more. Then we can…"

Indigo interrupted Hank and boldly shoved her way inside. "I don't think anyone's going to bite me," she said, trying to hide her irritation. "They're locked up, aren't they?"

"Well of course they're locked up, Indie." said Hank, jealously as he walked inside the jailhouse. He opened the back door where the cells were located. Jimmy Dean, ready to take the food down to Sam and Oliver, when Indigo suddenly grabbed the food from his arms and said sweetly, "Here, let me help you." Before he could answer, she swept inside the hallway, and went zipping down the dark hallway before Hank could stop her. All in a twitter, her eyes lit up when she saw Sam lying across a cot.

Oliver and Sam stood up, surprised to see her.

Hank was flabbergasted at the gumption of Indigo and flew down the hallway, hustled in front of her yanking the plates from her hands. "I'll do this. You can wait out front, not in here. Now, scoot. This is man's business. Not for pretty little ladies," he admonished.

Indigo fumed as she was ushered out the door that slammed in her face.

Jimmy Dean handed the platter to Oliver – keeping a safe distance, lest the Indian tried to grab him. Hank shoved Sam's plate through the opening. "Here's your grub," he growled.

Sam grabbed the plate before it fell on the floor, and he scowled. "Would you check the phones, please. I still want to make my phone call!"

"Don't be talking to me about your phone call. Take your

business up with the sheriff," Hank said. "You're lucky you didn't get strung up last night right along with ole Red in the next cage. Phone call should be the least of your worries, and I wouldn't be causing any more trouble if I was you. So, eat your food, and zip it. Anyway, sheriff said the phones are down," He turned to leave, and, as he opened the door, Indigo almost toppled into him.

"Hey, Indie. What are you doing listening at the door? You can't be snooping and spying around here or trying to get in with those felons."

Indigo stiffened at Hank's words. "How can you call them that? Oliver didn't do anything but look at your stupid old truck and Sam was just sitting at the bar, having a drink. You can't bring made-up charges just because you don't like Indians… or outsiders."

"Well, the sheriff thinks differently. He's sending for Judge Ellis who'll be here in a few days. They'll have their fair trial."

Indigo's face burned at the comment.

"You know you can't be interfering in your dad's business. He's the law. He won't be happy to see you put your cute little nose where it don't belong." Hank wagged a finger at Indigo and gave her nose a tweak.

Indigo slapped his hand. "Shut up, Hank. This isn't the old wild west where you do whatever you want. We have laws."

"Indigo!" Janet whispered in alarm, walking up to her friend. "This isn't helping matters. You won't get anywhere by getting all riled up and losing your temper. Not with Hank or the sheriff. Come on," she said, pulling Indigo.

"At least Janet has some sense, Indie. You should listen to her," Hank said with a smile. "Even if she if a J…" he let the words drift off, after a scathing glare.

"You should watch your mouth," Indigo said, and stubbornly crossed her arms and pondered Janet's plea.

Hank sidled up to Indigo and smiled. "Why don't you girls

come on back to the bar tonight and have some fun? We can shoot some pool, have a few drinks, and forget about those two in jail. You don't want to cause trouble with your dad."

Indigo ignored him and walked outside with Janet.

"I know you're upset, Indie. So am I, and so is Sally, but doing this won't help! We need to be clever about this, and outsmart your dad… um… I mean, the sheriff. He's no one to mess with. And with you showing partiality to two total strangers, and one of them being an Indian is not going to look very good. If the sheriff gets a whiff of that he won't let you within an inch of the jail, let alone the cell."

Indigo sighed as she walked down the street. "I know. It's just so irritating. I'm so angry I could explode. Plus, I'm really worried about Sam and Oliver."

Janet interrupted. "That is obvious. Come over to my house and calm down. My mother will make some potato latkes with applesauce. Your favorite. Sally was still asleep when I left this morning. If she isn't up when we get back, we'll wake her. Then we'll put our heads together and come up with a plan. We don't have much time but we're not going to let them hang Sam and… what's the other guy's name? I don't like calling him 'the Indian'."

"Oliver," Indigo said, and squeezed her friend's arm. "And thanks for talking some sense into me. I get so carried away that I don't think straight. I hope I didn't get that from my dad. I can't believe I'm related to him… makes me sick to think about it."

"Well, then don't," Janet said. "Stay with me for a while. My parents won't mind in the least."

The girls turned the corner by the church and ran into Pastor Goodwin, who was sporting a nasty bruise on his jaw and a cut lip. Indigo and Janet waved to him and shouted out, "Hi, Pastor."

"Good morning, girls. It's another blessed day!"

Indigo grimaced at his upbeat words. "Well, good morning

back to you. Not so sure about it being a blessed day. They have Sam and Oliver locked up and…"

"Yes, yes. I know, but at least Hank and the boys didn't do anything drastic last night. It was quite a brawl, though," Percy said, touching his jaw. "First fight I've ever been in… But it felt good to fight for the Lord and justice. I do so happily… no matter the bangs and bruises I incurred."

"Pastor," Indigo said, nervously. "Glad you're happy to fight for the Lord, but there is going to be a trial next week. The judge happens to be a friend of the sheriff, who by the way is my dad, I'm ashamed to say. It might look like justice has been done, but I can say with near certainty, it won't be."

"Now, now girls. I'm sure the sheriff will uphold the law," Percy said. "He seems pretty adamant about that."

"What law?" Janet interrupted, frustrated by the Pastor's naivete about the sheriff and the people in this town. "The law is what it says it is."

Pastor Percy walked up to the girls and put his hand on their shoulders. "I can't believe the sheriff would go against the judge's order. That would be criminal. I'm sure he will follow the letter of the law."

"That's what I'm trying to tell you," Indigo said. "The judge will do what my father tells him to do."

Percy sighed. "I'm on my way to see the two prisoners…"

"Their names are Sam and Oliver," Indigo said, irritably.

"Let me talk to them and get their story. I promise I will do anything I can to help them. Now, don't worry. I'm certain it will all be fine. Praise be to the Lord. Goodbye girls."

Indigo and Janet watched Percy head over to the jail. Indigo said, "He's really nice. And I truly believe he thinks he's going to help, but he seems a little gullible to me."

"Yes," Janet agreed, looking at the preacher. "I admit that he's way better than that porno-watching Pastor Tynes. What a hypo-crite he was! I'm glad he's gone. He always gave me the creeps."

Indigo whispered conspiratorially. "I overheard the sheriff say that Tynes liked to look at young girls as well. Peek in their windows at night. I wonder what the good Lord would say about that."

"Oh, I imagine he'll be gone for a while, then he'll come back pious, repentant, cleansed of his sins… hallelujah and amen." They both chuckled at the ridiculousness of that thought.

*

Deputy Ben sat at his desk, busily cleaning his gun when the door opened and in walked Pastor Percy Goodwin. "Hello, Pastor. What can I do for you?' he said amiably, wiping the edge of the gun barrel with a dirty rag as he looked out the window. "Say, did you happen to see that big bunch of crows flying over here a while ago? They made quite the racket, squawking real menacing like. It would've been hard to miss them."

Pastor Percy was amused by the question. "No, I can't say that I did," he joked, "Did they do something illegal?"

Deputy Ben stiffened at the wisecrack. "Well, I never seen anything like it before. They were flying around the jail like they were conspiring… There were hundreds of 'em circling and cawing… making such a racket I had to cover my ears. I've seen crows before, but this was different. It was a terrifying scene." Deputy Ben appeared on the verge of hysterics. "Look at my arm," he blustered, showing Pastor Percy the deep gash. "One of those nasty things flew right down at me, evil like, like he was gonna peck my eyeballs right outa my socket. I tried to shoot at 'em… the whole bunch… but for some odd reason, I didn't hit a one… and it was weird 'cause I can shoot a rat's ass a mile away." Getting hot under the collar, he paced back and forth.

Taken aback by the deputy's strange behavior Pastor Percy exclaimed, "My dear soul, let me help you. I see that you are overwrought. I shall pray for you extra hard tonight that you don't get frightened by God's creatures… or so upset. Yes, there might have been a flock of crows, but to think that they would be evil, is another matter. Crows, I understand, are very smart. Uncannily smart, not evil. It could be all the stress put upon you – by your work, perhaps."

Deputy Ben Willis glared at the preacher and fumed, "Why don't you go to that cell back there and preach to those two felons… They're gonna need it a helluva lot more than me. I was trying to tell you something seriously wicked blew into town last night and it's still here. I don't care what you say!" Raising his voice to a high pitch, he sputtered, "I was trying to tell you something important and you mock me. Save your prayers for those two crooks!"

Deputy Ben unlocked the door with a clang leading to the back. Percy looked at the man, concerned for his mental state. "Thank you, Deputy," was all he said, as he walked down the narrow hall, and thought how damp and dark it is, as he made his way to the cells. He noticed a small, barred window above each cell and, easing his way to the bars, he called out, "Hello, gentlemen."

Oliver and Sam looked at the man curiously, wondering what he wanted. Oliver remembered the pastor from last night, coming into the bar and getting into the middle of the fight with his Bible in tow. He admired the slight man for his courage and determination. *He would be considered a good brave*, Oliver thought, surprised by the notion.

"My name is Pastor Percy Goodwin. I'm sorry about what happened to you last night. I did try my best to help, but I'm afraid I fell short…" He grinned sheepishly. "I came here to see if there's anything I can do for you… perhaps bring you something. Are you hungry?"

Oliver said, "Thank you, Pastor, but they did feed us."

"Wonderful," Percy said. "Then perhaps I could pray for you

both. I don't know what your faith is, if any… but it doesn't matter. God loves everyone and takes all strays into his flock. Would you care to join hands with me so we may pray together? I will ask Him for guidance and mercy from…" Percy paused, uncertain how to phrase his next sentence. "Ask Him for help in this terrible situation you're in."

Sam stepped up to the bars and said, "If you want to do something, Pastor, help us get out of here. We didn't do anything wrong. Oliver is innocent, as I am. He discovered his father's '54 red pickup truck out there – the one that Hank drives around. His father has been missing for a few years and he wanted to get to the bottom of what happened to him."

"I'm so sorry to hear that," Pastor Percy said.

Sam spoke with an urgency. "I was just passing through this town yesterday minding my own business. Now, I'm in jail for nothing. We both are. I can't even make my phone call. So, like I said, if you want to do something for us, get me a phone or call this number, so we can get help and get out of here."

"Well, of course. I'd be happy to help," Percy said enthusiastically.

"Do you have anything to write on?" Sam asked.

"Percy pulled out a note pad and a pen. "What's the number?" Sam gave him the number and Percy quickly scribbled it down.

"This is Bernie, my friend in Los Angeles. Bernie Sacks. Tell him my circumstances and where I am. He'll help, I'm sure."

"I'll call as soon as I get back."

'Be sure to tell him it's urgent."

"Yes, yes, don't worry. Now I will say a quick prayer, if you don't mind." Before Sam could object, Percy closed his eyes and began. "Dear Heavenly Father. I am asking for your…"

Sam interrupted. "Amen, Pastor. Thank you, but I think that phone call could answer our prayers."

Momentarily taken aback, Pastor Percy said, "Of course. God

bless you both." He gave a half wave as he hurried down the hall and knocked on the door.

To Percy's surprise, the sheriff opened with a loud greeting. "Glad to see you saving souls, Pastor Percy, but I wouldn't waste too much time on those two back there," he said, smacking Percy on the back.

Percy said, slightly miffed. "No one is a waste of time, sheriff. We all have redeeming qualities."

"Why, of course, Percy. That's why you're here." The sheriff looked at Percy's hand, squishing something together in his palms. He frowned. "What have you got in there, pastor? Are you hiding something?"

Percy's face paled at the comment, and he put his hand behind his back. But the sheriff reached down before he could successfully hide the note. The sheriff pried open Percy's hand and grabbed the crumpled paper inside his sweaty palms.

Sheriff Joe's lips twitched and snarled. "You shouldn't be trying to hide things from me, Percy. You may be new in town, but know this… I don't tolerate anyone interfering in my duties."

"No, no," Percy said, backing away. "It's just a phone number, that's all. Sam said the phones weren't working here, so I thought I would make a call for him. I was trying to be a good Samaritan, sheriff. That's my job. Besides, they are entitled to a phone call. Right?"

Sheriff Joe's eyes bore into Percy's while escorting him to the front door. "You tend to your preaching, and I'll tend to the law. Tomorrow's a big day. It'll be your first sermon and I'm curious to hear what you'll be talking about. Got to make sure it's not too racy. We Baptists like to keep it strict, and we've got certain protocols you must adhere to… no fanciful embellishments either. I hear you've been taught a different faith," he sniffed, "not quite as strict as I would like, but we needed a pastor on short order, and that's why you're here. Might be a little loose around the edges…"

he paused with a grimace, "but we'll remedy that soon enough. Now, good day to you. Remember, keep your snout in the good book and send over your sermon before days done."

Pastor Percy was a little confused by the sheriff, and thought, *I'd best follow the rules here, and stay out of the sheriff's business. I'm sure he'll do the right thing. He's a man of the law and of God. And the sign in his office says, In God We Trust.*

That thought put his mind at ease for a moment. But as he walked on, doubts started to trickle in, making him nervous. "I'd better pray mightily. I fear I will need all my strength and more, living in this town." He quickened his pace down the sidewalk.

CHAPTER SIX

THE GIRLS

AT THE HERSHELS' house, Janet, Sally, and Indigo sat together in the warm and comfortable living room. Soft, squishy sofas and wide-berth chairs meant for lounging lined the room, filled with beautiful paintings. It felt like home to Indigo.

Her father's house was large, and some would say really nice, but to Indigo it was cold and ornate. She couldn't believe that the couch was still covered with plastic and sitting on it made her clothes stick to her. A housekeeper came once a week and meticulously cleaned every inch of the house, and, when she finished, the smell of bleach and floor cleaner was so strong, Indigo would have to hold her nose as she walked inside and proceeded to open every window. With its high wooden fence surrounding the one-acre property, it felt sterile to Indigo, so she stayed in her room most of the time and counted the days until she could leave this place.

On her nightstand, she kept a picture of her mother, which she would kiss every night. She missed laughing with her, going to the movies, and dancing together around the house. On weekends, they would stay up late, bake cookies, and watch old movies on TV. Then her mother got lung cancer. Her mother's college friends told Indigo that marijuana helped with the pain, so they made sure she never ran out. Even when her mother was close to dying, she still had a great sense of humor. Near the end, she made Indigo promise to go live with her father. "Get to know him," she said. It would only be for a few years, then she could go off to California, her lifelong dream, and pursue acting, or writing, which she excelled in at school – trying out for every part, big or small. She learned from acting to put on a good front around her father, but it was hard to contain her dislike of him and this town. Cattle and horses were prized above all else… except for pick-up trucks. The trademark in town was your Ford or Chevy and the number of cattle and horses you owned. No fancy Camaros around here. And then, along came the intriguing Sam Colton – so different than anyone she had ever met. Her heart melted, just thinking about him. There weren't any men like that in Miners Gulch. She did like her girlfriends, though. They made her life bearable in this town.

Janet Hershel was smart, shy, and had a good sense of humor. Indigo always told her, "You need humor around this place." But smart was the key word for Janet. She got straight A's in school and was already accepted at all the colleges of her choice. She was a whiz at science and biology, which baffled Indigo, since she hated those subjects. But it was Janet's academic skills that were one of the main reasons she was so impressed with her. Janet wasn't popular in school. Some called her names, which Janet tried to ignore. But Indigo could see that she was hurt by the comments. She hated how cruel kids could be, and they formed a bond.

Sally Bennett came from a battered and alcoholic home. Her parents fought a lot. Sometimes Sally felt the brunt of their alcoholic rages, and occasionally would come to school with bruises. Her dad worked in the silver mine. Her mom stayed home and took pills to keep calm. As soon as he was out of school, her older brother left home to join the military. But the one thing the girls couldn't talk Sally out of was her obsession with Hank. Sally would go on and on about his being a football star, so handsome and strong. His picture hung in the school hallway, with his big bold smile. "He was going to be a pro-football player," Sally would say, gushing. Then she would go on about his injury and how bad she felt about him losing his chance for the pros. Everyone in town knew about it, and he returned to Miners Gulch embittered.

Sally did odd jobs for the Hershels. In her spare time, she painted, but she had a dream to be a professional stripper. She heard they made some real big money and there was a town, about sixty-plus miles away that had a real nice strip joint. She hoped to get a job there and show Hank she could amount to something. Hank came around her house occasionally. But that was generally after the bars had closed and he had been drinking a lot. He would invite her to The Gravel Pit for a drink and have his way with her. If Sally questioned him when she saw him again, he would get angry. "Don't ask me when I'm gonna see you again. You're lucky I see you at all." Then he would drive her back home and dump her out at the end of her long driveway. Sally would say, "See you soon." Hank would say, "If you're lucky." And he would tear off down the road. Sally was always crushed by his comments and vowed to be better the next time. *I've got to stop whining so much,* she would think, miserably. *Then he might treat me better.*

No matter how many times Hank verbally abused her, and on occasion, struck her, Sally couldn't stop herself from seeing him. He was her drug, and she was heavily addicted. She thought if she could dance seductively and men found her appealing, Hank might get jealous and want her for his own. *Maybe one day he'll marry me,* she told her journal.

The three girls sat together in Janet's room trying to come up with a plan.

"It's going to be really hard to get inside the jail and see Sam and Oliver," Indigo said. "Sheriff Joe will have someone there twenty-four hours a day. Maybe I could get Deputy Ben to let me go inside. I could say I'm bringing some extra food for them."

Janet smiled. "I don't know about that, Indigo. Ben sucks up more to your father than he does his guns and nightly beers. For starters, he wouldn't trust you, and the sheriff would skin him alive, if he let you in."

They both turned to Sally. Indigo suggested. "What do you think? Ben's an odd duck, for sure. I don't know if he dates anyone around here… he's too busy kissing the sheriff's fat ass. But maybe you could do a little dance for him. You could practice your stripper moves. Ask him if he thinks it's sexy enough." Indigo frowned. "Look, I know my father will get this trial going as fast as he can, so we probably have less than a week. If we're gonna get them out of jail, we need a solid plan."

Janet was thoughtful, then said, "I have an idea that will take the three of us to pull off, and we'll have to be extra cautious… but it might work."

Indigo sat up, brightened at the prospect.

CHAPTER SEVEN

FIRE AND BRIMSTONE

SHERIFF JOE WAS sitting in his office going over some paperwork and talking to Deputy Ben. "I want you to keep the door locked at all times and keep the key in your pocket when you leave." He thought a moment and had a great idea. "No, better yet, I want you to stay here overnight. We'll get a cot for you and a few of your belongings. It shouldn't be for too long. I spoke with Judge Ellis. He'll be here in a couple days. He will also bring his friend, an attorney – a good ole boy from upstate. He'll represent the two felons. So that should get the ole ball a-rolling on this case and get things back to normal around here. Gotta nip the nuts right off the ole bull." He grinned.

Ben slapped his knee laughing at the sheriff's words. When he stopped laughing, he asked, "What are you going to do about your sassy daughter, sheriff? She's a handful and might be itching to cause trouble."

"Well, that's where you're dead wrong. She can't do a damn thing. It's set up all legal. Law's the law, and I'm following it to the letter. She may grumble and complain and say, 'how awful.' Can't wait till she leaves. She's a big pain in my ass, and bossy as hell. Makes my head hurt. If I wanted that, I would've taken a bride. I'm guessing the Lord's been teaching me a big lesson with that girl. Takes all my manhood not to wallop her but good. But I've gotta set the standards around here. Keep the town running smooth that way."

Ben nodded his head vigorously. "That's for sure, sheriff. I'm honored to work with you… learn the ropes an all. You're a real hero in this town."

Sheriff Joe grunted. "Well, the ropes you need to learn is how to tie one real good, so when you're about to snap a neck or two, gotta keep 'em from slipping loose. Get working on those skills, Ben. They'll come in real handy. Now, we got church service tomorrow with the new pastor. I'm a little wary of this one. Can't believe they sent that simpering Percy to replace Pastor Tynes. That man could get you shaking in your boots with his fiery sermons. Kept everyone obeying God's law – just like the job calls for. But damn, he should've kept his stash of porn locked up better… so his son couldn't find it and show it to his friends. Well, after that, the shit hit the fan and word spread like wildfire. People gossiping… asking me what I was going to do about it. I had no choice but to send him packing. Maybe, after a spell, he could come back… explain how the Lord spoke to him and forgave him for being weak. But… I don't know. All the congregation could think about after that is him watching porn, while he's up preaching the Lord's Gospel."

Ben burst out laughing again. "When you put it like that, you're right… he mighta screwed himself." He made a nasty gesture with his hand.

"Knock it off, Ben. Gotta be above that. Now, I'm going over to see what the new pastor has in store for us tomorrow. I don't want any surprises. Got more than enough going on right now." Sheriff Joe straightened his holster and walked out the door.

The church was a few blocks away, off Main Street – old,

worn, and sturdy. A couple of years back, the town took up a collection to install a big cross on top of the church. You could see it all the way across town, and it was lit up at night. Then a while ago a big storm came and blew the thing right off the roof. It was a little banged up, so the sheriff asked the repair shop at the auto dealership to fix it. "Nice to have it back," the sheriff said, walking by. "Looks almost as good as new."

As Sheriff Joe got closer to the church, he heard faint sounds of music emanating from within. *Must be Agnes practicing for tomorrow's service,* he thought in delight. But when he opened the door, he heard music that didn't sound like proper Christian music. It wasn't solemn or holy. As he walked further inside the church, his eyes bulged at the sight of Pastor Percy, hopping up and down, singing something vulgar that sounded like, "Some kinda bitch…" – the only words he could make out. The rest was gibberish. Sheriff Joe couldn't believe the audacity. He thought about getting his gun and shooting the pastor for this horrid display of blasphemy in church. "Maybe I'll shoot the piano first – and then him," he fumed. Instead, he stomped up to Percy and whacked him hard on the shoulder.

Seeing the murderous look in the sheriff's eyes, Percy jumped about a foot off the ground. Red faced and sweating, Percy wiped his face. "Hi… um… hello, Sheriff J-Joe. Was just having a bit of… um… practice… a musical number."

Sheriff Joe bellowed out in disbelief. "What in the hell was that you were playing… and, in the House of the Lord? You're lucky the good Lord doesn't come down and smite you on the spot… after that vulgar display of disrespect."

Percy shuffled his feet nervously and tried to explain. "I was singing an Elton John song. I've always admired how he could dance around while playing the piano. Such a talent… " Percy hesitated, unsure if he should continue as he watched the sheriff's face turn a deep shade of red – afraid he would rupture a blood vessel. He somehow gathered the gumption to continue. "You know, my faith doesn't condone dancing it up a bit. I look at it as good exercise for the body. Moving and shaking gets your heart rate up and removes tension."

Sheriff Joe couldn't believe the gall of this... this mouse of a pastor. "I heard you singing something about a witch... or a bitch...!" he exploded.

"Oooh... I know it wasn't appropriate, but I love that snappy tune. I just got a little carried away is all."

The sheriff directed his furious gaze at the pastor. "You best not let any of that stuff slip out tomorrow in your sermon or I'll save the Lord the trouble of coming down to smite you. I'll do it myself. And Agnes... she'd tar and feather you if she caught you playing such sinful tunes on her piano."

All Percy could do was stand meekly and nod.

"You know, God is a Baptist, and He would be appalled at your behavior. A might too loose for our town. Now, tell me what your sermon will be about tomorrow. You never brought it over, and I thought you needed help. By the looks of things, I'm certain you do."

Percy found his notes and said, "I was going to preach from the book of Psalms. About the shepherd and..."

"No, no, no! Give the good folks something worth coming for. Use a passage from the Old Testament. A real tongue-burning sermon. Talk about the Devil and his sidekick... *You* know... get them groveling and then strike at the right moment. Especially the ones that have been a bit naughty during the week. Fill 'em full of fear, ready for next week..."

Pastor Percy tried not to show his amazement at the sheriff's demands, and said stiffly, "Why yes, sheriff. I see what you mean. I'll get on the passages right away."

Sheriff Joe eyeballed the pastor. "See that you do. Like to see everyone coming back for more." He turned to leave, then stopped. "You play any more of that Devil-worshiping crap and I'll more than smite you if you get my drift. This is the House of the Lord. You show respect."

Percy stood and watched the sheriff leave. He was baffled by the man. On the outside, he seemed friendly enough, but underneath it all, the man was chilling. He worried about Sam and Oliver. He wondered if they got their phone call. *Well, at least, they should be getting a fair trial,* he thought. He took his tattered Bible and sat down in his office to go over tomorrow's sermon. "I'd better make it a real good one for my first day. And if the sheriff wants fire and brimstone, that's what he'll get."

The next morning Percy rustled around his small house, getting ready for his sermon. Service on Sundays were held at ten o'clock, sharp. Sheriff Joe didn't want the service any earlier because, "folks got to let off a little steam on Saturdays. More of them show up that way."

By a quarter till ten, the church had begun filling up. Most parishioners were curious about the new pastor in town. Rumors had already circulated about Percy's tussle in the bar. Some wondered what kind of preacher he was that would get into a brawl in the saloon.

"Looks pretty scrawny to be fighting in the bar," one of the ranch hands remarked with a grin.

"Maybe he'll be preaching today on how to fight with your Bible – and get whooped."

A few guffaws were stifled under the glaring eye of Mrs. Binns, a local spinster, who expressed her disdain. "None of this is proper or funny, boys. Mind your manners. You're not in the saloon." Then her eyes fell to the Hershels, who walked in and sat in the very last row, seemingly subdued. Mrs. Binns craned her neck in shock, and whispered over to her friend, Mrs. Jones. "What in God's green acres are they are doing here in our church?"

"I heard word the sheriff told them, since this is the only

church in town, they should respect the community and attend. I rather like them. They are always so polite when I go into their store, and the quality of goods is top notch. So, if they come here to our church, for whatever reason, I welcome them." Mrs. Jones smiled at Mrs. Hershel.

The pews were full now, and Sheriff Joe stood to the side, pleased by the large turnout. *A little excitement in town doesn't hurt every now and again*, he thought, giving a big smile to Hank Sr. and his wife. *Just wait until they see who's next*, he chuckled to himself.

Just then, Deputy Ben arrived with Oliver and Sam – his guns drawn. Ben nudged them down the aisle to the front row near the sheriff, so they could keep a sharp eye out in case of an attempted escape.

The parishioners gasped at the sight of the convicts.

"I don't know which to find more shocking here today," Mrs. Binns said haughtily. "The Jews or the convicts. I heard tell those two came to town for a crime spree and…"

"My, my," Mrs. Jones said, looking at them with a hint of intrigue.

"Well, just imagine, we could all have been robbed or even worse," Mrs. Binns crowed indignantly. "Indians have been a curse to our genteel nature ever since we came to this land. That tall one looks like a savage, with his long hair."

"I don't know. I think he's quite magnificent," said Mrs. Jones with a smile, as Mrs. Binns held her chest, shocked at her friend's admission.

"Well, don't be vulgar," Mrs. Binns said through clenched teeth. "They send chills down my spine."

Janet, Sally, and Indigo were the last to enter and sat in the back row with the Hershels. Indigo was surprised that the sheriff had Sam and Oliver attend church services. She wondered what he was up to.

Pastor Percy, neatly attired with a clerical collar and black suit, walked to the pulpit a bit nervously, and sat his notes down as he looked at the assembled crowd. He gave a surprised glance at Sam and Oliver sitting in front. Retaining his composure, he tepidly hit his gavel on the podium, and began his sermon.

"What a great pleasure to see the House of the Lord filled with the townspeople of Miners Gulch," he squeaked out. "My name is Pastor Percy Goodwin. I hail from the eastern part of the country – namely, Connecticut. I am so pleased to be asked to come to this most… unconventional town. A bit different from the east coast…"

Sheriff Joe "harrumphed." He glared at Percy, showing his annoyance.

"What I mean to say is… a very fine town, with a… a wild west… feeling… a truly unique place." Pastor Percy was upset he couldn't get the right words out. He shuffled his feet nervously, then he said solemnly, "Thank you all for coming. I look forward to getting to know each of you. I will be holding prayer service in the coming weeks for you to learn more about the Good Book. I will let you know of more future events as time goes."

Percy looked directly at Sam and Oliver and smiled, then raised his voice a few octaves. "Welcome, brothers, to our House of the Lord. I shall pray for your souls and that your upcoming trial may be swift and fair." Percy looked at his notes, then at the awaiting crowd. "Fire and brimstone. That is my topic for today." He cleared his throat and started with; "Upon the wicked He will rain snares: Fire and brimstone and burning wind will be the portion of their cup, a horrible tempest…" Percy looked at the sheriff, who nodded his head in approval, so Percy continued. He even banged with zeal on the pulpit a couple times for show, then cleared his throat and walked around and continued. "But even the Lord that showeth his wrath also showeth His love for all humanity, for all races, and He forgives all who ask." Percy started feeling a bit strange. He couldn't figure out what it was, as his breath quickened, and he felt lightheaded. He took a deep breath to stop his jitters. Determined to put on a good show, he stretched his hands toward the heavens, raised his voice, and shouted at the top of his lungs, "God will bring down the wrath of the evil dwellers walking upon the earth. May he smite the sinners in their path and make room for the true believers!"

Percy was on a roll now getting all revved up and he felt he was pleasing the townsfolk and the sheriff. But suddenly a string of bizarre words started spilling from his lips as he whirled around the platform. He felt as though something, or someone, had completely taken over his body. He tried to stop it, but he totally lost control as he started to dance around the pulpit wildly. His legs moved up and down of their own accord, and he felt like a lunatic as he suddenly fell to his hands and knees and began howling like a wolf. It was as if he were watching a story play out in real life. And it was himself that he was watching.

Then Percy abruptly stood up and once again began to dance around in a circle. He heard himself chant the strange words, "Kawewe, kawewe," as he hopped on one foot, then the other. Percy could hear the distant beat of drums in his ears and then let off a blood curdling scream. "Forgive me my heathen friends. My teachings were all about my vanity… about *me*. Father, forgive me, for the sin I have committed in Your name against the Indian children. The injustices I committed caused them great harm. I can see that now. The children will be set free… and, for my sins, I WILL BURN IN HELL…! BURN BABY, BURN!" Percy was screeching at the top of his lungs, dancing around like a madman.

The parishioners were shocked by what they had just witnessed from the pastor as they sat glued to their seats, stunned.

Sheriff Joe clamped his mouth shut and ran up to Percy and hissed. "What the devil is wrong with you? Are you touched in the head?" When Percy didn't respond, he gave him a sharp kick in the leg.

Percy jolted back to his senses, rubbed his head, making sure this was really him and not some apparition. He could still see visions of a tall gangly man with bushy eyebrows that appeared from out of thin air and was pleading for forgiveness. Percy forced himself to speak, hoping his words were his own… not like before. He breathed deeply, as beads of perspiration popped. *Well, whoever that person or apparition was, I hope it goes away and never comes back. What an embarrassment, and on my first day…* he thought miserably, wishing he could disappear, like that apparition.

The sheriff kicked him again, a little more forcefully this time. "What are you doing? You look like a raving fool. I asked for a fiery sermon, but… but this is too much."

Percy's eyes started to clear. "I don't know," he said baffled. "I don't know who or what that was. It surely wasn't me… Someone – something other-worldly seemed to take over my sermon… asking for redemption."

Sheriff Joe's hands trembled as he restrained himself – ready to choke him if anything else went askew.

"Well, you best get your senses together, and I mean pronto. I don't know what kind of weird shit that you were doing earlier, but it better not happen again, or I'll give you an apparition you won't forget." He eyed the parishioners, who sat unmoving with eyes agog. "Now you get back to preaching. You'd best make up something good, for this… this… odd behavior of yours. Better not happen again, either!"

Pastor Percy nodded weakly, still baffled, as the sheriff turned and addressed the congregation with a forced smile.

"The pastor here was trying to show you, with a little too much zeal, perhaps, what happens if the Devil comes skulking around. He takes right over. Not a pretty sight," he added for emphasis. "Now the pastor will get back to preaching and finish his Sunday sermon. Hallelujah."

Percy looked mortified as he faced the parishioners and mumbled some awkward apology about being overly zealous in his first sermon. *He hoped it wasn't the Devil talking… can't even think of that right now,* he thought, as perspiration streamed down his face.

Percy did his best to continue. He couldn't even recall what he said during the rest of the sermon. He was so relieved when service was almost over, he forgot to announce it was time to pass around the collection plate, when he heard the sheriff, "harrumph," loudly. He panicked for a moment. Then in a high-pitched voice, he managed to squeak out. "To our good citizens… Collection plate will now be passed around. Please be generous in thy giving. The Lord has many needs, as does the church."

Agnes hurried to the piano, as she looked at the odd preacher. She sat down and began playing vigorously, as the silver plate was passed around and down each aisle. Parishioners still stunned, shoved money into the plate, anxious to leave.

The parishioners were almost as glad as the pastor when that ridiculous service was over as they hustled out of the church.

Deputy Ben was the last to leave, ready to take the prisoners back to the jail guns drawn. "Nice sermon," he said with a wicked chuckle.

Indigo waited around the corner, hoping to talk to Sam. When she caught sight of him, she popped out of her hiding place and said, "Good morning deputy. Hello, Oliver. Hi, Sam… Can I have a word with…"

Deputy Ben immediately cut her off. "Whoa there. You're not to interfere with my duties or the prisoners. The sheriff already told me to not let them speak to anyone, or he'll have my hide. Now, shoo." He admonished Indigo and then brandished his gun at Oliver and Sam.

As Deputy Ben shoved them forward, Sam caught Indigo's eye and smiled.

Indigo felt her heart beat a little faster. She was determined to do something… anything. She *had* to. But what? She felt like a prisoner, herself, forbidden to see Sam. She went back to the church to see if she could find her father – to plead with him about visiting the jail. As she entered the church, she heard her father yelling at Pastor Percy, so she hid behind the door.

"What the blazes were you doing up there?" Sheriff Joe asked, furious. "You made a mockery of this church and me, and I look like a fool for bringing you here. It was bad enough that our last pastor had a liking for… oh, never mind that… but *you*! Not sure who was worse."

Percy was wringing his hands nervously and said, "I honestly don't know what happened… what it was."

The sheriff interjected, "What are you? A retard? A moron?"

Percy shook his head, humiliated. He swallowed hard, not trusting his voice.

"I ought to kick your ass from here to next Sunday." Sheriff Joe snarled. "I will tell you one thing," he threatened, poking Percy in the chest with his beefy fingers, spittle flying as he spoke. "It had better not happen again, or I'll run your scrawny butt right out of town on rails. You won't be preaching anywhere, when I get finished with you. You hear? Not ever!" He turned and stomped out of the church.

Indigo felt this wasn't a good time to bring up anything about the prisoners to her father. So, she poked her head around the corner and saw Percy holding his head in his hands, looking dejected.

Indigo walked up to him and said sweetly, "I heard what he said to you. Most folks around have been the brunt of his rage one time or another… and it's not pleasant." She tried to make him feel better and said, "I thought your sermon was… well, entertaining. For once I didn't fall asleep, and just tell them next Sunday the Lord has a strange way of talking to His disciples. He was adamant. Basically, you could tell the parishioners almost anything if you're convincing enough. All you have to do is say it enough times, over and over… doesn't matter if it's not true, they'll believe you. Tell them you are a person of the higher order and have knowledge that they don't understand. Say it may seem a bit strange, but this is what He conveyed to you." She smiled mischievously. "I think you're a really nice man, and you mean well. You're certainly not like Pastor Tynes. He was a repulsive person, pretending to be so pious, but he was a real judgmental ass. This town is stuck in the past and the folks here cling to their old ways of thinking. They dislike anyone that's different from them. I can't wait to leave this place. But what is most urgent right now is Sam and Oliver. I'm afraid what might happen. I beg you… we have to help them."

Percy wiped his nose and looked at Indigo, grateful for her encouragement. "I was thinking that very same thing, about Sam and Oliver needing help," he said, blowing his nose, and looked closely at Indigo. "That's very kind of you to say those things. I fret that I made a terrible first impression. The sheriff was livid with me, understandably. Probably no one will show up next Sunday. They must think I'm a fool or worse. I'm used to preaching about the goodness of the Lord and of Jesus helping the sick and poor – not the fire-and-brimstone kind of preaching. I want to talk about the love of God, not the fear of Him. I guess I'm not a good fit for this town."

"Well, I think loads of people will show up next Sunday, just to see what happens next," she said with a giggle. "Nothing like a little excitement to fill the pews."

Percy lowered his voice and looked around warily. "You know, all during the sermon I felt as if the Lord was speaking to me through someone from the past. I heard his name so clearly… Preacher Jim. It seemed he was here seeking redemption. I could almost see the man asking for forgiveness – with his bushy eyebrows and frightened pale eyes. When the sheriff kicked me, the vision left. I was as surprised as anybody when that happened."

Indigo smiled and said, "I'm not a super religious person and the only reason I go to church here is because I have to. My father, the sheriff, insists that I go. So, I do it to save all the headaches it would cause if I didn't. Everything the sheriff does is for show. He just bought a new Bronco. My guess is he likes it because of the horse hood ornament. Now he's going to keep Sam's Camaro. Frankly, I think he seems to be more of an outlaw than a 'sheriff,' but no one seems to mind. A lot of folks around here like him… a real tough guy… the John Wayne type."

Indigo stood. "I should go now. I'm going to stop at the jail and see if I can get inside, somehow, to see Sam. Take care, Pastor Percy." She kissed his cheek before heading out the door and down the street to the jail.

Deputy Ben was sitting at his desk, cleaning his guns. He had them spread out on his desk while he was taking the chambers apart and, with his little brush, cleaning each one individually. Ben barely looked up when Indigo came inside and grumbled. "What can I do for you?" He scowled at the interruption, completely engrossed in his array of disassembled guns.

"Hi, Ben. Oh, sorry to interrupt you from your work." She leaned in close. "I heard about the swarm of crows that tried to attack you. Gotta be ready, I guess…" Indigo added with a big grin. "They actually sound more dangerous than the two you have locked up back there. If you wouldn't mind, I would like to see them… find out if they need anything, like toiletries or clean clothes."

Deputy Ben grunted his displeasure at being interrupted and grumbled, "Now, Mary…"

Indigo snapped at him. "My name is Indigo, so stop calling me Mary." Wanting to whack him upside his head with one of his many guns, instead she said a little more sweetly. "Now, back to… Sam and Oliver."

Deputy Ben, shoved his chair and leaned back, rocking precariously. "Now, don't get all in a twizzle. You know very well, In-dee-go," pronouncing each syllable with exaggeration. "You know very well you can't go back there. So, go home like a good girl and mind your father before you get into trouble."

"What an oaf," Indigo fumed.

"Sticks and stones can hurt my bones…" he chastised sarcastically, "but words can never harm me… so stick it, Indie!"

"Your disgusting! You've got your nose so far up my… uh… the sheriff's behind… it's revolting," Indigo fumed and slammed out the door. She headed over to Janet's house grumbling to herself. "There has to be a way."

Maybe Janet and Sally would like to go for a walk with me. I need to think.

She couldn't believe the sheriff had made the Hershels attend church. *They have their own faith and are such nice and kind people. And they never get angry when people speak ill of them.* Not long ago, some locals painted out the word, 'kikes,' on their building. They never complained. They just went out and cleaned the offensive words off the side of the store. *I bet it was that Jake Austin who did it. It's going to be a while before things change around here,* she grumbled to herself.

As a red truck turned the corner, she heard the engine pop and sputter coming in her direction. She wished she could hide, but it was too late, as the truck rumbled down the street, idling up beside her.

"Hey sexy," Hank shouted. "Wanna go for a ride? You could come out to the ranch, and we could go for a swim in the pond. I hear skinny dipping is good for you."

Indigo shrugged and said, "Oh, geez! The offer sounds so tempting, I can hardly refuse. But on second thought, I will." She hurried to the side of the street and kept on walking. She liked to annoy him.

"Oh, gosh, Indie," Hank said. "You had my heart pounding

real hard for a minute. I thought after that weird sermon today you might want to have some fun. Where the heck did that guy come from, anyway? What a looney-tune! I bet the sheriff's sorry he brought him here."

"I like Pastor Percy. I don't care that he acted a bit strange up there. He was probably nervous… or something. I'm going to see Janet – so goodbye and enjoy your swim."

Hank hopped out of the truck and caught up with her. "You know your dad doesn't like it with you hanging out here all the time. He thinks you should spend more time home… learn to help around the house. Maybe try your hand at cooking dinner sometime. You never know when someone might just pop the ole question to you. Gotta be ready."

"Don't be stupid. I'm not Joe's servant and Harriet keeps things neat and tidy. She can cook for him if she wants."

Hank persisted. "Say, Indie. Why do you always take up with the underdogs, like that odd preacher, and the Hebrews – not to mention Sally. She's just trailer-trash."

Indigo went to slap Hank, but he ducked before she could hit him. "Hey, I would rather hang out with the two of them than you. I really don't care about how odd the preacher acted today He's a nice man. I'd say the schools around here need to teach more history so people wouldn't be so stupid – including you." Indigo stormed off without another word and raced into the Hershels' store.

*

Percy sat alone in the church, going over the earlier events from his sermon. He rubbed his sore leg where the sheriff had kicked him, still trying to understand what had happened. He thought, *I had everything prepared, just as the sheriff asked me to, even though I didn't like his suggestions of hellfire and damnation, I did it. It always takes away from my message of good and compassion. I guess that doesn't work around here so much. The sheriff seems to prefer stark warnings, always thinking the Devil is waiting to snatch up wrongdoers and whisk them off to Hell. I could kick myself for acting like an ass in front of the congregation.* He felt his face burn from the humiliation of his outburst. *It just seemed to come from out of nowhere.* He remembered preaching something about Satan's clutches when, out of the blue, something took over. *I had no control of what that… that apparition was saying.* He held his head in his hands and moaned. "How am I ever going be able to show my face in this town?" *The locals will surely think I'm a bit off.* He looked up, closed his eyes, and said a silent prayer. A moment later, he felt something brush against his shoulder and stiffened. Out of the corner of his eye something uncanny caught his attention – a hazy silhouette mysteriously shifted, ever so slightly and floated nearby. Percy gasped in alarm, and, without another thought, dove under the pew and froze. "Oh, dear Lord, help me. I must be going mad." His heart thundered so loud in his chest, he thought he might faint. He took a deep breath and waited for the form to disappear, but instead it drifted closer and started to take shape. Pale faded eyes popped out from bushy eyebrows and a ghostly voice called out. "Pastor, I am not here to harm you."

Percy was afraid that if he spoke, he might howl like a wolf again, or dance around like a madman as he had earlier. Under his breath, he said, "I'm not doing that again. I don't care who this is." And he refused to budge.

Bushy eyebrows came close, as the form peered underneath the pew, and held out an ethereal hand. "Come." The fuzzy shape wavered, watching him with interest.

Percy's body quivered in fright and wiped his lips as beads of sweat popped.

"Please do not be afraid."

Percy slowly inched his way from underneath the pew, rubbed his eyes and looked in disbelief at the spectral form. It was wavering so close, he could smell a moldy odor and quickly put his hand over his nose to blot out the putrid smell that wafted across the room. He choked out, "Who are you? What do you want?"

"My name is Preacher Jim, Percy," he whispered hoarsely. "I have been in the darkness for a very long time. When I was among the living, I did terrible things… terrible things to the Indian children at the boarding school under my care. I accused the children of being sinners because they prayed to their Great Spirit… whom I have since come to know and respect. I called the children heathens and worse, thinking I was the superior one, and that I alone, could lead them on a path of righteousness. I was an egotistical fool. I cannot move on from the depths of despair until I make redemption. Hidden Spirit, whom I once envied, told me Oliver, was in grave peril. Once I redeem myself from my egregious actions, then I can go with the light and out of the darkness."

Percy was too stunned to respond. For a brief moment, the wavering form became real. Preacher Jim sat down as cool as a cucumber on the pew, crossed his long legs and swung them idly back and forth and stared, bushy eyebrows bobbing.

"Now I am here to help. Do not fear me, pastor."

Percy stood transfixed, staring at the man. He wanted to ask the Lord, "What have I done to deserve this?" He had a million questions, but before he could speak, the man vanished in a blink, as a whisper of air whooshed past, and the icy image faded into crystals of misty drops, leaving behind the ill-smelling odor.

Percy felt a chill pass through him as he stood up and looked around, stunned. His eyes twitched nervously, and he grabbed the side of the pew so he wouldn't topple over. *Maybe I'm not going mad after all… I hope.* Trembling, he held his Bible to his chest. *Mental illness doesn't run in my family, and I only drink occasionally. The man obviously wanted my help.*

As he paced back and forth, and up and down the aisle, an

idea popped into his head. Clear as crystals. He had an overwhelming feeling that he must help Oliver and Sam to escape… if they were found guilty. He still wondered – *guilty of what?* From what he could see – nothing, and yet the outcome did not bode well for either of them. *Maybe I should talk with Indigo and her friends. I hope they don't think I'm mad.*

Feeling somewhat relieved, he straightened his shoulders and breathed out a sense of wonder. "I believe God sent me this vision." He felt at peace and started to hum as he walked out the door and said a quick prayer, "Please, Lord. Help the judge see the truth and set the boys free."

CHAPTER EIGHT

THE SCALES OF JUSTICE

OLIVER AND SAM were talking when the deputy brought in their supper of burgers and fries. "Got the judge coming soon, so button up your hats," Deputy Ben said. "Here's your grub. Enjoy it while you can," he taunted. "The judge don't take kindly to upstarts and no-goods coming to our town causing trouble… specifically Injuns. I'd start praying if I was you. Don't know if that jackass, who calls himself a 'pastor' can help, but I'll send him along if you want." Ben couldn't help himself and let off a loud snort.

Sam stood at the bars, staring at the deputy, ignoring his rudeness. "Any chance the phones are working? They can't still be out of order." The deputy gave him a glare, meant to silence him.

"You won't get away with this," Sam said.

Deputy Ben, grinned. "Looks like we already have, boy. Any more questions?" His hand rested on his pistol, fingers twitching.

"You will pay for this when I get my attorney." Sam yelled in disbelief.

Ben eased up to Sam and clicked the trigger. "I said the phones are out of order, so don't be calling me a liar, boy, or we'll tack on extra charges for belligerent behavior. I'd say you got enough charges already." Having made his point, Deputy Ben turned to leave.

Sam wished he could grab Ben's gun. He wasn't too handy with a gun but would seriously consider shooting him. He paced back and forth in the small cell. "If we get out of this place I'm going back to Los Angeles and see if I can find someone to investigate what goes on in this town so they can bring the sheriff to trial. It's a joke in this town… law and order."

Oliver looked at Sam calmly and told him the facts. "You'd have to get rid of half the people that live here. They would just get someone else like Sheriff Joe or worse. Don't you know we've been fighting these kinds of people ever since the white man invaded our country? They've called us names of every kind, then stole our lands, kidnapped our children, and now treat us like invaders. Don't you know anything about our history, Sam? The half of you that's Indian should want to know about what goes on in our culture…"

The door swung open, and Pastor Percy walked in with a scowling deputy right behind. "Look, Pastor. It's okay if you want to say some prayers and such… not that they're gonna do any good, but the sheriff's gonna be livid if you try some underhand stuff. So, hurry up talking with the Man upstairs. An don't be smuggling any more notes outa here."

"Oh, pooh," Percy said in exasperation. "You act like I'm going to bust them out of here."

"Well, like I said. Don't you let them give you anything, or any kind of information. You only got just a couple minutes, and I mean *a couple*. Say a quick hallelujah, then scoot on out of here."

"Of course, deputy, whatever you say. It's my duty as a servant of the Lord to help the ones in need."

"Ha!" Deputy Ben snorted, "Not sure what you were in church…" Then he said under his breath, "Idiot of the Lord would be closer." He slammed the door shut. "I'm timing you, too."

Percy leaned in close to the bars and whispered to the two men. "I want you to know, I am here to help if… if the judge finds you guilty. I have a feeling that man won't be lenient. Word is, he's a friend of the sheriff. I'm on my way to talk to Indigo and the other two girls to see if they will join me in my quest for justice. I believe you are both innocent and…"

The heavy door swung open again and this time Deputy Ben came scurrying down the hallway. "You got thirty seconds left, Pastor."

Percy bent down and said a prayer, "…and may the Lord save you from the inequities of destruction…"

Deputy Ben grabbed Percy by the back of his collar and pulled him to his feet. "Okay, enough now. Out!" He snickered and said, "I'm checking your pockets and any other cracks and crevices you got for hiding contraband. So bend over," he chortled, "and let's see whatcha got."

Percy looked at the deputy in disbelief. "This is outrageous," he sputtered incredulously. "What kind of place is this?"

"Just joking, Pastor. But need you to empty your pockets."

Percy did as he was told with great annoyance. "I believe you are taking things a bit far."

"That may be, but orders are orders."

Then the door banged shut.

Sam was floored by the deputy's abhorrent treatment of the pastor, but he was pleasantly surprised by his offer to help. He jumped up with a thought.

"Hey, Oliver. If they do manage to get us out of here, we could hide out for a while at my Aunt Alice's house, which is around sixty miles or so from here… and maybe borrow Uncle Fred's truck or something."

Oliver looked at Sam. "Sheriff Joe will put a warrant out for our arrest. Everyone for hundreds of miles around will be looking for us. It will be dangerous. We will have to prove our innocence.

I also need to prove that the '54 Ford is my father's. Finding out whoever stole it might lead to information about the disappearance of my father. I fear it is too late to help him, but I need to know what happened."

"Whew. Not sure how we'll do that," Sam said, still pacing. "But we'll find a way. Someone in this town has got to know something."

*

Percy felt he was now on a mission, especially after the strange visit from that ghostly figure. He wondered who the devil he was and why he came to him. *As weird as it seems, I believe that preacher. Guess it's never too late for a chance at redemption,* he thought, and hurried over to the Hershels' mercantile store hoping to find the girls there.

Percy opened the door and peeked inside the mercantile. *The only business open on Sunday, besides the Blue Sky Saloon.* He knew the Jewish people celebrated the Sabbath on Saturday. He had no problem with that. He respected all religions and views. *We are all one under the eyes of God.*

Sally was sitting behind the counter and looked up when Percy walked inside. She nonchalantly said, "Hi," and went back to reading her magazine.

Percy noticed she had a sad look about her and that her nails were bitten down so short her fingertips were bleeding. Sally's long blond hair always seemed to hang over her face and for some reason that Percy couldn't fathom, he wanted to brush it away and comfort her. There was something about the way she turned her head and tossed her hair about that struck him as innocent and sweet. His heart warmed just looking at her. But the faded bruise that her makeup failed to conceal made his face burn. He immediately thought of Hank, who had the reputation of a lady's man. Word was, he was a spoiled and entitled rich kid, full of anger about his football injury… *but that's no excuse,* he thought. He heard that lots of girls had a crush on the guy, including Sally. *Probably smitten by his good looks,* Percy thought, with a hint of jealousy. He cringed at that thought. *It is unbecoming of a preacher — a man of the cloth.* But still, the feeling lingered, and he smoothed his hair.

Last week at the barbershop, Percy saw Hank come in bragging about his prowess on the previous night. "Gotta fight the women off like a swarm of mosquitos trying to get at me." The barber laughed at his remark and overheard some crude comment he made about Sally.

Just as he sat in the chair, ready for a shave, Sally walked in, visibly upset, pleading with him.

"Hank. Can you come outside? I want to talk to you."

Hank made a face, but grudgingly went outside with the girl.

Percy overheard Hank say to Sally, "Not sure if I wanna see you tonight. I might have other plans. So, stop bugging me."

Hank came back inside saying, "Good Lordy. Women are a pain in the ass. Can't live with 'em or without 'em."

Jimmy Dean came rushing in the door carrying two cups of coffee, and Hank gratefully took one of them. "Now Jimmy Dean here takes real good care of me. I don't have to listen to the broads hounding me," he said, smacking his lips. "Gotta say I get pretty sick after a while of at all that loving."

The boys laughed at Hank and slapped him on the back. The banker, Mike Stull, grinned. "Oh, I remember the good ole days. My pappy always said, if the gals give you trouble, just ignore them. If all else fails, give 'em a smack or two. Shuts 'em up real quick."

Hank puffed up his chest, "Yep, got that part down real solid," he said, taking a sip. "That's real good coffee, Jimmy Dean. Real good. But damn, my head hurts."

Percy knew right then and there he couldn't stomach the guy and that he would have to pray extra hard for his unkind thoughts.

But harming a woman was inexcusable. God might even forgive him his unkind thoughts, but he wasn't sure the good Lord would forgive Hank.

As Percy stood in the doorway looking at Sally, he collected himself enough to say, "Hello," and give her a warm smile. He was at a loss for what to say. He knew she wasn't interested in him. Why would she be? He had made an ass of himself earlier. He wanted to say, "Would you like to come over for supper tonight?" Wow! He couldn't understand this feeling that seemed to come out of nowhere. He felt clumsy and awkward and could feel his face redden. Thankfully, Janet and Indigo came out from the back to rescue him from his thoughts.

Janet said with a smile, "What can we help you with, Pastor?"

Percy took his gaze off Sally, and suddenly remembered why he came. "Um, yes. Well, you know the trial is set for some time next week. That's what I heard. I think, that is… I was… I wondered if you'd be willing to help… help Oliver and Sam get away if things don't go well," he blurted out. Looking around, awkwardly, he continued. "I'm worried about the outcome of the trial. We don't have much time, but we could at least try."

Indigo's face paled thinking about the outcome, then smiled at Percy, grateful for his willingness to help.

Sally and Janet looked at Percy, unsure what to say.

Finally, Indigo spoke up. "We were just talking about that very thing. You know you could get in big trouble, helping us. That could get you fired from your position at the church. Not to mention the sheriff might hang you as well, if he catches wind of our plan."

Janet ventured a timid, "That is really very kind and brave of you, Pastor."

Indigo said, "We were trying to figure what to do. Now, I think, between all of us plotting and planning, we might come up with something."

"I certainly think we could," Percy agreed. "Would you girls like to come over for dinner tonight?" His eyes wandered over to Sally. "We could relax and then talk about our plans."

Sally lowered her eyes and cringed, uncertain of what to make of this pastor. She looked to Janet for help and rolled her eyes. *He's not anything at all like Hank,* she thought. *He's not rugged or handsome. In fact, he's awkward and odd. Anyway, why would he like her?* She was wild for Hank, no matter what he did – and she didn't even care if he was a little rough with her. *That's all I've seen most of my life.*

Percy said, "I… I… m-mean, if I'm not imposing."

Indigo didn't hesitate. "Of course, we'll come."

Janet looked at the pastor in surprise and delight. "What time, Pastor?"

"Call me Percy. Please. It's so formal using 'pastor' all the time. How does six o'clock sound?" Janet and Indigo both agreed. He looked at Sally. She simply nodded her head.

"Perfect. I'll make my special BBQ ribs if that sounds okay with everyone."

Janet said, "We have some fresh potato salad my mother made earlier."

"Wonderful. See you then," Percy said, and he almost skipped out the door, feeling giddy and light as air at the turn of events.

After Percy left, the girls were silent for a moment. Then Indigo said with a smile, "Did you notice the pastor looked at Sally most of the time he was talking?"

"Oh, my gosh! What if he has a crush on you?" Janet said with a giggle. "He seems really nice. Not at all how you expect a pastor to be… I think he's pretty cool, even though I laughed all after-noon thinking of him howling like a wolf in church this morning. Did you see the shock on the sheriff's face? And I thought old Binns was going to fall off the bench, she was so appalled by his… whatever it was."

"I think he was as surprised as everyone else at his behavior," Indigo said. "He was embarrassed by what happened and told me the vision or ghost he saw warned him that Oliver and Sam are in danger. It really shook him up. So, as hilarious as it was, we can't make fun of him. We know the guys are in big trouble, and I'm grateful he wants to help."

The girls looked at Indigo, digesting what she had said. Sally finally spoke. "I'm glad he's not anything like that last 'pervert' who was the pastor. He always looked as if he was undressing you with his 'divine eyes,' as he would say – then he would preach to us about our sins. Ugh!"

"He was definitely a pervert," Indigo said. "Okay, so we're on for dinner tonight at six. I'd better go home for a bit first, then I'll see you guys at Percy's house."

As Indigo walked into her house, she cringed when she saw her father sitting at the kitchen table, eating a plate of raw hamburger with vinegar, and salt and pepper. He shot her a look, wiped his mouth and said, "It's time we have a talk, Mary."

Indigo fumed. "Why don't you call me by the name my mom and I chose?"

"Because you have the same name as my mother – and the Virgin Mother. You should feel honored."

"Well, that was then and, guess what? This is now – and my name is Indigo, whether you like it or not. I'm not part of the Virgin Mary or your mother – whom I've never met, by the way."

Sheriff Joe took a huge forkful of his raw meat and chewed furiously, trying to decide if he should strike his obstinate daughter for her disrespectful tone. He chose to restrain himself.

"So, I'll tell you straight. You best not interfere with those two fellas sitting in the jail. Hank said you seemed a little too friendly with one of them the other night at the bar. Then Ben tells me you went to the jail and tried to get in to see them. Now, there will be a trial this Tues… uh…" he paused, looking at his daughter, and said, "I meant next week. Judge Ellis will get to the bottom of why they were here and what they were intending to do. Randy seems to think they were planning to rob the bar. He found a note on the counter outlining the layout of the town. Everything was there, including the bank with an X on it. So now, if you try to interfere in any way, I'll lock you up as a conspirator. You understand?"

Indigo shoved her shoulders back in defiance and glared as her father continued. "This town is my town. I keep everyone here safe. Outsiders that come here could cause all kinds of trouble. So don't think, just because you're my daughter, you get special privilege. Don't know for a fact you're my blood, either. Your ma could've been lying so she could try an weasel money out of me."

"That would be the best news of all," she said, "not to be related to you!" and stormed into her room.

Sheriff Joe finished his lunch in one last bite. *That girl gives me an ulcer, with her smart mouth. I'll be glad when this is over, and things in this town can get back to normal.*

*

That night, Percy opened his front door and welcomed the girls inside. They were pleasantly surprised by the comfortable setting with the lights dimmed low and a tantalizing aroma drifting from the kitchen. Musk-scented incense was burning, and soft music was playing on the record player. The girls' eyes widened at the sight of the dapper preacher, dressed in beige khaki slacks and a light tan sweater with a yellow pinstriped shirt underneath. *He looks rather handsome*, Indigo thought, with a smile. She was amazed that he was able to turn this sparse place into something so warm and homey, with an oversized sofa and ottoman, a recliner chair, and decorative lamps. The colorful paisley curtains added a nice touch too, she surmised, looking around the room.

Percy said to the girls, "Thank you for coming." He smiled at Sally and asked, "May I take your sweater?"

Sally hesitantly took off her cardigan and handed it to the preacher.

Janet and Indigo looked at each other, as Percy's hand rested a little longer than necessary on Sally's shoulder.

Percy caught himself and blushed, then quickly ushered the girls to his dining table. "Please come in and sit down." He looked at Janet holding her potato salad, and quickly took it from her. "Many thanks, Janet. This will be a great addition to our supper." He pulled out the chairs from the table and beamed, "Please make yourselves at home. May I bring you something to drink? I have coke, water, orange juice… and of course, after dinner, I have a little cognac if anyone would like to indulge with me."

The girls all said, "Coke, please."

Janet nudged Sally. "Why don't you go in the kitchen and help him?"

Sally balked. "Good grief! I'm not so sure about all this. Can't say I'm really interested in Percy. He's a preacher, for God's sake. Can you imagine what he would think if he knew I want to be a dancer? That seems pretty weird, to me," she said, chewing her fingernails.

Indigo jumped up, rolling her eyes at Sally, and went in the kitchen to offer her help. Percy gladly accepted and poured four glasses full of Coke. Indigo added some ice.

In the meantime, Percy turned his attention back to the stove. He pulled out the rack of ribs and set them on the counter ready to slice. With a large butcher knife, he sliced the succulent meat, shooting steam into the air. He piled the platter full, carried it out to the table, and set it down in the middle. He said with a charming smile, "Bon Appetit."

The girls echoed "Bon Appetit," then inhaled deeply.

"Shall we pray?"

"Just make it a short one, Percy…uh… Pastor. We're all starving."

"Please, please, call me Percy, please. Pastor is so formal among friends… I hope that is what we shall be. And, yes, I will make it a quick one. The Lord doesn't mind, knowing that we are grateful for what we have."

Everyone bowed their heads. "Dear Lord. Thank you for the wonderful company in my midst tonight, and the bountiful feast we are so fortunate to have. Amen."

Indigo added her own sentiments. "I would like to thank the Lord for sending you here."

Janet first and then Sally replied, "Amen."

Percy's face beamed brightly then reddened. "Thank you for those kind words, girls. That is very considerate." Then he helped everyone fill their plates with the succulent, aromatic ribs and freshly made potato salad.

All was quiet for a few moments as they dug in with gusto. "This is beyond heavenly," Indigo gushed, chomping on a tender piece of mouth-watering meat.

"These are possibly the best ribs I've ever tasted," Janet said, licking her lips in delight. Sally echoed her friend's comment, and, warming a little to the pastor, she said timidly, "You know, Percy, you could get out of the salvation business and open a restaurant."

"The doors would bust down to get these ribs." Indigo agreed, holding one in the air. "You could save a lot of people hungry for ribs."

Janet giggled, as she patted her lips with a napkin.

Percy said, "I'll give it some thought, he smiled. "Not sure how the Lord would feel about that, but it's not a bad idea."

Sally ate heartily. Indigo was glad to see Sally smiling, for a change.

After they finished the meal, the girls all helped Percy do the dishes and tidy up in the kitchen.

Percy said, "How about a glass of Cognac, girls? Goes down pretty smooth, and it's great for digestion."

"Yes!" Indigo was the first to answer.

"Sounds good to me," Janet said.

"How about you, Sally?"

"I've never tried it before, so… just a small one."

Once Percy had poured everyone a drink he sat down on the ottoman. "I've been thinking about what you said, Indigo, about the judge and the sheriff. Do you really believe the judge will do the sheriff's bidding?" He looked at Indigo. "Oh, I didn't mean to imply…"

"Don't worry, Percy. I've heard all about the judge. He's a squirrely fellow for sure. I would bet anything he'll recommend a 'hanging.' And the sheriff will likely say, the faster the better. Then the townsfolk will have a big party."

Janet and Sally gasped at that thought.

"So, Deputy Ben, I assume will be on duty around the clock. He has the keys, I'm sure. Any suggestions on how to distract him, without making him suspicious?"

Sipping their cognac, everyone sat lost in thought, contemplating.

Then Janet spoke up. "Ben is like a bulldog, guarding the jail. It won't be easy. I know he sees some girl occasionally from Westin, and he doesn't really seem interested in anyone else. But maybe you could sway him with a kiss, Sally… or…?

"Oh, my gosh… ugh!" Sally said, wrinkling her nose. "But what if I took him over some supper and added a sleeping pill to it, ground up inside. Maybe even two…?"

"He eats at the bar a lot, so, not too sure about that. But he might take it home for later," Indigo said, thoughtfully.

"Who could be more trustworthy than a preacher with a bottle of whiskey," Percy said, with a grin. "No, really… I would go and tell the deputy I want to get to know him and just sit with him and talk. Tell him that's my mission in Miners Gulch… to get acquainted with everyone, so I can get to know them better."

"Well, I know he loves guns," Indigo said smartly. "Tell Ben you want to learn how to shoot… that you want to learn every-thing you can about guns… you hear he's a crack shot and the guy to talk to on the subject. Then he'll most likely talk your ear off."

"Then I could come over and bring a pie… with rat poison laced through it," Janet said laughing.

"Oh, my gosh, Janet," Sally said. "That's even better than my idea."

"Not enough to kill him, of course. Just enough to make him a little sick." Janet said, astonishing her friends. "Or… on a more serious note… I'll bring over Mom's signature apple pie and add a little laced rum for flavor. He'll lap it up and he'll never know what hit him."

Indigo added, "Or, we can just put a strong sedative in that bottle of whisky you take over to the jail for him, Percy."

"Great idea!" said Janet. "My parents keep some at the store locked up. And if that doesn't work, we'll just knock him out and grab his keys." Janet surprised Indigo and Sally by her bravado. She was usually so calm and sweet-natured.

"That might be the best idea," Percy said, though somewhat amused by Janet's plan. "I'll spike Ben's drink, so when he gets a little tipsy, and he will, he'll fall asleep… and when he does, I'll get the keys and free Oliver and Sam. But we must be smart about this. If the sheriff gets wind of what we're planning, we'll all be locked up. And then, we'll be of no help to Oliver and Sam."

"I'm not so sure about all this," Sally said nervously, picking at her nails.

"It will indeed be a risk, Sally, and we definitely need to be careful, but I do like your idea, Percy," said Indigo. "Are you sure you're destined to be a preacher and not a detective?"

"Well, I hadn't thought of that idea," replied Percy with a grin.

Everyone was quiet for a moment, contemplating.

Then Sally blurted out. "I'm scared of what might…"

Before she could finish, Percy said, "We'll be careful. I understand your fears, so please know that I will have everyone's safety in mind."

Janet said, "I agree that if we get caught, there could be big trouble, but to do nothing is far worse."

Indigo said, "I'll see if I can find out where Deputy Ben keeps the keys, so when Percy goes for his 'little visit' to see Deputy Ben, he'll know where to look."

Percy stood. "Let's all have faith in the Lord, that we shall overcome the villains."

"I think we should go over our plan one more time, since we have just until next week. It leaves so little time."

"Would everyone like to pray?"

"I appreciate your thought of good tidings, Percy, but maybe after we leave you can say a prayer for all of us," Indigo said sweetly.

*

It was around nine o'clock and the Blue Sky Saloon was quiet, with just a few regulars sitting at the bar, having a drink. They nodded to Sheriff Joe as he walked in. The sheriff scanned the bar, saw Hank and Jimmy Dean Hinkle talking with Randy, and headed over to chat with them.

"Howdy, Sheriff," Randy said. "What can I get you?"

"A big shot of rye," replied Sheriff Joe, and pulled out a chair, sat down and took off his hat, then pulled out a great big Cuban cigar from his pocket – a gift from Hank Sr. – and sniffed it gratefully. He leaned back, lit it, savored the aroma from the pungent tobacco, and closed his eyes as he exhaled great plumes of smoke. *This is a little taste of heaven,* he thought, *having a fine cigar, a glass of rye whiskey, and a town I run. Life is not bad.* He took another puff of the cigar and a sip of whiskey, then looked at Hank and said, "Your Pa has good taste. Mighty fine cigar. Want one?"

Hank banged his beer mug on the bar and shrugged his shoulders. "Naw! Don't care much for those things. Got sick on one when I was younger and never wanted another. Maybe Jimmy Dean here would like one, though," He looked at his friend and nudged his shoulder.

"Hey, you wanna try one of these fine Cubans, my friend?"

Jimmy Dean slugged down his beer and slammed the bottle on the counter, copying Hank. Then he added, "Woo-wee." That'll cross your eyes." He avoided looking at the sheriff and said, "Sure, Hank. I'll take a stogie."

Hank grinned and asked, "You ever smoked one of these before, Jimmy Dean?"

"Can't say that I have, Hank." Jimmy Dean squirmed, unsure what he should do. He didn't like to smoke, but felt he should look manly, especially with Sheriff Joe around. That guy made his palms sweat. He knew the sheriff didn't like him, always giving him a dirty look. And he liked to impress Hank whenever he could. This seemed like the perfect time to do that. He just hoped he wouldn't gag.

Sheriff Joe frowned, watching Hank, hand Jimmy Dean one of his prized cigars. *I only smoke these on special occasions,* he thought. *Can't believe he's giving one to this simpering guy. I hope he chokes on it.* The sheriff tapped the counter with his empty glass, and Randy came over. "I'll take an icy long neck along with another rye, Randy."

"Right away, Sheriff." Randy poured a generous shot and set it down on the bar. "Here you go. Say, heard earlier the church service was pretty unusual and that pastor was… well, entertaining. Folks were carrying on, laughing about it. Sorry I missed it."

"Not too sure what to make of that tenderfoot," Sheriff Joe grumbled. "He's a strange one, for certain. Not so sure I like him or his soft stance on preachin', either. This is cowboy country, with strong-willed men around here. Every now and again they need to hear about the Devil – to scare the shit outa them… keep them in line for a while. Not saying I don't believe in the Devil and all, but I need a preacher to deliver the message. Percy looked like a damn fool up there today. Best not try that load of crap again next Sunday," he grimaced.

Hank and Jimmy Dean leaned in close, listening to the sheriff. Hank smirked and said, "Well, not sure where you got that guy, but it was like something got loose inside his noggin and pecked at his brain."

Jimmy Dean laughed. "That was a damn good description, I'd say," he said, while holding the Cuban cigar close to his nose, and giving it a good sniff. "Guess I'd better have another round before I fire this big boy up." He looked at Hank, who nodded. "Yep, fill 'er up there," he said and shoved his shot glass over to Randy. "Take a Gentlemen Jack, this time… not the cheap stuff."

Hank struck a match for Jimmy Dean, who took a big puff on the cigar. His face turned a couple of shades of pink, red, and then purple. Starting to choke, he tried to catch his breath, but all he could do was gasp for air. He thought he was going to be sick or worse… die.

Hank started pounding on his back.

"You all right there, Jimmy Dean?"

Jimmy Dean could only get out a whimper then gagged trying to catch his breath. "Oh, my," he gasped, wiping his eyes. "I'd better get to the restroom and get myself right. I'll be back." He flew off the barstool and hustled into the men's room and heaved into the toilet.

Sheriff Joe sat there in amusement watching him go. He noticed the way he walked, and especially the way he looked at Hank Jr. A bit too feminine in the way he talked, too. *Why would Hank hang out with this character? Hank likes people fawning over him, but still, there's got to be a limit. I guess since he's not a football hero anymore Jimmy Dean fills the bill.*

Sheriff Joe looked over at Hank and lowered his voice. "You think Jimmy Dean is a bit of a poofer? *You* know – a fruitcake – if you get my drift."

Hank thought for a moment, then sucked deep on his beer.

"Jimmy Dean's got a soft spot, yeah. He takes care of his ailing grandma real good. Cooks up a storm and makes sure she eats. A real good cook, too. Can make a meatloaf taste like a sumptuous steak… and he's neat as a pin. He may not be as macho as some of the cowboys around here, but he's a real friend to Hank. Can't go wrong with that, if you ask me."

"No, guess you can't," the sheriff said, begrudgingly. Still, he was not a fan of that pussy boy. That kinda stuff didn't sit well with him, but he wasn't going to push the point with Hank Jr.

A pale Jimmy Dean wobbled slightly as he walked over and sat down carefully on the bar stool and wiped his brow. "That was a mighty strong cigar," he said. "Not all that sure I care for them."

Hank shoved a shot of whiskey his way, and said, "Looks like you need a drink, partner."

Jimmy Dean nodded and took a long sip.

Sheriff Joe thought irritably, *damn waste of a fine cigar.* The sheriff had a sharp eye for people and could size them up in a second. He'd bet his last nickel the guy was as queer as they came. If word got out about Jimmy Dean's preferences, he'd be in for a wicked time in this town. Good thing Hank was well-liked and had a powerful dad. Regardless, Sheriff Joe was going to keep an eye out. *If this queer tries any funny business, I'll string him up right along with the Injun and the half-breed.*

He took a sip of his rye thinking he couldn't wait for this damn trial to be over and get things back to normal. *Then the only thing I'll have to worry about is guys having too much to drink and getting rowdy… shooting off their guns and all. Don't mind them getting into a tangle with a filly now and again. Can't blame them. Women caused most of men's troubles, especially when they get too high-minded. Can't abide that, that's for damn sure.* He shook his head and ordered another beer and rye.

It was around midnight when Hank and Jimmy Dean said, "Night, Sheriff," and stumbled out of the bar.

Sheriff Joe stayed a while longer, wanting one of Gladys' burgers and fries – and maybe a little extra later on.

Outside the bar, Hank was walking along the street when, up ahead, he saw Indigo. He rubbed his blurry eyes, stopped Jimmy Dean, and grabbed hold of his shirt.

"Hey, Jimmy Dean. Lookie what's up ahead!"

Less enthusiastic, Jimmy Dean hiccupped. "Oh, yeah. Looks like that Indee-go-go."

Hank tugged Jimmy Dean's arm. "Let's hurry. I wanna see her." With Hank leading the way, they staggered down the street.

Indigo was busy talking to Sally, and neither had heard the guys coming. But when she felt a tap on her shoulder, Indigo jumped and whirled around.

Sally's eyes lit up as she looked into the face of the guy she was crazy about and secretly hoped to marry one day. *Maybe he'll want company tonight,* she thought hopefully.

"Jeez, Hank. You startled me. Sally and I were…"

Hank slurred his response. "Say, little lady," taking off his hat and bowing. "How'd ya like to go on a real date with me? Take you to a real fancy steak house over in Troutdale. Heard the steer, mean steak melts right in your mouth."

Indigo looked disgusted by his drunken suggestion and Sally was devastated and embarrassed by his obvious feelings for her friend.

"Look, Hank. You must have marbles in your head. I told you earlier I'm not interested in you or your steer or your pond. I see how you treat women… punching them around whenever the mood strikes."

Pointing to Sally, Hank tried to defend his behavior. "She was giving me a hard time, so I accidently…" Before Hank could finish, he felt a whack across his face, then another.

Indigo hollered at him, her face burning. "Is that how you do it, when you think she's bothering you?" She smacked him again, and this time she balled up her fist and slugged him as hard as she could. He reeled back into the arms of Jimmy Dean before he could fall over. "Well *you're* bothering me… so get lost."

For a moment, Hank was too stunned to move, and gingerly touched his jaw. "Damn." He yelled. "Good thing you're the sheriff's daughter or I'd bust you a good one." He turned to Sally. "And as for you, you groveling bitch… don't come 'round me no more. You're homely as a hedge hog tied to a barn door. Ain't that right, Jimmy Dean?"

Jimmy Dean grabbed Hank's arm and pulled him away. "That's the truth. Now let's go and leave the ladies to their business." As they staggered off down the street, Jimmy Dean said, "Yer too drunk ta drive home. Come and stay at my house."

Indigo watched Hank and Jimmy Dean sway their way down the street.

Sally watched in dismay, near tears. She felt humiliated, her heart broken. She wished she could simply disappear.

Indigo put her arm around Sally. "Don't pay any attention to Hank. I know you like him, but he's not nice to you – plus he's a real loser. All he has going is his dad's money. I can't stand that he treats you so awful. You put up with that kind of treatment at home; you don't have to take it from Hank. I've tried not to judge you, but I have to tell you – you deserve wa-a-ay better than Hank and it's time you stood up for yourself. The guy may be good looking, but his soul is another story." Indigo hugged her friend and smiled. "On a happier note, I have a feeling that Pastor Percy has an eye for you."

Sally kicked a stone down the pavement and commented, half-heartedly. "He's not very handsome or masculine. He's kinda skinny and… well, he's a *preacher*, for God's sake!"

"And he's a really nice and sincere man," Indigo countered. "I bet he would never hit you or call you names like Hank does. Don't end up like your mom and get stuck in an abusive relationship."

"It's pretty weird," Sally said, "thinking about a preacher who actually 'likes' me – that way. I've never even been fond of going to church, so, it seems kinda crazy…"

"Let's go to my house, where a real happy home life awaits," she grinned. "My dad is a lot of things, that mostly I despise… but he doesn't beat me. He does insult me, though, mean with his words," Indigo shrugged. "But I don't care. His words mean nothing to me. He's a tyrant with a badge and a big mouth."

Sally shook her head, agreeing with her friend. "He is that for sure."

"The sheriff's probably over at Gladys's house right now. He thinks he's a real tomcat, with all the women after him. They must think they'll get… I honestly don't know what they think they'd get from him, but… yuck!" Indigo said with a shudder.

"I'm just glad he's not here," Sally said, as they walked into Indigo's darkened house. "He makes me nervous."

"That stupid-ass Deputy Ben, might be trouble," Indigo said, yawning widely, showing off a row of straight teeth. "It might not be so easy for Percy to let him inside the jail for a drink."

"I hope the judge will be lenient at the trial," Sally said hopefully.

"I bet anything the sheriff will convince the judge to hang them both. He'll say it's too expensive to keep them locked up. Taxpayer's expense, and all."

The girls talked a bit more before falling asleep.

*

Tuesday was a big day in Miners Gulch. Judge Ellis was coming to town, to the surprise and shock of his daughter and her friends. *Wanted to give them a big surprise*, he thought wickedly, *catch everyone off guard.* Sheriff Joe Jenner was ecstatic, not only to see his old friend, but to get this trial behind him. It had been a while since the town had a trial of this magnitude. Typically, he addressed traffic violations or drunk driving, which might land you in jail for a night or so. Whatever the charges were, Sheriff Joe handled them swiftly, so nothing got out of control. The sheriff's word was final, and no one disputed it. There were a couple incidences in which someone dared to question the sheriff's authority, and, in neither case, did it bode well. Tom Berringer, for example, who fought the sheriff on a theft charge, was found dead a month later. That was just one example.

But now, a big case was set for trial. Judge Ellis came to town on Monday to go over the details of the case and review matters at hand.

Judge Ellis was in his late sixties, tall, and knock-kneed. He wore wire-rimmed spectacles about an inch thick that made his dark brown eyes appear to protrude out of his face. His speech was slow and precise. The judge's great-great-grandfather, Ronald Ellis, died with General George Armstrong Custer at the Battle of Little Bighorn. His family proclaimed him a hero, and the story of his bravery was passed down from one generation to the next. That was a history lesson Judge Ellis was fond of retelling. So, when he heard about Oliver and Sam, he was ready for battle. Like his family before him, the judge wished that every Indian had been killed off long ago and still secretly liked the idea of a bounty on their heads. The sheriff and the judge shared a similar disdain for Indians.

Judge Ellis and the sheriff hadn't seen each other for a while, so they had a lot of catching up to do, so they met at the Blue Sky Saloon for a couple drinks.

The judge stayed at a small boarding house with Betty and Dick Vincent. Dick was the local handyman around town and Betty cleaned houses on occasion and, on Monday nights, she cleaned the Blue Sky Saloon.

Judge Ellis heard the charges against Sam Colton and Oliver White Cloud. He had Hank come over and describe the scene of the "intended burglary." Jimmy Dean accompanied Hank and provided his own view of what happened that night.

"I think you're right. A jury trial would be in order. You have the jurors lined up, sheriff?"

Sheriff Joe's rotund belly shook, as he swiveled in his chair. "Sure do. Want to see them before the trial, Judge?"

"No, I don't think that'll be necessary. You're familiar with these folks enough, I'm assuming?"

"Yes, sir… every one of them. It should go real smooth and quick. Stuff like this that lingers too long causes folks to get anxious. Don't want that. People need to be able to sleep at night, knowing they'll be protected and kept safe from dangerous elements… like those two snakes that rolled into town. One's a half-breed and the other's a full-blood. Definitely in cahoots."

Judge Ellis shifted his legs and rubbed his chaffed knees. "So, when you're ready, let's go take a look at the two 'alleged criminals.'"

Sheriff Joe drove the judge to the jailhouse in his new truck. Once inside, the sheriff unlocked the door that led into the cells. Sheriff said, "Nice and cozy back here. Got all the comforts of home. Plus, three squares a day."

"Three squares, you say. That's mighty generous of you. I see you're upholding the law and taking good care of the prisoners."

"And that's real generous of you to say, Judge. That's why I got me a smooth- running town. Now, need to let you know, one of them is complaining about his phone call. Says he didn't get one. I told him the phones have been outa order, so…"

"So, who's complaining about their phone call?" the judge asked, agitated, as they neared the cells.

Sam looked up. "That would be me. The sheriff here has denied me my rights. I am entitled by law to one phone call."

"Well, the sheriff says the phones have been outa order for a spell. I've got you boys an attorney already lined up, so no need to fret about your phone call. He's a real upstanding fellow and he knows the law real good out here. I'll send him over directly so he can talk to you boys, as soon as he gets to town." He turned to the sheriff and said, "Okay, I'm done here."

The door banged closed behind them, sending an ominous boom that reverberated throughout the cell and shook the bars.

Sam looked over at Oliver who was sitting on the bed, cross-legged. It irritated him that he didn't seem bothered… he just looked so serene, as if he were praying.

"Oliver," Sam said softly. "I have a feeling we're in big trouble. They're gonna do what they want, and no one will be able to stop them. No one will care, anyway… except maybe the girls and the pastor. And even if they told someone, the sheriff would simply claim he upheld the law… that they had a trial and…"

The door abruptly swung open and in walked a balding, wheezing middle-aged man.

"Howdy, boys. Name's Rory… Rory Calhoun… and I'm here to represent the two of you."

Deputy Ben brought in a chair for him. Rory thanked him and sat down, Took a pad of paper, and started to write.

"The year is 1980, 28th of August. Defendants are: Oliver White Cloud," he said with a snort. "Injun, huh? What tribe?"

Oliver didn't respond.

"Okay. I'll just put 'redskin.' That should cover it. And you…?" He looked at Sam. "Sam Colton, right? Should I put half-breed for you, or would you prefer something different?"

Sam jumped up, outraged. "What the hell kind of lawyer are you?"

"The kind that's going to give you a fair representation. That's the kind I am. Now you want to get all smart alecky with me or do you want me to do my job?"

Sam glared at the man and spat. "I don't think it'll matter much one way or the other. You'll just do whatever the judge and sheriff want you to do."

Seething, Rory shoved back his chair and got to his feet.

"Look, I was sent here to help you, to defend you. And all I get is smart-mouthed hostility. This is your last chance to tell me your side of the story. That's why I'm here." Controlling his anger he said, "Now, what's it going to be?"

"Would it make any difference what I say?"

Rory grinned. "Well of course it would." He sat back down and said, "Let's start at the beginning. Now, tell me why you came here to Miners Gulch, and how it happened to be on the very same day this, um… Oliver was here. You seem to be a smart guy and it shouldn't be too hard to explain."

Rory took notes as Sam told him the story of his passing through town. Oliver even told him a little about his father's red '54 pickup truck.

Rory nodded and said, "I think I've heard enough. Got a good case for you. See you tomorrow in the courthouse. We should do just fine. No need to worry." He knocked on the door. A moment later Deputy Ben opened it and led Rory to the exit.

Sam called over to Oliver. "Have you noticed how original these people are with their names? Jimmy Dean, Hank Williams… and now Rory Calhoun. Any minute now, I expect to meet John Wayne… or Elvis Presley. Wishful thinking on their part, no doubt."

*

It was a steamy hot Wednesday, and there was a buzz about town. Everything was hopping. Cars and trucks lined the main street as far as you could see. It didn't seem to matter it was on such short notice. Hordes of people gathered and wandered the town in anticipation of a party and the trial. The barber shop was buzzing with excitement. The local diner was filled to capacity with a waiting line out the front door and down the street. Of course, the Blue Sky Saloon had been packed since 9:00 a.m. with shots of whiskey lined all the way up and down the counter. Randy and

Gladys could hardly keep up. A little before 10:00 a.m., as the courthouse started filling up, the bar began slowing down.

The twelve jurors, hand-picked by the sheriff, were mostly ranchers and cowboys, and a few businessmen including Mike Stull, the banker and Bertie Dawes, the barber. Escorted single file into the courtroom, they took their seats near the judge.

Indigo, Janet, Sally, and Pastor Percy were stunned by the news of the trial, and that it had happened so fast. They were the first to enter the courtroom and pushed their way up front, and sat behind Oliver and Sam, who were already seated with their attorney, Rory Calhoun.

Sheriff Joe and Deputy Ben sat on the opposite table up front. Going through a small stack of papers in front of him, the sheriff was the acting prosecutor for Miners Gulch.

The energy in the courtroom was frenetic, with everyone talking and gossiping about the trial and on betting whether there would be a hanging or prison time. Some folks had come from a hundred miles away and drove all night to see the trial. Sheriff Joe Jenner had a big reputation. Most felt the rumors running rampant of a hanging was imminent. The folks wanted to stick around for that, so they came prepared with tents, chairs, and coolers filled with food and drink. A party-like atmosphere prevailed.

At 10:00 a.m. sharp, Judge Ellis came out of the back room, his black robe fluttering like a bat ready for flight. The bailiff, Harold Cummings, stood and said, "All rise. The honorable Judge Ellis will be presiding over the case of the State of Wyoming versus the defendants, Oliver White Cloud and Sam Colton." He cleared his throat and continued. "The case involves alleged theft, burglary, attempted murder, disorderly conduct, resisting arrest, and punitive damages in the amount of twenty thousand dollars… and an additional five thousand dollars to house the criminals."

Everyone in the courtroom stood, crammed together, as an anticipated hush filled the room.

Judge Ellis banged his gavel and said, "This here is a trial in Bedford County, in the municipality of Miners Gulch, docket number #12410. The day is 30th of August, in the year 1980. The charges are of a serious nature.

First charge: Attempted theft of a said 1954 red Ford pickup truck.

Second charge: Conspiracy to commit burglary in the Blue Sky Saloon and elsewhere in Miners Gulch and environs.

Third charge: Causing distress to the owners of said saloon and thousands of dollars in damage.

Fourth charge: Threatening to kill Hank Williams Jr. and Jimmy Dean Hinkle. Now, how do the defendants plead?"

Rory Calhoun stood, motioning for Oliver and Sam to stand, as well.

"Mr. Colton. How do you plead?" the judge asked.

"Not guilty, your honor."

Mr. Cloud… I mean, Mr. White Cloud. How do you plead?"

Oliver's eyes slowly scanned the courtroom. "Not guilty." Then he added, "As if that will make a difference."

A bang with the gavel rang out. "Okay, Mr. White Cloud. That's enough. You will be held in contempt of court for any further outbursts in this courtroom. Now let's begin, shall we? Rory… uh… Mr. Calhoun – are you ready for your defense?"

"Yes sir, I am," he said loudly, blotting his forehead with his kerchief.

"Defendant Mr. Oliver White Cloud states that his father, Looking Spirit, a resident of a South Dakota reservation, went missing a couple years back. He further states that his father has not been seen since. According to Mr. White Cloud's testimony, his father was heading west from his reservation in a '54 red Ford pickup truck to look at a horse for sale. He claims the truck he saw in town looked like his father's truck. He further claims that when he saw it, he inspected it, but he had no intention of stealing it. He was just sitting inside of the vehicle."

Rory Calhoun gathered up his papers, and said, "Now, onto Mr. Sam Colton. Mr. Colton states that he was just passing through town. He wouldn't say where he was going other than, 'just passing through'. Sounds plausible enough, right? A man from glamorous Hollywood, California just passing through our quaint little town. Most likely curious to see how 'real men' live." A few chuckles erupted in the crowded room. "Now, Mr. Colton states that he entered the Blue Sky Saloon around 4:00 p.m. on the 24th of August, 1980. He said he had had a long drive and wanted a few drinks to unwind and relax. He further stated he enjoys watching people… could be, maybe to scope them out." He looked at the jurors and winked. "Harmless enough, wouldn't you say? Then he played a few games of pool with Mr. Hank Williams, Jr."

Someone in the courtroom shouted out, "And he's a cheater, too."

The judge banged his gavel and said, "That'll be enough."

Rory Calhoun continued. "Then, according to Mr. Colton, he played a game of pool with Mary, the sheriff's daughter, who now calls herself, Indigo – like the color of yarn," he grinned. "Then Mr. Colton had a few innocent dances with Mary or Indigo, as well. Now the jury can see what an upstanding man from Hollywood, California looks like. I checked where he worked in Hollywood, and they told me he was no longer employed there. I believe he was fired. So that shouldn't make you suspicious, should it? Both Mr. White Cloud and Mr. Colton deny knowing each other previously. Now Mr. Colton thinks he knows the law more than I do, because he's from Hollywood, where everything is make-believe, including the people. These two men claim their innocence, but I'll leave that up to the jury to decide…"

Sam Colton had heard enough. He stood up, interrupting

Rory Calhoun's argument. "Your honor, I would like permission to speak in my own defense. This man, this Rory Calhoun, is not representing me or Oliver White Cloud properly. He's acting more like a prosecutor than our defense attorney."

Judge Ellis was apoplectic at the interruption and banged his gavel in protest. "You will sit down this instant, Mr. Colton, or I'll have you removed from this court of law. The gentleman you're speaking of, Mr. Calhoun, is a very fine attorney and doing the best he can under the circumstances. You're lucky I don't fine you. Now, sit down, and shut up!"

Rory Calhoun grinned and said, "I think I'm finished with these two, your honor. Thank you."

Sheriff Joe stood slowly and cracked his neck as he walked up to the jurors. He stopped and nodded at each one. "I thank each of you for giving up your time on this marvelous, but somber, day. Now, as you can see, we have two defendants claiming their innocence on multiple charges, but I would like to prove otherwise. Now, as most of you know, I uphold the law in this town… in a firm but fair way, as most townsfolk will attest. This Injun, excuse me, I mean to say, Indian, is making a false and accusatory claim about one of our most respected and upstanding citizens. Hank Williams Sr. is a Christian man, who attends worship services every Sunday. He is a successful rancher and employs a lot of folks in this town. Now it appears that Mr. White Cloud is accusing Mr. Hank Williams Sr. of stealing a raggedy, old, broken down '54 red Ford pickup truck. Mind you, Mr. Williams Sr. is a man with a proper upbringing and has no cause for stealing a battered truck. Nor would he even contemplate doing so, being a man of impeccable character. I'd say Hank Williams Sr. could buy a hundred or more of those trucks with his pocket change alone. So, why would he steal one? We don't even know if the Injun… Indian, Mr. White Cloud, is fabricating his story. Making false claims is a very serious crime here in Miners Gulch as is defaming one of our most prominent citizens. Now, the other defendant, Mr. Sam Colton, who I can see is some sort of half-breed, has been telling falsehoods since he arrived. I believe he was concocting a plan to rob our Blue Sky Saloon. Truth be told, he was acting suspicious, and then he caused a huge brawl in the saloon with substantial damage. We can't be having law breakers coming into our town and thinking they can get away with it. Now, there's a real big sign outside of town that plainly states: 'No Indians.' So far as I can see, these two willfully disobeyed the sign, and then maliciously broke the law. So, we got Mr. Hollywood and Mr. White Cloud, obvious criminals, waiting for you to decide their fate. I know each one of you will make the right decision. Remember one thing. Breaking the law in our town – we take that seriously. Maybe this case will deter other such motivated individuals from coming here. Don't like to waste our taxpayer dollars housing criminals. Doesn't sit well with me."

The judge rapped his gavel and spoke to the jury. "I think all the evidence has been shown in a fair and equitable manner. Both sides presented their case and now you the jurors will go back and decide… guilty or not guilty." He banged the gavel and announced, "Court dismissed."

The bailiff quickly hopped up and stated, "Everyone rise," as the judge left the chambers. The bailiff instructed the jurors to go to the back room. They all filed behind Jake Austin, the head juror, and sat around a long table on hard plastic fold-up chairs.

Jake said, "Okay, let's begin our deliberation. All twelve of us need to agree on the outcome, so let's not waste a lot of time. If anyone has questions, get to it." Jake looked around the room and added, "Anyone got a complaint about hurrying along?"

Most everyone shook their heads, no. "Okay. Now we heard what those two were up to in town. I say, without a doubt, they are guilty. Let's take a vote. Raise your hand for guilty on all counts."

Eleven of the twelve jurors raised their hands. Betty Vincent was the exception. Jake eyed her and said, "What's the problem, Betty? Why aren't you raising your hand like everyone else?"

"I'm not sure we should be so hasty. Those boys will…"

Jake cut her off before she could finish and stated the facts as he saw them. "Now, you heard everything like we did… the very same stuff. How is it you can't see they're guilty like we all did? Practically caught them red-handed. You want to go against all of us here in this room – all your friends and neighbors? We stick together in this town."

*

Out in the courtroom, after most of the people had left, Deputy Ben talked to the sheriff. "Should I take the two prisoners back to the jail while we wait for the verdict? It's been over an hour. I kinda thought they might be finished by now – but guess not. Looks to be a holdup or something…"

Sheriff Joe wiggled in his chair and yawned. "Yeah. Take 'em back. I want this over as soon as possible."

Deputy Ben pulled out his gun and signaled for Oliver and Sam to get up. He checked that their cuffs were still on, and said, "Let's go, fellas – back to your cozy cell." He ushered them toward the door, then hooted out, "Bet you boys can't wait to see what our law-abiding citizens will have to say about the two of you."

Sam and Oliver ignored the deputy. They knew the outcome wouldn't be in their favor.

Deputy Ben gave them a push outside and gloated. "Don't hold your breath for a not guilty verdict." The sunlight glared down as an anxious crowd gathered outside the wooden door.

Indigo, Sally, Janet, and Percy were huddled together under a tree near the courthouse. "What the hell kind of attorney did Sam and Oliver have?" Percy asked, outraged. "Excuse my language, ladies."

Indigo was fuming. "The kind my father likes – the rigged

ones he pays off. He has a list of 'special people' he likes to use who are beholden and at his whim. It makes me sick." Just then her eyes landed on Sam, as he passed by with the deputy. Words caught in her throat. She wanted to give him some kind of encouragement, to tell him that she and the others still had a plan. But before she could say anything, Deputy Ben hustled them toward the jail.

The crowd gathered near, and some shouted. "What's it gonna be, Deputy? A hanging?"

"We'll have to wait and see. Now, no one will be allowed inside the jail." He waved his gun for show, shoving people out of the way as he ushered Oliver and Sam inside, and shut the door.

As soon as the door closed, the bailiff came running out of the courtroom and hollered out. "Verdict's in. Sheriff says the jury has made a decision."

A throng of people crowded their way back into the court-room. Once inside, rumors flew about the verdict as everyone waited and wondered.

The door banged open as Deputy Ben hustled Oliver and Sam back to the front and sat down.

A few minutes later the judge made an elaborate entry. His robe swished out as he sat and banged his gavel. "Please be quiet."

A moment later, the jurors filed out of the back room and assembled in their seats. Once situated, the judge said, "Hear ye, hear ye. I ask the jurors. Have you reached a verdict in the case against the two defendants, Sam Colton and Oliver White Cloud?"

Jake Austin rose to his feet and addressed the judge. "Yes, we sure have, your judge's honor." A smile tugged at the corner of his mouth.

Judge Ellis looked at Jake, eyebrows cocked, then over at the packed courtroom, then back at Jake and said, "Mr. Austin. Will you please read the verdict?"

The silence was so deep you could hear a pin drop as Jake opened the paper and read.

"The jury finds White Cloud and Sam Colton guilty on all three charges: mayhem, murder, and mischief."

The judge looked at Jake and wondered for a moment about this guy's smarts.

A roar went up in the courtroom as the announcement was made.

"Hear! Hear!" the judge shouted while banging away with his gavel, trying to restore order to the courtroom. "Settle down." He rapped his gavel several more times until finally the courtroom quieted to a low buzz.

"No more outbursts in my courtroom," Judge Ellis warned. "The next one to make a sound will be arrested. Am I understood?" He cleared his throat. "I will now pass sentence on the two men. Oliver White Cloud and Sam Colton, will you please stand for the court?"

Oliver and Sam looked at each other, stood up slowly, and faced the judge.

Judge Ellis waited a few moments before saying anything. It seemed like an eternity as he sat on his perch, looking down at the two with unflinching eyes. Finally, he banged his gavel to the relief of the waiting crowd and spoke in a strong voice. "I hereby decree, under the law of the great State of Wyoming, in the town of Miners Gulch, that Oliver White Cloud and Sam Colton shall be hung by the neck until dead." For a moment, it seemed everyone was in shock at the sentence.

Judge Ellis continued. "I would say that should deter any more outsiders from coming into our great state and small towns with the intent to commit heinous crimes. Tomorrow seems like a good time to carry out the sentence… wouldn't you agree, Sheriff?"

Sheriff Joe said, "Yes, your honor."

"Then, take them away, Deputy."

The bailiff hurried up front and yelled to get everyone's attention, but to no avail. He screamed out, "All rise." But it was too late, as pandemonium broke out in the courtroom. Boots were stomping wildly, revving up the crowd, followed by hoots and hollering. The judge paid no mind as he checked his watch, got up from his seat, and left the courtroom. He was starving.

Sheriff Joe beamed over the verdict. *I'll arrange it tomorrow by the 'hanging tree' behind the Blue Sky Saloon. A real nice tree, too – good and strong. Been a while since we've used it,* he thought feeling giddy.

You would think a national holiday was just declared as everyone seemed to dance their way out the door. A ranch hand cried out, "This calls for a big celebration…"

Bernie said, "I'm going to get drunk as a goose," and he clicked his heels together. "I'll bring my fiddle and get Harold and some others to bring their guitars and stuff. Let's have us a real big jamboree."

"Sure glad the judge seen fit to uphold our law," Jake Austin hollered gleefully. "Gonna get mighty drunk, myself."

The crowd outside the courtroom was in a frenzy by now, as Deputy Ben, accompanied by the sheriff, came outside with the two prisoners. Sheriff Joe called out, "Okay folks. Let's all disperse now. Trial's over. Tomorrow we'll carry out the verdict. Now, skedaddle. Thanks for your support and for coming to the trial."

A cheer went up in the crowd, and they started chanting:

"Sheriff Joe, you're our man

The reds can't escape

Your hangin' hands."

Sheriff Joe smiled and doffed his hat, with one arm firmly wrapped around Oliver's, while Deputy Ben held onto Sam.

"Move," the sheriff said eagerly. "Gonna be your last day, so let me know what you boys want to eat for… we'll just call it your 'Last Supper.' Except you'll have no disciples to join you."

Randy let off a loud snort, "That's a good one sheriff. I like it."

"Well, got to have a little sense of humor… right boys?"

Sam was still in a bit of shock and didn't respond. Oliver stared straight ahead.

"I'll get Gladys to fix your supper tonight, a real good one too. Anything you want. Probably worked up a hearty appetite," he winked. "Been a helluva day."

As Deputy Ben slammed the cell door shut, Sam and Oliver looked at each other.

"You didn't expect anything different, did you, Oliver?" Sam asked quietly.

"No, not really. I just didn't think they would hang you, as well, since you're not a full blood. Guess it doesn't make any difference. I'm sorry you got mixed up in this mess." Oliver said, sitting down.

"Hard to imagine this is our last day," Sam said. "I'm not sorry I met you though. I wish someone knew about this town and what goes on here. They can steal your people's land and treat you guys like vermin. Guess I'm vermin, too," he said sardonically. "Or, at least, half of me is. I hid being Indian for so long, I almost forgot myself. I cut my hair, left my aunt and uncle's place, and never looked back… that is, until now. I'm really sorry I never got the chance to learn more about my people and my heritage."

CHAPTER NINE

AS THE CROWS FLY

OLIVER LOOKED OUT the small window and noticed a few crows flying overhead. He stood up on his bed and watched them as they flew around in circles over the jail and landed on a light post on Main Street. Then a few more of them gathered. They weren't squawking or cawing – they just sat there, still as statues. Oliver watched them with interest, wondering what they were up to. A thought suddenly struck him. He stepped off his bed, looked at Sam, shaking his head in wonder. "I believe help has come…"

Sam walked next to Oliver's cell and looked at him like he was crazy. "What? Have you seen someone out there that's going to blast us out of here…? Or maybe it's the pastor bringing his Bible for a weapon, or maybe the girls are going to have a shootout?"

"The crows are back. I believe they will help us."

Sam looked at Oliver incredulously. "I hope the crows know how to pick a lock. Maybe you can tell them where the keys are… wrapped around the deputy's belt."

Oliver didn't respond. He just kept looking out the window at the crows.

Sam said, "I'm a little worried if that's what's going to rescue us," and shook his head. "Well, I certainly hope they get some backup." He stood on the bed, looking out the small, dingy window and then over at Oliver whose eyes were brimming with curiosity and was humming.

"They have come to help us," Oliver said calmly. "I'm not sure what they will do… or how… I just know it. He turned to Sam. "You have no idea how incredibly smart and crafty they are. It's been known they remember faces, hold grudges and, yes, even pick locks, I would bet. For generations, our people have greatly respected the ravens and crows. Their intellect is really quite astounding."

"Well, I don't want to pin my hopes and my life on a bunch of crows!" Sam said.

Oliver just stood silently watching the crows – with a faint smile of hope.

Sam finally stood on his bed and looked out the small window. He was amazed at the number of crows gathering outside, and suddenly excited. "Look at them all perched in the trees… on streetlights… and on tops of roofs… and even on that fence post right outside our cell. It looks as if they're waiting… for…" Sam let his words trail off as he watched in amazement as the crows pointed their beaks into the air, quietly clacking like they were communicating with each other in a secret language. He felt a shiver run up his spine and thought, *Oliver might be right.*

Suddenly a big fat crow with huge yellow eyes swiveled his head and flew at the window, startling Sam and he jumped back. It landed with a thump and its long beak pecked at the glass. He swore he heard the crow say, "Doubter."

Sam backed away from the window and hopped off the bed. "I could swear that crow with those weird yellow eyes called me a doubter."

Oliver uncrossed his arms and looked at his friend. "Like I said… they're pretty smart birds."

"Um… I don't know. I guess… well, it seems pretty crazy to have your life depend on a bunch of birds. Maybe it's just being desperate – clinging to anything at this point."

Oliver said, "I guess we'll find out tomorrow, my friend."

Sam wanted to shake him and tell him… "Tomorrow we're going to die. How can you look so calm?" He wasn't sure he wanted to hear any more about the crows. His nerves were on edge – and jumped when he heard someone rattling the keys in the lock.

The door swung open, and Sheriff Joe came walking down the hallway, hands on hips, looking like a bear that had just devoured a tasty salmon.

"Well, boys. This is your last night and I'm here to make sure you enjoy every minute of it. I've asked Gladys to cook you up a real nice steak… fresh from the local rancher. She'll add in some mashed potatoes, gravy, butternut squash, and sourdough bread smothered in butter. That'll perk you up. Bring it over around six tonight. Might even throw in a long neck to celebrate your trial. Sorry you lost."

Sam and Oliver quietly stared at him in disgust.

"I got the ropes ready, and that big ole Sycamore is strong enough to hang the both of you boys at the same time," Sheriff Joe said, off-handedly. "Been a spell since I used it."

Oliver could feel his anger swell. He stood and faced the sheriff. "Is that the same tree where you hung my father? That's his '54 Ford truck that I…"

"Well, let me tell you something, Red. If he was an Injun coming though this town, he wasn't using his head. Most come here drunk looking for trouble, and that's exactly what they get… the kind that ends poorly for them. So, I don't want to hear any sob story about your daddy. Ain't got no use for Indians in my town. Besides, you redskin sonsabitches killed my hero, General Custer. Now, there was a darn good soldier – a brave man – and what kind of hero you Injuns got? Sitting Bullshit, that's who. As far as I can see, you're both getting your dues. And you're lucky I'm giving you boys such a nice sendoff, so shut your trap."

Sheriff Joe slammed the door shut behind him.

Sam fumed. "I can't believe this kind of crap is still going on. It feels like we're stuck in the old west… like the 'Shootout at the OK Corral.'"

Oliver said, "In case you didn't learn it in school, General Custer was a thief who discovered gold on our lands in the Black Hills… and brought in the U.S. army to seize the territory for him. The rest is history, so to speak."

Sam pondered Oliver's words. "Seems like our people 've been fighting a losing battle for a long time," said Sam, as a terrifying realization washed over him. "The people in this town seem just like that General, lying, and worse. So I don't care how many crows there are outside… not sure how they're gonna help us escape the noose." A quiver of hatred surged through his veins. "Guess I'm discovering what it's like to be an Indian around here – and it looks pretty bleak, even for a half-breed."

Oliver and Sam sat, both lost in their own thoughts, until they heard a sharp popping sound at the window. They both hopped up and looked out.

Indigo was standing below the window, waving, alongside Janet, Sally, and Pastor Percy. Indigo said excitedly. "We'll be back tonight Sam and…" She stopped mid-sentence when Deputy Ben hustled around the side of the jail, his eyes bulged out at the sight of the group standing below the window.

He huffed angrily. "What are you doing back here, Indigo? The sheriff 'll have my hide if he finds out. Now get. People might get the wrong idea – and think you might be aiding and abetting the prisoners… maybe even help them escape. Could land yourselves in jail with your shenanigans. You, too, Pastor. What kind of example are you setting in this town?" Before anyone could answer, Ben rattled on. "I'll tell you, not a very good one – that's for dang sure. Now shoo! All of you. Skedaddle." He waved them away with a flap of his hands.

Indigo mouthed an apology. "Sorry."

Sam sat back on the bed. The brief ripple of joy and spark of hope quickly vanished. His spirits sank even lower, and he slipped into a depressed state. There was no way they were getting out of here. He didn't care what Oliver said about those crows and their magical 'woo-woo' powers.

At six o'clock sharp, the door jangled opened. The deputy balanced a tray filled with plates piled high with food – just like the sheriff promised.

"Looks like you boys are having a real feast – fit for a king, by the looks of it." He leaned over and took a big sniff. "Ooh, that smells good. I wouldn't mind one of these steaks myself. Pretty damn lucky if you ask me. The sheriff's being mighty generous with you boys." He pushed the plates through the opening. "Been fed pretty well since you been here, I'd say. Fatten you boys up for the killing, just like we do a hog, 'cept we ain't gonna eat your red ass. We'll just give your carcasses to the pigs to snack on." He laughed at his crude joke and banged the door shut.

The smell of the steak, potatoes, and squash filled the air. Oliver looked over at Sam, who sat looking at his plate with distaste, then shoved it away.

"I think we should eat, Sam. I have a feeling we're going to need all of our energy for what lies ahead."

Sam hesitated. "I'm not sure I can get any food down. Feeling a bit sick to my stomach, thinking about tomorrow. I think you have more faith than I do – in us somehow being freed… Can't say I feel the same."

Oliver smiled as he cut into a tender slice of the New York

steak. "Not guaranteeing anything, but just in case something unexpected happens tomorrow, you might wish you had eaten. Need to be ready, is all I'm saying." He cut into another morsel of the tender beef, and chewed, contemplating.

Sam's stomach growled, and he thought, *what the hell?! Live or die, I might as well eat.* He dug his fork into the pile of mashed potatoes and gravy and realized he was hungrier than he had thought. Every morsel of food quickly disappeared from his plate.

Deputy Ben came back an hour later and collected the empty plates. "Glad to see you didn't waste the food. Best get a good night's sleep," he said with a chuckle. "Oh, on second thought, you might want to stay awake and enjoy your last hours – I'm guessing you'll be getting nothing *but* sleep soon enough…" then paused, "or roasting your backsides."

It was getting dark now, and Deputy Ben was sitting at his desk, yawning. He was looking to be on duty all night and thought he might play solitaire to pass the time. As he began shuffling the cards, he heard a rap at the door. He got up, pulled out his gun, walked to the door, unlocked it, and opened it just a crack. He pointed his pistol through the crack, and asked, "Who is it?"

Percy thought warily. *It's not going to be as easy as I had imagined.* He said, "It's me, Deputy. Pastor Percy."

Deputy Ben opened the door a little further. "What do you want? No one's allowed inside."

"I thought I'd come over to give the last rites to the prisoners and have a drink with you afterwards… maybe keep you company for a while," Percy said.

Deputy Ben hesitated. "The drink sounds mighty tempting, but I have strict instructions from the sheriff. Can't let anyone in tonight – no exceptions. Guess that includes you, Pastor. You can give them their last prayer or whatnot tomorrow – at the gallows." He shuffled his feet. "Hell, for all I care, have a big prayer service.

But just not tonight… sorry." And Ben shut the door before Percy could say anything more on the subject.

Deputy Ben sat back down at his desk, reshuffled the deck of cards, and laid them out – liking what he saw.

A short while later, Deputy Ben heard another knock at the door and grabbed his gun. *Damn! I got me a winning hand, too.* He stood, annoyed by the interruption. Probably the pastor again. "I'm gonna tell him to get lost." He unlocked the door a slight crack and saw Mary – smiling sweetly. He couldn't believe the gall…

"I brought you a homemade apple pie, Deputy. Still warm out of the oven. I felt bad with you being here all alone tonight, and thought you might like something to sweeten your night…" She tried to hide her disdain and forced out a big smile. "I could help you pass the time away."

Ben's head reeled. *That Mary has never ever been this nice to me before,* he thought suspiciously. *Why now? I bet she wants in because of that half-breed,* he fumed. *She can't believe I'd fall for her crap.*

"I ain't supposed to let anyone inside," he growled. "Especially you, Mary. That's orders from the sheriff. He thought you might be up to some funny business. So, no! You can't come in."

"I didn't realize you're afraid of my dad. I guess you're just a chicken, like everyone says," Indigo said, taunting him. "More like a jackass with a pistol."

"You got a foul mouth on you, Mary! So get!"

Unable to help herself, she flipped him off, then stormed down the street.

"You're a big pain in the ass," he shouted after her. "I wouldn't go for you, anyhow." Ben was furious at her comments about him and slammed the door so hard it rattled on the hinges. "She's a real sassy bitch," he muttered. "If I was the sheriff, I'd lock her up on account of her vile tongue."

Ben lost interest in his winning hand and threw the pile on

the desk, wishing he had a bottle of whiskey instead. "I should've taken the preacher's bottle. I would've drunk the whole dang thing." He shoved his chair out and leaned back. "Can't wait for this damn night to be over."

Around midnight, he had just dozed off and started to snore when a slight 'tap-tap-tap' woke him up. His eyes flew open, and he almost fell over in his chair in his hurry to get up. He brushed the sleep from his eyes, and he grabbed his guns, ready to shoot the intruder. "I don't care who it is either. Sick of being bothered!" He grumbled. Easing his way to the door, he cracked it open slightly. Nothing seemed to be out there as he swiveled his eyes back and forth and heard nothing. So, he opened the door a bit wider and poked his head out a little further and peered into the darkness. *No one was there.* "Musta been a dream," he said under his breath. And then a sudden shiver shook him alert. "Better keep my eyeballs propped open. Something fishy is going on." He rubbed his arms as goose bumps shot all the way up to his shoulders. Then he felt a whisper of breeze surround him. He sat up, wondering if he had left a window open. Suddenly the soft breeze turned into a blustery gale as it whirled around his entire body, vibrating from the intensity. Then he saw the door swing open, and someone or something knocked him back against the wall. Eyes agog, he looked down in amazement, and saw a troupe of crows in a single line march in and encircle him. They didn't make a sound. Looking like a row of little soldiers marching into battle, lifting their scaly feet, the birds tilted back their heads, fluffed out their feathers and spread their wings, ominously. Opening their mouths, they clacked their sharp beaks in unison. It sounded like a barrage of firecrackers, exploding around him.

Deputy Ben stood watching this bizarre sight, paralyzed and too frightened to move. He wanted to shoot every one of those damn birds, but his arm was frozen to his side. He wondered for a moment if he was having a nightmare and shook his head. He realized he was awake and then snarled viciously. "Get out of here!" He tried to kick a silver-winged crow, but he couldn't lift his feet, and almost toppled backwards from the effort.

The silver-winged crow glared at the deputy with its glowing eyes, spread its wings wide, then marched up to him with beak poised, let off a loud 'caw' and dove at his leg. The pain was so intense, it shot all the way up his leg – it felt like he was pierced with an arrow. He tried to scream for help, but his mouth was abruptly clamped shut.

Right before his eyes a ghostly form materialized – shifting in the air. "Hello, Deputy. Gettin' ready to hang some skins tomorrow?" the apparition whispered eerily. "I don't think so."

Deputy Ben froze in fear. *I must be either dreaming this… or I'm hallucinating.* He couldn't speak. His breath had caught in his throat.

"I'll bet you're wondering who I am," the wispy form said, now starting to take shape. Ben gasped as he saw a tall, lanky man with bushy eyebrows and a gaunt face with hollow, pale blue eyes, grin. "Why don't you sit, Deputy…?"

Abruptly pushed back into his chair, Ben's eyes were popping out at the apparition.

"I am your worst nightmare, Ben… don't go anywhere. I have someone to see…but I'll be back…" The form quickly vanished as it slipped through the wall and entered the cell, where Oliver lay asleep.

"Oliver! Are you awake?" the shadowy form asked. When he got no response, he poked Oliver's face with his long bony finger, jolting him out of bed.

"Harken to thee… can you hear me?"

Oliver blinked his eyes and stared at the ghostly form.

"My name is Preacher Jim. I am here to tell you a story of a time long ago, when I knew your grandfather, Hidden Spirit – one of the finest warriors I had ever met. I have to tell you that

I was obsessed by him – envious of him – of his long, black, shiny hair. I knew that hair held Samson's power – and I wanted that power. He was fierce. I couldn't believe God would gift this 'heathen' with such incredible strength and I fervently prayed to Him to unlock the mystery that lay hidden in that boy. I was no match for him, though, so I ranted and raved like the lunatic I had become. I used God as a weapon to bully and scare the children at the school. I tried to scare Hidden Spirit, but he was fearless. Now, I am here to seek forgiveness for what I did – for the terrible injustices I inflicted upon your people. Hidden Spirit walked a far truer path than I. Ironically, my favorite saying at the boarding school was, 'Suffer little children unto me.' Unfortunately, I took that message far too literally. I know I will be seeking forgiveness for some time… I was hoping that you might forgive me, Oliver White Cloud."

Before Oliver could answer, the ghostly form continued. "Have faith that things will turn around, brave one. I have come at your grandfather's plea. Sleep well, my friend."

Before Oliver could ask a question, the apparition vanished.

Outside, Deputy Ben sat frozen in his chair, thinking, *all this work and stress is taking a toll on my sanity. I must be going crazy…stark raving mad.* He stared at the crows, who were watching his every move. Then, out of the blue, the tall, lanky apparition appeared next to Deputy Ben again. It seemed vague and shadowy. Then the hazy form reached out and slapped his face, so hard, his head swiveled sideways. "Sticks and stones, brother Ben… enjoy your night."

Deputy Ben looked in alarm, on the verge of hysteria, as the form now floated so close, he could smell its putrid breath. He was totally bewildered as a slight buzz of electricity zinged up his legs, sending jolts of electrical currents that shocked him. Then the form leaned in and blew icy air into his ears. Deputy Ben abruptly slumped over on his desk, face first.

*

Sheriff Joe came bounding into the jail at 8:00 a.m. and opened the door. "You would think this is a grand holiday out there," he chortled in delight, "like the fourth of July. The town is packed. People are sleeping in their pickup trucks. Tents are set up on lawns and on sidewalks. Coffee and whiskey is breakfast. The Blue Sky Saloon is open and crowded, bringing in a lot of business – gonna be a mighty fine day." He looked at his deputy and frowned. "What the devil is wrong with you? Looks like you've seen a ghost. Come on, get up and get moving. Gotta lot to do."

His hair disheveled, eyes bloodshot, Deputy Ben straightened, sat up in his chair and looked around the room, shaking his head. *Where the hell am I?* He spoke in a troubled voice. "I think I had a visitor last night…"

"What the dickens are you talking about?" Sheriff Joe bellowed. "You know I specifically told you that no one was allowed in here. Damn! I best check on the prisoners. If for any reason they're not here, I'll hang you instead!"

The sheriff flew in back toward the cells, banging on the metal bars. "Wakie, wakie. Your big day has arrived, boys."

Sheriff Joe saw Oliver sitting on his bed, looking relaxed and entirely at ease. It rankled him. So, he said, "You boys are gonna be the honored guests at the lynching party. Like your last cup of coffee?"

Oliver remained calm. "No, thanks."

Sheriff Joe looked at Sam and offered him the same. He got the same response except that Sam looked far more rattled than Oliver. That pleased the sheriff. "Well, suit yourself. We'll be leaving within the hour, so, best say your last boo-hoo or chant to your spirits or whoever the hell it is you talk to. Pastor Percy will be at the gallows to pray for your sorry asses." He turned and left, banging the door behind.

Sam looked at Oliver. "Doesn't look so good, my friend. It's been a real pleasure getting to know you. Big mistake passing through this town. Can't imagine that this is going to be our last day alive…" He wiped away a tear. "Sorry I don't have faith in those crows like you do Oliver… Just hard to believe is all."

Oliver said, "We'll see soon enough."

Sam sat back down on the bed and thought bitterly. *What a sham! The trial… this town…* He held his head in his hands. Sam could feel the blood pounding in his ears – the only sound he could hear. He thought about praying but couldn't imagine it would make a difference. Besides, what was there to pray for? That the Sheriff would let him and Oliver go free? Fat chance of that happening. He looked over at Oliver and saw his lips move, as though he were talking to someone. *Probably praying to the Great Spirit.* Sam wished he knew more about the Great Spirit and his gifts, other than the earth, the sky, and animals… his mind reeled with confusion.

Before Sam knew it, the door clanged open, and he jumped. The sheriff was all smiles and puffery as he threw the handcuffs to his deputy and looked over at the two. "Let's get ready. There's a parade of people out there waiting to cheer you on to your 'happy hunting grounds.' Sounds like the perfect place for you skins to go." He chuckled at his cleverness.

Deputy Ben 's face was pale, and his hands were shaking as he asked each of the guys to put their hands out through the small opening, so he could cuff them – Oliver first, then Sam. That done, the sheriff opened the cell door.

"Get moving, boys." Sheriff Joe said, noticing Oliver's ponytails hanging down – almost to his waist. "We could give the folks a real show, Ben. I'll get the scissors and snip those pigtails and auction each one of 'em off to the highest bidder. The folks could take home a little memento, remembering this fine day and the thieving Indian and his half-breed cohort."

Deputy Ben was quiet, thinking about last night and his bizarre dream. *It really was a dream, wasn't it?* In a panic, he reached down and felt his leg which was sore and bloodied – and he almost toppled over in fright. *I don't dare say anything,* he thought in desperation, unable to move his feet.

Sheriff Joe whacked him on the head. "What's wrong with you?" he hissed. "You best get your shit straight, 'cause you're acting mighty stupid. Don't mess up this day either! Now, get your guns ready for action and let's go."

He gave the deputy a push and glared at Oliver who cracked a smile. Sheriff Joe said, "You won't be smiling for long, Red."

The day was sunny and bright, no clouds overhead with the promise of a hot, summery day. A buzz filled the air as the locals were anticipating the big event.

Sheriff Joe marched Oliver and Sam along the streets, parading them through town, strutting like a peacock. Tipping his hat, he waved to the ladies making them holler out in excitement, and he called out. "Glad to see everyone could make it to this momentous occasion."

The crowd cheered excitedly, waving flags as he rounded the corner and walked behind the Blue Sky Saloon.

No one seemed to notice the crows gathering quietly, almost hidden in the trees and on rooftops and telephone poles. Soon hundreds had arrived – beaks poised, ready for action.

Oliver shot a glance upward and whispered, "Hamkamya upo."

Inexplicably, Sam felt incredibly at ease. He couldn't put his finger on why, but the feeling persisted as he began to feel surrounded by a soothing balm in the midst of all this chaos. He looked at Oliver, who seemed poised and confident as he walked.

Near the back of the saloon, was a rickety sign painted in big bright letters; 'herein lies the hanging tree!' It loomed large. Underneath the Sycamore tree was a newly constructed platform made of pine that smelled of a freshly cut tree. Two nooses dangled from the huge branch and swayed eerily in the dappled morning sunlight – back and forth back and forth, looking like ghosts fluttering in the wind.

The back of the Blue Sky Saloon was already crowded as Sam's eyes caught Indigo staring intently at him. A sad smile filled her gorgeous face. Beside her stood Janet and Sally. Pastor Percy was already on the steps, Bible in hand – his pale face distraught and full of worry.

Sheriff Joe nudged Oliver and Sam up the platform with his gun, enjoying his grand entrance as he waved at the crowd. He waited until the roar died down, then held up his hands to quiet the others. Some people had never been to a hanging before and were excited about the impending event – jostling their way to the frontlines. Others wondered if they could stomach watching two young men die, while others placed one-dollar bets on the length of time it would take for the feet to stop twitching. Estimates ranged anywhere from three seconds to five minutes.

Randy and Gladys had set up a barbecue out back for the occasion and Hank had brought a stack of beef ribs to cook, compliments of his father. The savory smoke filled the air as the ribs crackled on the flames. Kegs of beer had been placed against the back wall of the saloon along with jars of hard-boiled eggs, pickled pigs' feet, and salted tongue.

It's going to be one helluva party, the sheriff thought, pleased. As he looked around and took off his hat, he yelled to the crowd. "Gotta couple pigtails I'm gonna cut off on this here Indian." He pointed at Oliver. "Don't think he'll be needing them any longer, so I'll auction off each one to the highest bidder. Any takers?"

A roar of excitement pulsated through the crowd.

Sheriff hollered out, "Randy – get me a pair of scissors!"

Indigo shook with rage at the unspeakable thing her father was going to do. She had had enough and felt she would explode if she didn't do something. Desperate as she was, she didn't care what her father might do or how he might react. Nothing mattered right now, except Sam. She couldn't bear to watch him hang and she couldn't bear to leave him. Her heart refused to believe that this would be the last time she would see him – her mind whirled between a crazy mixture of hope and fear. There was that deep connection she couldn't explain.

Janet and Sally and Percy were anxious to help. Everyone's nerves were on edge. They were still plotting, trying to think of something… anything. Time was running out. Randy came hustling out with the scissors and yelled. "Whack them tails off. I'll bid for one of 'em to hang it up in the bar as remembrance of this glorious celebration."

Indigo suddenly snapped. She ran up to Randy and yanked the scissors out of his hands and shouted at the top of her lungs to the assemblage – much to the dismay of Sheriff Joe. "You will not treat these men like they are up there for your amusement. You and the sheriff and that bigoted judge are a joke… about as crooked as they come… bought and paid for. These guys, Sam and Oliver, are innocent and do not deserve to be hung," she pleaded, panting in terror, as the crowd looked back at her and "booed."

Sheriff Joe was taken aback – infuriated by his daughter's defiance. He had to shut her up before things got out of control, as the crowd was getting restless, and hurtling insults. So, he ran over to her and shook her hard. "What the devil do you think you're doing?" he hissed furiously. "You best shut your mouth, before you cause any more trouble, or I'll have you removed. Do you hear me?"

Indigo wrenched her arm away from her father, and looked at him in disgust, but she refrained from saying anything more, as he looked ready to kill her. She stomped off as Janet and Sally took her arm and led her away from the crowd to the side of the platform.

Sheriff Joe calmed the crowd by saying, "My apologies for my willful daughter's outburst," he grimaced. "She has trouble with our kind of 'swift' punishment under the law. I'll forgive her this once for interrupting our event – and I will forego the pigtail snipping. That Indian can take his locks with him to the grave." He turned to Pastor Percy. "Okay, Pastor, get your ass up here and give the criminals a quick prayer so we can get this show on the road. Got some celebrating to get at."

Pastor Percy thought his legs would give out as he walked up the platform steps to where Oliver and Sam stood. He had tears in his eyes as he saw the nooses pulled taunt around their necks and he stifled a sob. He struggled to compose himself and bit down hard on his lower lip trying to stop it from quivering. "I would like to say a prayer and ask that everyone quiet their minds and still their hearts for a moment while I begin…"

Boos and jeers went up in the crowd. Jake Austin threw a beer can at Percy, who ducked his head just in time, missing him by inches. Someone else hollered out, "Forget the prayer, Pastor. If we want to hear that crap, we'll attend your service." A thunderous wave of laughter filtered through the crowd, as eggs and rotten tomatoes were hurled at the platform.

"Yeah," another guy yelled. "I say give 'em a drink and send 'em off drunk. Where they're going, prayers don't follow." The crowd let off an earsplitting roar, followed with clapping and jeering.

All the while, a stiff breeze blew up out of the west sending hats mysteriously flying into the air. Spouts of dirt devils erupted and whirled in ever-changing circles. Then, out of the west's stiff breeze blew in a flock of crows, landing silently in the Sycamore tree, covering the branches with feathers and beaks. Then more and more gathered until the flock of crows looked as big and massive and dangerous as a thunderous black cloud. The crows remained silent as they perched unseen in the nearby trees and rooftops – blanketing the yards as their wings spread wide, poised, ready for action.

Percy ignored the jabs and jeers – determined to say his prayer, raised his Bible high in the air, shouting above the noise. "I ask our Father in heaven to look down and shower Oliver and Sam with blessings and love. May their Great Spirit be near as they pass into the ethers of light. Let these two fine young men find their way to the gates of Your heavenly bosom – and mostly I ask that you forgive the wrong that was laid upon these innocents…"

More boos and jeers and curses erupted from the onlookers, as Sheriff Joe hustled over in shock and pushed the pastor out of the way. He shouted above the roar. "I think you've said enough, Pastor," he said irritably. "I don't know what kind of prayer that was, but it's over. Now get down, before I shove your ass off the platform."

The crowd booed Percy, as he stepped down, ducking the rib bones and other debris being hurled at him. He looked back furtively at Sam and Oliver.

Sheriff Joe took off his hat and waved it in the air to get everyone's attention. "We shall now commence with the business at hand. Hope you all are enjoying yourselves on this fine day. So, let's get on with the hanging." He turned to the deputy and said, "Make sure those nooses are secure. Wouldn't want the felons slipping out and getting away," he snorted. The crowd was wound up, ready for the show.

Deputy Ben walked up to Oliver and Sam hesitantly, not sure what to expect. His face quivered in fright as he neared Oliver, who stared at him fearlessly. His eyes seemed to mock the deputy with their startling blue gaze. Ben quickly checked the knot and, as he did, he felt a queer feeling – like a stinging wasp buzzing around his face. He swatted at the air and felt a brush of wings flap against his ear. He was so frightened, he ducked his head, trying to get at his guns while at the same time checking the nooses. "All secure," he shouted, running off the platform and into the crowd.

Sheriff Joe wondered what was going on with people today.

First that damn cockamamie pastor with that simpering prayer and now his deputy who looked like a fool up there with his shaking hands, afraid of… who the hell knows? "Gonna have a talk with him later," he muttered, as he hustled up the steps, smiling at the anxious crowd.

"Okay folks. I think it's time to send these two criminals 'to meet their maker.'"

Jake Austin and his friend, Clyde, snorted loudly and hollered, "Getta snapping… Ooooh, my neck! What we waiting for?"

With a grand gesture, Sheriff Joe yelled, "Okay folks. Let the show begin." As he reached for the lever to release the slip, a large screeching crow with huge yellow eyes, eerie and haunting, dove down directly at the sheriff – all the while snapping its large beak. It punctured his thumb with such force, the flesh ripped open, and then pecked his arm.

Sheriff Joe howled in pain and, before he could react or pull the lever, another crow swooped down and poked his head. Then another lunged at his back and tore into his shoulder.

A gasp arose from the astonished crowd. Mouths agape, they looked on in horror at the sight and froze – unable to comprehend what had just happened. And before anyone could move or react, it seemed as if thousands of crows appeared and swooped down in unison – darkness descended – as a mass of wings, beaks, and claws ravaged the frightened crowd. Screams of anguish and shouts erupted into chaos. The screeching and cawing of the crows were deafening as people rushed in every direction, trying to shield themselves from the onslaught of the birds, while ducking for cover.

The sheriff hollered the loudest and covered his head and scrambled as fast as he could for refuge under the platform, cussing as he went. "Goddamn crows! Goddamn day!"

Indigo recovered just enough from the startling events, and, without another thought, raced onto the platform, amidst the swarm of crows while Janet and Sally quickly followed.

Percy was already up the steps and onto the platform – the girls were right behind. He shouted out, "I'll untie Oliver. You get Sam?"

The girls didn't bother to answer. They were already fast at work, untying the knot. Finally, they freed Sam from the noose. Percy finished with Oliver, and all flew down the steps in unison. Janet waved them along, and shouted above the noise, "Follow me to my house. You can hide there."

Oliver and Sam nodded, and without hesitation, followed the girls. Adrenaline had kicked in and they ran through the side streets and alleys as fast as their legs could go, somehow managing to stay out of sight. Halfway to Janet's house, Percy stumbled and started to fall. Oliver quickly grabbed his arm to steady him and asked, "can you make it? Winded and breathless, his face drained of color, he managed to wheeze out, "Yes. Thank you." In a minute they caught up with the others.

In the distance, the crows seemed to hover over the edge of town, as if waiting for Oliver to get to safety. The big fat crow with yellow eyes flew overhead and sat on a lamp post – watching – cawing.

Winded and frightened, Janet led them to the back entrance of the mercantile store and banged furiously on the door, praying her parents would hear. It seemed to take forever, but just a few minutes later, Janet's father, Norman, opened the door and gasped in surprise when he saw his daughter, wide-eyed and frightened, with Sally and Indigo and the new pastor. His eyes bulged at the sight of the two that were set to be hung. He wavered slightly, then corrected himself, and held out his hands. "Welcome. You must be the boys that…"

Mr. Hershel stopped himself, embarrassed. "Oh my, come in, come in," he said warmly, pulling them inside. "Please forgive my rudeness," and quickly slammed the door shut and bolted it.

Janet's mother, Gilda, came running into the room when she

heard the commotion and clutched her chest. She quickly recovered her shock, and said, "Please, everyone, come into the drawing room. Let me get you something to drink. Then we must get you boys to safety." Her eyes scanned the group, and she felt her heart thump.

Gilda and Norman knew what it was like to be persecuted. They lived that way in Germany when they were rounded up and taken to a concentration camp, fearful for their lives. Gilda poured tea with shaky hands, wondering how the two had managed to escape their fate. *It had to be a miracle*, she thought.

Once everyone had caught their breath, Janet said, "I would like to properly introduce you to Oliver White Cloud and Sam Colton. I know you heard about the… well, what the judge ruled. I cannot express how grateful I am that they are alive. I'm not even sure… I can't really explain how this happened other than a huge flock of the crows swarmed the crowd. It gave us enough time to free Oliver and Sam from the noose and… well, here we are… they managed to escape."

"It seems like a dream. The first crow attacked the sheriff, and then hundreds more came, and… before we knew it… pandemonium broke out." Indigo smiled. "Isn't it glorious?!"

Norman exclaimed, "It's certainly by the Grace of God you boys survived, I would add."

Indigo asked hesitantly, "We hate to bother you, or put you in jeopardy, but do you think they could hide out here for a while? You must believe that they are innocent."

"We do, my dear, and please, you do not need to explain to us," Norman exclaimed. "We very well understand the prejudices in this town and the sheriff's tactics. Yes, of course we will help. Whatever we can do." He looked at Oliver and Sam and asked, "Are you boys injured or hurt?"

"No," Oliver said. "Thank you for understanding. You are both so kind."

Sam sat quietly, dazed by the turn of events. He couldn't believe that they actually got away. *It was a really close call.* He looked at his friend and thought, *Oliver was right about those crows.* He was just so grateful to be alive he wanted to hug him and jump for joy. But, instead, he looked at Mr. Hershel and calmly asked, "Any chance you could help with these handcuffs?" He showed his cuffed wrists.

Norman said, "One of the many tricks I learned at Auschwitz. So, yes, I can. But time is crucial, and we must hurry before the sheriff comes sniffing around." He got up and instructed, "Follow me."

They walked through the large mercantile shop past the hardware section and dry goods and came to the feed supply section, where large bags of oats and grain were stacked to the ceiling. Mr. Hershel deftly moved several bags of grain and oats and kicked aside a battered rug, hiding a cellar door. Norman pulled on the corroded handle that led to an underground basement. As he started down, he turned to Oliver and Sam. "Out of habit, I always keep this place stocked with food and cots in case of an emergency. I guess it still stems from my days at… well never mind. I'm just glad to help you boys out." Norman lit a kerosene lantern and signaled for them to come down. "You've got all the comforts of home," he said, smiling. "I'll bring down water in a moment." He put his hands on their shoulders. "Whatever we can do, we both do it gladly. We're happy that you both escaped the… hanging noose. We have witnessed too many of those… enough to last a lifetime," he said with eyes brimming. "You should be safe here – for a while, at least."

Gilda came over with a bucket of water and Percy quickly took it from her hands. Pointing to the girls, he said, "Do you think it would be all right if we all go down and talk with Sam and Oliver for a moment?"

Gilda said, "How about five minutes? We'll come back and – if all's clear, we'll open the door."

Norman climbed the steps and said, "If you hear voices overhead you can be pretty sure it's the sheriff or his deputy searching for you. In that case, please extinguish the lantern and do not make a sound."

Percy and the girls traipsed down the stairs, and Norman quietly closed the door. Looking around the well-appointed cellar Percy was impressed. "Mr. Hershel did a fine job making this a comfortable space." The color was returning to Percy's face. "I do believe a miracle just happened… whether it was the work of crows… your Great Spirit… or the Holy Spirit… it doesn't matter. You are safe and hallelujah!" He closed his eyes and said a quick prayer. "Please dear Lord, bless Oliver and Sam and help keep them safe Amen." He looked at the faces staring at him and quickly said. "Just know I will be right beside you – we will be right beside you – every step of the way."

Indigo, for once, was at a loss for words. She sat next to Sam, trying to put the day's events into context. "Well, all I know is that, I LOVE CROWS! I used to be afraid of crows and thought that they were pesky creatures. I *had* heard rumors they were evil or something… but now, I rather like them." She smiled, "maybe you both have friends in high places that you didn't tell us about."

Percy added, "I would add, very high places. Amen, to that Indigo."

They heard a rap on the cellar door. Norman's voice sounded urgent. "Please, everyone. It's time."

Indigo said nervously, "Let me do some digging around. Maybe I can uncover something about my father. He's a real shady character. And I'm sure he's got stuff he's hiding. She looked directly at Sam. "I realize that my father is worse than I ever thought… he's a monster… I really hope you don't think I'm anything like him?"

Percy said, "You would be more like an angel, than a monster, I assure you. But I'm afraid it's time to leave." He gave her a push toward the steps. "We must hurry."

Indigo turned her gaze back to Sam – walked up to him and hugged him tightly. Then, she looked into his dreamy eyes and impulsively, kissed him long and hard on his lips, unable to let him go.

A surprised Sam gently pulled her arms away. "Just what I needed, Indigo. I hate to see you go, but I know you must. Thanks, doesn't even begin to tell you how grateful I am for your help and how lucky I am to have met you. He kissed her again and said, "that's for luck."

Indigo wanted to melt right there. His lips tasted like heaven. She had to pull herself away from him as she whispered, "I wanted to do that from the very first moment I saw you."

Sam smiled and whispered, "Good minds think alike."

Everyone gave a quick round of hugs and said their goodbyes, as they reluctantly clamored up the steps. Percy looked back and said, "God works in mysterious ways… or so it seems."

Norman helped everyone out and quickly shut the door and covered it with the burlap rug that blended in with a layer of hay and then added a few bags of grain on top.

Everyone stood there for a moment, not sure what to do next, or where to go. They were all still in a daze.

Gilda came back in the room, dabbing her eyes, struggling to keep desperation out of her voice. "Everyone must go now. And, please be careful."

Norman agreed. "You must all disperse in different directions," he gestured with a sweeping motion of his hand, "at once. The sheriff and the deputy will be out looking for Oliver and Sam everywhere – and for anyone who helped them escape. You must not act guilty. Act as surprised as everyone else about this tumultuous day."

Indigo nodded, "It's imperative that we be calm. The sheriff can spot fear like a bloodhound – and he's relentless. I think we all know that though."

"Now hurry, please." Norman opened the back door. Indigo scurried out, looking in all directions, then motioned to Sally. They hurried down a side street, unnoticed. Percy went out the front, carrying a bag of scones that Gilda gave him.

A blustery gust of wind kicked up out of the west, sending large, thorny tumbleweeds rolling across the street – whirling like wild phantoms – stirring up dust devils along the way. Percy looked up at rooftops and trees for any sign of the crows. But nothing. *They disappeared as mysteriously as they had arrived. What an unusual way for the Lord to distract the people,* he thought with a smile. *It certainly was effective.*

As Percy continued up Main Street, he heard engines roar to life as pickups and cars rumbled on down the street, most likely looking for Sam and Oliver. He shuddered. Percy took a deep breath trying to calm his jitters. Looking around the street, seeing no one, he sprinted on down the sidewalk, hoping to avoid the sheriff. He knew it was only a matter of time before he came over to the church, and he had to be prepared. Once at his house, he raced inside, and locked the door. He clicked on a low light and went to his desk drawer… pulled out a bottle of 'Mr. Beam,' as he like to call it and poured himself a glass of the golden liquid. He stopped when it was half full. *Better not get carried away,* he thought wryly. *Need to keep my wits about me.* He held the glass to the light, gave it a twirl and said, "To soothe my soul, dear Lord." Ready to take a sip, he heard a knock at the door. His body stiffened, his hands shook wildly, and his glass sailed out of his hands and shattered on the floor. He didn't move. Then he heard, "Percy. It's us. Indigo, Janet, and Sally. Are you in there?"

Relieved by the sound of the girls' friendly voices, Percy opened the door and quickly ushered the girls inside.

Indigo said breathlessly, "Percy. We are all on edge and wanted to come over and see how you're doing… maybe go over what to say when the sheriff questions us. It'll just be a matter of time before he comes sniffing around – sooner or later, we'll have to answer about the incident."

"Yes, yes. Splendid idea. I was trying to soothe my nerves with a nice glass of bourbon, when I heard a knock at the door and dropped mine… I'm embarrassed to say, I panicked for a moment. I know everyone's nerves are shot, so how about a glass of bourbon before we get started?"

Everyone nodded their approval.

Percy threw a towel over the broken glass, leaving it where it was, then poured the drinks. "This will help calm you," he said as he handed a glass to Sally, who looked pale and frightened.

Sally took it shyly and smiled at Percy. "Thank you."

Percy smiled back. "Sip it slowly. Guaranteed to relieve your jitters."

Sally took a sip. A feeling of fire slipped down her throat, and she coughed. After a moment, she took another sip, and began to relax.

Once everyone had their drinks, Percy said, "Let me say a prayer for Oliver and Sam." He closed his eyes and began to pray, but Indigo interrupted him.

"I appreciate your good intentions… but really, if you don't mind, I think we should focus on what we're going to tell the sheriff when he starts grilling us. You know he'll come looking. Just a matter of time. He's cagey and if we act nervous, he'll know we're lying. We must not falter, just look him squarely in the eye and say, 'The crows came at us, and we took off running – looking for cover. So, we rushed to the church for safety. We had to run for our lives. And we're still pretty freaked out."

"What if someone saw us coming out of the mercantile store? Then my parents will be in huge trouble. I'm not certain how they would hold up," Janet said worriedly.

Percy took a long drink of the whiskey, enjoying its calming effect. "We could say we went to warn them about a flock of crows flying all over the place and attacking people – so they needed to stay inside."

"Well," Janet thought, "That sounds plausible. Then we came over to the church to welcome people in – in case they needed a place to get to safety and away from the crows."

"That's good." Indigo said. "We must deny ever seeing Sam and Oliver – EVER. We cannot waver on that, or their lives will be over, and we will be to blame."

Sally raised her glass and stood, "I will deny it, no matter what."

Janet and Percy and Indigo all raised glasses and clinked a toast to Oliver and Sam.

"I thank the Lord for this day," said Percy, "for this miracle… and for meeting you girls."

CHAPTER TEN

THE HUNT FOR OLIVER AND SAM

THE SHERIFF COULDN'T believe his eyes at what just happened when he saw those *"vicious birds!" Blasted things came from out of nowhere and attacked him.* He crawled out from under the platform from where he was hiding and hauled himself up, arm shaking. To his amazement, not only had those blasted crows disappeared, but the two felons, as well.

The deputy crawled out from the platform behind the sheriff, jittery – and brushed the dirt from his pants. He pulled out both guns and told the sheriff, "Don't you worry… I see any more crows lurking about, I aim to shoot 'em dead." He jumped when he heard the sheriff holler at him.

"Why didn't you shoot those things when you had the chance? You musta seen they were attacking me? AND, where in hell did that Indian and half-breed go?"

Deputy Ben twiddled with his guns and said nervously. "I-It's the strangest thing I've ever seen," he faltered – feeling his sore leg. "Those birds flew at me before I could get at my gun and tore into me something furious. I didn't have a chance… I swear."

A growl vibrated up the sheriff's throat. "Well, if you see any crows hovering around… don't hesitate this time… shoot!"

Throngs of people stood silently nearby. The air was thick with highly charged emotions. Everyone was still baffled by the incident. Everyone was on edge, frightened by the menacing flock of crows that had nearly pecked their eyes out.

Jake Austin limped over, whimpering and bleeding from where a crow had pecked away at him. "That damn bird about took my ear off."

His friend, Clyde, bragged half-heartedly. "Lucky it was just your ear… I'm damn lucky to be alive."

Hank slid out from his hiding place near the beer keg. He picked up his prized Stetson that had been knocked off in the flurry and smacked the dirt from his hat – then hustled over to the sheriff.

"Heard tell the Indians and crows are in cahoots. My dad swears those Injuns are downright crazy. He saw some crows swarming around their rez a while back and do some witchcraft stuff when he ran into a chief on their lands. That shit got him twitchin' and a shakin'… scared the hell right outa him and he took off like a bat outa hell. The demon crows were chasing right behind… my dad hasn't been back there since."

Sheriff Joe cut him off, furious. "So, you're telling me it was witchcraft? You think that's what happened, Hank? Witchcraft? Maybe those crows got into some kind of poison you ranchers like to put out that made them go crazy. I say, forget about those blasted birds. We need to be on the lookout for those two sneaky felons. Can't have gone too far yet… unless they magically flew off with those nasty birds." Gathering his thoughts, the sheriff straightened his holster and took command. "Deputy Ben. You take the south end of town and scour every inch of it. Hank, you patrol the northern sector on the outskirts. I'll start in town, knocking on every door – see if anyone is hiding them. It shouldn't take long – they're handcuffed and on foot."

"Yes sir, boss," said Deputy Ben.

"Get right on it," Hank nodded and took off in his truck.

Sheriff Joe cut a path down the wooden sidewalk, huffing with fury. *This was supposed to be a grand day, a celebration. Let the townsfolk see how I handle thievery in our midst... especially by a redskin and a half-breed. I'm so mad I could kill 'em with my bare hands, then I'll string 'em up for those crows to peck. Bastards won't make a fool of me again. And whoever might be hiding them, I'll string them up, too.* Fuming, he kicked a post with his boot as he strode on and peered inside windows and rattled doors to see if any stores were open. As he walked past the barbershop, he saw a couple of ranch hands inside, talking with the barber.

He stepped inside and took off his hat. "Hello, fellas. You seen any sign of those felons skulking around?"

"No sir, sheriff," A lanky young ranch hand said, "If'n I do, I'll shoot 'em... if you like."

"Well, that's mighty thoughtful of you but I'd just as soon handle this matter myself. Just let me know if you get wind of anything suspicious or see them," Sheriff Joe said, tipping his hat.

"Say, Sheriff, that was really something, huh? Never seen anything like that before... a flock of crows like that so huge, I swear covered the sky," the barber said, sharpening his scissors. "Can I crop your hair a bit while you're here? It's getting a bit unruly, and it'll only take a minute."

"No, thanks. I've got work to do... felons on the loose an all. My job always take precedent. Maybe next week. Just need everyone to keep their eyes sharp and let me know if you see anything peculiar."

The barber said, "Will do, sheriff. Think you might need to find out where all those crows came from, though. The town's kinda spooked..."

Sheriff Joe nodded his head and walked out the door and continued down the street. He stopped at the gas station and checked out the entire building – including the restroom, parked cars, and garage. While he scanned every square inch inside the empty building, a strange feeling crept over him – and an unsettling sound buzzed past. *Must be from all the chaos earlier*, he thought, swatting his beefy hands over his face.

Next, he walked a bit further down the street, heading toward the mercantile. As he neared, a faint smell of fish wafted past. *Bet they're cooking up some real nasty shit,* he thought viscously. He couldn't stomach those kikes. He thought they were "a blight on the community." On the other hand, there were those hefty monthly paychecks… always on time too.

Sheriff Joe banged opened the door to the mercantile. It was quiet and no one was at the counter, so he pounded on the bell. "Any Jews home?" he asked, sniffing the air. "Or ya eating that foul-tasting 'mazza balls soup' you try to push off on people? That kinda stuff don't sit well with me."

Norman came hustling out of the back, and his face blanched at the sight of the sheriff. He asked as calmly as he could. "Good day sheriff. May I be of assistance to you? Perhaps a tasty rump roast that Gilda just cooked, or perhaps some…"

The sheriff interrupted. "I'm not here for supplies. And, if I want a rump roast, I'll get it from one of the ladies in town. What I want to know is if you or your 'old hen' have seen those two felons that escaped a while ago… and under some pretty strange circumstances, I might add. A huge flock of crows that no ones ever seen before, flew into town like a battering storm and disrupted the hanging. Then they disappeared. Now, I suspect you might be a little sympathetic to those two… being from a Jew tribe, an' all."

Norman felt beads of perspiration pop on his forehead, then slowly drip down his face and onto his trembling lips. "We've seen no one, Sheriff," he squeaked out. "And we've been here all morning."

The sheriff stared at Norman with merciless eyes. Noticing his tremors Sheriff Joe stuck his face close to the nervous man and queried. "You seem a little jittery. You hiding something from me? I can smell fear a mile off and spot a liar just as well. And if you're aiding and abetting those criminals, I'll string you up right along with them. So, you best be straight with me." The sheriff thrust out his chest. "I run this here town, so don't lie or play games with me. I ain't in a playing mood. Now let's get your wife out here and see what she has to say. She might be a little more prone to telling the truth, you piss-ant."

Norman froze, staring at the man.

"Get your wife out here!" Sheriff Joe boomed. "And I mean now!"

Norman was so flustered he could barely talk as he ran toward the back. "G-Gilda, d-dear. Could you come out here? The sheriff wants to speak to you."

Gilda wiped her hands on her apron, took a deep breath, and collected herself. She walked out of the bakery bringing a freshly baked strudel with her – its tantalizing aroma wafting behind. Every weekend she baked an assortment of cakes, cookies, pies, and strudel – and they were all sold-out by the end of the day. She took another deep breath and stepped out into the front with a forced smile. "Good day to you, Sheriff. I brought you a fresh strudel – apple," she said carefully.

"I'm not here for strudel, Mrs. Hershel. I just want to know if you're hiding any fugitives in here?" He stared at Gilda, watching her every twitch.

Gilda swallowed hard then breathed out and said, "This is my baking day, Sheriff, and thus far I have neither seen nor heard anything afoul – and, of course, if I did see anything afoul, I would notify you immediately. We are law abiding citizens." She hid her shaking hands in her apron pocket… and desperately tried to hide her fear and loathing for the man.

"Well, I would still like to take a look around your shop… which you people practically stole…"

Gilda had to bite her tongue to not respond to the man. Instead, she said politely. "Of course, Sheriff. Please look around all you like. We have nothing to hide."

Norman ushered the sheriff through the adjoining rooms, walking past the bakery and hardware and into the feed supply section.

Gilda's heart skipped a few beats as she followed the sheriff and her husband. She prayed there wouldn't be any unexpected noise from below. Trying to keep her voice steady and her nerves intact, she inquired, "Is there anything in particular you want to see?"

"I wanna know if you have a secret cellar or hidden door that they might have slipped into… without your knowing, of course." The sheriff replied with heavy sarcasm. "This room looks the most likely for someone to hide out in." His eyes carefully searched every corner and door of the large space for loose floorboards, or a secret door. He looked in between the bags of grain, and aisles of corn, rows of wheat, and bales of hay stacked against the wall. He kicked the loose hay around the floor with his pointed alligator boots and he shifted his holster, hand on his gun, ready to shoot anything that moved as he slowly inched his way throughout the room.

Standing still, the sheriff pondered their whereabouts. *I know they couldn't have gone far… crows or not.*

He continued investigating the area, kicking the hay around the floor, suspecting there had to be a cellar somewhere in the area. At the end of an aisle, he came to a stop, rubbed his chin, and tried to figure out where it was. Continuing his search, his boot stumbled upon the edge of a rug, covered in hay. This was it. He knew it. Hurriedly, he kicked more hay out of his way – and then shoved the stacks of grain and kicked the rug away. He spotted the handle! "Here it is!" he screamed, feeling the adrenaline rush through his body. He bent down and yanked on the handle. The door was heavy. He grunted as the door creaked then slowly opened. *Gotcha now*, he thought, giddy with visions of killing those two. He knelt on the floor on his hands and knees and peered inside the dark opening. A slight breeze wafted up and brushed against his collar. He couldn't see a thing. The cellar was shrouded in darkness. *It's black as an ace of spades down there*, he thought, inspecting the opening.

The sheriff hefted himself up and hollered out excitedly. "Get me a lantern, and be quick about it, Hershel. If I find any funny business going on down there, the whole lot of you'll be in jail for harboring fugitives."

Gilda felt her legs turn to stone. Fleeting thoughts of torture raced through her mind, as she rubbed the scars on her arm. Standing motionless, she put her hands to her mouth to hold back a scream. On the verge of collapse, she let out a gasp, when suddenly the cellar door slammed shut, trapping the sheriff's hand.

Sheriff Joe howled in pain. "Eeooowch!" He frantically tried to open the door that had entrapped his hand. He grunted and snorted in fury. Finally, he managed to lift the door just enough to pull his hand out, then cursed at Gilda. "Why the hell didn't you help me? You just stood there, watching, like you were enjoying it," he fumed, wishing he could strangle her.

Gilda concealed her trembling hands and managed to get a few words out. "I-I'm sorry, Sheriff. I was so shocked by what happened, it… it caught me off guard."

The sheriff growled, not believing her. "And where the hell is your husband?"

"He… he must be out front… waiting on a customer," she said in a strained voice.

"If I thought any of this was intentional, I'd…"

Gilda finally found her strength and resolve. She looked him directly in the eyes and said, "I did not cause this. How on earth would I know that the cellar door was stuck?"

"Because you people are devious, that's why. I'm going down

in the cellar, that you claimed wasn't there. And when I get back up from looking around, I want answers. And if I find those two felons, you're going to jail. Now get me a light!"

Norman came racing into the room. "I'm sorry. I had a customer to attend to…"

"Just get me a blasted lantern or something!" Sheriff Joe screeched. "I'm in a hurry."

Norman did as he was told and hustled back with a lantern in hand and lit it for the sheriff.

This time when Sheriff Joe yanked on the cellar door, it opened with ease, and he almost toppled over. He checked the hinges, puzzled, then inched his way down the steps cautiously, holding the lantern high. After the first couple of steps, he thought he heard a faint groan. The hackles on his neck rose. Then a sudden breeze whooshed through the cellar. His skin prickled. He thought, *a window must be open.* He paused, and for some reason, it unsettled him. He slowly eased his bulky frame back down the ladder. *Something's fishy going on down here*, he thought, *and I'm going to find out what it is.* As he stepped onto the ground, he held the lantern high and saw a silvery shadow flicker on the wall. His whole body tightened. A crackle of energy shot up his back and he thought in glee, *it's those two felons. Got 'em now.* Gun pulled, he looked around the room, slowly inching forward, then in a flash… the image was gone. "Damn," he muttered. "Where the hell did they…" his words died off as a sudden blast of icy air froze on his lips, and his teeth began to chatter. The icy wind encircled his legs in a freezing grip, and he shivered from head to toe. He was not a man that frightened easily, but this – whatever this was – scared the daylights out of him.

He steadied his gun, and hissed, "Whoever you are… you lousy Indians… you're gonna be dead. He fired off a couple rounds as the bullets ricocheted around the room and one whizzed right past his ear. "Damn it!" he swore, as he ducked.

He tentatively inched his way further into the darkness, still shivering, and held the lantern high. Then he heard a weird sound. He tilted his head and listened. It was like beaks clacking. At first it was subtle, then the sound of clacking beaks intensified. Then the clacking sound stopped, as if warning him. He remained still for a few minutes, waiting, then slowly moved his feet forward. Nothing happened – until, suddenly, the clacking sound started again and boomed so loud that it shook the room. He stopped dead in his tracks and quickly covered his ears to drown the sound out. He fell to his knees in fright and looked cautiously into the shadows. The air hummed a foreboding warning. He leaned back and moaned, "Oh, no!" He saw beady red eyes glaring at him… blinding him with their pulsing beam of light that seemed to mock him. Not bothering to aim, he simply cocked the trigger and fired at the beady red eyes. He wasn't sure where the bullets landed and didn't really care. He just wanted to get out of this place.

Then the beam of light surged, turning his gun into a red-hot piece of iron. He gasped as the gun burned his hand and dropped it to the ground. Another blast went off in the darkness. He backed away, shaken, picked up his smoldering gun, and fled up the ladder as fast as his bulky frame would take him. He saw the Hershels standing nearby… staring at him in alarm.

Pale and stunned, Sheriff Joe gathered his wits and tried to convince himself that what had just happened was all in his imagination. He glared at the Hershels and pointed to the cellar. "What the hell do you have down there – the Devil's sidekick? I'll tell ya, it's something wicked… and you're probably in league with it. If I find out you've had anything to do with *any* of this… this… malarkey, I'll hang you myself. It would be good riddance, too."

Sheriff Joe gingerly touched his gun, which was still hot… a tinge of smoke coming from the barrel. He glared at the Hershels and snarled. "I'll be back," he threatened, and stomped out of the store, slamming the door so hard, the glass wobbled.

Bewildered by the sheriff's behavior, Gilda tentatively peered down into the cellar and called out softly. "Oliver. Sam. Are you down there?"

A huge crow with yellow eyes fluttered up, beating its wings lightly, and flew over to a small opening by the door – then, sailed off into the sky.

Oliver answered calmly. "Yes, we are here… we were lucky this time… had a little help, but too dangerous for us to stay much longer. We'll leave as soon as it gets dark."

Gilda was simultaneously relieved and sad. She wanted very much to help the two boys, but she knew if they got caught, it would wreak havoc on her family, and they would most likely perish with them. Her husband and she had been through so much in that awful camp, but she also knew that hatred has many faces. Before walking away, she said, "I will make a nice bag of food for your trip."

Norman peered down to the boys and said, "And, don't worry about those handcuffs… I'll be down in a minute to get those things off you." Then he closed the cellar door and he and Gilda sank to the floor. Hugging her tightly, he said, "We'll get through this, my dear."

*

Meanwhile, the sheriff was on a rampage through town – banging down doors and ranting at whomever crossed his path. When he reached the church, he stormed through the entrance, sweating profusely. At the sight of his daughter and her friends in the company of that 'damn pastor,' he shouted belligerently. "Nice little party I see… why aren't you out there with the other townsfolk, helping to find the felons? And you, pastor – if one could call you that!" He said, pointing a beefy finger at the girls, "What's the meaning of this… serving drinks to these girls in the House of the Lord. Doesn't exactly look good for you. Your job is to keep the lechers from straying too far from the words in the Bible… spouting goodwill, and all. Not corrupting our young and innocent." The sheriff walked up to Percy and stood nose to nose. "I've got a real good suspicion you've been a might too sympathetic to that Injun and half-breed. You hiding those fugitives in here, Percy? I'll have your hide and then some if I catch wind that you are." He ground his thumb into the preacher's chest and practically foamed at the mouth while bits of saliva sailed across the room. "Just know… I've got my eyes on you."

"I pray to all that are in need, sheriff. As for the girls… everyone was in distress, and I thought a little whiskey might calm their nerves… can be God's remedy in frightening times like these…."

Sheriff Joe grunted his displeasure and looked over at his daughter and said, "Why don't you do something useful, like answer the phones in my office while I'm out looking for those runaways?" Then he glared derisively at Janet. "Why don't you scoot on home and eat some of your un-American food," he smirked. Finally, his glance landed on Sally and his voice softened slightly. "Now, Sally. I hope you're not involved in of any this skullduggery stuff around here… I'd be very disappointed if you were." He looked at each of them in the eyes. "Now! I hate to break up this little gathering, pastor, but I have a gut feeling you might be plotting something – especially the way you looked when I walked in… which was guilty as Hell. I can spot a lying mug a mile off."

Percy's throat constricted. Then he let off a long slow breath and said calmly. "We were gathering here in friendship and comfort, not plotting anything, Sheriff. And that is the Gospel." He lied without a blink and stared directly into the sheriff's glaring eyes.

"Well, best not be plotting. If I can't trust the pastor of this town, who can I trust?" the sheriff said derisively, while walking through the church, checking closed doors and peeking under the pews. "I'll just say it again. If I catch anyone helping those two escapees, you'll end up in a heap of trouble. So best keep your noses clean."

Percy forced a smile and said, "I assure you – I will let you know if I see anything." He looked at Sally and said, "I'll be happy to walk you home Sally… must be watchful of any suspicious happenings."

The sheriff grunted. "I think you've done enough, Pastor. I'll take Sally home. You best concern yourself with your next sermon… and it better be a whole heap better than your last one. You were a disgrace to our congregation and to the Lord." He turned to Sally and grabbed her arm, "Come along."

Sally was shaking in fear. She was not a good liar, and thought, *what if he asks me questions? What will I say?*

Percy sensed her hesitation and fear. So, he put his hand on her arm and squeezed tight. "Stay strong, sayeth the Lord and have faith. All will be shown in divine time." He smiled at Sally, trying to give her courage.

The sheriff pulled Sally along and walked her out the door. "I'll say it again. You best let me know if you see or hear anything."

With Indigo and Janet leaving, as well, Percy was left with mixed emotions, watching Sally go. He was surprised by his feelings toward the girl, who seemed lost and at odds with the church and its teachings. He was at odds, himself, as he looked out the window and heard gunshots in the streets. People were firing their guns while carrying drinks as they meandered down Main Street and onto the side streets. It was early, and some folks were already drunk – chatting excitedly about the unusual events that happened earlier at "the hanging tree."

As they were walking down the street, Jake spotted a large crow up ahead. He said in between gulps of beer. "Look at the big ass thing, sitting on that lamp post. Gonna be a goner."

The crow let off a raucous caw that sounded more like a jeer, as the bird noisily clacked its beak.

Jake pulled out his pistol and said, "I'm gonna shoot that thing, dead. Watch me." So, he fired a few shots in the air – missing the bird but hitting the lamppost and knocking out the light. The broken glass splattered across the sidewalk and the crow dove off with lightning speed – disappearing into the trees. Then, seemingly from nowhere, the bird reappeared and flew directly above Austin's head where it dropped a big splat on his hat. Clyde bent over laughing unable to hold back his glee and slapped his knee. "Like I told ya, Jake. You're full of shit… and look what happens."

Jake whacked his hat on the post, trying to knock off the bird droppings, fuming. "Ever since that Indian and that Hollyhoo guy came to town, all kinds of weird shit started happening… bringing a whole heap of trouble with them."

"We need to send for John Wayne. Now he's a guy who could ride into town and catch a crook in a shake of a lamb's tail," Clyde bragged, and let off a bark of laughter.

"Well, I like that Custer dude. There's pictures of him all over town – got the guy plastered in the courthouse and a great big one in the sheriff's office."

The two guys walked back into the Blue Sky Saloon, still arguing who they liked better.

Everyone was still trying to piece together earlier events – and most wondered aloud, "What the hell happened?"

The sheriff's temper flared at the turn of events. *Can't have people doubting me*, he thought, and that he couldn't abide. So as evening approached, and there was still no sign of those two convicts, he became enraged. He had everyone on the lookout, barking out orders, " I want every road, alley, house, barn, and train searched or under surveillance." But, still, not a peep about Oliver and Sam. *It's as if those two just up and vanished,* he thought. *But that couldn't be… Someone had to have helped those bastards.*

He had retraced every detail in his mind. The only thing that made sense, he thought, it had to be those *Jews*. He was getting angrier by the moment. *I just know it.* He wanted to go back to that cellar of theirs and take another look around. This time more closely. But that cellar gave him the heebie-jeebies. *He'd be damned if he showed any signs of fear.* In this town, he was the man people feared – looked up to – and he wanted to keep it that way. Then an idea struck him. *I'll send Ben over there. He can go through that cellar. Let's see what happens to him, down there… see if he sees any-thing strange. He's handy with a gun, and he ought to be since that's all he does all day long – shoot cans, sit in the office on his ass, go out on an occasional dispute. And, in between, he shoots more cans. Let him earn his wages, for a change.*

Dusk was setting in as rounds of shots ricocheted in the streets. People were shooting at anything that resembled crows or Indians. He thought he had better calm things down before they spun out of control, and they shot someone they hadn't intended to shoot.

But first, he headed over to his office to see if any leads had come in on the case. He saw Indigo sitting inside… sulking. Brac-ing himself for a confrontation with his headstrong daughter, as he walked inside where Indigo welcomed him with a glare. *Damn, she's a pistol,* he thought. His life would be easier if she got her ass out of town. *Can't wait for that day to come.*

He tried being polite and asked through gritted teeth. "Any calls or leads on the felons?"

"Just your usual jerks making up stories."

"What stories?"

"Heard some assholes want to go out to the reservation and shoot up the place… kill some Indians."

"Who says that?" the sheriff asked.

"The barber," replied Indigo."

"Well, who is it threatening to do that?"

"*You* know… Jake Austin and his ass-wipe buddy, Barnes. The real educated ones, that make stuff up," Indigo fumed. "And I can't believe they still talk about that creep, Custer, either. I guess they think they're real wild cowboys out to 'tame the west.' Real nice town, Sheriff." Indigo spat out.

"Well, it *is* a nice town," the sheriff said, puffing up his chest. "I keep the streets safe for women and children, and I keep out the trouble-makers. Like the ones I'm gonna hang, soon as I find them – and find them I will. You can bet your sweet behind on that, dear. Now, mind your manners, and stay out of trouble… not so sure about you hanging out with that pastor, either."

Sheriff Joe grabbed his bullhorn, walked out the front door and slammed it behind him. Lifting the bullhorn to his mouth, he yelled out his directive. "Time to stop the shooting before some-one gets killed. Put your guns away." He waited a moment, ready to holler a little more forceful next time. Most folks grumbled, but all complied and soon enough disbursed – mostly in the direction of the barbecue. That settled, he set out to find his deputy. Winding his way through the streets he passed by the Blue Sky Saloon. He stopped and looked at his watch and thought, *It's past five already. This has been one helluva day and I could use a drink.*

He walked past the barbecue and the hordes of people, stop-ping for a quick "howdy," glad everyone was having a grand ole time and most were pretty drunk by now. He swung open the door and walked inside the saloon, and quickly covered his ears against the blaring sound of guitars screeching. "What is this godawful tune playing on the jukebox?" he seethed. How he hated that hippie shit! As he walked up to the bar, he about ruptured a vessel as he saw Randy, feet up, strumming his guitar – like he didn't have a care in the world.

Sheriff Joe knocked Randy's feet off the bar and hollered over the loud music. "That shit is so loud, my ears are about to burst. You know I can't abide that kinda hippie stuff. Turn that crap off before I break every damn record in the jukebox. This is about the umpteenth time I told you," he said with a glare. "I don't want to tell you again, either."

Randy hopped up, ran over to the jukebox, and quickly put on a country tune.

"That's more like it," the sheriff said, still riled. "Good all-American music that folks like to listen to. Now this, you can understand what they're singing about. Why don't you strum along to *that*, instead of the shit you were playing earlier?" He banged his fist on the bar. "Now get me a drink."

The Blue Sky Saloon wasn't too busy yet. Most folks were either at the barbecue or lounging around outside on this balmy summer night, leaning against their pickup trucks, talking about ranching and the weather forecast for the following week – and of course, the mishap earlier and "those blasted crows." Tongues were wagging like crazy as everyone tried to spin a different tale.

"You seen my deputy around, lately?" the sheriff asked Randy, annoyed that he hadn't seen him since this morning.

"No, sir. Last I saw, he took off driving south outa town. Most likely looking around for the Injun and his cohort. What do you suppose happened to them?"

"I got my suspicions," sheriff said, taking a long drink. "Who ever helped them is gonna be in a big heap of trouble."

Soon, people were drifting into the bar and things started to rock.

Hank Jr. walked into the bar around seven with a shaken Sally sporting a fresh black eye and a cut lip. Hank shoved her into a chair near the jukebox and walked up to the sheriff. "I might be able to help crack the case for you. This little tramp here's acting suspicious like. She seemed real nervous when I asked her about those convicts. I gave her a bit of a punch to get her to talk, but she started crying like a baby. So, I'm gonna try again later… use another tactic on her… maybe have ta get a little rough."

Sheriff Joe looked over at Sally who was slumped in the chair. "Whatever you have to do to bring justice will be fine by me."

"I'll get it handled, sheriff," Hank grinned and ordered a drink from Randy.

A while later, Percy walked into the bar, at first unnoticed, squinted his eyes and looked around the dimly lit room. His eyes widened as he spotted Sally sitting by herself at a table and was ready to walk over when the sheriff spotted him and yelled loudly, "Say, pastor. Shouldn't you be at the church saving souls… or maybe working on your Sunday sermon? Sure the shit could use it," he guffawed at his remark. "I don't think frequenting a bar is setting a good example for the locals. You need to be in the House of The Lord, where you can be in touch with the 'Big Guy'… up there." He indicated, pointing upward.

"The Lord doesn't mind where I go, as long as I have Him with me in my heart," Percy replied, with a newfound verve. "Besides, you never know who I might convert in the most unlikely of places." Percy hustled over to the table where a frightened Sally was seated. She tried without success to hide her battered face. His eyes widened in shock. "What in the world happened, Sally?" He turned her face around and frowned at the sight of her black eye and cut lip. "Who in God's name did this to you?" Percy was livid. "I bet that…" He was interrupted by a slight shove.

"Pardon me, pastor. I think you're barking up the wrong tree. Now, skedaddle. Me and the little wh… I mean, little lady… have some unfinished business to get at." Hank promptly sat down, and glared at Percy, almost daring him to interfere.

Hank, ready to take a slug of whiskey nearly choked on his drink when he saw the preacher raise his fist and cry out. "Abuse will not be tolerated by me or by the Lord," he shouted, a little more bravely than he felt. "He would frown on your behavior and call it, 'a most grievous sin.'"

Hank let out a loud snort. "Now, pastor. I don't want to hurt you, but if you don't take your scrawny ass outa here, I'm gonna throw…"

Wham! Percy landed his boney fist alongside Hank's chin with enough force to swivel Hank's neck a good one. Adrenaline rushed through Percy's veins, spurring him on, and before a stunned Hank could react, Percy landed another blow… this time connecting with Hank's Adam's apple.

Hank shoved his chair back and bowled over choking in disbelief.

Percy looked at his fist in amazement. "The hand of the Lord shall smite the evildoer." Smiling, he went to Sally and grabbed her arm. "Let's go!"

Sally hesitated, looking at Hank – hating and wanting him at the same time.

Percy pleaded. "We must get out of here before Hank hurts you even more. Please."

Hank recovered from his shock and in one long stride, grabbed Percy around the neck – lifting him off the ground with one hand, and with the other hand balled into a fist, he was ready to knock his teeth out. "I'm gonna teach you a thing or two about turning the other cheek, pastor," Hank snarled. But before he could swing, a normally meek and mild-mannered handyman, Dick Vincent, spoke up. "You can't hit the preacher, Hank. He's a man of God."

"Well, now, just watch me," Hank said, grinning wickedly. "Show you how it's done!" He slammed his fist into Percy's stomach and Percy doubled over, gasping for breath and in pain. Then Hank walloped him on the side of his head, foregoing his teeth.

Percy fell to his knees. Hank hit him again and he flew forward, skidding on the floor and landed against a table, wheezing… he felt a rib crack.

Dick's face burned with disgust, and instinctively jumped into action. He struck Hank across the back of his head with his long neck, beer bottle sending glass shattering down Hank's shirt, along with his blood. Hank shook his head, looking stunned. Then an all-out brawl started. A few cowboys staggered in the door and shouted, "fight," and jumped into the middle of the action. Soon the whole bar erupted into chaos.

Percy managed to get up and deftly dodged the wild punches being thrown every which way. His ribs ached and he wasn't anxious to get hit again.

Sally noticed Percy's injury and ran over to help him. They managed to get out the door together, as fists and boots and bottles were flying haphazardly across the room.

Once outside, Sally broke down and sobbed. "I'm so sorry. I seem to cause trouble wherever I go. Guess my dad was right... I'm just no good."

"I want to be your friend and help you, Sally," Percy said kindly, catching his breath while holding his stomach. "I can't let Hank bully you anymore," he wheezed out. "You have to remain strong, and, most importantly, you are far better a person than you give yourself credit for. I think you're... well... really quite wonderful. Now remember, you can't say anything about Oliver and Sam. We must keep them safe until they have a chance to leave this place. If not... he let his words trail off, unable to comprehend the consequences."

The sheriff watched Percy and Sally leave and chuckled to himself. He couldn't believe that Percy had the balls to go at it with Hank. *I wished Hank would've knocked the shit outa that pastor. Set him straight on what's what around here... acting like a real jackass at church service. Best not try any of that horse crap again, or I'll cut him a new one. And what's he doing with that Sally? I'll get to her later.*

Sheriff Joe was about ready to put a cork in the brawl. He didn't mind that the boys let off a little steam, once in a while. Looked like a good fight and he was itching to get into the thick of it... but he was the law... and supposed to be above all that. So, he sat and watched, lit one of his fine Cubans and sipped his drink for a while, enjoying the spectacle.

Then things started to get out of hand, so Sheriff Joe made his way to the front door and rang the bell furiously, until he got everyone's attention. "That's enough, boys," he shouted. "Settle down now and get a drink. I don't want to lock anyone up tonight."

Soon, everyone complied and stumbled back to their seats, holding their sore jaws, bloodied lips, and torn hats, ready for more drinks. Someone turned up the jukebox and the mood suddenly switched to a party-like atmosphere.

Deputy Ben entered the bar looking rumpled and found the sheriff. "I've been driving down every road I passed and even stopped at a few farmhouses and ranches. No one's seen hide nor hair of those two felons. Not a blasted thing. You know if I had caught sight of them, I would've shot 'em deader than dead." Ben shifted his gun belt and said, "I swear, I don't know what the dickens happened earlier with those crows and stuff. Just thinking about them gives me the willies." He looked at the sheriff who was watching him with fury in his eyes and added nervously. "I could sure use a long, tall drink right about now. I'm about as parched as that pavement I was driving on." He knocked on the bar to get Randy's attention. "Get me a real cold brew. It's hot as hell out there."

The sheriff shifted in his seat and said, "Before you get yourself a big, tall brew, why don't you head on over to the Jews' place. They've got a cellar in there, and I want you to scour every square inch of it. See if they're up to any funny business… like harboring those felons."

Reluctantly Ben stood up, licking his lips, itching for a beer, and said, "Yes, boss." He headed out the door. As his boots clunked heavily on the wooden boards, he muttered to himself. "Damn. I'm one tired hombre."

A few long blocks down the street, he reached the mercantile store and jiggled the door handle. It was locked. He jiggled it again… a little more forcefully. "Open up. It's Deputy Ben Willis. Sheriff wants me to come in and take a look around."

He didn't hear a reply, so he shouted louder this time. "Hurry up, before I blow a hole in your door." He shook the door again.

Gilda peered out a window, and said, "We're closed for the day, Deputy. Come back tomorrow. Please."

Ben rattled the door again, thoroughly agitated. "Open up! Police business. Sheriff wants me to come in and take a gander in your cellar. See if you Jews are up to some funny business."

Gilda stalled and said, "Just a moment, please." A rustling of feet followed, along with a series of hushed whispers.

"Say, what's going on in there?" Ben demanded, shaking the door furiously.

Pale and visibly shaken, Gilda finally swung the door open, her eyes closed momentarily, trying to hold her emotions in check. She then spoke in a calm voice. "Come in, Deputy. The cellar is through here." She led him past the bakery and into the feed supply room. "The sheriff has already been down there once today. You're welcome to look around again." She pulled up the cellar door, and said, "The stairs are a bit rickety, so watch your step, Deputy." Gilda held her breath as she waited for him to go down.

Deputy Ben hesitated and pulled out his guns and looked around the store suspiciously. "I want to know what took you so long to answer the door… an' what the devil's going on in here? I heard voices whispering… then it sounded like a bunch of people running. You'd best come clean, or I'll take you to the sheriff's office and lock you up for lying. He thinks you're a sneaky bunch over here, so let's have it. Who ya hiding?"

Having overheard the deputy, Janet hurried into the room, with Percy and Sally right behind. Janet quickly intervened and answered for her mother, who was on the verge of tears.

"Hello, Ben," she said sweetly, sliding between him and her mother. "Are you looking for some nice fresh scones we just baked earlier today?"

"It's Deputy Ben, to you." He replied annoyed by the girl.

"And no, I don't want any of those scones. I wanna know where the skins are. Sheriff thinks you're hiding them in here."

"Don't be ridiculous 'Deputy Ben. We're not hiding anyone or anything. And if you heard voices… it was us you must have heard talking. Didn't mean to make you nervous or suspicious. There's been a lot going on today, and the towns going crazy. There was a big brawl at the bar earlier and the pastor was injured. He needed some bandages, so I helped him out. Feel free to look around… again. Accusing us of harboring fugitives… dear me, Deputy Ben, that would be against the law."

"Just doing my job is all," Ben said in his defense.

"Here's a lantern," Janet offered. "Careful down there… It's pretty dark in the cellar. Be a shame to have you trip," she said, holding back a smile.

Ben snapped the lantern out of her hand, and started down the steps, slowly. The glow from the lantern cast eerie shadows in the darkness, so he stopped halfway down. His skin prickled… a feeling of dread followed. His thoughts went wild and wondered what was down there. Hesitating, he tentatively took a few more steps – then suddenly, he heard the cellar door bang shut.

Upstairs, a smile danced upon Janet's face, as she covered the cellar door with the rug, and brushing the hay from her hands.

"What the hell is going on up there?" Deputy Ben screamed in alarm, as a buzzing noise encircled him, and he swatted wildly. Then a moment later a sizzling sound whoosh zoomed past… something bit his leg. He banged on the door in fright. "Let me out! Something wicked 's down here."

Gilda was almost faint with fear as she handed a large satchel to Percy.

"You best get me out of here or I'll start firing," Ben shrieked, pounding furiously on the door. "Open the door!" Suddenly, his hands were glued to his side. He thought for a moment that he might faint and swore he saw eyes glowing in the dark… eerie and haunting.

Percy hurried to the back of the store behind a stack of hay where Oliver and Sam were waiting, and he handed them the satchel.

"Godspeed, the two of you. May He watch over you on your journey," said Percy solemnly, holding back tears.

Gilda and Norman arrived to bid Oliver and Sam goodbye. The two young men looked at everyone gratefully. Gilda hugged them both, and they responded. "No words can express our gratitude. Thank you for your kindness and bravery, Mrs. Hershel," Oliver said softly.

"You saved our lives, and you and your husband will never be forgotten," Sam said, kissing Gilda's cheek.

Gilda wiped away a tear and pulled out some money from her pocket. "Here, take this. It's not much, but it might come in handy on your journey."

Norman hugged both men and bid them farewell.

A mournful shrieking was coming from beneath the cellar door. "Help me," Deputy Ben pleaded. "I don't want to die down here amongst the wicked." He let out a sob.

Janet smiled.

"We'd better hurry," Oliver said, hugging Percy and Sally before racing out the back door.

"Be safe," everyone mouthed, watching with fearful eyes as the two slid out the door.

Dusk was settling in, and Indigo was outside waiting for them. She ran up to Sam and whispered, "It was like a dream meeting you." She kissed him softly on the mouth.

"Thank you, Indigo," Sam whispered in her ear. "You are so lovely."

"Can you tell me where you are going? It won't be safe out there. The sheriff will be looking everywhere for you and Oliver."

My Aunt Alice and Uncle Fred live near Brighton. We'll stay there until we can figure a way out of this mess. It's around seventy miles or so from here."

"I hope one day to see you again, but I am grateful you're both alive," Indigo said. "Remember, we will always be here to help." She pulled a piece of paper from a pocket. "Here's my phone number… but be careful if you call. We have open lines where people can listen in. Might be dangerous."

Indigo hugged Sam again, barely able to let him go. She could feel his heart race as they held each other. A flurry of noise inside, jarred Indigo out of her reverie.

Oliver said, "We must hurry!"

Sam reluctantly let go of the red-headed beauty. "Goodbye, Indigo." Then the two sped off into the night.

Indigo whispered after them, "Please be careful."

She waited a moment before hurrying back inside, and heard the deputy plead for help.

"I'm trying, Ben, but the door seems stuck. Give me a minute," said Janet, who was normally reserved but stood valiantly guarding the locked door – waiting to see that Oliver and Sam had made it out the back safely.

Indigo saw Janet waiting and nodded her head, indicating all was clear.

Janet waited another minute or so before she opened the cellar door. Everyone seemed to hold their breath, partly from fright, but mostly from elation – knowing they helped save the two men from certain death.

Janet finally opened the cellar door and spoke sweetly to Ben. "Was there a problem down there, Deputy?"

Deputy Ben looked pale and frightened, then with a suspicious sideways squint, he shrugged his shoulders and found he could move his hands.

"So sorry we didn't hear you. We were on the other side of the store. Oh, and that door… I guess it tends to stick on occasion… did the same to the sheriff. I hope it didn't frighten you." She held out her hand to help him up the steps, but he smacked it away and gathered his strength, hauled himself up and burst out of the cellar, sweating furiously. His disheveled hair stood on end, and he looked frightened as he drew out both his guns and pointed them at the Hershels. "I know you're up to something here," he said with a growl. "I should lock up the whole bunch of you. Had something to do with those felons I bet. You just wait 'till I tell the sheriff."

"The only ones we were trying to help is you Deputy Ben," said Janet with a straight face. "Sorry you got locked down there."

"Sorry, my ass. I don't believe any of you," Deputy Ben's face was brimming with fury.

"We'd better get that door fixed right away," Janet added.

"I still think you were up to something… I'd bet my shirt on it," he said with a snort. "And you got something mighty wicked down there that blew out my lantern, so you're lucky I don't shoot the whole bunch of you for lying and interfering in police business," he rambled.

The Hershels stared in dismay at the frenzied deputy.

"Put away your guns, Ben," Indigo said, stomping up to him. "What's wrong with you… threatening these people?"

"I'll tell you what's wrong with me," he said. "These people got the evil eye. I can see it and I don't like it one bit."

"Look," Janet said calmly, looking directly at the deputy. "The cellar door was stuck. I told you it does that sometimes. There was nothing down there earlier, and there's nothing down there now, so I'll go back down there with you, if you want, and I'll show you."

"What I want is for you to show me where the two felons are hiding at," Ben said. He was so angry his hands shook, and he could barely hold his gun steady.

"Walk around the entire place, if you don't believe us," Janet said, defiantly. "We have nothing to hide from you."

Percy walked up to the deputy to try to calm him down. "What you say is terrible… accusing the Hershels, who have done nothing more than help me in my time of need. So, forgive us if we didn't hear your cries for help." Then he smiled. "The darkness can be truly frightening. If you came to church more often, you would know there is no reason to fear the darkness. The Lord protects us in our times of need."

"What do you know about anything? You're a lousy pastor to boot, so don't go lecturing me about the church or my job. And look at you, hanging out with ole trailer trash, a Jew and the sheriff's daughter, that's got a vile mouth on her.

Indigo heard Ben's comment and yelled at him. "How dare you talk like that? Why don't you shut up, and get out of here?"

Ben glared at Indigo. "You should be ashamed. What kind of daughter are you, anyways? Sheriff Joe took you in and gave you all you needed. You're a traitor to him."

"I'll show you what kind of daughter I am." Indigo swung a bag of oats at Ben, knocking him on the back of his head.

Ben staggered backwards from the blow. "You little witch! You've been tainted with the evil eye. No wonder your father thinks…"

Indigo wasn't finished and banged him again with the bag of oats. "I think you should leave while you can still walk. Get out." She shoved him toward the door.

It took all of Deputy Ben's willpower to keep himself from shooting her. He slid his gun into his holster and slammed out the door. "I'll be back."

CHAPTER ELEVEN

AUNT ALICE AND UNCLE FRED

SAM AND OLIVER raced off into the dusky night, slipped into the shadows and melded into the darkness – heading north. They had around seventy miles to go, not far from the South Dakota border. Fighting the urge to panic, Sam followed Oliver, who seemed instinctively to know the way. They stayed off the main road and didn't speak for hours, as they needed to be alert to any sound or movement. Sheriff Joe would have everyone searching for them and Oliver was determined to get away. He wasn't going to end up like his father, where no one would ever learn what happened to him. So, he kept up a grueling pace, and walked and ran until Sam, out of breath, could no longer follow.

"Do you mind if we rest a minute?" he panted

They must have gone at least fifteen miles or better, but not nearly far enough in Oliver's estimation. It was getting late, so Oliver relented when he found a secluded spot, a ways off the main road and under a large tree. They opened the satchel of food that Mrs. Hershel had prepared for their journey – grateful for the freshly baked bread and cheese. It tasted delicious.

Lost in their own thoughts, Oliver and Sam ate in silence.

Oliver thought about the crows that had saved their lives. He had never really believed that crows could be so powerful – more like crafty and smart, and maybe even a touch of clairvoyance. But in large groups they were a sight to behold – a real force to be reckoned with. When he was younger, his father had told him, "The crows will help protect you. They are your totem sent to you from your great-grandfather, Hidden Spirit."

Oliver thought his totem was weak. He had asked his father why he couldn't have a bear for a totem, or a wolf or mountain lion. He was ashamed now, thinking back on his shortsightedness. He wasn't convinced when his father told him that the crows are not only smart, but that they could foretell danger ahead and their intellect is almost human-like in their retention of facts and their ability to converse in multiple dialects. Oliver realized now that he should never have doubted his father.

"It's been a long day," Oliver said. When he looked over at Sam, he saw he was already asleep, with a hunk of bread still in his hand.

Oliver lay down and thought, *it's going to be a real short night. We have to be up in a few hours.*

A moment later Oliver drifted off into a troubled sleep and woke when the stars where still high in the sky. He jumped up and shook Sam, and said quietly, "It will be light in a couple hours. We need to get going." He handed Sam a hunk of cheese and some bread, "We can eat on the way. Let's go."

Thoughts of Sheriff Joe and his posse kept them moving, as they wound their way through the grassy plains and off-beaten trails. They heard sirens blowing and dogs barking in the distance – reminders they were fugitives on the run.

It had been three-and-a-half days of grueling travel since they left Miners Gulch. Oliver thought it was a small miracle they had made it, so far, undetected. Oliver knew all the back trails from when he used to hunt with his father, and he followed his instinct on the best route to take. It was with great relief that they finally made it to Sam's Aunt and Uncle's aging farm. They were both exhausted.

The two sat for a moment on a hillside overlooking the small ranch, battered by time. Sam thought that the farm seemed a little more dilapidated than what he remembered. The wraparound porch slung low with a few broken steps in the middle. The white paint was chipped and faded gray, but still showed signs of life. There was a large garden with tomatoes trailing up a pole, and stalks of corn rising high, almost ready to be plucked along with rows and rows of cucumbers, squash, and numerous other vegetables. Chickens were running around the yard squawking, and a huge red and gold rooster crowed loudly from a fence post – as if warning the hens to seek cover from intruders, since he was the keeper of the flock. A black and white Holstein cow named Pepper was contentedly grazing in the pasture. Sam smiled as he looked at the old girl, glad to see she still among the living. A rickety fence where Pepper slept looked ready to topple over in the next big storm.

It had been a while since Sam had been on this twenty-plus-acre farm where he was raised. Uncle Fred was a kind, mild-mannered man, who was completely smitten with crazy Aunt Alice. He remembered how she loved to dance around the house every afternoon while listening to the latest hit songs on the radio. Said she needed to stay sharp and practice her moves, "a stripper's job is grueling work," she used to say, going off to work in a nearby town. Uncle Fred didn't mind that she made a living 'dancing' for men… as long as she was his. Alice was Fred's life, and he was hers. She liked the freedom he gave her, and Fred liked that she came home every night.

Sam and Oliver walked slowly toward the farm and paused at the gate before going up to the house. Sam hadn't been here since he left for Los Angeles, right out of high school. The same Chevy truck was still there, as well as Aunt Alice's '69 Mustang convertible. It was rusted a little, but otherwise, in good shape. He thought the cherry red car matched Aunt Alice's nail polish and the glossy pink lipstick that was a permanent fixture on her face.

Sam inhaled deeply trying to relieve his jitters as he headed toward the porch and up the broken stairs, where he lightly rapped on the screen door that hung off its hinge. A moment later Aunt Alice peaked through the screen wearing skin-tight short-shorts, a pink halter top, and pink high-heel shoes. Her platinum blond hair was pulled back into a ponytail with a bright pink ribbon hanging down her back. Clinging to the door for support, she was at a loss for words and could only stare at the boys.

Sam finally broke the silence. "Aunt Alice. It's me… Sam. I know it's been a while since I've been here, but I'm in… a bit of trouble. *Big* trouble."

Aunt Alice closed her mouth and responded, wide-eyed and still in shock. "Sam," she whispered. "Is that really you?" She blinked back tears. "I can't believe it. It's been such a long time. I've been worried about you."

"I know I didn't call much. I wish I had a good excuse for that… but I don't. I'm sorry."

Aunt Alice recovered her shock, looked him up and down with admiration. "Well, I understand Sam. You musta been real busy in Los Angeles. I'm just glad to see you, and that you're well. You've turned into a fine young man… and real handsome to boot!" she gushed warmly.

"Aunt Alice… This is my friend, Oliver… Oliver White Cloud."

Aunt Alice turned her attention to the quiet man, who was observing the reunion.

"Well, hello and howdy-do to you," Aunt Alice said with an awkward curtsy. "What a fine-looking specimen of a man you are, I would venture to say… Indian." She stared intently at Oliver before continuing. "Are you a member of the… Cheyenne… or the Sioux tribe?"

Oliver nodded his head. "Yes. I'm from the Lakota tribe. Good guess."

"Well… you're one of the most striking Indians I've ever seen. Look at those gorgeous eyes. Blue as the ocean. I would kill for those. Get you fine self in here," Alice said, patting him on the behind. She swung open the screen door, which was ready to separate itself from the hinge holding it in place. "Your uncle has been meaning to fix this for a spell. One of these days I suppose he'll get to it." she said, brimming with happiness and welcoming the two inside.

Sam hoped that Oliver wouldn't be offended by his crazy Aunt Alice and her wild ways, and he gave him a look. But Oliver seemed just fine, so Sam glanced around the room for Uncle Fred, wondering if he was outside tending to chores, or in the kitchen cooking up one of his favorite dishes – lima beans – the bigger the better.

"Freddy, get over here and see who just walked in the door," Aunt Alice cried out excitedly.

Uncle Fred came rushing out from the kitchen, wiped his hands, and then stopped in disbelief. He dropped his towel as he hurried over to Sam and gave him a big hug. "Well, I'll be a monkey's uncle. It's so good to see you, Sam. We certainly have missed you around here. I can't tell you how much. But now, I see you're all grown up. I guess time has wings… it goes by so fast."

"I missed you, too, Uncle Fred." Sam replied with a stab of guilt, then looked at Oliver. "Uncle Fred, this is my friend, Oliver."

Uncle Fred smiled wide and extended his hand. "Hello Oliver. Any friend of Sam's is more than welcome to our home. Come on in and sit down. You boys look pretty bushed. How about some coffee, boys? Freshly made."

"I would love some. Thank you."

"Me too, Uncle Fred. If it's not too much trouble."

"You're never too much trouble, Sam. Never have been."

Uncle Fred brought over the pot and set it on the table. "Here you go, boys. There's cream and sugar right here on the table. I've just made some sourdough bread that's piping hot and a big pot of beans. Can I get you both a bowl?"

Oliver and Sam nodded enthusiastically. "Yes," they said simultaneously, while sipping on their hot coffee.

"Say, sweet cheeks. Can I fix you some lunch? A nice big bowl of beans and some of my homemade bread?"

"Good Lord, Freddy. Keep feeding me those darn things, and I'll blow a hole clean through my britches. I'll take a liverwurst sandwich, instead, with some ketchup and onions, sugar plum. And don't be sneaking any of that pickle berry jam, on my sandwich and ruining it," Aunt Alice said, making a face. "Ugh!"

"Comin' right up," Uncle Fred said with a big kiss on her cheek and a big smile.

Aunt Alice patted her belly. "Got to watch my weight, boys." She pinched a roll of loose flesh that drooped out over the top of her shorts. "Need to lose my middle that's been bulging out from all your Uncle Fred's fine cooking. I swear he's going to get me as fat as those hens outside. I gotta stay in shape for work or I won't be getting any big tips from the boys at the bar," she winked. "Gotta keep 'em going wild when I shake my hoochie on stage. So, the more they clap, the wilder I get an' the more I shake. The Slippery Elm still brings in a pretty good size crowd," she said, with a grin. "Your aunt's the breadwinner around here, Sam. We got the ranch paid off, and even tucked away some savings… so we're doing pretty good. Uncle Fred grows most of our food, and takes care of me and the animals around here, so I can't complain…"

"Complain?" Uncle Fred said with a big smile, giving her a kiss on top of her head. "You never do, sweet cheeks. Now, eat up boys. You must be starving." He sat the bowls down and watched them eat with gusto.

Aunt Alice picked at her liverwurst sandwich while watching Sam. In between bites she lit a Virginia Slim and exhaled slowly.

"You know, Sam, Sheriff Joe came by the Slippery Elm a few days ago. He told me that you boys were sentenced to the gallows for attempted robbery and other crimes. Said he was all set to hang you both, and then just as he was ready to pull the latch, a big ole flock of crows came barreling down, from outa nowhere, and attacked the crowd – but somehow you boys managed to escape. He warned me that if you came asking for help, I was to tell him right away. And if I didn't… well… he said I'd be mighty sorry and that harboring fugitives is a crime."

Aunt Alice fidgeted nervously in her chair and said worriedly. "I've seen a nasty side to him that makes my blood run cold. I remember what he did once to one of the girls at work because she lied to him. He slashed her arm and she had a bunch of stitches where he cut her up." She took another drag from her Virginia Slim. "It was awful. He said he'd do the same to me. I want to help, but that man scares the daylights outa me. I love you, Sam, but you boys put me in a bad situation."

Uncle Fred hurried to her side to calm her down, as she started to cry.

"Now, now, sweet cheeks. That sheriff is a mean son-of-a-gun, but we can't throw these boys out, no matter what he threatens. We'll be real careful. We're not the kind of folks to turn our backs on our relatives. Besides, I know that lousy bum just wants any excuse he can find to hang an Indian." Uncle Fred rubbed his wife's shoulder. "It's like a notch on his belt. Anyway, I can spot a car coming for miles off down that dirt road. I'll get the boys a real good hiding spot in case that scum comes sniffing around."

Aunt Alice sniffled, then blew her nose in Uncle Fred's handkerchief. She was deep in thought for a few minutes, then took another drag on her cigarette, and tapped her long red fingernails on the table, pondering the situation. She looked at Sam and let off a sad smile. "I would never turn you in, honey. You know that don't you? It's just that the sheriff makes me nervous. But don't you worry none about that. I can lie real good." Then her eyes drifted over to Oliver. She loved the color of his eyes, and thought, *how unusual he is, with his stoical face — and those glorious blue velvet eyes that must be straight out of heaven.* She shifted her shoulders back and smiled brightly. "You boys are welcome to stay as long as you like. Forever, would be all right with me."

Sam squeezed her hands together in his. "Thanks, Aunt Alice."

"I could never kick you boys out, and, as you can see, I've got a real big heart." Pridefully, she patted her generous bosom, then looked at Fred. "Why don't you set something up real nice out in the barn for Sam and Oliver — up there in the loft, if it's sturdy enough. That way if that nosey bastard comes looking…" She stopped herself. "Pardon my French, boys. Don't mean to cuss like that. Just meant to say… it might be a good hiding place. I don't think he could get his fat ass up the ladder, anyways."

Uncle Fred nodded. "My sugar plum always comes up with the best ideas. I knew you wouldn't turn these boys out." He patted her face, and looked over at Oliver and Sam. "Are you okay for now, staying in the barn. We'll make it downright homey as we can and bring up a bunch of hay and blankets and such.

Sam breathed out a sigh of relief. "Sounds like heaven right about now… Thanks to you both. I really appreciate it… and again, I'm really sorry it's been so long since I've called."

"We understand, Sam," Uncle Fred said kindly.

"I see in you that you're a very brave woman," Oliver said sincerely. "You would be honored in our tribe. I wouldn't want any harm to come to you or your husband."

"Thank you for those kind and thoughtful words, Oliver. We'll just keep our eyes peeled open."

Uncle Fred said, standing, "Well, now that's all set, with you boys staying. Now if you're up to it, I could sure use some help around the farm. Gotta few things been meaning to get at… as I'm sure you saw."

"We'd love to help you, Uncle Fred," Sam said. "Anything you need."

Oliver stood and walked over to the screen door. "I see that this is about ready to fall off. If you have a couple nails and a screwdriver, I'll get to work on this, if you don't mind."

Uncle Fred halfway out the door, with a quick smile, said, "I wouldn't mind at all. Been meaning to get at the door for a spell." He went off and came back in a couple minutes with the supplies for Oliver.

Oliver went to work and managed to fix the door in just a few minutes. "I think it's all set," he said, swinging the door back and forth. "Should hold you for a while."

"Well now, isn't that something… got a door that's working like new. I think your friend is going to be a Godsend around here," Aunt Alice gushed, smiling at her nephew. "Come and sit near me," she said, patting the chair. "It's been too long since I've seen your sweet face. I just want to look at my handsome boy for a spell."

"Yes, it has been a long time," Uncle Fred said, pouring more coffee. "Your Aunt and I, well, we were worried about you. We weren't sure what you were doing in Los Angeles. Your pa came around a few times asking about you, but we didn't know anything, so we just said we hadn't heard from you for some time." Uncle Fred took a sip of his coffee. "I know it was real rough on you when he dropped you off here to live with us and how hard it was to be without your momma. You were such a young tike when you came here – smaller than a sack of potatoes when you arrived with your pa and little suitcase. Jesse told us, 'If he starts whining and crying and carrying on like a little baby, just box him in the ears a good one. That'll shut him up.' Then he told us, 'There's stuff I gotta get after. So, I gotta leave him here with you.' We never found out what 'stuff' he was referring to, but we surely weren't gonna turn you away."

Sam swallowed hard and choked back his anger.

"I'm glad he left you with us 'cause he wasn't a good pa and we loved you like you was our own…"

Aunt Alice interrupted. "Now just hold on a bit. Your pa, who happens to be my brother… did the best he could. He was a wild one, for certain. Hard to tame and settle down. Couldn't help himself, I guess. He had a weakness for the three D's. Drinking, dames, and dancing – then throw in some gambling to boot. Your pa never liked to stay in one place for too long. Said he got restless looking at the same thing, day in and day out. Same with his women, too. Real sorry about your mama, Sam. I only met her a couple times or so. Jesse used to say, for an Arapaho squaw, she wasn't bad. Not sure how she died. He said, one day she just keeled over. That's all I know."

Sam sat rigid, burning, with fury at the mention of his father. He wanted to shout out, "Can't you see what a scumbag he is?" It took all his will power to restrain himself. He and Oliver needed a place to stay and couldn't afford to cause any trouble… They had already had enough of that.

Oliver looked at his friend's face and changed the subject. He quickly asked Aunt Alice about her work.

"That's real sweet of you to ask. And since you both might need a little perking up, I'm gonna give you boys a sneak-peak at the new act I'm working on. I need the practice anyway… so hold onto your britches. Gotta real nice treat for you boys." She squeezed Uncle Fred's shoulders and kissed his cheek. "I'll be right back." She shoved her chair back and hustled into her bedroom to change.

Oliver and Sam looked over at Uncle Fred, who winked. "You know how your Aunt Alice is, Sam. That little lady loves to dance."

Oliver held back a grin… and politely nodded his head.

A few minutes later the door burst open, and Aunt Alice came parading out in her costume – a pink satin robe revealing a shiny satin gown underneath.

Oliver couldn't believe Sam's aunt and resisted a laugh.

Sam shifted uncomfortably in his chair, dreading what was to come.

Aunt Alice pulled back a linen curtain in the corner of the living room and said proudly, "This is my dance studio, boys. It features a floor-to-ceiling pole that Uncle Fred installed for me." She sauntered over to the record player and waited for the music to begin. Suddenly the song, "You Sexy Thing" blasted out. She slowly wiggled her hips to warm up, then sashayed back and forth to the beat. She slowly straddled the pole, gave it a big hug, then gyrated seductively around it. The tempo picked up. In her fervor, Aunt Alice twirled around the pole, wildly… her gown flung out from her ankles and whooshed up above her hips. As she twirled and in sync, she pulled off her robe – and sent it flying across the room. With abandon, she really let loose… her pelvis bumped and grinded naughtily, alluring, while she stretched her left leg as high as it would go. The pace was even faster now, and she thrust her hips back and forth, bumping and grinding against the pole, her legs encircling it tightly. Enjoying the attention, she gave the boys a wicked smile as she twisted in circles and slowly removed her silky top – flinging it across the room. She kept twirling around and around the pole in a dizzying whirl, as her bosoms threatened to spill out – all the while twirling a baton.

Sam moaned, "Oh, my God!" as he watched his aunt's ample bosoms flouncing around in an unbelievable spectacle.

Uncle Fred was clapping and cheering her on. "Woo-hoo, baby! I'm digging it!"

As the music was reaching a crescendo, Oliver and Sam tried to keep their mouths closed as a scant lacy top came flying across the room, landing on Oliver's lap.

Oliver eyes popped, as he looked at the top, not sure what to do with it.

Sam groaned and held his head in his hands, waiting for this embarrassing spectacle to be over.

What seemed like an eternity, and to their relief, the song finally came to an end.

Aunt Alice did a little curtsy to the boys and spoke breathlessly. "I can still get those guys at the Slippery Elm riled up with my moves. Might not be as young as I once was, but I still can shake it pretty good. Not too bad with the ole baton from my cheerleading days, either." She grinned at Uncle Fred as she put on her robe and walked into the kitchen wiping her brow. "I worked myself up into a sweat. How about a nice little gin and tonic for your dancer?"

Uncle Fred hopped up, ran to the liquor cabinet, and pulled out the bottle of Bombay Gin. He clinked some ice into the glass and poured the tonic, adding a slice of lime.

Aunt Alice's high heels clicked on the linoleum floor as she walked to the table and sat down in a flounce. "You can tell them boys back in Hollywood that your Aunt Alice has some fancy moves. I could shake it up with them glitzy girls I see on TV... If they want me to come out there and try out, I'd be willing. I could put on a 'special show' but, they'd have to pay a pretty penny to see me in all my glory."

Sam wasn't sure how to respond to Aunt Alice, so he quickly stood and shoved his chair back, almost knocking it over in his haste to get out the door. "Well, um, thanks Aunt Alice..." he stammered, "for the show... er... your dance..." then muttered under his breath, "or whatever that was."

Oliver quickly stood and handed the silky top to Fred, anxious to leave. "We should get going to the barn. Thanks for the food and the... uh... everything." He hustled out the door, right behind Sam.

Uncle Fred was fanning Aunt Alice lovingly. "That was quite the show, sugar plum. I think I should help the boys get started on the loft before dark and get them settled in." He kissed her brow and headed out the door.

Uncle Fred walked over to where Sam and Oliver were standing. "Sorry, boys. Got a little sidetracked by the show." He gave them a wink and led them down to the barn – about a hundred yards from the house. On the way, they passed a portion of the garden, where sugar peas vined up thin poles, prickly squash blossoms spread out on the ground, ripe cherry tomatoes hung heavily in clusters, and large beefsteaks that could easily win the county fair. Uncle Fred stopped and sniffed a ripe tomato – then picked two of the ripe beefsteaks. "Take a bite out of these beauties. Sweet as can be. I usually can a bunch of them, and they last me all winter." As the boys took a bite, he boasted, "Isn't my sugar plum something? Your Aunt Alice… she could shake a leg right off a cow… if she'd a mind to."

Oliver and Sam looked at each other in amusement, not sure what to think. They just nodded their heads in reply and continued to eat.

Sam remembered eating his uncle's tomatoes right off the vine when he lived here. He took another bite as juice dribbled down his chin.

Oliver sucked on the ripe tomato, enjoying the tangy sweetness that reminded him of the ones his mother grew back home.

As they headed down the path to the barn, only a few splashes of the red color remained; the rest was a weathered gray. The missing front door lay stacked against the wall. Inside were a few bales of hay piled up at the far end of the barn, with a stall for Pepper and a steep rickety ladder led to the loft that was riddled with holes and rotting boards.

Sam looked around the barn and remembered it well. He used to play in here by himself and would sit and daydream about his future. Uncle Fred thought it was a wonderful place for a boy to explore – inside this very same loft, where he and Oliver would stay. He never thought he would be so grateful to be back here.

It seemed that every Sunday, all those years ago, his cousins would come to visit. Sam hated those times, and he couldn't stomach Skip and Wilbur. They were ten and eleven to his seven years, and they loved to play Cowboys and Indians. Sam was always the Indian... and Skip and Wilbur were the cowboys... and always won. They would tie Sam's hands behind his back, and do a pretend war dance, hopping around him and singing, "Pee-yew, pee-yew, wamp 'um, wamp-pu... I'm gonna shoot you." They would take their BB guns and hide in the bushes, and, as he ran from them, they would shoot at him. The BB's stung like crazy and made him cry. Then they would taunt him – calling him a "big baby redskin." They would yell, "Why don't you go back to your Injun squaw?!" Other times, out of boredom, they would chase him around the barn – and, if they caught him, they tied him to a tree. Once he stayed there until dark and screamed until his uncle finally found him. From much practice, Sam became expert at finding hiding places in the barn. He had dreaded his cousins' visits more than anything. When he told Aunt Alice what they had done, she would say, "Now, sweetie, they're just playing. Don't be so sensitive about being part Indian. That's just the way of it, honey." Then she would go back to painting her nails or bleaching her hair. Uncle Fred was usually busy in the fields and didn't want to bother him. So, Sam's childhood was frustrating and, at times, lonely. And to this day he could remember those taunts from his cousins and how much he wanted to leave this place and forget his Indian blood.

To this day, Sam still thought about his mother, Singing Dove. He remembered *she had a beautiful voice and would sing to him every night, and he would fall asleep in her arms.* Being here brought back those memories and how deeply he missed her.

Sam looked around the barn, and made his way to the loft, carefully easing himself up onto the precarious slats of wood.

Oliver was right behind Sam.

Uncle Fred surveyed the area, and said, rubbing the stubble on his chin. "You're gonna need to put some boards up there, where the missing ones are – or I should say, *aren't*. Hate to have you roll over in the middle of the night and come tumbling down," he said joking. "I've got a bunch of boards in my shed that should work pretty good.

Oliver gingerly walked across the loft, careful not to fall through the large cracks and rotted floor. "I think with a bit of work this should be just fine," he said.

"We'll haul up a bunch of hay for your bed, and Alice could give me a few of her sheets and blankets," Uncle Fred said.

Oliver and Sam were grateful for the hayloft even though it would take some hard work. Oliver remarked, "I have to say that this is way better than the hard ground we slept on for the last few nights." Sam readily agreed, as they both climbed back down the ladder.

"Well boys, let's get to work," Uncle Fred said with a smile, happy to see his nephew and his new friend. "Gotta say I'm mighty grateful for the company – and some help around the ranch."

"Well, the loft sounds pretty darn good to me," Sam said. "It's gonna be our new sleeping quarters for a while, so I guess that's the least we can do is help out."

They went to the shed where Uncle Fred had stored an array of wood. He found a large piece of plywood laying on the back wall and with Oliver's help, managed to cut it to the right dimensions. With a bit of maneuvering, Sam and Oliver hauled the pieces of wood up to the loft.

Oliver said he could fix about anything, so Sam followed his instructions.

Uncle Fred brought more wood for the boys with the tractor.

After several trips up the ladder, Sam and Oliver had the upstairs loft mostly finished.

Uncle Fred asked, "How you boys holding up? We been working a couple hours or better. So, why don't we take a break? Then, if you're done up there and you've still got some energy left, I've got a few more chores to get at – that is, if you don't mind giving me a hand. Been a lot to take on by myself since Harold had to leave."

Oliver looked around the ranch and blew a long whistle. "I can see there's a lot to be done. I was checking out your fences on my way here… I'd say they're in pretty bad shape."

"It seems like I can never catch up… fix one thing, and then something else falls apart. The summertime is busy. And then, fall is right around the corner and then the long cold winter sets in. Now before all that, a lot of wood needs to be chopped, and I've got to move bales of hay from the fields into the barn so the animals will be warm and well fed. Then the chicken coop needs to be repaired, and so does the leaky roof in the barn and the one in the house," Uncle Fred said. I know you boys are here because you're in a load of trouble, but what a godsend that you came. I'll do my darndest to help keep you boys safe."

Sam looked at the axe and said, "I remember chopping wood Uncle Fred," and flexed his muscles for show. "I'd be happy to help… just hope I still know how to swing an axe." *I think living in the city has made me forget a lot of things.* He didn't realize how much he missed being in the country. For some strange reason, it felt good to be here. As Sam stood quietly looking around the farm, he bent down and plucked a bright orange Tiger Lily… his mother's favorite flower. He swore he saw an image of her smile at him as he inhaled the fragrance… he touched the silky petal and stuck the lily into his pocket. His heart constricted. He wished she were here with him. He would tell her that he was sorry for being ashamed of his Indian heritage. *Being part of you is so much better than being part of Jesse. Why did you ever marry that man? He wondered. He took me away from you. If he ever comes around here looking for me, it'll be a sad day for his sorry ass.* Sam picked up the axe near a woodpile and swung it – splintering a big log into several pieces and imagining it was his father. "I'll knock his block off," he grumbled, as he picked up another piece of wood and, with one furious swing, sliced it right down the middle. *Maybe I'll kill him… then, they can hang me for something I really did.*

Uncle Fred came around the barn and watched Sam for a minute, then walked up to him. "Gotta lot on your mind, I see."

Sam just nodded and looked away.

"Sorry about all that's happened, Sam. I'm just glad you boys got away. That Sheriff Joe is a real mean bugger. He's evil and cunning. Your Aunt Alice is afraid of him, and she doesn't frighten often. We'll need to be a mite careful. I fear he won't give up till he finds you…"

"I'm sorry to come back this way, putting you both in danger, especially after I've been gone for so long."

Uncle Fred patted Sam's head, like he did when he was young. "We'll be sure to cover all our tracks and be on guard at all times. Not going to let that man get you boys."

Oliver came over, hay spilling over his hair and down his shirt. "Got the last of the hay in the loft. Should have a real comfy place to sleep tonight. How about I fix the barn door? It looks pretty beat up, but if you've got a strip of metal or something I could get it back up and working."

"I think I have what you might need," Uncle Fred said on his way to the shed. A minute later, he came back dragging a long strip of metal that was once used around his old silo and had seen its better day. "Think this this'll work for you, Oliver?"

"Let's measure and see. Then I'll cut a few strips and have this door as good as new." Oliver winked at Sam, who was watching – wishing he were that handy.

After a couple hours, they had the door fixed and ready to be hung. Oliver, Sam, and Uncle Fred were working up a sweat when Aunt Alice walked into the barn carrying a big jug of lemonade – wearing her signature look: high heels, short-shorts, and halter top. As she bent over to pour everyone a drink, her bosoms poured out, as well. "I must say, you boys are a sight for sore eyes… all sweaty and hot."

She looked at Oliver's long, lean muscular body with sweat dripping down his bare chest, and she gushed. "Lordie have mercy on me – you're a sight for sore eyes."

Oliver blushed, embarrassed. He wasn't sure how to respond to Aunt Alice, so he looked down at his feet and nodded his thanks.

Aunt Alice handed Sam his glass.

"Thanks, Aunt Alice," Sam said, downing the drink in one gulp.

"Off to work I go. You boys stay outa trouble now," she said, and blew them each a kiss.

Oliver and Sam watched Aunt Alice as she sashayed with even greater exaggeration to her car. She opened the door then turned and waved. "Be careful of eating all those beans," she said with a laugh, as she lit a long Virginia Slim cigarette, then slid into her cherry red Mustang convertible. Putting her key in the ignition the engine groaned for a second, then roared to life. Aunt Alice deftly shoved the gear into first, and sped off down the driveway, blowing smoke and more kisses as she drove past.

Uncle Fred shook his head, with pride. "She sure is a handful, that's for darn certain," he said, watching her drive off down the road. "I love her more than all the violets in the world."

Sam and Oliver both looked at each other – happy for Uncle Fred, but relieved she was gone.

After they rested and finished the lemonade, Uncle Fred suggested mending the chicken coop. "There's a coyote coming round, looking to get at my hens – and I'd like to keep my girls safe. The coop needs a bit of propping up – and made more secure. I lock 'em in at night, and so far it's kept them from becoming dinner. But as you can see, it won't take long for those wily coyotes to figure out how to get inside."

Oliver walked over to the chicken coop, bent down to inspect the perimeter and decided the weakness was around the foundation. The boards were rotting underneath, and the wire was loose. The entire coop was wearing out. "Do you have some cement? I could add more slats of wood around the edges and fill it in. Nothing will get through that."

Uncle Fred said, "That would be real good. I don't want to shoot the coyotes. They have a right to be here on God's earth. It was meant for us all – wolves, included. A lot of ranchers around here hate 'em 'cause the wolves get after their cattle. But we all gotta share the land with the critters. That's one thing you Indians sure got right. I have a lot of respect for your people… they know how everything is connected to everything else. You take one thing away, and, like dominos it all falls apart."

Oliver's blue eyes widened at Uncle Fred's astute observation. "You sure you're not part Indian?" he joked good-naturedly. "We always believe nature and the outdoors brings us closer to the Great Spirit and the earth and sky is our church… makes it easier to pray outside."

"I think that sounds about right. I have met me a bunch of ignorant folks in my life, for sure," Uncle Fred said, as he pulled out a dusty bag of cement from the shed. "Now, I don't mean to say unkind words about your father, Sam, but he is one of those ignorant jackasses that I could never stomach. Your Aunt Alice always defended him, and I couldn't go against her, you know…"

"I know he dropped me off here when I was young. I remember back then I didn't like him. He scared me.

"He's a low-life bugger," Uncle Fred said with a growl. "I only met your ma a couple times, when you were just a little thing. She was real quiet, but I could see that she loved you more than the moon. She cradled you the whole time, singing her songs. Your dad was mad because she loved you so much, I think. Thought she should be paying more attention to him, when he was around. One time I saw him smack her upside her head when she didn't answer him quick enough, and he knocked her right off the chair with her holding you. She protected you from the fall, that's for sure. I wanted to kill him, but your Aunt Alice intervened before I could do anything. I heard him mutter under his breath, 'Whiny redskin bitch… Get your ass off the floor and go get me a brew from the truck.' I didn't see him again till he dropped you off – saying he had stuff to do and was in a real big hurry."

Uncle Fred watched Sam's reaction, but only got a stoical look back – so he continued.

"Aunt Alice put up a fuss at first. She told me she could hardly look after herself let alone a youngster – with all the preening it takes to be a dancer. She said, 'I got my workout routine, a beauty regime, and on top of that my fussing routine. How am I supposed to look after a kid?' Well Jesse stomped around the house, mad as a wet hen. Then you came out of the bedroom, asking for your mama, and you started to cry. Your pa slapped you and told you to quit bawling like a little baby. Said, 'shut up or I'll give you another slap. You sound just like your ma… a whiny little bitch.'

"If I had to listen to that much longer, I would have shot him, so I took you outside. You were crying real hard. I hugged you for a while, then I walked you over to the barn and introduced you to Edna. She was our milk cow. It was dark, but I lit a lantern and we sat just there, looking at Edna… and you patted her for a long time, tears running down your face. I felt helpless as I watched your little heart break in two. Mine broke, too, and I started to cry with you. We were both sniffling, so then I thought I needed to do something to get you to stop crying, so I took you over to the chicken coop. The hens were asleep, but I told you that in the morning we would get us some fresh eggs. I said it was like playing a game. If you could find the eggs, I would cook them up for breakfast. You finally stopped crying. All you could talk about was the chickens… and I saw your first smile. That's when your pa drove off. Didn't even say goodbye to you. Scumbag. That's what he's always been. Hit the bottom of the barrel with that one. I can't believe your Aunt Alice is related to him. She's a real corker, for sure, but she has a big heart, and she cares about you, Sam. Even if she has a strange way of showing it. And she likes you too Oliver."

Sam shoved his hands in his jeans and stared at the ground. He had started to let his hair grow out, and his dark brown locks were already below his ears. He wore a bright blue cloth around his forehead and tied it around his head, leaving the long strands hanging down his back. Just having longer hair made Sam feel proud, more connected to his roots – to his mother. He choked back the tears and anguish and pain he had held inside for so long. He gritted his teeth to stay strong. Right now, he had more pressing matters to deal with. The tears could come later.

Oliver and Uncle Fred were quietly watching Sam.

Sam looked at Uncle Fred and Oliver with tear filled eyes. "Here I am… a grown man who wants to hug his mother one more time, more than anything in the world." He stood up straight and announced with pride. "I finally can say that I am proud to be an Indian… Arapaho. I love the name, and the smooth flow of the sound… Arapaho," he whispered softly. "It gives me the chills, just saying it." So, Sam said it again: "Arapaho." And then closed his eyes. "It rolls off my tongue, like thunder… like a force rumbling through me." He smiled and swore he could feel his soul awaken-ing. He could feel his power rise in him, which had lain dormant for such a long time. It was as if he had been waiting for this his whole life. "Arapaho." He whispered again. He loved saying it. It made his insides bubble with joy.

Sam looked at Oliver and Uncle Fred, and said, "I wish I were full blood… not partly from someone like Jesse. I can't call him my father. He is nothing to me, except a distant haze of trash. As far as I'm concerned, I'm Arapaho. It was something I used to be ashamed of. And now I want to shout it to the world. I want to discover more about my ancestors and myself. With the blood of my mother that runs through me, I feel like the me inside myself has finally come alive."

Oliver smiled at his friend's transformation. He watched Sam standing tall and proud. "You are looking more and more like a warrior, my friend." He put his hand on Sam's shoulder, and grinned. "You would make a fine brave."

Sam brushed aside a stray strand of hair from his face – liking the feel of his long hair – it had the feeling of power.

Uncle Fred said, "I want you to know that I am proud of you and that you are nothing like Jesse. I can see your mother in you. The quiet way you have about yourself… your goodness… just like she had in her. Arapaho. That sounds real good, Sam. I like it, too. You should be proud."

Sam shoved his shoulders back, feeling the weight lifted from him, "I'm lucky to have you and Oliver, Uncle Fred. But, enough about me. I say, let's get going on that chicken coop, shall we?"

"That'll make the hens sleep better, knowing they won't be dinner anytime soon," Uncle Fred said. So, they set out to work digging a trench under the coop, removed the rotted boards, then laid a layer of cement with new boards to secure the bottom.

Oliver set about making a new door, and replaced all the siding around the chicken coop. Then, together, they fixed the roof, which was long, tedious, work. It was getting close to sunset when they finally finished – exhausted and thirsty.

Uncle Fred said, "How about we call it a day, boys? I'd say we've done a month's worth of work in a day and I'm mighty grateful for your help. Surprising how fast something can get done with six hands."

They walked to the shed to drop off the tools and supplies.

"I could rustle us up a big pot of beans," Uncle Fred said. "And I have some sourdough bread and Lemonade to wash it all down."

"That sounds good to me," Sam said, rubbing his sore muscles as he walked toward the house. "I could eat a back end of a… never mind what. I'm starving… and real stiff."

Oliver noted Sam was limping a little and teased him. "Looks like it's been too long since you've seen a good day's work."

"Well, you should be fit as a fiddle in no time," Uncle Fred said, grinning.

At the outdoor pump, Sam held his head under the water while Oliver pumped. When he cooled off, he stripped off his clothes and let the water run over him. "Ooohh, this feels good," he said, as the silky cool water splashed over his lean body.

Uncle Fred came out with a bar of soap, and Sam lathered himself in a frothy scent of honeysuckle.

"That's Aunt Alice's favorite soap. I snuck a bar of it for you boys. Thought you might like to smell something other than cow manure and chicken poop for a change. We don't have to tell her we used it," Uncle Fred said with a laugh.

Next, it was Oliver's turn under the pump, and Sam managed the handle. He doused himself in the water and soaped up, scrubbing away the days' worth of grime. He didn't mind the stench of the chicken poop as much as the stench of the jail. Thinking about it made him scrub even harder.

Uncle Fred smiled at the two young men. He had really missed Sam, and found Oliver smart, eager to help, and a very proud young man. *He must have that warrior spirit,* he thought, watching him. *Maybe it's something in the way he walks, or perhaps how his startling blue eyes level you with his gaze. There's a fierceness inside him. That boy has something not many have… eyes of the spirit… great power.*

Uncle Fred was an avid reader of all sorts of books. He liked to study the many different tribes and their ancient powers, and he wished he had some of their knowledge. He found himself in awe of Oliver, and the strength he possessed. Maybe Sam hadn't been taught much about his people and he didn't know who he was yet, but it wouldn't be long before he did. *But… that Oliver is a force to be reckoned with.*

Uncle Fred was just north of fifty. He had grown up in Wyoming and would be there until the end of his days. He loved the land, the wildness of it all. He had passed through some reservations when he was just sixteen years old and felt great respect for the people. They spoke little, but when they did, it was powerful. Uncle Fred never forgot the time he met an elder from the Shoshone tribe, who spoke of the coming times for the white man and the destruction they would reap. He taught Uncle Fred in that short time about the creatures that roam the earth and of their importance. The Shoshone lived under terrible conditions on the reservation, but that elder seemed to rise above it all, and had majestically retained his power. Oliver reminded him of that elder.

So, when Uncle Fred was getting supper ready, he told the boys the story how he met Alice. "My greatest joy was meeting your Aunt Alice – Alice Price at the time. Alice was all I could think about in high school. She was a cheerleader, and real popular. All the guys fell all over themselves to get her attention. She was all bouncy and cheerful. "Rah-rah-rah," was her favorite saying. I was real quiet and shy and didn't have a lot of friends, but I secretly admired her. I knew my chances of ever getting Alice to notice me, let alone talk to me or anything else, was out of the question.

"I worked on the farm with my dad and brother and every morning at five, I milked our twenty cows. Then, I would gobble something down for breakfast and run out the door to catch the school bus. I never had time to wash all the barnyard smell off me, so most of the kids avoided me, and teased me and said,

"You smell like a barnyard." Whenever I saw Alice at school, my eyes would light up and my heart would flutter. One day I practically dribbled saliva down my chin when I passed her in the hallway. She was wearing pink lipstick to match her tight pink mohair sweater and pink pants, which showed off every curve of her incredible body. Everything jiggled as she flounced down the hallway, golden blonde ponytail swinging, as well. I felt drips of perspiration slide from my armpits, and I had to grab hold of the locker door to steady myself. I must've looked like a fool with my mouth wide open, gawking at her. Pete Hardy came by and shoved me against my locker, when he saw me looking at Alice. He laughed out loud and mocked me. "Fat chance, barnyard." He also told me to keep my eyes off his girl and slammed me hard in my stomach with his beefy fist – then he kept walking down the hallways. The other boys with Pete mocked me, too. They all had their mouths open, mimicking me, as they passed by and gave me a shove. All of them were on the football team – Pete was the captain, of course. But that incident never stopped me from secretly admiring Alice Price. I would've given my right big toe, just to have her smile at me.

"And one day I got my wish. It was a late Saturday night, and I was on my way home from the grocery store doing some shopping for my ma. As I turned down the dark gravel road, I saw blinkers flashing up ahead, and pulled over to the side. I hopped out of the car to see if I could be of help, and I got the surprise of my life. Inside the car was Alice Price and Pete Hardy. The windows were all fogged up, and Pete didn't see me, but I heard Alice screaming in the back seat. 'Let me go!' she yelled. I froze for a moment, not sure what to do. Finally, I got my nerve up and knocked on the window and asked if they needed any help. I was shaking like a leaf on a tree in a storm, real hard, when Pete slammed out of the car, his pants partway down. He shoved his finger in my chest and told me to 'mind your own beeswax, if you know what's good for you.'

Then, he shoved me again and said to get lost. Something in me grew bigger than my fear. So, I picked up a nearby rock from the ground, and as Pete went to get back inside the car, I bashed him on the back of his head and watched that big quarterback slowly slither to the ground. For a moment I was afraid I had killed him. Alice saw me, let out a shriek, and flew out of the backseat. She was sobbing real hard and wrapped her arms around me real tight. Finally, when she was able to catch her breath and stop crying, she looked up at me and asked, "What's your name?" I couldn't believe she was talking to me, and I stood like a fool in disbelief. She told me that Pete had almost… well… *you* know, had his way with her, and that if I hadn't come along when I did, well… I rescued her just in time. She told me that she would never forget how brave I was… saving her from that brute. Her words were, 'I used to think he was cool, but he's nothing but a bully.' We've been inseparable ever since… and she told me she didn't care if I smelled like a barn."

Uncle Fred kept stirring his pot of beans and continued. "I didn't have a lot of extra time to spend with Alice, after working on the farm and with homework, but she didn't care. I stole her heart in her time of need, and she was devoted. We went out every Saturday night and I still couldn't believe my good fortune. The girl of my dreams was mine. I inherited the ranch a couple of years after I graduated from high school. My father died in a car accident and my mother didn't want to stay here, so she went to live with her sister in Michigan. My brother didn't want the farm, either, so he moved away. I was grateful to have the farm for my own and I have been happy here ever since. Shortly after I inherited the place, I married your Aunt Alice. I thought I must've died and gone to heaven."

Uncle Fred brought in the soup and steaming hot bread fresh from the oven and set it on the table. Everyone dove in, piling mounds of butter on the crusty bread, and ate heartily.

"That was quite a story, Uncle Fred," Sam said, as he took a big bite of bread – then dipped it in the soup. "I never knew any of this. Thanks for telling me."

Oliver smiled at Uncle Fred as he poured each of them a big glass of Aunt Alice's lemonade. Then they discussed their plans for tomorrow.

"I think we should work on the fence, which is falling apart," Uncle Fred said. "If that's okay with you boys."

"Fine by me," Oliver said, and Sam echoed the same while stuffing his mouth.

"I can't tell you enough how much I appreciate your help today. Your Aunt Alice plucks a tomato or two in the garden. She says she gets exercise bending over – and a tan at the same time. She always likes to look good for work. I don't mind she flirts some. That's what she was made for, men looking at her– and she loves it – but the important thing is she always comes home to me. So, I don't mind. I'm not the smartest guy or even all that good looking, but in her eyes… she thinks I'm the best thing since liverwurst and ketchup. I've got to be the luckiest guy in Wyoming."

Oliver and Sam laughed and agreed with Uncle Fred, who was, indeed, lucky. He noticed the bowls were empty and hopped up and brought in more beans and bread. They finished that, as well.

Soon Sam started to yawn and rub his stomach. "I'm so full right now, I could bust. Think I'll head to the loft. Sounds like heaven to me."

"Right behind you, Sam," Oliver echoed, stretching his tired muscles. "Thanks for the food, Fred."

"Oh, call me Uncle Fred, like Sam here does. I like the sound of it, and I like you. Again, I really appreciate your help and I'm glad you're here. Sleep tight and see you in the morning. I'll fix us a pile of the best-tasting eggs you've ever had. The hens are good layers, and they pop out some jumbos. I talk to the girls every morning and tell them how much I appreciate them and their fine eggs. Then I pet each one and call them, 'my little beauties' as they strut around the yard like feathered goddesses. So, in return, they always give me nice plump eggs by the basketful. Guess I have a way with the ladies." Uncle Fred winked and said, "Goodnight, boys."

Oliver and Sam woke the next morning at sunrise, as bits of light filtered through the cracks in the barn. Sam had slept deep and hard, not sure if he had budged an inch. Oliver yawned as he stood and peered through the slats.

As the guys dressed, they made their way down the ladder and walked outside, breathing in the crisp fresh air. Entering the kitchen, Oliver commented, "Smells good in here." He sniffed the air appreciatively.

Uncle Fred smiled as he poured each of them a hot cup of coffee. "Morning, boys." Hope you slept well in the loft. No critters got ya, I hope."

"My head didn't even hit the pillow before I was gone," Sam said.

"I slept pretty well myself," Oliver said, grateful for the cup of hot coffee as he sipped.

"Well, it's a mighty fine day, we have… but gonna be a hot dogger, for sure," Uncle Fred said, as he whipped up a large bowl of eggs, ready to pour into the skillet. Next, he sliced some of his homemade sourdough bread and put it in the toaster. He was zipping around the kitchen, smiling, right at home doing the cooking.

Sam and Oliver watched him in amusement as he bustled about humming. He pulled out a jar of jam from the fridge and set it on the table proudly. "This here is my pickle berry jam. Made it myself from scratch with all the stuff from my garden… hope you like it. Pretty much make everything, and I thank the good Lord I have all I need right here. Gotta nice piece of land and my sweet cheeks by my side – and now you two boys show up right when I need you. I know I've said it a hundred times, but I can't thank you enough for your help."

A bleary-eyed Aunt Alice came stumbling into the kitchen and sat down at the table with a flounce. Uncle Fred smacked her on the cheek with a big kiss.

"How's my girl, this morning?" Uncle Fred asked, while hurrying to get her a cup of coffee. "You're up early this morning, sweet cheeks. Did we wake you?"

"No," Aunt Alice said, while stifling a big yawn and situating herself in the chair. Her night dress slipped open in the front, revealing her bountiful cleavage. "I wanted to tell you some news, Sam," she said, taking a sip of her coffee. "Jesse came into the lounge last night. He says he wants to see you. Says he's real sorry he wasn't around much when you were little… and wants to make it up to you. Says he can't wait to see how you've grown."

Sam sat rigid and silent.

"He said to tell you he's a changed man and that anything he can do to help, he will. He heard about your trouble with the law and your close call with… uh… in Miners Gulch." Aunt Alice sipped her coffee, made a face, added more sugar, and stirred — watching Sam's reaction.

"You can tell Jesse I've got no use for him or his help."

Uncle Fred rubbed his head, worriedly, eyes following between Aunt Alice and Sam. "Well now, sweet cheeks," he said, a bit nervously. "You can understand how Sam would feel about Jesse after all these years. He's been gone most of his life and now, all of a sudden, he wants to see him."

Aunt Alice sighed and took another sip of coffee, then she went over to Sam and kissed him on top of his head. "I'll tell him whatever you want, my dear. No need to fret. But don't be surprised if he just shows up. You know he's unpredictable that way. Hard to anticipate what he'll do."

"Thanks, Aunt Alice, for understanding," Sam said.

"He brought some woman in with him last night. Said she was a real peach." Aunt Alice frowned. "She didn't look like a peach to me – unless he meant 'over-ripe.'"

Uncle Fred stood, patted his wife's head – proud of her humor. "We got a load of work to do today, sweet cheeks. Want to get at it before the heat gets rolling in." He bent close to her ear and whispered, "I don't think Sam's interested in hearing any more about his pa." He turned to the boys and said, "Ready for a good day's work?"

"Sure am, Fred… I mean, Uncle Fred," Oliver said as he jumped up. "Thanks for breakfast. The eggs were some of the best I've eaten. You weren't exaggerating about how good they are."

Sam didn't say anything as he walked outside toward the barn, jaw clenched, thinking about what Aunt Alice had said about his father.

Uncle Fred handed each of the boys a shovel, and he grabbed some wire to mend the fence. No one mentioned anything about Jesse, even though he weighed heavily on each of their minds.

Sam put extra strength into digging holes for the wooden posts at a pace that made Oliver and Fred smile. It was close to noon and boiling hot when they looked up and saw a cloud of dust rise in the distance and heard the whine of a car barreling down the dirt road.

Uncle Fred set down his shovel, wiped his brow, and looked at Sam worriedly. He had an inkling of who it was coming down the road.

Sam tensed his shoulders in anticipation of the unwelcome visitor.

Oliver eyed Sam, noticing his jaw muscles flexing. He walked over to him and put his hand on his shoulder. "Stay calm, my friend. I'm right here with you. Holler if you need me."

CHAPTER TWELVE

DADDY DEAREST

A FEW MINUTES LATER, a '69 Buick Skylark flew down the long driveway and came to a stop, in a flurry of dust and gravel. A wiry, weather-beaten man of about fifty, or so, with bloodshot eyes and a skin-tight T-shirt, clinging against his sweaty chest, stepped out of the car in a haze of smoke and looked around the ranch. As his eyes finally landed on Uncle Fred, he threw his hat up in the air, and hollered. "Well, I'll be a monkey's uncle. Hot damn! Sure is good to see you, Freddie boy."

Uncle Fred bristled as he looked at Jesse. He hated being called Freddie boy and slung a growl at the unwelcome visitor. "Alice 'll be glad to see you," he hollered over, and turned his back and continued to dig another post hole.

Hearing the commotion, Aunt Alice came bursting out of the house with bleach in her hair and Saran wrap laced around her head. Wearing her high heels, short-shorts, and halter top, she scurried over to Jesse and gave him a big hug and kiss. "My goodness. I've barely seen you these last few years, and now, here you are – two days in a row. This is wonderful," Aunt Alice gushed and squeezed him around the neck.

"Mighty good to see you, sis, but I came to see my son. He must be all grown up by now," Jesse said, squinting his crinkled eyes. "That must be him over yonder with Freddie boy. Got him workin,' I see."

She gushed. "Yes, that's Sam. He's so handsome now… and so sophisticated. Got a real good job in Los Angeles, too."

"Well, it's no wonder. He got the smart genes from me, not from the squaw, and that's a fact. I wonder if he's as smooth with the ladies, though, 'cause I see he's got the looks from me, too. I could teach him a trick or two about taming the broads." He gave Aunt Alice a wink. "All ya gotta do to reel one in is tell 'em how you love her and can't live without her. Then, bam! You got her hooked, line and sucker." He slapped his leg and laughed. "Even if you smack 'em around a bit it don't matter… I swear, they even likes ya more."

Aunt Alice winced at those words, wondering what had happened to her sweet younger brother. She started to worry about Sam, with all his trouble – and now with Jesse showing up, it all made her stomach twist.

"Say, Alice… who's that big Injun over there? Freddie boy got himself a low-life worker, I see. Sam shouldn't be hanging out with that one. He looks mean as hell." Jesse noted, eyeing the muscular Indian, who was staring back at him, shooting daggers. Jesse involuntarily winced.

Jesse hollered out. "Well, if it isn't my son, come back home to roost. How about a big hug for your pa, who drove like a bat outa hell to see ya."

Sam ignored him and continued digging another post hole.

"Hold up there, partner! Where's your manners? It ain't polite to ignore the one who brought you into this world. Gave you my seed. You gotta be grateful for that…"

Jesse's words died off as he watched, albeit a bit nervously, as Sam stomped over to him, looking ferocious.

"As far as I'm concerned, I don't have a pa... so save your breath and shut your mouth. I hope I've got none of your rotten 'seed'..."

"Hey! What kinda way is that to talk to your father?" he blanched. "I did as good as I could under the circumstances, so don't disrespect me. I haven't been around as much as I wanted to, but I've always wished the best for you. Right now, I'd like to get to know you a bit better... if you're willing to let go of the past and don't begrudge me for being a man. Got my needs, ya know. Ladies say I'm like that Marlboro dude you see on all those billboards alongside the roads."

"Sorry you wasted your time. Like I said earlier, I'm not interested in you, the Marlboro dude or your manly needs. You wouldn't know what it's like to be a man, anyway."

"Well, if you ain't an ungrateful one," Jesse said, fuming. "You know, I wouldn't be such a smart ass if I were you. I hear you boys gotta big reward out on ya. Five- thousand smackers is what they're offerin'... for each of ya. Best watch your back. Sheriff might just come sniffing around these parts and find ya both."

Sam spit in between his shoes.

"Looks like you and your ma are just alike. She wasn't grateful either... an' look how she ended up."

Sam's entire body burned with fury – shaking so hard he could hardly hold his hands steady.

"You might be heading in the same direction if you ain't careful an..."

Before Jesse could finish Sam ran over and swiftly landed a solid punch with his fist that slammed into the side of his face. Jesse's head went spinning, and he fell over. Sam's anger spilled over into a boiling rage... thoughts of killing Jesse filtered through his mind.

Jesse's eyes glazed over as he looked at Sam... a hint of fear surfaced briefly. He slowly pulled himself off the ground and staggered to his feet and spat out a mouthful of blood from his split lip. Alice watched in horror – torn between her brother and Sam. She stood stunned – not sure who to go to first. She winced at the sight of Jesse holding his jaw while blood trickled down his face.

"You gotta rag or cloth for my head?" he asked, angrily. "That boy's gotta bad temper that's gonna land him in trouble… real soon, I 'spect."

Aunt Alice could barely speak. She needed to regain her senses. "Yes, I've got a cloth for you," she said, hurrying into the kitchen, with Jesse following closely behind – throwing Sam a warning glare.

Uncle Fred looked at Sam, amazed at the boy's grit. "Got to say I'm glad you stood up to that scum, Sam," he said proudly.

To Uncle Fred's mind, Sam seemed like a good steady worker, but not actually the fighting type. *Thought Sam was softened a bit by the big city living. Apparently, he was wrong.*

Oliver grinned. "That was quite a punch, Sam. Guess it's been inside you for quite a time. That guy deserved what you gave him, and more. I wanted to take a swing at him myself, but you clearly didn't need my help."

Holding his bruised hand, Sam looked at Uncle Fred and Oliver and smiled. "Must say, it felt real good to do that. I think my mother would've approved."

A moment later, Jesse came storming out of the house holding a bag of ice to his face. A worried Aunt Alice trailed behind him and asked, "Are you sure you can drive? Your face looks pretty bad."

Ignoring her, Jesse opened the car door with such force, it swung back and banged shut. Growling incoherently, he opened the car door again, with less vigor this time, and hopped inside. Once he had lit a cigarette and popped a can of Hamm's beer, he fired up the engine. Aunt Alice hurried over to his car, and he spat out. "That ain't no son of mine, Alice. You can have him." He put the car in reverse, gravel spitting out from the tires, then turned around and roared off down the road.

"Don't do anything foolish," Aunt Alice cried out after him, wringing her hands in despair. She flicked the ashes from her Virginia Slim cigarette and took another long drag. Then she jumped in alarm, put her hand to her Saran-wrapped head. "Oh, my Lordie. My hair's gonna fall out if I don't wash out this bleach." She yelled to Fred, "Bring the boys inside and feed them. I'm all in a tizzy. Might need a stiff gin and tonic to calm myself, before I go to work." She hustled up the steps, high heels clattering on the wooden boards.

They all watched her in amazement as she ran into the house. Uncle Fred turned to the boys with a grin. "You hungry? I've got some spam I could fry up and I'll make you boys some of my famous pickle berry pancakes. Of course, they're only famous with me," he said, chuckling. "Maybe get us a big glass of lemonade, as well. Hot as blazes now, so let's mosey on inside."

Oliver threw down his shovel, wiped the perspiration from his brow, took off his sweat-soaked shirt, and hung it on the post.

Sam did the same. In just a few days of work, his arms were filling out, his waist trim. He was stronger – and it felt good.

Oliver and Sam headed to the outside pump and took turns putting their heads under the cool water. Oliver's bronzed body glistened with the droplets that ran down his back, and his long hair dripped with moisture. He shook his head, sending his hair and droplets flying into the air. As they walked toward the house, Uncle Fred handed them a towel to dry themselves.

"That Jesse is a real sonofabitch." Uncle Fred grumbled, more to himself, as he followed Sam and Oliver into the kitchen.

"I really don't remember a lot about Jesse, other than that he was mean to my mother. Didn't like him then, and don't like him now. He used to scare the daylights out of me. Think I got over the scared part," Sam smiled. "It felt good to knock the crap out of him. Never thought I could kill before, until now… and for one brief moment I wanted to. Had to hold myself back… didn't want to give the sheriff a *real* cause to hang me."

"That thought crossed my mind, too." Oliver commented wryly. "No one could blame you if he landed in a ditch somewhere. He's got a coward's way… the kind that smiles on the wrong side of their face. Seen a lot of those people in my lifetime." He stopped as sparks of anger flashed from his deep blue eyes. I agree with Uncle Fred that he's a no-good bugger, but he's not worth getting into trouble over," Oliver said, and sat down at the table.

Uncle Fred poured the boys a large glass of lemonade. They saluted each other and drank it down in one gulp.

When Sam emptied his glass, he filled it again. He turned to Uncle Fred. "What do you think Jesse 'll do? He was steaming mad when he left. You don't think he'll turn us in do you?" He twirled his glass in circles, a worried frown creased his brow.

"One never knows with that one Sam. We'll be extra careful," he said thoughtfully. "Like I said. He's a real sonofabitch and I was only polite because of your Aunt Alice. She would have been real upset with me if I caused any trouble or said anything bad about him."

Uncle Fred hurried into the kitchen, whipping up his special pancakes. He added a couple of dollops of his pickle berry jam to the mix, then cracked a couple eggs, and began to whip up the mixture.

Soon, Aunt Alice traipsed out of the bathroom, her hair wrapped in a worn yellow towel, wearing her pink paisley robe. She sat down at the table, lit another Virginia Slim, and inhaled deeply – blowing a puff of smoke in the air. Her robe slipped down as she reached over for an ashtray. Oliver and Sam quickly averted their glance.

Uncle Fred came out of the kitchen with more lemonade and grinned at his wife.

"Ooopsy-whoopsy, boys," she said, pulling up her robe. "I swear I can hardly get anything big enough to fit around my curves. I'll let you in on a little secret," she said, conspiratorially. "That's why all the guys at the Slippery Elm come in… to take a peak." She smiled and took another long drag on her cigarette.

Oliver and Sam shifted in their seats uncomfortably, averting their eyes. That woman made them uneasy with her unconventional and loose ways. But Uncle Fred was used to her outrageous behavior and not only took it in his stride but was tickled by it. In the kitchen, he was cooking up a storm and chuckling heartily at his wife's wild ways.

"Say, sugar plum," Aunt Alice said, sniffing the air. "Are you making those pickle berry pancakes? Those things stink up the whole house." She whispered to the boys, "And taste even worse." She winked at the boys. "Thought I'd gag when I took a bite. That was enough for me. I can't believe he likes them… or thinks anyone else would. But that's my Freddie." She giggled and blew out a huge plume of smoke.

"Thought the boys might appreciate them, sweet cheeks." Uncle Fred said, dipping a cup in the batter and pouring it onto the griddle to sizzle.

Aunt Alice snorted out a reply. "I'll take a spam sandwich, if you don't mind. And be generous with the relish and put some extra horseradish on it as well."

"Coming right up, sugar plum," Uncle Fred called out and came out later and set down a pile of pancakes on the table. "Dig in, boys. Hope you like them."

Sam and Oliver eyed the pancakes with suspicion, and asked, "What did you say were in these pancakes, Uncle Fred?"

"Well, you know, my prized pickles from the garden, along with my other secret ingredients. If I tell you I'd have to… oh never mind. I was trying to be clever but realized I wasn't clever at all."

Oliver peered at the pancakes and picked one up with his fork to inspect and then shrugged his shoulders. He didn't ask any more questions about the "famous pickle berry pancakes" and piled a stack on his plate, poured on extra syrup, for cautionary measures, and began to eat. He was starving. Uncle Fred brought out a platter of fried spam along with Aunt Alice's sandwich.

Aunt Alice took a bite of her sandwich, wiped her mouth primly, and looked at Sam with a feeling of pride. *I'm so proud he's my nephew*, she thought. A stab of guilt ran through her as she thought of her brother. "I'm real sorry about your dad, sweetheart. I'm sure he didn't mean those things he said to you earlier. I think he's just frustrated that he hasn't found himself yet. I'm sure he will… one day." She took another bite of her sandwich. "He's a late bloomer, dear. Very immature, is all."

"Why do you defend him after all these years, Aunt Alice? He's never going to change… except maybe for the worse. He acts like he's something real cool and special, but he's far from that," Sam said with a mouthful of food. "Comparing himself to the Marlboro Man, is ludicrous… and I don't care how many Marlboros he smokes, he'll never be that guy… doesn't even come close."

"I know he's always admired that good-looking hunk in the commercials," said Aunt Alice. "I smoke Virginia Slims, but I don't call myself Virginia – let alone Slim. Gotta have something to shake." She grinned wickedly and gave a little wiggle in the chair, then paused. "I can't imagine your father will tell anyone you're here or turn you in. He's got his issues an' all, but he wouldn't do that to you, Sam. You're his son, for heaven's sake."

Uncle Fred set down his fork on his plate. "Now, I know he's your brother, sweet cheeks, but he's got a side to him you choose to overlook."

Oliver and Sam raised their eyebrows, looking at Aunt Alice frown, as she took a bite of her sandwich, her jaw working furiously.

"That's not fair. I know my brother hasn't been a real good role model for Sam or much of a husband, for that matter. But deep inside he's got a good heart. I just know it. I tried to teach him that growing up." Aunt Alice wiped away a tear. "I did my best."

Uncle Fred put his arms around his wife and crooned, "Don't cry, baby. It's just that… well, I haven't seen that good side to him yet. How about we change the subject. Let's talk about the weather and how it's been a while since we've seen some rain. Now, eat your spam sandwich, dear. You don't want it to get cold and hard, plus… you're gonna need your energy for your show tonight."

Aunt Alice straightened her shoulders, took another bite of her sandwich and wiped her eyes. "This is delicious, sugar plum. Thanks for looking after me." She chewed for a few minutes, contemplating, then turned to Sam. "I hope you understand that I care about you and your well-being. If I thought that Jesse would turn you in… well, I'd be done with him. I want you to know that sweetie." She pulled back her chair and walked around the table to kiss Sam on the cheek. "You're my handsome, boy. Always will be… even if you didn't call me much after you left. I suppose I was an embarrassment to you," she said, solemnly. Then, suddenly, she smiled and started twirling around in circles. "Well… how many guys can say they have a real hot auntie?" She pinched his cheeks, "and," she exclaimed, turning to Oliver, "look at this noble friend of yours. I can't leave *him* out." And before Oliver could move, Aunt Alice grabbed him around the neck and kissed him firmly on his lips. "Just a little something to remember me by," she said in a purr, stroking his long black hair. "You're a handsome one," she said, staring into his eyes, then added in a more serious tone. "I see in your quiet demeanor a soul that runs deep as a river… swift and strong. Real special." She pulled her eyes away and said, "Ain't that right, Freddie. This boy is powerful, through and through."

Uncle Fred cleared his throat and spoke thoughtfully – with pride. "My Alice here can spot a no-good wanker in a blink, so when she tells you that you're something special, you best believe she knows what she's talking about. And I couldn't agree with her more." He looked adorningly at his wife. "I know she's a firecracker and loves to kick up her heels and dance around and flirt with the fellas, but she's sharp as a tack, and I know she loves me." He leaned over and kissed Alice sweetly. "And I love her more than the stars and moon in the sky. So, I don't mind if she has a bit of fun with the boys… keeps her young and happy. Got a happy wife… you got a happy home."

Oliver looked at Uncle Fred and admired the guy for his honesty. But Aunt Alice… she was something else. She may have a keen observation of people, but she made him uncomfortable with her suggestive glances… That aside, he would always be grateful for their kindness and, most of all, for their willingness to help. And regardless of her unusual ways, it was hard not to like *Aunt Alice*.

Aunt Alice stood up to excuse herself. "Gotta paint my toes, boys. I like to dangle 'em in the men's faces when I'm working. Keeps the bacon rolling in so my Freddie can cook it up in the kitchen. That's why I love him," she cooed sweetly, sashaying across the room. "He is the best thing that's happened to me since hairspray."

Sam was learning more about his Aunt Alice. When he was younger, she would embarrass him. When he discovered she was a dancer, he was mortified and wanted to flee. But as he sat here with Oliver and Uncle Fred, he came to realize that, yes, she was different than most women, but she had spirit and an enormous heart. He was thankful for that, even though she danced seductively around his friend, trying to kiss him. But that's who she was. Seeing her through different eyes now, he started to admire her.

"We have more work to do, and the day is still young – so I guess we should get going," Oliver said. "Oh, and thanks for the pancakes… they were, umm, unusual," he grinned and stood and looked at Uncle Fred. "I could finish up with the chicken coop. It shouldn't be much more work… only a couple more hours or so. Plus…" he smiled, "gotta keep the girls safe from the hungry coyotes."

Sam rubbed his stiff shoulders and stretched out the ache from digging the posts. "I'll get the chicken wire and help Oliver. Once we get that done, we could start patching up the barn."

Uncle Fred looked like he was going to cry as his eyes filled up and he sniffled. "I appreciate you boys thinking of me and my girls, but it's time I start to get you boys a safer place to hide, in case the sheriff happens by. I don't trust that Jesse as far as I can throw him – and, trust me, I'd like to kick his ass from here to Timbuktu. I've got a root cellar I use for my canning goods and stuff. It's not real roomy, but it'd be a good place to hide in case of snoopers and such coming by."

Oliver agreed with Uncle Fred about Jesse and said, "I gotta hunch that guy would probably turn us in for a nickel. He's the type to do it. I hope if Indigo, were to hear anything about the sheriff heading this way, she could get word to us. Unless we're able to clear our names, we won't be safe – anywhere."

"You got that pretty straight, Oliver. That's why we're going to be extra vigilant."

Sam agreed they should be extra cautious.

"Well, if you boys are ready to get back at it," said Uncle Fred, with thumb in pocket, "I'm ready. If you want to wait awhile to rest your sore bones, though, that's okay by me."

Sam and Oliver were already standing by the door. "No need to, Uncle Fred," said Sam, flexing his newly formed muscles, and grinning. "I'm ready."

"Yep, let's get going," Oliver agreed, heading out the door. "Gotta hunch we'd better hustle," looking up at the sky, and shivered. *It feels like something is in the wind, and it doesn't bode well,* he thought, but kept his feelings to himself.

Sam glanced at Oliver, noticing his concern. He thought

Oliver seemed unsettled and wondered if he had a premonition of things to come – so he watched his friend closely and hustled along.

"Just remember. Our biggest defense is you can detect a car coming from miles away," Uncle Fred said, as they headed to the cellar on the south side of the house. "So, at the first signs of dust blowing, you boys 'll need to skedaddle down there. First, though, we need to get it fixed up a bit for you." Uncle Fred opened the cellar door and walked down the rickety stairs. He turned on an overhead light, which was a single bulb hanging down in the center of the room that flickered and swung back and forth, casting an unsettling glow throughout the damp room.

"Okay, boys. Come on down." As Oliver and Sam walked down the steps, a musty smell drifted up. The cellar had a dirt floor with rows and rows of wooden shelves that lined the side of the wall with canned goods.

"Here's a whole section for my pickle berry jam," Uncle Fred said proudly.

Sam held back a grin and wondered why he made so much of that stuff. It certainly wasn't his favorite and he wondered where he got the recipe. He managed to sell a bunch at a local store, but to him it tasted like salty brine mixed with sugar.

Oliver's face cracked a slight smile at the mention of the controversial jam.

"Okay, boys. I got a small room in the back," Uncle Fred said, yanking on the old, rotted door. "I think you two might fit in there. It'll be a tight fit for sure, if you don't mind being squeezed a bit," he grinned, "but it'll hide you pretty good."

Sam cringed as he peeked inside the small cubicle. "Looks like a lot of spider webs in there. Maybe we could sweep a few cobwebs out before we give it a try," Sam said, shuddering, then reminded himself they were part of the natural order.

"Is there a broom down here? I'll give it a sweep," Oliver said, noticing Sam's reluctance to go inside.

Uncle Fred found a half-worn broom and handed it to Oliver. "Soon as you're done, let's Give it a try and see how you fit."

Oliver swept the tangled webs out of the cubicle and shook free any of the spiders outside. He knew every creature had a purpose, and spiders were no different. As he banged the broom outside on the cellar door, he stopped and tilted his head to listen. Everyone stood motionless as they heard the rumbling of a car coming down the road.

Uncle Fred ran up the steps to see. Someone was flying down the road, heading toward his house. "Stay down here, boys. Let me see who it is." He quickly slammed the door shut, hurried to the front porch, and sat down – acting as though he were quietly passing the fine afternoon away. He watched with curiosity as an unfamiliar Chevy truck skidded to a stop in the driveway.

A lean guy, about thirty years old or so, stepped down from the truck and hollered out, "It must be my lucky day. Is that you Uncle Fred? It's me, Skip. It's been quite a spell since I last seen you and Aunt Alice. How ya both doing these days?" Not waiting for an answer, Skip moseyed up the path toward Uncle Fred and pulled a toothpick from his mouth. "How's Aunt Alice? I wanted to come over and see if you're both doing fine and whatnot. I heard there could be trouble heading this way." He picked at a front tooth with his toothpick. "Word is, Sam and another Indian fellow escaped from a noose in Miners Gulch, and neither's been found yet. Word scatters around these parts pretty quick, ya know… especially being runaways." His eyes swiveled back and forth, scanning the area.

"Well, if you came out here for gossip, I don't have any… and if you came out here looking for Sam, I'd say you wasted your time," Uncle Fred said, with a warning undertone.

"I don't mean to cause any trouble or anything, but if you're harboring fugitives… you might be in a world of trouble. I know Sam's your nephew an' all, but…" His words drifted off for a moment and he kicked a couple stones. Then, he continued. "That'd be a darn shame to see you and Aunt Alice get into trouble. Ya know how Injuns are, Uncle Fred – even the half-breeds. Unpredictable as hell. So, I'd just want you to be real careful. You don't wanna get yourself caught up in a mess…"

"I'd say, not looking for your advice, so…" before he could finish, his noxious nephew, Skip interrupted. "Heard there's a big reward out for Sam and the other Indian fellow he's in cahoots with. Not a bad thing to have a little extra cash on hand. Times are a bit tough now… not that I would turn in my cousin, ya know." He kicked at a few more stones, like he was nervous. "Heard they were planning a big robbery of some sort. Always kinda thought Sam was trouble from the git-go."

"Well, I don't listen to gossip, so I wanna know what did ya come out here for?" Uncle Fred asked, angrily. "You waited all these years to show up, and now you're looking for incriminating information about your cousin. I'd say you came a long way for nothing." He was on the verge of telling him to leave when Skip said, "You don't need to worry none about me," he winked, with a slap on Uncle Fred's back.

"Been meaning to come out here for a spell now… well, since I'm here, would you mind if I said hello to Aunt Alice? I've been meaning to stop over at the Slippery Elm, but it's a long drive. She's really something," Skip said, with a big grin. "Always been my favorite aunt."

Uncle Fred hesitated. He didn't want to invite Skip inside but realized he shouldn't act like he was hiding something. "Well, I'm sure she's pretty busy, but maybe she has time for a quick howdy. She's most likely primping – getting ready for work." He said, and quickly turned his back on Skip and hustled up the steps, hoping to discourage him from staying long.

Uncle Fred opened the screen door and called out, "Sweet cheeks! You remember nephew Skip? He stopped by to say howdy. Are you decent?" He called out, and then turned just in time to see Skip stumble on his way into the kitchen. He thought, *serves him right coming out here, itching to cause trouble.*

Skip mumbled something incoherent and then suddenly lost his balance and fell hard against the kitchen counter and crashed to the floor with a loud 'boom!'

Uncle Fred looked on in horror as Skip started to thrash around wildly… his legs jerked in odd angles and his body shook uncontrollably. Blood was dripping out of the side of his head, and he was drooling profusely from his mouth.

Uncle Fred hollered out in alarm. "Oh, my heavens, Skip."

Hearing the loud commotion, Aunt Alice came flying out of the bathroom and nearly fainted when she saw Skip bleeding from his head and convulsing. His eyes were rolled back in his head, and he was gasping for breath. She held on to the door and asked, "What on earth happened, Freddie? Did he have a heart attack?" She sobbed at the sight of him. "It looks like he gonna die – right here – in our house and on my kitchen floor."

Uncle Fred wasn't sure who to attend to first and stood frozen, trying to figure out what to do. He shook his head to clear it and then said as calmly as possible. "I'll call an ambulance. He needs help."

"Oh, my Lordie, sugar. What are we going to do?" Aunt Alice cried, running around the kitchen – her high heels clacking furiously on the floor. Then she started to panic. "We can't let him die here. The sheriff will surely come out and…" She stopped.

Uncle Fred was usually a rational person, but this scene shook him up. Suddenly the screen door banged open and in flew Oliver and Sam. He breathed in gratefully. "Oh, thank God you're here."

Sam was a bit shaken. "We heard all the commotion up here, so we busted out of the cellar door and came running."

Oliver looked at the man lying on the floor and spoke to Uncle Fred in a controlled voice. "Take Aunt Alice to the bedroom and get her to calm down." Then he looked at Sam. "I need a cool cloth and some water."

Oliver flew into action and kneeled beside Skip. Ancient instincts took over as he placed the cloth on Skip's cut to stem the flow of blood, then put his hands on Skip's head and closed his eyes. For reasons he couldn't explain, he focused on his grandfather, Hidden Spirit, for guidance. He began to pray in his Lakota language – language he had not spoken in years, but which now came flowing back with abandon. Feeling a whisper brush against his ears, encircling him, he held out his hands to the Great Spirit and sensed a smooth stone slip into his palm. His entire body began to vibrate, and a warmth spread throughout his body, as if a balmy summer breeze had entered his soul. As the whispers intensified, he squeezed the stone against his heart.

Oliver felt the man on the floor had stopped moving... his life force was slipping away. He panicked briefly, then heard a soothing, reassuring voice from somewhere far off. As soon as he heard the words, "Cokata hiyupo, mi-thakoza. Come to the center, my son." He felt himself being lifted up... lingering above his body... waiting. He suddenly lost concentration and faltered... then remembered to relax. He looked across the room and saw Skip, floating above his body, staring at Oliver – disdain written all over his face. He was tempted to slap away the look.

A loud voice thundered. "Do not seek vengeance upon the ones who are dulled by hatred. The unenlightened ones do not understand."

Oliver gasped at the voice that pierced the void. He willed himself not to lose his connection to the spirit world. So, he focused on his breath and calmed his emotions and concentrated on his task before him. His gaze wandered over to Skip, who now looked terrified. The disdain on his face had vanished, and now

– visions of his life – from childhood to present floated past him in a vivid string of cringeworthy events… then, just as quickly as the vision arrived, it dissipated. Skip floundered and flailed wildly. "Please! Someone, help me!" he wailed. Instead of heading toward the light flickering in the distance, he started to fall… down… down… down into the darkness.

Oliver looked on in disbelief. Skip was heading toward a fiery abyss – his body flailing out of control, screaming for help. A roaring blaze and a fiery whirlwind scorched the air, ready to suck him into the whirling vortex. Oliver heard Skip shout, "Forgive me. I'm sorry…" as his words ricocheted off into the ethers.

From somewhere in the outer realm, Oliver heard a voice. "Hanta yo. Clear the way." Oliver quickly sped off and sailed through the ethers and into the abyss. Just before Skip was sucked into the raging inferno, he barely managed to pull the guy back from the brink. Oliver was sweating profusely as he held the limp body in his arms, then let go.

Then with a loud thud, Skip found himself on the floor, opened his eyes and looked around, wondering if he were alive or if he had slipped into that big, black burning hole. He moved one finger at a time to make certain he wasn't dead. Then his eyes began to focus, and he slowly sat up. He felt oddly transformed… he couldn't believe the calm and peaceful feeling that filled him. The turmoil and prejudices he had created most of his life seemed to have vanished, right along with his bitterness. He rubbed his injured head, vaguely remembering he had been somewhere in the outer realm, talking to a young virile Indian with long flowing hair and astonishingly blue eyes, who helped him. Skip shuddered– grateful he hadn't landed in the fiery depths of… well… that possibility was too much to consider right now.

Skip closed his eyes, and wondered… *Was all this just a dream, or a nightmare?* He shivered remembering the vision. He remembered crying out for help. *I'm just grateful for another chance to live.*

Skip wasn't particularly religious, and only occasionally went to church – mainly Easter and Christmas.

He strangely wanted to change – become a better person. *It might take some doing, but I could start by telling Sam how sorry I am for treating him so badly when we were younger… and for my hateful thoughts – mostly against Indians.*

Skip looked at the people staring at him in concern – his Aunt Alice, Uncle Fred, his cousin, Sam. Then his eyes landed on Oliver. He looked closer at that virile young Indian, sitting next to him, who… who saved him from… from where, he couldn't be sure. *A moment ago, I held this man in contempt, and now…* He reached out to touch his face, to insure he really wasn't dreaming. *Without him, I would not be here. Was it all just a dream… or was it something more…? I thought I was going to die and be forever tormented for the cruelty I had inflicted.* He was determined to live a life with meaning. Without thinking, Skip reached out and hugged Oliver tightly, as tears filled his eyes. "Thank you," was all Skip could manage.

Oliver was almost as surprised as Skip at what had just happened. He couldn't believe he had been in the outer realm, helping this man and wondered why he was sent out there.

Oliver felt for the stone – in awe of its power. *It must carry some wicked-powerful magic,* he thought. He loosened a few fingers, anxious to glance at the mystical stone holding a secret mystery… but the stone was no longer there. He looked upward… and saw no one… then listened… and heard no one. *I've got a lot to figure out,* he thought, then looked over at the man who had mysteriously survived. A brief smile touched his lips.

Skip stood up slowly as he grabbed the table and looked around the room. He felt almost giddy, seeing everything from a different perspective now and was inspired to make amends with his cousin. "It's nice to see you, Sam. I know it's been a long time and I don't blame you if you harbor ill feelings toward me. I know

I treated you badly when we were younger, and I hope someday you might forgive me. I was a fool."

Sam was taken aback and didn't respond at first. This whole incident left him shocked. It might take a while to trust his cousin.

Skip looked at Sam, scooted his chair close, and spoke in a low tone. "I can't explain what just happened, but I could see my entire life float past – right in front of my eyes – like I was watching a movie. I was a worthless, spiteful coward," he said, full of remorse. He stared at Sam as if seeing him for the first time. Tears began to well up in his eyes and he started to sob, deeply, for several minutes. When his tears subsided, he blew his nose and glanced sheepishly at Sam and said, "I don't think I've ever shed more than a single tear in my entire life – but look at me now… bawling like a baby," he spluttered, wiping his face with the back of his hand and grinned, "but have to tell you, it feels good to let go of all those pent-up feelings. My heart was so full of hate… it was killing me."

Sam sat listening – amazed and stunned by the transformation of his long-despised cousin. For the first time in his life, he thought he might actually like the guy. Maybe it was time to let go of the past.

"I'm sorry about the trouble you're in and I'm embarrassed to say what I was going to do. Maybe someday we could spend time together to talk… if you would be open to it," Skip said, solemnly.

Sam nodded in agreement. "I think I would be open to that, Skip. Can't say I was before this, but glad you're alive."

"That makes two of us." Then, Skip went on to ask a few questions about what had happened in Miners Gulch.

Sam told him a few of the details about the sheriff and their escape, not wanting to discuss too much, just yet.

Soon after, Skip said his goodbyes with big hugs for everyone. "I surely would love to come by another time, if that's okay with you, Uncle Fred. Anything I could do to help, give me a holler."

Uncle Fred, still shaken, assured Skip that would be fine, and added, "Come by anytime you'd like."

Aunt Alice teetered over to the table in her pink satiny high heels, reeling from the earlier trauma of seeing Skip collapse on her floor. She told Uncle Fred, "I sure could use a gin and tonic right about now, with a bitty extra gin. Maybe a teeny bitty more than a bitty. My nerves are shot," she moaned, and stumbled into a chair and sat down. "I wasn't sure what was going to happen. I thought Skip was going to die right there on my kitchen floor," She fretted, and lit a Virginia Slim and then looked at Oliver in amazement. "You sure are something, is all I can say… surely something powerful. I knew it the moment I looked into those big, beautiful heavenly blue eyes."

Uncle Fred hurried back with her drink, set it on the table, then rubbed her shoulders and gave her a kiss. "This will soothe your jitters, sweet cheeks. Just take a few sips and now you can relax. We have Oliver to thank for saving Skip. That's for damn sure."

Aunt Alice raised her glass in admiration and said, "I'll drink to that," and downed her gin and tonic.

"I'll take some coffee, if you have some handy, Uncle Fred," Oliver asked.

Uncle Fred made a whole pot and sat it down at the table, along with some fresh biscuits, and he buttered some for the boys.

"How about I butter one for you sweet cheeks?"

Aunt Alice said she would pass. "All that dough bloats me. You know I have to watch my figure."

"Yes, dear," Uncle Fred said.

Sipping coffee, and eating biscuits, everyone's eyes soon landed on Oliver, looking at him in wonderment. "I'm so glad you were able to help, Oliver. That man would've surely died on Aunt Alice's kitchen floor… what a disaster that would've been," Sam said scratching his head.

Sam wanted to pepper Oliver with questions, and hesitantly

asked, "How did you save Skip? I saw you sitting there talking to me and in the next minute… you seemed to be elsewhere… I can't explain it, but it's like one minute you were here and then you weren't… seems kinda crazy and amazing at the same time." Uncle Fred watched Oliver out of the corner of his eyes, curious.

"I'm not entirely sure myself. I'm just as amazed as everyone else. I saw him looking at me with pure hatred, then… it seemed like some forces were going to take him to a dark place. He was screaming for help and said he was sorry. That's when I went after him, and next thing you know, he's back…" Oliver paused, "I guess I need to figure all this out myself."

"That's one heck of a story, Oliver. We have to be some of the luckiest people around to know you," said Uncle Fred.

"I've been telling you all along, Freddie, this fine, young, dashing Indian, is real special… I could see it in his eyes," Aunt Alice winked proudly. She stood, kissed Oliver on the cheek and announced she was getting ready for work.

Everyone hopped up at the same time, full of nervous energy, and headed outside, ready to take their minds off the earlier events and get to work.

Uncle Fred wanted to make sure the tiny room in the basement would be virtually undetected and finished sweeping away the cobwebs that dangled freely while Oliver fixed the latch on the door so it would lock securely from the inside. Sam swept the debris off the floor and patched the shelves that were ready to fall so Uncle Fred could add more jars for storage. Once all that was completed, Oliver suggested they start on the sagging porch. "A few steps are broken, and the railing is wobbly," he said. Wouldn't want Aunt Alice to trip and fall in those high heels of hers."

Everyone was happy to keep busy banging hammers, pounding nails, and sawing pieces of wood to replace the warped and broken boards. Uncle Fred said, "I've tripped on these darn things before, and I feel bad I didn't get around to this sooner. My sweet cheeks could've broken her neck the way she likes to traipse around in those spikey heels of hers."

Aunt Alice swung the screen door open, and said, "Did I hear my name being brandied about? Hope it was good." She looked at the guys hard at work and smiled. "My, my. You boys sure are a sight for sore eyes. I would love to stay and watch, but I've gotta show to put on tonight. So, off to work I go. See you later boys." She bent over and gave Sam and Oliver a kiss goodbye.

Uncle Fred hurried over to her side and held out his arm. "Let me help you down the steps dear." He proudly announced. "Got the railing and boards all fixed up for you, so your pretty shoes don't fall through the holes."

"I'd say that quite a few miracles happened, today," she gushed out. "That was real thoughtful of you boys to help my Freddie so I don't go crashing through those darn steps." Aunt Alice kissed Uncle Fred goodbye and meandered to the car with a couple wiggles for show and slid into her car… the Mustang sprung to life as she started the engine. She sat in the driveway for a minute letting the car idle, then she slipped it into gear, tooted her horn, then sped off down the road.

That night while preparing dinner, Uncle Fred said, "I got me an inkling… a bad feeling about that sheriff. We need to be real careful in the coming days."

"I agree," Oliver said, while helping him with the finishing touches in the kitchen.

Supper complete, Uncle Fred hurried over to the table and set a steaming tray of meatloaf on the table, fresh out of the oven, and hurried back with yellow summer squash – garnished with edible flowers fresh from his garden, along with big red beefsteak tomatoes, and topped off with some fresh basil and freshly made cheese… complements of Pepper.

"This dinner looks worthy of a five-star restaurant, Uncle

Fred," Sam said, appreciating the array of food and inhaled the wafting aromas.

"Dig in, boys," said a smiling Uncle Fred. "We sure worked up an appetite."

"That we did." Oliver said, admiring the beautifully arranged food. He took a big helping of everything. "Smells and looks delicious, Uncle Fred."

"Appreciate that but can't forget my sourdough bread. Be right back," said Uncle Fred as he hustled off to the kitchen. Back at the table, he sat down and fiddled with his food. Finally, he said, "I never really cared for Skip and his brother Wilbur. They were downright mean. My older brother didn't teach them to be respectful. He was full of demons from the war, I guess. He didn't treat the boys real good either… I suppose they carried *his* demons, as well."

Sam wiped his mouth and said, "Pretty amazing to see the change in him, Uncle Fred. He didn't seem like the same asshole Skip that I remember when he used to come over to the house." He took another bite of meatloaf, then said between mouthfuls of food, "I really wish Oliver could work some of his magic stuff on the sheriff… turn him into a poof of air and have him disappear with a snap of a finger."

Uncle Fred smiled. "I like that idea, Sam. Well, at least we got Skip off our backs. Gotta be thankful for that."

They all sat around for a while drinking coffee, and then everyone pitched in and helped Uncle Fred clean up the dishes. Darkness was coming and Oliver yawned. "I'm bone tired. Ready to turn in. Been a wild day."

Sam agreed, stood up, and patted Oliver on the back. "It has been one of the wildest days I've ever seen," he grinned. "Night, Uncle Fred."

"Night, boys." Uncle Fred said. As an afterthought, he added, "That was really something that you did, Oliver, saving that boy's life. I just can't stop thinking about what you did. Real glad I got to know you, and glad that you and Sam met."

"Feeling's mutual, Uncle Fred. But what you and Aunt Alice did by taking us in was pretty courageous, itself. I'd call you a warrior… someone our elders would be proud of. Goodnight, now."

As the boys made their way to the barn, Sam asked Oliver, "Do you think the sheriff 'll be coming for us soon?"

Oliver said, "We'll definitely need to sleep with one eye open until things get settled. We know it's going to be just a matter of time before he comes or someone else does, so we'd better head out soon. I just hate to leave with us being called 'felons' and hunted down by every red neck or ranch hand for miles around… especially with that reward out for us. They're 'll be dead or alive posters all over the place."

"Damn. We'll never be safe, no matter where we go. We need help, but for now we'll just have to watch our backs," Sam said sullenly. "Goodnight."

CHAPTER THIRTEEN

THE SHEDDING OF BLOOD

OLIVER LAY BACK on his pillow in the loft and thought about the smooth stone that slipped into his hand earlier when he was helping Skip out in the ethers. *It's not a stone I've ever seen before… both hot and cold… sizzling and freezing.* "I wish I still had it so I could examine it more closely. Maybe you will come back…" he whispered a prayer. "So, I could know your secrets… know where to go, or if I should stay and fight." As Oliver thought about the stone he squeezed his hand tight, and suddenly, he felt a gentle vibration and a warmth spread throughout his body. *It was the stone!* He thought excitedly as he stared into its depthless beauty. The feeling was not only comforting but soothing as well… soon the stone lulled him into a sleepy state. Just as he closed his eyes ready to drift off, he felt a sudden jolt burst up his spine. His eyes flew open, and he gasped – visions of death whisked on by. Then he saw blood pouring out of a headless body, flowing like a faucet. He covered his eyes to still the haunting vision. *Whose body is it… whose blood, is it?* He wondered nervously, as he paced back and forth in the loft, unable to sleep, pondering his disturbing vision. *Visions don't always mean what they seem*, he thought, and he tried to clear his mind and think rational. *It must be my imagination playing tricks on me.*

"Maybe I should pray to the Great Spirit, so I can understand the meaning of the vision." So he leaned his back against the wall, crossed his legs, and waited. Waiting for what, he wasn't sure – maybe a miracle. He continued to pray. After an hour or more passed his eyelids grew heavy. He shook his head to stay awake, but soon the lure of sleep overtook him, and he dozed off into a comforting dream in which he saw the face of a young Indian girl smiling at him and felt the smooth stone pulse in his hand. Then he heard a far-off whisper. "Careful, Mi-thakoza. Keep your eyes sharp… they are coming."

Oliver's eyes suddenly flew open. He eased himself up on his elbows and listened carefully in the darkness, wondering if this was a dream, *or did I actually hear a voice talking to me?* Prickles started to rise on his arms then spread over his entire body. He heard a slight snore from Sam. The chirp of the crickets seemed irritating as he listened for suspicious sounds in the night. He squeezed the stone in his hand, then held it up to a sliver of light shining through the crack in the barn. A faint voice warned, "Watch out for the Wachicus!" Then a young girl's voice cried out, "Run, Oliver. Run!" He knew right then the stone held mystical powers.

Oliver's heart pounded so hard he could feel it pulse against his chest. He was wide awake now, jumped up, threw on his boots, and shook Sam. "Wake up! They're coming!"

Sam sat up, not sure if he was dreaming, and rubbed the sleep from his eyes. Then realizing it was Oliver shaking him, he asked, still groggy. "What is it…? What's going on?"

"We must get out of here. Now!"

"Is someone coming? Did you hear something?"

"Come," Oliver said, worried. "I think the sheriff is close. We need to get out of here… fast as we can… as silently as we can across the yard to the cellar. Ready?" he asked. Not waiting for an answer, he pulled Sam up.

Sam didn't bother putting on his boots as they both slid down the ladder and opened the creaky barn door just wide enough to slip though. They waited for a moment, hoping no one had heard them. Ears sharp, muscles taunt, holding their breath, they waited a moment and saw nothing suspicious. But Oliver's skin prickled with apprehension. He remembered the vision and moved like lightning. Feet barely touching the ground, they flew across the yard heading to the cellar. Sam was right behind Oliver, panting, and they quickly opened the door, just as dawn was beginning to break. Oliver scanned the landscape and almost dropped the cellar door in surprise at the sight of a few crows flying overhead, then landing in a nearby tree, clacking their beaks. Sam shivered and said, "It's the crows Oliver. Maybe they're here to help?" The sight of yellow eyes glowing from the trees like a beacon, gave them a glimmer of hope. The birds squawked, and then flew into the shadows of the leaves and branches, waiting silently.

Oliver and Sam raced down the rickety cellar steps that seemed ready to give at any moment. Sam lamented the fact he hadn't fixed the steps yesterday. He hoped they wouldn't go crashing down *now*. It was pitch black inside the root cellar as they inched their way to the back, groping around for the door. Oliver found the latch and pulled gently on the old handle. As they squeezed their way inside the tiny space, they heard a loud crash upstairs as someone stormed up the steps.

The front door was knocked off its hinges and slammed to the floor. There was shouting and cussing and boots stomping on the floor.

"Alice Evers! Get your ass out of bed and get down here! I mean, pronto! That is, if you want to see another day. You too, Fred."

Aunt Alice, still groggy, cracked her eyes open, and stumbled out of bed, smothering a cry. "Oh my God! It's the sheriff, Freddie!" She threw on her silk robe that lay on a nearby chair with her high heel slippers.

Fred jumped up in alarm and looked at his wife with frightened eyes. He spoke softly. "Don't be afraid, sweet cheeks. Just act calm and deny everything. Those boys are safe in the cellar. I'll be right behind you. Try to act surprised when he starts questioning you."

Aunt Alice nodded, quietly left the bedroom, and hurried into the kitchen, heels clicking on the linoleum floor. It was five-thirty in the morning and the sheriff had all the lights turned on. Alice stopped cold as Sheriff Joe hurled his bulky frame next to her, pistol drawn, and shoved the barrel right between her eyes – blurring her vision.

Her entire body was frozen with fear when she heard the sheriff growl in a deceptively soft voice. "Where the hell are those felons, Alice?" he questioned. "I know they're here." He grabbed her face, hard. "You lie to me and I'll plug you so full of holes no one will recognize your pretty face, which'll look like a bloody stump." He cocked his pistol in warning. "You best spit it out right now."

Aunt Alice's mouth was so dry she could barely speak. "I… uh… I…" She didn't want to die, but she couldn't tell the sheriff where to find the boys, as thoughts of dying flashed through her mind. She wanted to cry, but she was so frightened she couldn't shed a drop.

Fred came bounding out of the bedroom, shirt unbuttoned, mouth agape. He saw the sheriff with his gun pointed at Alice and grabbed his quaking heart. He couldn't let her die. She was the love of his life. He loved Sam and Oliver, as well, and he could feel himself torn as he stared at the sheriff.

"I… why are you accusing me…?" Alice asked, shaking from head to toe.

Then, WHAM! Sheriff Joe bashed her in the head with the butt of his pistol, and she slid to the floor in a heap, moaning… blood dripping down her face.

"I told you not to lie to me, bitch."

Uncle Fred's legs managed to work, and they got him over to his wife. "You've got no right to barge into our house without a warrant!" The sheriff stopped him at gunpoint.

Sheriff Joe leered at Alice and nudged her with his boots. "I'll shoot your lame-ass husband first, Alice Evers. You can watch him die, then I'll shoot you next if you don't start singing outa tune real fast. I am in a hurry and out of patience!"

Suddenly, the screen door banged open and in traipsed a disheveled Jesse, Hamm's beer in hand, strutting like a wild turkey. His hair was askew and was sprouting a half-grown gray beard.

Sheriff Joe wasn't sure if he was happy to see Jesse barging in. He looked him up and down and noticed a huge hickey on his neck.

"Say sheriff," he said, wheezing. "Hope I'm not too late. Just wanted to make sure that big ole Injun didn't escape. Thought I'd see if I could give you a hand," he grinned, while taking a swig of his beer. "Checking to make sure my reward is… uh…" He was flustered under the sheriff's scrutiny. "Well, you know… I… uh… my money that I got coming…"

Sheriff Joe cut him off. "Shut your dumb ass mouth. You're telling me you're worried about money at a time like this? I should lock your ass up for being stupid, barging in here and question-ing me."

"I wasn't doubting you, Sheriff," Jesse said contritely, and slurped another drink of beer. "I wanted to let you know, Sam, my son… well, he ain't a thief. He's got a big ole chip on his shoulder for sure, thinking he's some sort of big wisecrack living out there in Los Angeles, an' all. He can't help it. He left Wyoming to go an' live in the land of the hippie-dippie doo-dah shit. Gotta lot of queers out there I hear that might-a messed with his head."

"Shut up, Jesse, before I shoot you for running off at that big fat mouth of yours. I already know most of that crap." Sheriff Joe turned back to Alice. "Now your sis, here," he said, kicking her in the stomach with the tip of his alligator boots. "She's got some real nice titties that she likes to shake around at the Slippery Elm. But right now, she'd have to do a mite more than shake those things around me… that is, if she wants to live."

He pulled on her blood-streaked hair. "Okay, now, you big titty bitch! Get your ass off the floor and show me where you and ole Freddie hid those two felons… Sam and Oliver."

Uncle Fred walked up to the sheriff, hands shaking like a shriveled leaf, and said, "My Alice hasn't done anything, and she doesn't know anything, either. It was all me! You can lock me up or shoot me, I don't care, but leave her alone."

"Well, ain't that dang sweet – 'bout melts my heart, an' boo-hoody-hoo," he mimicked viscously. "I'll shoot the both of you if you don't start singing… real pretty like – right here on the spot. Best tell me what you done with them, or I'll bring in every bounty hunter I can find and send in for more troopers from every county in the state if I have to. Then I'll knock every square inch of this broken-down place to the ground. Then, I'll torch it. One way or the other, I'll get 'em. Your choice, Freddie boy. Live or die!"

Suddenly everyone jumped at the sound of a loud clattering below the kitchen floor.

Sheriff Joe's eyes widened like a cat ready to pounce, and quickly sprang into action, waving his gun around like a madman. He yanked Alice's arm and in one swift motion and went clamoring out the door.

"You got them hiding in your cellar?" he asked, furiously, and shook her until her head almost snapped off. "I should plug you full of holes right now." He yanked Alice's head back and cocked his pistol. "Show me to the cellar door."

Alice started down the steps. But before she could move, the sheriff spotted Oliver and Sam running across the yard. Shoving Alice aside, he went barreling after them, gun aimed – his bulky framed looked like a huge barrel… jiggling and bouncing as he ran. He wasn't as fast as Sam and Oliver, but his adrenaline kicked in and his feet were pounding surprisingly fast. He shouted at the top of his lungs, "Stop before I shoot!"

Sam and Oliver kept running, heading toward the barn as a few shots were fired.

Aunt Alice looked on in horror with Uncle Fred at her side, holding her. She wiped her eyes and blew her nose. She couldn't believe her nephew and Oliver were about to die. She shoved her shoulders back. From somewhere deep inside, a ball of gumption rose up with a flourish, filling her with determination. She would not let that bastard bully her any longer. AND, she would not let him murder Sam and Oliver. She adored them both more than anything. Those boys gave her the mighty strength of Samson. So, she flew up the stairs, yanked open a closet door, and hauled out a great big shotgun. It was kept loaded for emergencies – and this was an emergency. There were only two bullets in the chambers. *That should kill him twice as good.*

Uncle Fred saw Alice come downstairs with the great big shotgun. He pleaded in dismay. "Sweet cheeks! What are you going to do? That shotgun is about as big as you are. I beg you – don't go out there. He'll kill you."

Alice Evers was full of fiery determination. "I've had enough of fat assholes leering at me to last me a lifetime – and especially that fat asshole that just threatened to kill me. I'm done being scared of him," she fumed, "and his big mouth threats. This time, he has pushed me just a little too far. He's one mean sonofabitch, but I'll never let another sonofabitch threaten me or my family again. So, out of my way, Freddie. A new Alice has just emerged."

Fire burned in her belly as she sped down the steps. Renewed strength filled her entire body as she kicked off her high-heeled slippers and raced to the barn. Her insides pounded like thunder as she neared the barn and waited a moment by the door. Then she heard the sheriff bellow. "Better come out boys, before your ass is a goner."

She saw Jesse, gun in hand, follow the sheriff into the barn. It made her madder than a fighting hen. Her eyes blurred over at the thought he would sell out his son for money. *My own brother!* She'd been fooled by men before, but now she had visions of shooting them both. *Good thing there's two bullets.*

Scenes from the past raced through her mind of the sheriff taking her out in the back of the bar and having his way with her. She never told Freddie about what that scum had done to her. She had kept those memories locked away for a long time… that is, until now. Now, she was going to even the score. That loud-mouthed bastard was going to pay. She felt an even greater surge of strength course through her as she plowed into the barn. Her big shotgun wobbled in her hands as her eyes adjusted to the dim light inside and the shadows playing against the wall. As she waited, her heart pounded so loudly she thought it might jump out of her chest. She heard footsteps around the bales of stacked hay and willed herself not to faint. She concentrated on the image of that cruel, snarling face in the forefront of her mind. So, Alice took a breath and steadied her gun as she crept stealthily through the barn, steeling herself for what she was about to do.

The sound of Sheriff Joe's gruff voice set her hair on end. "I know you two are in here. Gotcha covered now. There's no way out, so better raise your hands and give yourselves up. Come out peaceful-like and I might give you a break and let you rot in prison."

Alice watched as a few pieces of hay floated down from the loft in slow motion as a flicker of light caught the pieces as they flittered about in the air. The sight held her mesmerized momentarily, and thought, *they look like fairies dancing in the light.* Startled out of her reverie, she heard several loud blasts go off. Her heart sunk and she screamed as she saw the sheriff firing shots, "Boom! Boom! Boom!" One after another.

Jesse came flying around a bale of hay and, at the same time, let off a few rounds as well. Bullets were flying every which way.

Alice steadied her hand, cocked the long-barrel shotgun, and let off a thunderous blast. To her amazement, she just shot the sheriff, who lurched forward and reached toward a post to support him. Unable to keep his balance he slithered in slow motion to the floor and landed with a thud. Blood pooled around his body and oozed out from underneath his massive frame. "Bye, bye little birdie," She whispered, as she slid to her knees and watched, almost hypnotically, as the crimson blood slowly spread into the hay, near her. Shaking, she managed to get to her feet and walk over to the lifeless body. *It's as if he's still watching me,* she thought. She tepidly reached out and closed his bulging, lifeless eyes. "May you rot hell, you bastard."

Then she felt sticky droplets dripping on her shoulder and falling onto her head. She put her hand to her hair and gasped. Blood was spilling down from the loft – and it wasn't the sheriffs.

Then Alice looked up, stunned to see Oliver half-stumble, half-fall down the ladder. Blood oozed out from his chest blanketing his shirt as he dropped onto the ground. Hunched over, grasping his chest, he looked almost ethereal as he pulled himself against the ladder, barely able to keep himself upright.

Sam slid down the steps, right behind Oliver, and cried out in alarm, looking at his injured friend.

Alice saw a slight movement out of the corner of her eye. *It was Jesse!* He had his gun drawn, while crouching around a bale of hay, looking at Oliver threateningly. "Best hold up right there, Or I'll land you deader than a deer!"

Eyes agog, and out of bullets, Alice gathered her wits and jumped into action. She snuck around the back side of Pepper's stall, determining her plan. All set, with shotgun in hand, she suddenly lunged at her brother and smashed him in the back of his head with the butt of her big gun. A crunching sound ensued. Jesse landed with a soft thump on the barn floor, his head lolled sideways.

Just then, Uncle Fred flew into the barn, face pale, holding a tiny pistol that he had found digging around in Alice's upstairs drawer, full of lingerie and robes. He felt kind of silly holding the small gun, but then he thought, *it would shoot a bullet just as good.* Looking around frantically for his headstrong Alice, Uncle Fred prayed he wouldn't be too late and wanted to kick himself for the time he spent looking for this silly weapon. Then, he spotted her in the center of the barn. She was – alive! He was so proud of her. She was standing in all her glory, barefooted and formidable, clutching the smoldering shotgun. Then his eyes landed on the sheriff, with a gouging hole in his back, blood pouring out. Over by the bales of hay he saw Jesse, sprawled on the ground, as well.

Sam called out to Uncle Fred holding onto Oliver who was gravely injured. Blood was spurting from his chest.

Oliver smiled faintly at Uncle Fred, whose heart constricted as he looked at the boy's peaceful expression. He hurried over to him, but before he could make it, Oliver had slumped to the ground.

Sam fell to his knees, still holding Oliver, and desperately tried to give him mouth-to-mouth resuscitation. But it was too late.

Aunt Alice gasped. "Oliver! Please, no! Come back!" She fell beside him and kissed his blueish lips. "You can't die," she said, shaking him. "You can't! You're the most amazing Indian – the most amazing man I have ever encountered, not to mention uniquely handsome. You *are* – you're simply magnificent." She threw her arms around him, lips trembling, "But to see you like this – it doesn't seem possible."

Sam stroked Oliver's long hair. This seemed like a dream. His friend – this incredible guy, whom he so admired, was gone. *My dear friend.* He sat looking at Oliver, captivated by his vivid blue eyes that seemed to be staring back at him. *He swore they were telling him not to be sad.*

Uncle Fred sat down next to Sam and bent over and kissed Oliver's cheek, tears flowing. Aunt Alice, Sam, and Uncle Fred all encircled Oliver, with pain-filled faces, all holding hands. They seemed mesmerized by Oliver's peaceful face with his beautiful smile that seemed to linger.

No one paid any mind to Jesse, lying nearby, out cold.

Everyone sat in silence, still stunned, trying to wrap their heads around the earlier events. Grief poured out from their hearts, as they stared lovingly at their unique friend.

Aunt Alice and Uncle Fred had come to care for Oliver as their own and thought that their hearts would break into.

Shattered emotions pulsed through Alice. *There has to be a way to bring you back to life,* she thought frantically. She leaned close and whispered in Oliver's ear and said a prayer. "I have loved you like my own, dear Oliver. I pray the spirits will hear my plea and help you, so that you may live. I can't bear to have you go." No longer able to hold back her grief, she broke down in tears. Uncle Fred did his best to console his Alice, but his heart was broken, and all he could do was rock back and forth, as they held each other, trying to ease their sorrow.

Sam stroked Oliver's face, and whispered, "You can't go. Not yet. Not like this!" Then he felt a tingling sensation – like an electrical current flowing through his veins. It shook him out of his grief. Something gave him a glimmer of hope.

Then surprising himself, Sam closed his eyes and started to sing a song his mother sang to him when he was little. He wasn't sure how he could possibly remember those words, but they came clearly – like cool and refreshing raindrops after a storm. It was a song of love and of longing about a wolf and a boy who wandered the earth looking for their mother. Sam's voice was crisp and clear and filled the room with deep emotion as he sang… and memories of his mother came flooding back.

While he continued to sing, Aunt Alice and Uncle Fred clasped their hands together, struck by the intensity of his song and listened with a pang of hope and glistening tears.

Aunt Alice wiped away the last of her tears. Her eyes were now drawn intently to Oliver, whose vacant eyes seemed to light up, like oceans of glass. For a fleeting moment, she thought, my prayer has been answered… *he's still alive.* Then she felt a light wispy brush on her brow.

Sam was still singing when a misty shimmer started to encircle Oliver's body. Aunt Alice gasped and squeezed her hands as a very weird apparition appeared out of the shimmering light.

Sam opened his eyes and stopped singing.

Oliver face was now luminous… glowing. He exuded a peaceful, serene vision.

Aunt Alice, Uncle Fred, and Sam were too stunned to move or utter a word as the billowy form started to take shape.

Aunt Alice clamped her hands over her mouth and tried to speak, but her throat was dry as she saw a tall, lanky man burst forth from the shimmering light, wearing a long flowing headdress. His bushy eyebrows bobbed up and down… his pale eyes burned strangely bright. He looked around the barn and then back at her and he pointed his long boney fingers at Alice, then poked her in the chest. "You're my kind of woman. Sexy and strong. Killing a deranged sheriff and knocking out your candy-ass brother makes my head spin out of control."

Alice could smell his stale, noxious breath, and held her nose, as he hovered close. Then to her amazement, he dropped a bloodied bullet in her hand.

"I see our friend is in dire need," he said, hoarsely. "I heard you ask for help, and 'lo and behold,' here I am… help has arrived."

The wispy form took shape and became clear. The tall, gangly man shook his arms and cracked his neck, then bent down and whispered something into Oliver's ear.

Oliver moved his hand.

Then the lanky man turned to the stunned group and stated:

"My cruelty knew no bounds when my lily-livered soul walked upon the earth. I have been trapped between the ethers and darkness for a very long time. Now… I'm gonna sing you a song, to let you know I'll soon be gone."

Then he started to dance in a circle – gangly legs awkwardly moving in all directions, looking like a scarecrow flailing against the wind. He croaked out,

"My name is Preacher Jim

I was cruel - and I have sinned.

But the gates of heaven are gonna let me in.

I've preached and prayed

And ranted and raved… YOU MUST BE SAVED!

I lost my soul and fell into the big black hole.

I was a liar, and that's the truth.

It's dark as hell, and that I can tell.

You… don't wanna go there, brother.

So, I have paid the price…

Peace and Love, Brothers and Sisters…

My soul is finally free…"

The wispy form slithered to his knees, leaned over, and gave Oliver a big wet kiss on the cheek and smiled at the shocked group. Before anyone could react, the wispy form bounded over to Sam, and Uncle Fred, and shook their hands. "You are my kind of people. Good and kind. But gotta say, that Alice is a real hottie. Need more of you around. Take care of Oliver, my friends. I bid you adieu!" Then he announced he was, "Going to where the sun shines all day long!" And he sang out, "Farewell to all. But before I do, I have a little wish. I have never danced before in my life." Preacher Jim zoomed over and grabbed hold of Alice. Before she knew what was happening, he pulled her up, held her tight, and started to undulate in a bizarre dance – his feet dangled in seesaw, clumsy movements. He bumped and grinded, hips swinging wildly off-kilter as he thrust his hips with abandon. Then he finally found his rhythm and he did a little jig. He felt like the kid he never was as he kicked up his heels and whirled, and whirled, round and round and round, laughing all the while.

Alice thought her head was going to fly right off, she was whirling so fast… her head was spinning in circles. Out of breath, and to her relief, the bizarre dance finally ended. Preacher Jim bowed to Alice, then plopped her back down and kissed her hand – tongue hanging out, as spittle dripped onto the ground. Then in a blaze of flashing light, Preacher Jim vanished through a small opening, leaving a trail of smoke and feathers behind.

No one could speak for a moment, dumbfounded by the sight. It was simply too much to comprehend or to put into words. They merely sat staring… mouths agape. Shocked silence filled the barn.

Sam was the first to stir and closed his mouth.

Then Aunt Alice stood, opened her hand, and showed the bewildered group the bullet that Preacher Jim had placed into her palm.

Uncle Fred asked, "Wh… what does this mean? Is Oliver…?" But he was unable to finish his thought.

Before any of them could grasp what just had happened, they saw Oliver move his eyes and blink… as if awakening from a long deep sleep. Then he twitched his fingers. First on the right side, then on the left.

Aunt Alice whispered, "First I dance with someone or 'something' that's not really real or human, and then our beloved Oliver springs back to life. I don't know what that guy was – maybe an answer to my prayer or maybe a ghost, or maybe I was just hallucinating. It has to be the shock of what just happened – or I'm seeing things. Or… it's entirely possible I'm going crazy." She looked at Sam, then over at Uncle Fred for their reassurance.

"I think maybe we *all* must be hallucinating." Uncle Fred said kindly. "First that unusual preacher man that came from who-knows-where and saved our wonderful Oliver, who was at death's door." Then Uncle Fred let off a wide grin. "I've gota say that man can't dance for a bucket of seeds, but all I know is I'm going to have a great big drink tonight with my twinkle-toes. It takes quite a girl that can kick up her heels with a phantom. I couldn't be prouder."

Before Sam could comment on Aunt Alice, they saw Oliver smile at them – a big, beautiful, wide, engaging smile.

Everyone bent close, to make sure their eyes were not deceiving them. Then they heard a faint, "That was quite the show, Aunt Alice. You danced with an apparition… once a preacher from long ago, who terrorized the children at the boarding school. He was cruel beyond measure. And now he's asked for my forgiveness. I gave it, along with my blessings, and he gave me my life back."

A big whoop went up in the air. Aunt Alice jumped up in delight, ran over and hugged Oliver tightly. Uncle Fred joined her, and then they swung around in circles – overjoyed with happiness.

Off in the distance a big fat crow with bright yellow eyes swooped down from the rafters and sat on a railing, looking down, eyes darting back and forth. Its beak clacked a singsong chirp that sounded like – "your alive… your alive… rat-a-tat-tat…" The bird took flight and fluttered down next to Oliver and pecked his cheek – gently, as if a kiss. Then it hovered near Oliver's wound, and with beak poised, it pecked delicately until there was nothing left but a red glow on his chest. Next, it skittered around Oliver, wings spread wide, fanning, squawking, and clacking all the while – as if talking to him in a language that only Oliver could understand… brushing remnants of death away. A moment later the amazing crow did another singsong chirp, then flew up and out of the barn.

Oliver inhaled deeply… it felt good to breathe again, and he let out a long sigh. He could feel his blood flow throughout his body, and it felt wonderful. His cold and stiff limbs came back to life and began to tingle. He wiggled his toes wondering how long he was gone. Where he had been there was no sense of time.

Aunt Alice, Uncle Fred, and Sam all looked like they had seen a ghost.

Oliver motioned for Sam to come close, and then whispered. "I saw your mother, Singing Dove. She came to my side as you were singing her song. She said to tell you she loves you beyond measure. You have turned out to be better than she hoped, and she is proud of you. Her greatest pain was in leaving you, but it was not of her choosing. Jesse is the reason – the reason she no longer walks the earth. But soon he will pay. Before you move on with your life, she wants you to go with me to the Black Hills… to learn who you are and discover the traditions of your people. She said, 'It's high up in the hills, where the wind whistles and whispers its magic as you sit with Mother Earth beneath you. It's a sacred place… where the sun and moon kiss the sky. Be still, and you will hear the spirits tell their stories of long ago – filled with hidden secrets. Tell the trees you love them, as well. For that is where I stay when I want to feel them sway in the breeze. It makes my spirit feel alive with the rush of leaves. And then, that very strange preacher that was here, zoomed over, took her hand – and then, she was gone."

Sam was astonished listening to Oliver. He couldn't believe it – his mother, Singing Dove, talking to Oliver. *He knew she was near. He always felt her presence. And that preacher… Oh, my gosh!* It was more than he could have hoped for – to hear a message from his mother. He brushed away a tear and hugged Oliver. "I could kiss you right now, my friend. You have no idea how happy I am to have you back. It might be a bit selfish on my part, but if I am to find my way, I will need your help."

Oliver looked up at the overjoyed faces of Aunt Alice and Uncle Fred. He closed his eyes briefly, then flickered them open. "I am glad to be back," he said, "but now I'm tired. It has been a strange day. One minute I'm here and the next... well... *you* know." Then he abruptly closed his eyes.

Uncle Fred's hands shook as he watched Oliver's eyes close. "Just don't think about dying," he joked. We can't go through that... again."

They all sat around, waiting. A moment later Oliver cracked his eyes open and smiled. "I'm not going anywhere. I just need to rest for a while." He closed his eyes and fell into a deep sleep.

"I'm not sure if I should laugh, cry or be afraid..." said Uncle Fred.

Sam went over to Aunt Alice. "I'm sorry to tell you this, Aunt Alice, but... whoever that preacher was that came from who-knows-where said Jesse had something to do with my mother's death."

"No, that can't be true Sam," Aunt Alice cried out in alarm.

"I'm sorry, Aunt Alice, but it *is* true. You know somewhere deep inside it is. I know you care for your brother, but he is not a good person, no matter how much you tried to help him when he was little. He's turned into a vicious man with no morals... he was going to shoot Oliver. Now listen to me, please. I have a plan, but we have no time to lose."

Aunt Alice sank back down and stifled a cry. She looked over at Jesse, who was starting to stir, then over at the sheriff's body, covered in blood.

"Look, Jesse is going to wake at any moment, and we have to do something."

"Oh, my sweet Lordie. Look at the mess I'm in. They're gonna take me away and lock me up."

Sam hugged his aunt. "You're not going to get in trouble for shooting the sheriff… we're not going to let you… trust me. I'm just glad you shot him… we all are glad."

Uncle Fred, chimed in and said, "You are the bravest woman I've ever met. We won't let anything happen to you." Suddenly everyone jumped when they heard a car off in the distance barreling down the road… the sound of a blaring siren wailed ominously.

Aunt Alice froze.

They all looked over at the sheriff, lying in a pool of blood.

Sam took her hand and kissed it. "You need to stay calm, Aunt Alice, and trust me." Turning to Uncle Fred, he motioned for him to follow. He took Jesse's gun that was lying beside him, picked it up and hid it under a bushel of corn. "Get the shotgun!" Sam hollered to Uncle Fred, "and hurry." He wrapped Jesse's hand securely around the shotgun and turned to Aunt Alice.

"I understand you love your brother, but, as you see, no matter how much you tried to set him right, he's turned into a man with an empty soul."

Aunt Alice numbly nodded.

"I'm sorry, Aunt Alice. I know this is difficult to do. Uncle Fred was right when he said you are one of the bravest woman I know trying to defend us, but you're not going to jail over killing the sheriff… Jesse is."

Uncle Fred's eyes lit up. "That's right, sugar plum. You did the right thing and now *he* gets to pay. Not you. When the law gets here, just stick to the story."

Uncle Fred pulled her close and held on to her tightly, reigning in his own fear as the siren blared and a car screeched to a halt in the driveway.

Deputy Ben slammed the car door open, with guns drawn. He took a few steps forward and looked around the ranch and hollered out, "Sheriff Joe! Where are you? Came to help you round up the felons." The deputy took a few more steps brandishing his gun and turned in a complete circle, scouring the entire perimeter. He abruptly stopped as his eyes happened to land on a big fat crow sitting up in a nearby oak tree… it's big yellow eyes bore viciously into his and the bird began to squawk and screech, loudly. He had to cover his ears from the sound – and stepped back. The all-too-recent memories of those birds attacking him, and then the crowd made him skittish. He pointed his gun and thought about shooting the damn thing dead… but he would save that for later. He had police business to tend to. "Gonna be your last squawk – real soon," he muttered angrily.

Inside the barn, Aunt Alice looked fearfully at Uncle Fred, then at Sam, who nodded encouragingly. "You can do this Aunt Alice… you *have* to. Remember you are brave!"

Uncle Fred hugged Alice tight. He couldn't let her see his fear, so he spoke boldly. "Just strut your stuff, sweet cheeks, right up to the deputy. Think of it as being on stage, with guys hootin' an' hollerin'. Don't be afraid… we'll be right beside you."

"Come on, Aunt Alice," Sam said. "You will do great. Let's go."

Uncle Fred was the first out of the barn and boldly shouted, "Deputy! Over here!"

Deputy Ben whirled around and hustled over to the barn door, both guns drawn and ready to fire. His face flushed as he skidded to a stop in front of Uncle Fred.

"Glad to see you, Deputy," said Uncle Fred. "You came just in time… I do believe the sheriff's dead."

"Dead? Well, what the hell happened, and who the hell shot him?" he shouted furiously. "I'll bury the bastard!" He cocked his guns as he heard a sudden movement in the barn – ready to fire. Then he saw Alice Evers poke her head through the door. He reprimanded her indignantly. "Need to be careful and not sneak up on a man with a gun. Could get yourself shot." Then he about fell over when he saw someone else standing in the distance. His beady eyes recognized the felon heading his way and shouted at Alice and

Fred. "Out of the way, you two. This here is the outlaw we've been looking for. Now we got us a murderer on top of everything else. This time, he'll hang for sure… or maybe I'll just blow his head clean off, while I got him." He steadied his guns and took aim.

Aunt Alice screamed in alarm, "Don't shoot, you fool!" Forgetting her fear, she tromped up to the deputy and shoved his guns out of harm's way. "Jesse killed the sheriff. He's in the barn on the floor. I knocked him out when he tried to get away. I know he's my brother, but I couldn't let him get away with killing the sheriff…" she added as an afterthought. "It might have been an accident though."

Deputy Ben looked at Alice dubiously and perused the barn. "Well now… looks like I got me a passel full of felons, a murderer – and who knows what else? I bet you're trying to protect this criminal, and that's a crime itself. Stick 'em up, lady." He said, pointing his gun at her.

Uncle Fred stepped in front of Alice and said, "Don't be an imbecile. Sam here didn't shoot the sheriff. He has no gun. There was a shoot-out in the barn… bullets were flying every which way, an' the sheriff and Jesse were hot after Oliver and Sam, trying to kill them. Jesse got carried away and shot the wrong one. If you don't believe me, go on into the barn and see for yourself. You got all the evidence you need, right in front of you. Take a gander."

Deputy Ben growled at Fred. "A shoot-out, you say. Well, they musta got lucky to get away. Now, I want you to tie this one up… and no funny business, either. I wanna know where the other felon is, too."

"The other one was injured and is in the barn asleep."

"Best not be telling me any tall tales, Evers. Don't know whether this one here killed the sheriff or not. All I know is… he's an escaped felon. And right now, it looks like I'm the law around here… so hop to it."

Uncle Fred stared at the detestable deputy, whose ego erupted since he thought he was in charge. "Don't have any rope handy. Besides, this boy didn't do anything other than step into your town. Nothing to justify a hanging. He's not going anywhere. He just needs to prove his innocence of all of these phony charges the sheriff concocted against him."

The deputy spat on the ground, "Well, I don't care what you say. I'll lock your ass right up along with him… and your fancy dancer wife to boot. She can wiggle her tail off in prison, if you don't do as I say." He cocked his gun and pointed it at Fred. "Here's my cuffs. Put 'em on the felon."

Uncle Fred grudgingly did as he was told. Deputy Ben scowled. "Smart man. Now let's get into the barn and you can show me where the sheriff's body is." He kept his guns cocked and ready. As they walked inside the barn, Deputy Ben hustled over where Jesse was stirring.

Jesse, dazed, looked at the deputy, sat up, and rubbed his head. "What're you doing here?"

"Put your hands up!" Deputy Ben shouted. "You're under arrest for shooting the sheriff."

Jesse shook his head, groggy and confused. He stared at the deputy for a moment to get his bearings. "What the hell are you talking about? I didn't shoot the sheriff, you idiot. I'm the one who turned the escapees in… told the sheriff where they were hiding out."

"Looks to me like you did. You got a big ole shotgun right beside you in your hand, and that's a big ole hole the sheriff's got in his back. Evidence seems pretty darn clear to me… 'sides, I got witnesses that saw you shoot him."

Jesse stumbled to his feet, scowling at the deputy. "The hell, you say. Why don't you arrest that felon over there, lying on the floor? He's gotta big reward out for him. *He's* the one you should be after, not me. And that one over there… he's, my son. Gotta reward out for him, too. No need to hang him, though. He's just a snot-nosed kid, thinking he's big time, being from the 'looney land' and all… but the other one needs his neck stretched." Jesse eyed the deputy with contempt. "An' you ain't taking me anywhere either," he said with venom. "From what I hear, you're just a lame-ass deputy that shoots cans all day long… so, go find some cans and get out of my face." Jesse looked around for his sister, and called out, "Hey, Alice. I'm as thirsty as a fish in the desert, so run on in and get me a beer, will ya? My head hurts, too."

Aunt Alice poked her head around the back of Fred and said, "Sorry, Jesse. Can't do that. You best do as the deputy tells you."

Furious, Jesse knocked the hay off his boots and stomped out the barn door. "What kind of kin *are* you?" he asked with a growl. Then he eyed the deputy and spat. "I'm owed a big reward for telling the sheriff where those two were hiding out. And you ain't locking me up, either. I'm leaving."

Deputy Ben stood there for a moment, unsure of what to do, and twiddled his fingers nervously on the tip of his gun.

"You best not let him get away, Deputy," Uncle Fred coerced, standing beside him. "You'll be the laughingstock in town, and you don't want that – especially if you're gonna be next in line for the sheriff's job."

Deputy Ben stood a little taller and adjusted his holster. "Sure as shit – I can't have that guy disrespecting me." He hustled out the door after Jesse who, by now, was almost to his car.

The deputy shouted after him. "Jesse! I'm ordering you to stop right there, or I'll shoot!"

"Kiss my royal flush ass," Jesse said, flippantly, as he yanked the car door open, "and eat my chocolate-streaked shorts while you're at it."

A nervous Deputy Ben yanked out his pistols. His lips twitched nervously. "D-do as I say, Jesse, or I'll fire."

Jesse smirked, turned around, and gave the deputy the middle finger. "Up yours!" Then he bent over, bared his butt, and made a vulgar sound. He grinned, ready to slide into the car seat, when there was a thunderous explosion. A searing hot pain shot up his back and he stumbled forward.

Deputy Ben's gun was smoldering from the several rounds he fired from his gun.

A frightened Alice ran over as fast as she could – just as Jesse slumped onto the open door – and pulled his limp body into her arms, then fell with him to the ground. Blood oozed from Jesse's stomach through the multiple bullet wounds. She covered the holes with her hands, trying desperately to stem the bleeding – but it was useless.

Jesse looked up at his sister and managed a few last words. "Haven't been a real good person, have I?"

Aunt Alice was crying so hard she couldn't respond as Jesse continued with difficulty. "Tell Sam, I shoulda been a better dad. S-sorry I turned him in." His breath was ragged, so she bent her head close to hear. "Sorry about his mother too…" Jesse coughed up a huge amount of blood as he gurgled out in a shallow breath. "I love you, sis… a bunch." His eyes rolled back in his head.

Sam walked over, stunned, took Aunt Alice's hand and squeezed. He sat down next to her as she was cradling Jesse. Through misty tears, she said, "He told me he was sorry, Sam… sorry about your mama and you. I guess it took his dying to be sorry," she said in a shocked whisper. "Why couldn't he have done this when he was alive? I guess something awful was eating at his insides and he could never get over it."

Uncle Fred kneeled beside her and stroked her blood-stained hair. "This is a lot to get a holda sweet cheeks… I know it is, but we'll get through this, together.

Deputy Ben stood looking in disbelief, his lips quivering. He couldn't believe he had just killed a man – seeing all the blood and pain it caused, with everyone crying and carrying on. *It was one thing to shoot a can and see it explode, but this is different… blood was everywhere… I'm gonna be sick.* He gulped back the bile in his throat. Unable to keep it down, he flew into the bushes in the back of the house and dry-heaved until he was weak. He didn't want to humiliate himself in front of everyone, but it was too much. He stayed there until he found enough strength to stand, and finally rose up on his shaky legs. Gathering every ounce of willpower that he could muster Ben strode unsteadily back to where everyone was waiting. He said hoarsely, "Guess I'd better call an ambulance… a couple of 'em is more like it with the mess we got here."

Blotchy streaks of red hues covered his face. Deputy Ben straightened his shoulders, slicked his hair back from his face and cleared his throat. He had to sound like a man with full authority and blurted out. "I'm in charge now so I'm gonna take the prisoners back to jail. Got unfinished business to get at… like a hanging." He looked at Sam and thrust his finger in his chest. "You're in big trouble… you and that other Indian – for escaping along with a whole bunch of other charges."

"I never broke the law or did anything to end up in jail," Sam spat out angrily. "I just came to your lousy town for a drink on my way out here to visit my aunt and uncle. Next thing I know, I'm accused of some phantom, bullshit crime that there was never any proof of… and then I end up being put in jail sentenced to be hung. Big trouble, you say? I say you look at the sheriff's suspicious activities. That is, if you're interested in the law, Deputy. He was crooked, and you know it. If you let this go without an investigation… you're as bad as he was. He thought he was a real tough guy and could write his own rules because he knew no one had the guts to question him – including you. Now, here you are… trying to be just like him, because you have a gun and a badge… arresting me without a trace of evidence!"

Deputy Ben was agitated, unsure of what to do, his eyes twitched nervously. Finally, he said, "Look, there was a trial… and you both were found guilty and…"

He was interrupted by a livid Alice. "Oh, hush up, Ben. That judge was a crock of hooey… paid off to boot. The whole trial business was a sham the sheriff cooked up… wasn't true and you know it. He simply despises Indians… as you. Take these boys in, and you're as bad as the sheriff."

Deputy Ben fingered his gun. He thought grudgingly, *there's some truth to her words. But damnation… I'm the law round here now, and I'm gonna enforce it, no matter what she says.* He kicked a few stones in the driveway, then said boldly. "Look, Alice. I'm not gonna be treated like some sort of simpleton. I'm the acting sheriff now, and, by gosh, you need to treat me with some respect."

A low cloud of dust rose on the horizon. All eyes looked up. Whoever was coming down the road was driving pretty fast. "I ain't called anyone yet," Deputy Ben hollered, guns ready. "Whoever it is, best be careful."

Uncle Fred shook his head, looking at the deputy, thinking, *he's two eggs short of an omelet.*

Everyone had their eyes peeled on the cloud of dust, wondering who was coming down the dirt road driving like a bat outa hell… going at breakneck speed.

CHAPTER FOURTEEN

ALL'S WELL THAT ENDS WELL

UNCLE FRED SAID, "By golly, someone's gonna wreck their car driving crazy like that."

As the car came closer, Sam about fell over when he saw his Chevy Camaro coming up the long driveway. A stab of excitement filled him. Then to everyone's amazement, it skidded to a stop, right in front of the onlookers, sending plumes of dirt and dust flying over them.

Pastor Percy was the first to hop out of the car, followed by an excited Indigo, then Janet and Sally.

Indigo's gaze found Sam, and she ran over and flew into his arms – kissing his entire face.

Sam couldn't help thinking, *what a day this has been! In the midst of everything that had just happened… here comes Indigo.* He was thrilled. "It's so good to see you," he murmured through his shock, and hugged her tightly. Then Percy came bounding over and nudged Indigo out of the way and gave Sam a great big hug and a bigger smile.

"I can't believe this! How did you ever find us?" Sam asked, incredulous… astounded by their determination to help and their friendship. "It's so good to see all of you."

Indigo explained breathlessly. "I was snooping around and overheard Sheriff Joe and Deputy Jerk, talking about their plans, when Sam's dad, came over to our house one night. I couldn't believe my ears when Jesse told the sheriff where you both were… he wanted the reward money. I was frantic. So, I did some digging around in my father's office and happened to find a drawer that he forgot to lock… I believe I found something that will free you both." Indigo said excitedly and hugged Sam again and whispered. "We have one thing in common, though – lousy dads."

Sam grinned and replied, "We sure do."

They were interrupted by a flustered Deputy Ben, who scurried over. He hemmed and hawed for a few moments, then looked at Indigo. "I hate to, umm… to say," he stammered and shuffled his feet. "I've got some real bad news to tell you, so you might want to sit down. Don't want you to faint – or cry like a baby an all." He blanched as Indigo gave him an exasperated glare, and awkwardly continued, "Well, Indeego, I hate to be the one to break it to you… but… your father's dead… he's over there in the barn. The fellow lying by the car, is Jesse, who shot the sheriff – and then I shot *him*. Now on top of all that, I got two escapees to deal with… an one you're getting cozy with. So, I'm telling you right now – I don't want any interference – give me any trouble an' I'll arrest the whole bunch of you, too. Just go back home… the whole lot of you and let me do my job."

Ignoring the deputy's threats, everyone's eyes flew over to the body, lying in a puddle of blood. A loud gasp was heard. No one in the group had ever seen a dead person before. Sally turned pale and held her hand over her mouth, looking like she might be sick. Percy hurried over to her noticing her distress just as she wobbled, then slid to the ground. Everyone started talking and asking questions at once. Uncle Fred tried to explain what had happened, without success. Just then Oliver just walked out of the barn.

Everyone shouted their joy and ran over to greet him with rounds of hugs and kisses. "We're so glad to see you – AND to see you're both alive," Pastor Percy said tearfully. "We were afraid we wouldn't get here in time."

Trying to get everyone's attention, Deputy Ben shouted above the noise. No one paid him any mind and kept on talking, so he let off a blast with his pistol. "Now hold on everyone and calm down. I've got business to get at and if anyone interferes with my duties, I'll lock all of you up."

Indigo had had more than enough from Ben, so she walked up to him, with eyes blazing. "You aren't arresting Sam or Oliver or anyone else, so just be quiet. You are not the sheriff, no matter what you think."

"That's right," Percy echoed. "What are you going to do, shoot us all?"

"Just don't make me mad and regret what I might have to do."

Sally felt a burst of courage rise up like molten hot lava... ready to erupt. Normally she would quake with fear, especially if it was a person of authority. But not this time... something had changed. So, at the top of her lungs, she bravely shouted. "You can go to hell, deputy..." she paused a moment, looking at surprised faces, then continued, "and rot with the devil." Astounded by her sudden outburst, she reddened at her boldness... then looked shyly at Percy. "Pardon my outburst, but it's something that needed to be said... for quite some time."

"I must say it was quite brave for you to speak up. I think the Lord gives us strength just when we need it.," Percy smiled in surprise. "I might add, I couldn't have said it better myself... those words were perfect," Percy said, beaming, then looked back at the deputy with a flutter of unease, and walked over and remarked, "These two young men you were going to hang did absolutely nothing wrong. I'm appalled at how easily you can hang the inno-cent… without regard or proof," he stated boldly. "You'll have to shoot me before you take them into custody."

Aunt Alice, Uncle Fred, Indigo, Janet, and Sally, listened with interest and all felt a fierce determination not to let any harm come to Sam and Oliver again, so they formed a tight circle around the two… and dared Deputy Ben to make a move. Percy hustled over and quickly joined in.

"If you try to take Sam and Oliver to town, you'll have to shoot every one of us," said Indigo adamantly, with fire dancing in her eyes, arms crossed defiantly.

Deputy Ben pulled out his gun and twirled it in frustration, looking at the determined group. Percy moved from the group and stood nose to nose with the deputy, shoved his gun away, and said, "You're not arresting anyone until you hear what we have to say."

Deputy Ben shoved Percy back, and raised his fists, ready to fight.

Uncle Fred stepped up. "All right, all right, everyone. Come on in and sit down. No one's going to shoot anyone or go anywhere."

Deputy Ben growled, eyeing Percy and then relaxed his fists slightly. "Well, I'm the law and I say what's what around here… so everyone best listen up!"

Everyone shouted in unison. "Shut up, Ben!"

"I've got all the proof you need against the sheriff right here," Indigo declared, and stomped up to Ben, and smacked him in the face with a well-worn black book. "This has all the dirty secrets my father has been doing for a very long time. He's threatened the merchants in town to pay him a percentage of their earnings… Blue Sky Saloon, included. He's stolen lands belonging to the Indian tribes, threatened to kill them if they put up a fuss, and then he turned around and sold it to the ranchers. There's even a bunch of notes right here," she pointed to a few pages, "about bribing ranchers to get them to vote him into office. And that's just a fraction of what he's done."

"Well, your fathers passed on now, Indie. I don't know what good this black book is gonna do… 'cause far as I can tell, he ain't coming back to account for his crimes. In the meantime, there's supposed to be a hanging, and, hell, I'm gonna see to it…"

Suddenly, a fist came barreling at the deputy, slugging him in the eye, knocking him backwards.

"You are nothing but a spineless coward," said Percy, holding his hand, "and a sonofabitch to boot!"

"You just hit me!" Deputy Ben shouted in dismay, looking at Percy with fury. "I oughta knock the crap outa you. And what kind of a pastor are you, anyway? Using foul language an' striking a man of the law…"

"Then *act* like a man of the law, not a pompous jackass. You can't hang Oliver and Sam. That was a sham trial. Why don't you be a man that God would smile upon, rather than an ignoramus who pursues hatred and prejudice… someone who upholds the law."

Sally grinned at Percy, becoming more smitten with his strange and uniquely righteous ways.

Uncle Fred said, "Let's try to calm things down here before more trouble starts."

But everyone ignored Uncle Fred, as they hurled more threats around.

The still-woozy Oliver extricated himself from the group and walked toward the house.

Deputy Ben stared incredulously at Oliver as he passed him by – like he wasn't even there. *Didn't seem too afraid of him, neither.* That irked Ben.

In the middle of all the ruckus, another car rumbled on down the road. A little slower this time. Everyone stopped shouting and looked to see who it might be. Oliver stood on the porch, a slight smile on his face. Uncle Fred stood beside him feeling a slight tremor throughout his body, hoping no more trouble was coming. He wasn't sure he could take it.

Everyone stood watching as a shroud of dust blanketed the vehicle coming down the road. Uncle Fred thought *it might be a posse.* When the dust finally settled and the vehicle came to a stop, they were all surprised to see it was an old red Ford pickup truck.

Indigo gasped and grabbed Sam's arm in alarm when she saw who was driving. The rest of the group stood unmoving, and in shock, as Hank and Jimmy Dean hopped out of the red pickup. No one said a word as he tipped his hat to Aunt Alice, and walked up the porch steps to Oliver, and handed him a set of keys.

"This belongs to you I believe. I think it's time that you knew that my father was in on this… and the sheriff. They found your dad and his truck when he broke down close to town. The sheriff arrested him for loitering… then took care of him at the hanging tree. I'm sorry for…"

"I know what happened to my father," Oliver said bitterly, as he took the keys and twirled them between his fingers, never taking his eyes off Hank. He wasn't sure if he wanted to strike him or thank him, so he did neither. His deep blue eyes bore into him, looking for any sign of deception or trickery. He saw none and relaxed his shoulders slightly.

"I think you know that my father is a wealthy rancher with a lot of influence around here. I know it's no excuse, but I always wanted his respect… so I started to act like him. I turned into a bully and worse – but, mostly as of late – I became bitter. Your people had land he wanted, so it was easy to despise them. Hell, everyone in town felt that way about Indians. Signs were up all over the place. But the sheriff was the worst of all. He hated Indians the most and everyone that wasn't what he considered upstanding citizens and pearly white. Anyone with darker skin was not welcome."

Oliver never blinked as he stared at Hank. Thoughts of strangling him raced through his mind. It took every ounce of willpower not to.

"Then that night, when I caught you looking at 'my' truck, I was livid. I was going to show the world I was a force to be reckoned with. But I got a big surprise. *You* were that force to be reckoned with. You were tough as hell and could fight like nothing I've ever seen… not to mention fearless. I was jealous. I was angry. I wanted to see you destroyed. I used my influence around town to do what I wanted. I'm sorry that my stupidity almost got you hung."

Jimmy Dean stood nervously on the steps watching Hank, then his eyes drifted to Oliver. He couldn't help but admire the guy, and thought, *he's got a real nice physique and eyes that could stop you in your tracks. Oooh… best let go of that thought.* He sucked in his breath, then refocused his eyes on Hank. His longing for him drove him nuts. *He has to know I'm crazy about him. But, if I was to say anything, that would probably be the end of our friendship.* Jimmy Dean hated hiding his feelings, but he felt he had no choice.

Hank continued. "The sheriff strung your father up behind the Blue Sky Saloon – the same place where they tried to string *you* up. I'm gonna be in big trouble telling you all this, but I figure at some point, I have to grow a spine."

Oliver looked long and hard at Hank wondering, *why he suddenly had a change of heart.* He figured he would find out soon enough… so with a grudging respect he said, "I don't think the sheriff will bother you – or, for that matter, anyone, anymore."

"What are you talking about?" Hank asked, curiously.

Deputy Ben walked up the steps and announced with a wave of his gun. "He's dead… that's what! Sheriff was shot in the barn… and this other fella, Jesse, did him in… so I shot him dead. Been a wild time around here. But it looks like I'm in charge now. Now, I got two felons I'm taking back to town. Anyone who tries to stop me… they get locked up, too."

Hank reeled with this information. He wanted to smack the infuriating deputy, but thought he'd better hold off for now.

Deputy Ben strutted on the porch like a peacock… back and forth… then stuck his guns in his holster, turned and walked down the steps over to his patrol car, and called for an ambulance, then grabbed a pair of handcuffs for Oliver. On his way back, he felt the hairs on the back of his neck rise. He turned and squinted his eyes. He noticed a feather was floating around his head, then it started to whirl about crazily as if in a windstorm. Then the feather suddenly stopped and hovered in front of his face. *This is mighty strange*, he thought, reaching for his gun. Then the feather zoomed down… its shaft pierced into the ground, looking like a spear, ready to attack. It gave him a queer feeling… like it was a warning. After staring at it for a minute, he thought, *how silly of me… afraid of a stinking feather.* He snickered then hauled off and kicked at it as hard as he could but missed and landed on his backside. Everyone laughed at Ben, who looked foolish.

Then suddenly, the feather shot up, swift as an arrow, and flew directly at his head. Deputy Ben danced around swatting his hands, trying to get away from the whirling feather. He squealed and ducked as the feather made a low-pitched buzzing sound and zinged past his head, stopped mid-air, then did a whirlabout, and headed straight for his eyeballs. In his haste to get away, he tripped over his feet, covered his head, and cowered. He thought, *this feather could do some serious damage… maybe peck my brains out.* He scrambled to his feet and took off in a run. The big fat crow with the yellow eyes, which had been silently watching from a tree branch, dove down, grabbed the feather in its beak, and chased the deputy around the yard, wings beating a rhythm, and cawing… 'run, coward, run.'

Everyone watched the deputy swatting wildly as the crow dove intermittingly, and pecked at his head, sending him racing at top speed, screaming in sheer fright. "Get away… get away!"

Howls of laughter rippled through the group delighting in the deputy's comeuppance at the whim of a crow and a feather. Jimmy Dean and Hank laughed the loudest, and Hank hollered out, "I think that crow is smarter than you, deputy. Best not to mess with it, or it might peck out what few brains you got."

Deputy Ben furiously reached for his guns, gritted his teeth, hating to be the butt-end of the laughter, and shouted. "You crows are gonna be some nasty-tasting stew tonight. I'm sick and tired of you bothering me." He aimed his pistols at the soaring bird that seemed to dare his every move. The deputy blasted away, firing with both pistols. Bang! Bang! Bang! The loud noise rippled through the air. The only thing the deputy struck was a smattering of leaves and twigs, which promptly fell on his head. The crow seemed to laugh at the shower of bullets, and let off a loud series of, "Caw! Caw! Caw! Then the crow dove down and pecked the deputy's fingers so hard with its long, sharp beak that it sent blood spurting into the air and the deputy's guns clattering to the ground. Ben screamed out in alarm cursing and hollering as he picked up his guns and ran for shelter to his patrol car. Panting hard, he slammed the door shut and started the engine. He had had enough of this insanity and thought, *to hell with those felons and everyone else. Let those crows peck their eyeballs right outta their sockets,* and ground the car in gear, lights flashing.

For a moment, everyone was held spellbound as they watched that incredulous sight. Then cheers erupted from the group as Deputy Ben sped off down the road. "Have you ever seen anything like this before?" Uncle Fred cried out, giddy with relief.

"Good riddance," they all chorused out their delight.

Pastor Percy raised his Bible in the air and did a little jig around the yard. He was shouting at the top of his lungs. "The Lord works in mysterious ways, wouldn't you say?" he exclaimed, jubilantly. "Sending that big, beautiful crow to protect Sam and Oliver. Thank you… Hallelujah… and praise the Lord!"

Uncle Fred picked up Aunt Alice and twirled her around in circles, kissing her bright pink lips.

Smiling, Jimmy Dean tentatively joined in and sang out softly, "Praise be to thee…" and hustled close to Hank and squeezed his arm. "Thank you for being my friend."

Hank slapped Jimmy Dean good-naturedly on the back. "You're all right by me, Jimmy Dean." Hank grinned as he watched Deputy Ben's car speeding down the road. "Could never stand that guy. Liked to think of himself as some sorta 'Wild-ass Hickock,' or some kinda crap with his guns." He cocked his eye and looked over at the crow sitting in a nearby tree. Made him a bit nervous, remembering what had happened in Miners Gulch. *At least, they got rid of the deputy*, he thought, shaking his head, amazed and alarmed at the same time. *Might need to steer clear of those birds though.*

Indigo jumped for joy and ran up to Sam in her snappy little floral-print dress and rhinestone sandals.

Sam's breath caught in his throat, admiring the beautiful Indigo as she came close, touched her lips against his jaw, that sent ripples of pleasure up his spine. He hugged her tightly and ran his fingers through her long auburn hair. "Thank you again for coming," he said softly.

Indigo swallowed hard, unable to speak. She struggled to keep her emotions in check as she looked at his dazzling face. "I was so worried about you and Oliver. I guess I've dreamed of this moment forever… I can't tell you how… well… I'm just so glad you're safe. My father is – or rather, was – the scum of the earth," she said defiantly, "and, I'm not sorry he's dead. That may sound horrible, but I don't care. It means you will be free and now no one can accuse you and Oliver of anything… thanks to Hank's help. I never thought I would say that or be glad to see him. I guess you never know when people might change. It's pretty amazing."

They stood for a moment, holding each other. Sam rubbed his hands across Indigo's back. "Speaking of amazing… we both lost our fathers on the very same day and neither of us could give a crap? I'd say we hit the bottom of the barrel with those two, but I think we came out pretty good though considering."

Sam smiled at Indigo and squeezed her again. "You are really something. But before I can say any more about my feelings or go any further… I have to figure out who I am. I want to get to know my Indianness… if that's even a word. For the first time I can recall, I am proud of who I am… an Indian – with Indian blood running through my veins… Arapaho. That's who I am, Indigo. I like saying that. It makes me feel authentic and powerful." Sam looked off into the distance. "I am going to honor my mother and her heritage," he said, as tears welled up. "I haven't seen her since I was a little thing, but I still can remember her face and my mother singing her songs that forever remain in my heart."

Indigo's heart melted watching Sam as he poured out his feelings. She started to tell him that she understood, when Uncle Fred walked over in the midst of their conversation and gave Sam a big hug. He looked at him with pride. "This has been one helluva day, son. I'm still a bit shaky and on edge after all the hullabaloo, but there are no words to express how happy I am that you are – finally free! You and Oliver. I don't know what I would have done if… well, let's forget all that now. I'm just grateful for the outcome… makes me want to cry," he sniffled. "I don't mean to get so emotional, but I can't help myself." Then he looked at the girl next to Sam in admiration.

"Uncle Fred, this is Indigo." Sam said.

"Well now, Indigo, is it?" Uncle Fred said with a big smile. "I heard about you, and you're even prettier than what Sam said. I'd like to thank you for all your help you gave my boys… mighty grateful to you… couldn't even begin to tell you how much." He heard Sam's stomach rumble and said, "how about you gather everyone up and come on in the house. I'll cook us up a bunch of grub like you've never had. I'm in my element in the kitchen... I love to cook."

Indigo smiled and said, "That sounds wonderful and I'm starving. Thank you."

Soon everyone was gathered inside the kitchen... chairs were pulled up and added an extension for the table that stretched out across the small room. Percy, Sally, Janet, Oliver, Indigo, Sam, Hank, Jimmy Dean and Aunt Alice were crammed in beside each other, all scrunched cozily together and talking up a storm... like they had been friends for years.

Uncle Fred was humming, while getting ready to cook all his favorite dishes. He threw on an apron and whipped up a big batch of his pickle berry pancakes, then added a pile of bacon on the hot pan and grabbed a smaller pan for some spam. He wrinkled his nose at the smell and wondered, *who would eat that stuff, besides his Alice.* Then he cracked a couple dozen eggs in a bowl, whipped them up and threw in a stick of butter in a skillet, ready to scramble. Next, he made a large pot of coffee. He inhaled the aroma, enjoying the sound it made bubbling on the stove. Once finished, he brought the pot of freshly brewed coffee to the table and sat it down.

Aunt Alice was smiling, looking around the crowded table, sipping her coffee. Sally went over and shyly asked if she could sit next to her.

Aunt Alice nodded and said, "I would be delighted. My name is Alice, Sam's aunt. Most call me, Aunt Alice. You can call me that if you want... makes me feel good."

"I'd like that, Aunt Alice. My name is Sally Bennett, and it's a real pleasure to meet you."

The two ladies instantly hit it off. Sally wasn't sure why, but she saw Alice as a mother figure... someone that she could relate to. Alice saw Sally as the daughter she and Fred never got around to having.

"I heard," Sally said shyly, "that you work at the Slippery Elm."

Aunt Alice smiled at the girl. "Yes, I do. Word gets around, I suppose, about my dancing."

Sally slid her chair closer. "I've always wanted to dance for a living. I'm not sure about taking my clothes off, though. Maybe you could show me a few of your moves. Heard you were pretty good."

Aunt Alice took a sip of her coffee and thought for a moment before she spoke. "Well, I suppose I could. The men sure love it when you show a little skin, especially your boobies, and the money is real good – but I think I'm done with all that. I'm sick of men grabbing at me and leering with their tongues hanging out… makes me sick. I want to do something besides take my clothes off and dance. For years, I've been bleaching my hair a buttery blond, and now it's so dry, I think it's ready to snap right off any day. Gotta keep yourself looking sharp all the time… keep the boys coming in. But from now on – I want a simpler life. Being out here on the ranch that I have come to enjoy with my Freddie sounds real good. I been thinking I might set up a vegetable stand and sell his beautiful vegetables… might even find some fans for his pickle berry jam." She smiled at the thought. "Maybe rescue some animals, too – the kind that don't stare at your boobs or care what you wear." She gave Sally a serious glance. "Isn't there anything else you would like to do besides dance in a bar?"

"Well," she said, "I like to draw pictures. I'm pretty good at that, but not sure where I could sell them. I paint landscapes, too."

"That sounds mighty fine. I wish I could draw and paint. I bet there's a whole lot of shops that would want to sell you pictures." She took another sip of coffee, grimaced at the taste, and added another scoop of sugar, stirred for a while then remarked. "Looks like that nice man over there likes you a whole bunch. I notice he can't take his eyes off you for more than a few minutes. Sam told me about him and how kind he was to him and Oliver. He seems like a unique guy for a Bible thump… er… I mean, preacher man. I don't mean any disrespect. He seems genuine and… kinda cute. I bet he doesn't make you feel bad about anything you want to do or what you done. I can spot a con man in a minute, and this guy is the 'real McCoy.'"

Aunt Alice watched Sally's eyes drift over to Hank with a shade of longing and sighed.

Sally said, "I used to be crazy about Hank. I chased him all around town like a fool… but I couldn't help it. I wanted him so bad I forgot about myself. I would've done anything for him… and I did a lot of things I'm not proud of. But now, I'm… well, I don't know how to explain it, but I kinda like Percy. He's grown on me – and he treats me like I'm something real special. Hard to get used to being treated so good. Sally leaned close and whispered in Alice's ear. "I never imagined I would be with a preacher guy… seems like oil and water, him and me, but he doesn't care about my past, or condemn me for things I did, soooo…"

"I'd wager you're a pretty smart girl. Some never let go of chasing after men that could give two hoots about you. I don't know you well, but I'm proud of you for staying strong… besides, who cares if this guy is a man of the cloth… he seems pretty cool if you ask me. Besides a little prayer now and then isn't such a bad thing… it can't hurt to have a little chat with the Big Guy upstairs."

Aunt Alice lit up a Virginia Slim, as the two women continued to chat the morning away.

Hank scooted his chair closer to Oliver and Sam and said, "I have to tell you that I owe you two a great big apology. I came out here to try to make up for my stupidity and I wanted to tell you a story. I used to be a really good football player… suddenly things changed when I got injured. I became angry at the world… mad that I hurt my shoulder in college and couldn't play football any longer. I was full of self-pity, so I took my anger out on a lot of people… Indians in particular. Then something happened I'm not sure I can fully explain." Hank paused with a sheepish look on his face. "I bet everyone's wondering why I would change, so suddenly." Hank waited a minute looking for a response.

Sam and Oliver didn't respond but gave him a nod to finish.

Hank cleared his throat and continued, "I'm not much for dreams and such… can never remember what they were, but a few nights ago I had this really weird dream… scared the crap right outa me it was so real. I saw as plain as day, this great big Indian come outa nowhere, like he was floating on air. And then that guy floated over and stood right next to me… so close I could feel him vibrate. He looked to be eight feet tall and was wearing some big ass war bonnet… and I can still, to this day, feel those feathers tickle my face. I about croaked when I saw he was carrying a real big tomahawk. I about jumped out of my skin, wondering who the hell this loony bastard was. I shouted for him to get the hell out and then I threatened to shoot him. He just smiled and stood near my bed. He said his name was Broken… uh… Feather, I think. He told me if I didn't set things right… he'd come back and, well…" Hank shuffled his feet nervously, "and well, he told me I wouldn't like what would happen… and if I didn't set things right, he might come back and use that big ole tomahawk on me. That got my attention damn straight."

Everyone at the table became silent and turned their attention to Hank as he continued talking in a worried tone.

"Then that big ole Indian did some kind of war dance around my bed… and all of a sudden, I saw a bunch of teepees with some withered old Indians smoking a peace pipe and praying… like I was right there. I could feel them staring at me, then I felt a stabbing in my chest, like a knife plunged right on in. Hurt like hell, too. Then that big ole Indian knocked me in the head. The old man said this was a warning… one I'd best heed. I stayed awake the rest of the night thinking about what he said, and what I saw, and for reasons I can't comprehend, I took stock of my life.

Something I'd never done before. Not a real pretty picture, it was. Made me ashamed to look at it. I guess it took the people I hated the most to make me see what a rotten person I had become – spitting on any Indian I came across, hitting girls, making fun of people, threatening others, and the worst of it was making untrue claims against Oliver and Sam here – just because I hated Indians. I didn't even know why, either." Hank looked at Sam and Oliver. "I'm sorry for what I had done… real glad you both got away and didn't get hung. I hope one day you might see me in a better light."

Sam stared, stone-faced, not sure if he could so easily forgive this guy that almost got him killed. He had to let things sit and jell for a while; then he would see. He couldn't help but smile at that dream Hank had. *Our people are really something*, he thought as a feeling of pride filled his heart. This day was so full of turmoil and surprises his head was spinning. Now he needed some time to process all of it – including Jesse's death.

Everyone was glued to the conversation as they sat around the table listening to Hank talk… not sure what to make of him and his confession, but all were relieved at his miraculous transformation. Before anyone could react, or ask a question, a loud clink on a glass pierced the air and tried to get everyone's attention.

Jimmy Dean stood. His innards were shaking as he grasped his glass. "I don't know you folks here too well, but I want to thank ya'll for being so nice and welcoming to Hank and me. Gotta say, I feel right at home here. Since everyone's been speaking their piece, there's something I have been burning to say for a very long time. Something I've been hiding my whole life and I don't want too anymore. Now that the sheriff's dead, I feel I can come clean without… well, ya know… getting beaten up, or worse. I want to tell you straight out… um… I'm gay. I don't mean the happy kind… the *man kind*. I hope I haven't offended anyone, especially Hank, because… because he's been a darn good friend and I love him. I wanted to say that for a very long time." He turned to

Hank, embarrassed, and said, "I hope you don't hate me, Hank, for speaking my peace."

Hank's fork fell out of his mouth. His face paled slightly, and he looked around the table at everyone's equally shocked expressions.

Hank finally found his voice and said, "Whoa there, Jimmy Dean. I… I think you're a darn good friend, one that I can count on, but I got a hankering for the ladies." He grinned sheepishly. "I don't care if you like guys, but like I said – I like the ladies. He looked at Janet sitting next to him and gave her a big smile. "I might be a changed man, but not *that* kinda changed."

Everyone let off a nervous laugh, unsure of what to say next.

"I gotta say, Jimmy Dean," continued Hank. "I'm not sure that would be a good thing to announce in Miners Gulch, or anywhere near these parts. Folks are still pretty close-minded, so be careful who you show your affection to. I'd hate to have to shoot the fella that might take offense and give you a bad time."

Jimmy Dean blushed as everyone sat around the table still wide-eyed. Not long ago, Hank and Jimmy Dean were not to be trusted, and now, here they were, baring their souls.

Percy was the first to break the silence and said, "I have to say Jimmy Dean, it took some nerve for you to admit all that." And to Hank, he said, "And it takes a real brave person to confront his faults and to be so honest. God loves a truthful man. Bless you both for that."

Uncle Fred stood with his coffee cup, and said, "Well, I don't care who you like, as long as you're a decent person." He took a sip of his cold coffee then raised his cup. "You'd be welcome in my home any day, young man. You both would."

Janet had been silent while taking in all the drama. She raised her cup of coffee and said softly, "I also know what it's like to be despised for who you are. It's not easy trying to ignore the hateful stares, sly comments, and derogatory remarks about you and your family. We have been called everything under the sun… that we're not real Americans… we're Jesus killers. It's hard to endure, all that talk, but luckily, I have some great friends to help me through rough times, and two wonderful parents. So, Jimmy Dean, here's to your courage for telling the truth. It seems so strange, like a lifetime ago, you were not anyone I could trust… at all… and now… well, here you are… here we are, talking like old friends.

"Be ye, who ye shall be, as long as you are true of heart." Percy smiled at Jimmy Dean. "A toast for your honesty."

Everyone clinked coffee cups and glasses together, as cheers went up around the table.

Uncle Fred shoved his chair back and said, "I got so carried away with listening to everyone talk I almost forgot about our breakfast," and hurried to the kitchen. He came back shortly, arms loaded with his pickle berry pancakes, bacon, eggs, sourdough bread, and, of course, Aunt Alice's favorite… fried spam.

"Dig in everyone," Uncle Fred announced proudly. "We even got spam for those who like it."

Aunt Alice blew a kiss to Uncle Fred, and then looked over at Sam and Oliver, as she picked at her fried spam and eggs. She sniffled, then wiped her nose, remembering what a close call it had been for the boys.

Oliver and Sam noticed that Aunt Alice was tearing up and slid their chairs next to her and kissed her cheek. She cooed, patting their heads, and said in a shaky voice. "I still can't believe my brother, Jesse, turned you boys in for a reward… and now he's dead." She started to tear up. "It's going to take some time to get over that, I suppose. But the most important thing is you both are okay… you don't have to look over your shoulders anymore. I'm sorry what he did to you, but just know that I love you boys more than the moon."

"We love you too, Aunt Alice," Sam said soothingly.

"That we do," Oliver said, then lowered his voice. "I didn't realize what a crack shot you are, Aunt Alice. You are my hero – you saved our lives – you and Uncle Fred."

"Did I hear my name?" Uncle Fred said merrily as he came back to the table setting his pickle berry jam down. "Everyone's more than welcome to take home a jar of my homemade jam."

Janet grinned, looking at the peculiar jam. "I'd love to. I'll even take a case and sell it in our store, if you would like. I'm sure it would be very popular, with something as unusual as this."

Uncle Fred beamed at the idea. "That sounds real good. I got loads of that stuff in my basement – as much as you need. I'll get a case ready for you when you leave."

Hank's head popped up and offered his idea, too. "I could see if Randy and his mom would like to sell some of that stuff at the Blue Sky Saloon. Could put up a new menu… say… pickle berry pigskin sandwich. That should go over pretty good," he laughed goodheartedly, "or pickle berry burgers." Suddenly he felt strange, almost giddy. Here he was sitting around the table talking to people who, a few days ago, he wouldn't have given the time of day – except for Indigo. And now, here he was interacting with a Jew, an Indian, and a half-breed. And then there was Sally, whom he had treated abominably. He even liked the pastor, who, not long before, he had engaged in a bloody fight at the bar. He rubbed his head still wondering about that dream that seemed to have shaken him up – helped him let go of bitterness that felt like an anchor around his neck. Now, there was a lightness about him – it seemed a little strange, but it was a good strange. He discovered that his family's wealth wasn't all that important anymore. If his dad could hear him talk like this, he would think him a weakling – maybe even disinherit him – but he didn't care. He felt better than he had ever felt before – brand new. He looked at Janet, who looked back at him and smiled. He felt bad about the names he had called her and her family. *I wonder if she could forgive me,* he pondered, perplexed by his feelings. This was a girl he would never have thought about before – except that he always admired her for being smart and sensible. And she had a real pretty smile that he never noticed before… But now, well, it was strange to see how things can change in the blink of an eye, or in his case – a dream. He smiled to himself, as he took a bite of those pickle berry pancakes. *They were pretty darn strange, as well.*

Everyone stayed late into the night talking and eating and laughing. No one wanted to leave, but it was getting late.

Indigo was distraught about leaving Sam again, but she knew he had things to work out and needed to go with Oliver. She was just glad they were alive! She wasn't so sure right now about going to Los Angeles. *Might put those plans on hold for a while and see what happens.* With her father gone, she thought things might be better – for now, at least – in Miners Gulch. Maybe when Oliver was ready to take his brother's work to publish in Los Angeles, they could all go together. She crossed her fingers.

Sally looked sheepishly at Hank, as everyone stood, heading toward the door. He was the one who had made her heart throb for so long, but now – the feeling wasn't nearly as strong. She couldn't be more surprised about that than anyone, but she had to admit she liked being treated special, by Percy. So, as much as she had wanted Hank, she was relieved that was over. She was going to pursue her drawings and paintings and – who knows – maybe a little dancing on the side – *for Percy*, she giggled. She thought about hanging some of her paintings in the church rectory. *I think landscape scenes would be perfect… maybe with some little lambs.* She smiled at the notion.

With everyone getting ready to leave, Hank and Jimmy Dean walked out onto the porch – then, stopped and turned around. Hank asked in amusement, "Say, could we hitch a ride back to town with you all? I seem to have left my truck… I mean *Oliver's* truck – with its rightful owner," he said with a chuckle. He walked up to Oliver and stuck out his hand to shake. "I can't say how big of an ass I've been. It took a dream with an Indian to wake me up. When you come back this way, I wouldn't mind talking to you more if it's okay with you. I know it was more than just a dream… I saw who I was, and it scared a whole lot of sense *into* me. Made me see things from a new perspective. I appreciate you being willing to listen to me and let me say my piece. I do want to be a better person."

Oliver nodded and shook his hand. "That'd be fine by me."

Indigo and Sam hugged one last time, then everyone crammed inside the Chevy and drove off amidst waves, cheering, laughter, and tearful farewells.

*

The next morning, Sam and Oliver walked into the kitchen, with bags packed. A tearful Aunt Alice, was sipping a cup of coffee, watching the boys with sadness.

Oliver kissed her wet cheek and said, "I will miss you Aunt Alice. I've never been around anyone like you before… it took a minute, but I am so glad I got the chance to know you. You're quite something you know." Oliver sat down next to her and poured a cup of hot coffee.

Sam sat on the other side of Aunt Alice and tried to soothe her. "I will be back, you know. You and Uncle Fred won't get rid of me that easily, so no need to cry. I never realized how much I would miss it out here."

"Got a great big breakfast for you boys… can't have you leave hungry," Uncle Fred said, coming from the kitchen, carrying a big platter of sausage, eggs, and pickle berry pancakes, and sat it on the table in front of Oliver and Sam. "So dig in. Sure are gonna miss you boys around here. It'll be mighty lonely, but I'm going to put my sweet cheeks to work in the garden to keep her busy… at least we got most of the fixings around here done and am mighty grateful for that. So, where you boys heading off to?"

"We'll spend most of our time in the Black Hills," Oliver said. "I'll take Sam where my father used to take me when I was younger… far back in the hills, and about as high as you can go… a place where most people would never find. There, Sam will begin to explore his roots and understand his people. Learn the sacred ways and find where his ancestors are buried… show him where his people have gone for millennium, "seeking sacred goodness.""

"Seems hard to believe I've never been to the Black Hills before," Sam said. "Oliver calls it, 'the Hills of the Gods.' I wonder what makes the place so special. It seems surreal that I used to run from who I was… like a lifetime ago, and now, I can hardly wait to discover the traditions of the Arapaho."

"Who knows what will happen," Oliver said with a smile. "Be prepared."

Oliver and Sam filled their plates full, as they talked about all that had just happened in the span of a couple days, and of course, Sam talked about Indigo.

Uncle Fred looked at Sam with warmth in his eyes. He spoke solemnly. "I've been thinking how strangely things have turned out, and what a miracle it has been. You are my pride, Sam. I'm real happy you will get a chance to know who you are… and be proud."

After breakfast, Oliver stood and said his goodbyes to Uncle Fred and Aunt Alice. "I'm going to get the old ford warmed up for our trip. I know I've thanked you a hundred times, but again… thank you for everything." He hugged them both. "I'll be in the truck," and headed out the door.

Oliver couldn't believe he was sitting inside his father's beloved truck and ran his hand over the smooth steering wheel… without apprehension. His eyes glazed over the interior, surprised to see the inside was clean and the exterior had been washed. He looked at every inch of the truck, remembering, then felt under the seat and found a small bundle of sage tucked in the back. His father had kept his special sage in a worn leather pouch for a special occasion. *This seemed like a good time to use it,* he thought. Oliver put the sage to his lips. The brittle leaves left a musky taste. As he lit a match, the smoke curled up and filled every nook of the interior with its pungent aroma.

His mind was filled with memories of his father. He inhaled deeply and gave thanks for the return of his father's truck and for his freedom. Oliver leaned back on the bench seat, feeling the worn leather against his back and closed his eyes. He could feel the smoke encircling his face, swirling around him like a caress. He smiled. For the briefest moment, he heard a wild, haunting melody ring in his ears and felt himself drift away.

Sam opened the door, and looked at his friend, in amazement. "Did I hear music, or was it my imagination?"

Jarred back to reality, Oliver shook his head and said, "I think the elders are beckoning… waiting for us to make our journey. They say the 'Paha Sapa' holds the magic in her belly. They want us to go to the hills to listen and learn. We may be there for some time, I think. I hope you like sleeping on the ground. We'll be doing a lot of that," Oliver grinned. "You will learn to start a fire with nothing but sticks – how to hunt and track an animal through the trees with a bow and arrow, skin it, and use every bit of the animal. Bait a line to fish, then clean it, like in the old ways – how our grandfathers before us did, learn to respect the land. Then I'll build us a sweat lodge and we will sit inside, and you will sweat like you have never done before. Then prayers – day and night. The Great Spirit will be our guide on this journey. Be ready. This is what we do to become warriors for our people."

Sam climbed into the seat beside him. He watched the smoke curl up and wind its way to his nostrils. He breathed in, and then relaxed. "My quest to discover the great mystery that has eluded me most of my life…" He exhaled out a long sigh… "I am ready."

Uncle Fred and Aunt Alice clung to each other watching them drive off, blowing kisses. "Don't be a stranger, you hear?" Uncle Fred called out.

"I miss you boys already. Come back real soon." Aunt Alice called out to them, tearfully.

Oliver and Sam waved back. "We'll be back before you know it," Sam said. "Have some pickle berry pancakes waiting for us."

"Those words make your departure easier to bear, sweetheart. I love you, both – more than you know."

CHAPTER FIFTEEN

NEW BEGINNINGS

I N A BRILLIANT burst of orange and purple and red, the setting sun turned the sky and distant hills ablaze with color. Oliver found a secluded spot to park his father's truck, then covered it with branches to shield it from prying eyes.

Then Oliver and Sam walked northeast, moving slowly and deliberately while searching for the elusive trail. After a few hours search, Oliver found it. The terrain was steep, and the path narrow as they crawled through the thick brush and brambles making their way up the hillside to the secluded spot on the ridge. Sam and Oliver trudged on, passing through a grove of ponderosa pines, walking for hours, when suddenly the warm air, abruptly turned cool and damp.

"This is where many of our ancestors lie," Oliver said.

Sam shivered as they passed by the Indians' sacred burial grounds.

Sam took off the red cloth he used as a bandana that wrapped around his head, held it to his heart, kissed it, then tied it around a fallen cottonwood branch, and stuck it in a mound near the burial grounds. He watched as the faded red cloth flapped gently in the breeze. "This is for you, Singing Dove – my mother. I am on my journey now, "seeking sacred goodness." May the wind and light always fill your soul."

Sam stayed a few minutes more, then followed Oliver as they climbed higher into the backcountry. Toward dusk they finally reached the top of the mountain and onto a wide expanse of the plateau that seemed to stretch into forever. They sat down on a ledge that overlooked the valley filled with flowing streams and trees and shrubs. Peace filled the evening as they sat in silence, listening to the sounds of nature, mesmerized by the beauty of the land. Then the sounds of hooves beating in the distance, interrupted their reverie, moving fast through the canyons below. Oliver and Sam peered over the side and to their delight, saw a herd of wild Mustangs galloping like the wind across the valley, manes and tails flying high – their silhouettes reflected mysteriously against the canyon walls. The dust rose in thick waves, spiraling up. Then a flash of lightning creased the sky. Out of the dust an enthralling voice pierced the air. "Oliver…" the voice whistled out.

Oliver's ears pricked at the sound. He listened. He heard his name being called again.

"Oliver."

Sam looked around, eyes wide, wondering who was calling out to his friend in the wild hills. After the horses were gone, silence had settled in. No more whispers were heard, so Oliver set about making a campfire. Soon a couple trout were sizzling in the hot coals along with dandelion greens he picked along the way. They both devoured the tasty dinner.

Sam quietly watched the sparks rise from the flames as Oliver stoked the fire – both seemingly lost in their own thoughts. Oliver began to hum a song he learned from his father, a tune that easily formed on his lips. Chills went up Sam's spine as he listened.

Sparks from the fire rose high in the air that crackled and snapped around them. The sounds were comforting.

Then a whisper, "Oliver," was heard, followed by a faint cry, and a whinny. In the distance, a silvery laughter tinkled gently on the night breeze. Sam and Oliver straightened as a burst of light shot up. Through the deepening twilight, a horse appeared, galloping at a tremendous speed, then skidded to a stop – the mighty stallion reared up through the haze.

Sam's eyes popped at the sight of a beautiful Mustang with its long flowing mane and eyes glowing bright as sapphires. Atop the horse sat a young girl, holding a shiny blue stone… emitting a bright light that bloomed like a halo, and twinkled like the stars…

A voice rang out of the mist, that sounded like silky pearls washing against the shore. "Oliver. It is me, Chasing Rabbit, Hidden Spirit's sister. Do you remember? Your brother, Spirit Bear wrote about me in his story. I am real… I was real in the book. I am thankful your brother is writing about us – our people – so our stories will be told to the world. He said to tell you that he is thrilled you will take his work so it will be shown," the voice sang out. "You have the magic, Oliver. It is in your eyes, wherever you look. Use it wisely." Oliver felt the strangest sensation fill him, as the elusive stone, plopped into his hands – once again.

Oliver was captivated by its alluring glow. He heard the girl, say clearly, "The stone holds many secrets of long ago, Mi-thikoza – magic." The voice, sweet and soft… seemed to emanate from inside the stone, sending bright shards of turquoise blazing up. Oliver couldn't take his eyes away from the beaming rays.

Sam was aghast at the fantastical sight and stared at his friend in disbelief, then back at the girl and the beautiful wild Mustang.

The young girl's gleaming silhouette radiated all around her while she held onto the horse's long golden mane… its hooves lifted stately… up and down… up and down… moving in circles… like it was dancing. Then the Mustang pawed the ground, arched its powerful neck back and forth and whinnied. A silky mist rose like a puff of vapor around the girl.

Chasing Rabbit pleaded, "You must protect our wild Mustangs. The future looks bleak for them. The ranchers want their lands. The ones that are supposed to protect them, are not. Soon, their freedom will be taken… like ours. They will be driven from their lands to be sold off and worse… it makes my heart ache. The horses will soon need our help… I see it in the future. Please help, Oliver."

Oliver looked at the girl, Chasing Rabbit, and knew her words rang true. The horse let off a shrill whinny, that set his back on edge.

Then the young girl's luminous brown eyes, looked over and smiled at Sam. "Singing Dove said to tell you, she liked the red cloth you left for her. She sends her love and is glad you are in the sacred hills to learn of your ancestors." Sam felt a surge of warmth encircle him, like a velvety blanket, comforting him.

Then in the distance, a sound of hoofbeats pounded the earth, shaking the ground with its intensity. A moment later, a herd of wild Mustangs appeared in a cloud of untamed dust, gathered near the girl and horse, and pawed the air. A storm was brewing in the distance. The wild Mustangs flung their necks upward, nickering and whinnying, clomping their hooves in time with the booming thunder and pulsing lightning that flashed with fury. Then a bright light bloomed within the clouds, the wind rose… the clouds swirled and billowed, turning into a wild, tempestuous storm.

"It is time for me to leave," said, Chasing Rabbit with a lovely smile. "The spirits have gathered in the gloaming mist and are watching. They are proud of you and what you are doing." A face of a wizened old Indian with a flowing headdress appeared from the haze. The old Indian reached out of the mist and touched Oliver's face.

"Being high up in these hills will free you of your troubles and the anger that has shackled you for so long. Drive that old truck carefully, Mi-Thakoza. I will see you on the other side – but not for some time. You have much work to do, walking the red road." Then the wizened old face, suddenly changed into his father's face, and beamed brightly. He smiled a poignant smile, then said something to the girl and snapped his fingers. The vision wavered a moment, then the old man, the girl, and the Mustangs, vanished into a luminous rainbow of colors trailing on the edge of the milky way – hypnotically into the night sky.

Sam ran over and stood at the cliff's edge and held his hands out to the sky, breathing in the energy of the landscape. He felt empowered. He swore he could feel the heartbeat of the earth rise in his chest. Then a splash of lightning lit up the sky. He could feel his legs tingle, as he stood looking up, anticipating what he might discover on his spiritual quest… he could feel it in his bones.

Oliver and Sam sat side by side in the moonlit night, eyes searching the skies and valleys in wonder. Sam spoke in a whisper. "I can hardly believe my eyes – seeing that wild Mustang with those blue eyes… and that young girl, riding atop… Chasing Rabbit! She seemed to know you." Sam shook his head, trying to fathom what had just happened. "And the most amazing thing was," Sam continued, perplexed, "was seeing that old Indian… your father…" His words trailed off… his eyes drank in the images, still floating in his mind.

Shooting stars lit up the night sky, soaring across the expanse of the universe in a blaze of light. "Being here, in the beauty of the hills… it feels like a dream of coming home," he paused, "after a long absence." Sam lifted his head as if speaking to the winds.

"I have much to learn about my people and even more about the Great Spirit and all its mysteries. I am deeply humbled for this incredible journey and being with you, Oliver. Many thanks for your friendship and for bringing me here… to this magical place."

Oliver smiled as they both settled in for the night, hands propped behind their heads, looking at the sky, hoping for one last glimpse of the Mustang and the girl and the wizened old man.

*

Acknowledgement

Cheryl Acosta is a beautiful soul and owner of a native made store in Alpine, Ca. I asked her to share a bit about her background:

My childhood was one filled with stories of culture, traditions, and pride. One of the first lessons I learned in life was to be proud of the people I hailed from, my Blackfoot mother and Taino father. I followed my dreams to become a schoolteacher and through my vocation I had the opportunity to teach children that their individuality made them unique, special and the carriers of the torch of their ancestors. Their charge was to remember where and who they came from so that they in turn could pass this knowledge to the next generation. As retirement from my profession drew near, I knew I wanted to continue in education and share the culture, trials, tribulations and amazing art of my beautiful Native brothers and sisters. Gathered: A Native Made Marketplace is the dream come true. My store is a place where I can showcase the First peoples, handcrafts and ignite a desire to learn more of the history of the Native American people from a prospective that wishes to dispel myths', change mindsets, and give a venue where Native artist could sell their wares. Gathered: A Native Made Marketplace welcomes all who want to make our world a bit smaller by sharing the stories of resiliency, awareness of continuing issues and carrying on of traditions of handcrafts.

Gracias, Eyay iihan, nitsiniiyi'taki,
Cheryl Acosta Hill

www.ingramcontent.com/pod-product-compliance
Lightning Source LLC
Chambersburg PA
CBHW072022110726
47910CB00005B/1839

9780999834848